THE LAST
CENTURION

Contents

Thursday 6th April 1

Wednesday 24th December 6

Thursday 25th December 16

Friday 26th December 29

Saturday 27th December 44

Sunday 28th December 57

Monday 29th December 83

Tuesday 30th December 96

Wednesday 31st December 111

Thursday 1st January 126

Friday 2nd January 151

Saturday 3rd January 166

Sunday 4th January 175

Monday 5th January 192

Tuesday 6th January 203

Wednesday 7th January 213

Thursday 8th January 222

Friday 9th January 232

Saturday 10th January 241

Sunday 11th January 252

Monday 12th January 271

Tuesday 13th January..288

Wednesday 14th January...306

Thursday 15th January 325

Friday 16th January..345

Saturday 17th January 365

Sunday 18th January 378

Monday 19th January 391

Tuesday 20th January..416

Wednesday 21st January..441

Thursday 22nd January..454

Friday 23rd January..468

Epilogue 481

List of Characters 490

INTRODUCTION

Thursday 6th April 1476

Abbot Etienne of Caen, a native of Normandy, had piercing blue eyes and was tall and very thin. In his youth he had pleasant facial features and the once black hair surrounding his shaved head was now snow white. He was the quintessential embodiment of what a pious holy man should be. He believed in obedience to his abbey seniors, charity, poverty and chastity. He was very studious in his younger days in the order and, by this study, he became very knowledgeable about numerous interpretations of biblical scriptures. His years of dedication to the church had brought him recognition for his devotion to the true cross and he had extended the influence of the Benedictine Order in this part of the country. His active mind had always sought ways of doing activities more efficiently and he arrived from Normandy with an unbounded zeal for success.

Since becoming Abbot ten years ago, he had organized building work at the abbey to provide additional hospitality to travellers and he had also been the main driving force in attracting a large number of new disciples to the rule of Saint Benedict. However he was now considered a church elder and these were turbulent and godless times. His abbey was under attack by a band of brigands and as Abbot Etienne looked from the high tower of the Benedictine church, through aged and dimming eyes, the desecration being caused in the grounds of his beloved monastery drove him to despair and he inwardly wept.

"O Lord in Heaven," he cried, "Protect this holy monument from the devil's henchmen. Give us your holy grace and bring law and the King's justice to this ravaged land."

It thundered and the clouds darkened and the Abbot was thankful that the fading light and his failing eyesight protected his great sense of loss. When he became Abbot his abbey had prospered and many influential landowners had bequeathed parcels of land to the abbey, in return for prayers to be said on their heavenly journey. In this way the wealth and prestige of the church, and the Benedictine Order, had been secured. One local and wealthy landowner had donated a large parcel of unproductive and marshy land to the abbey in the knowledge that his place in heaven would be assured. This land had been drained and was now very productive and the brothers of the abbey happily tilled the soil and grazed the sheep and cattle. The only son and heir of the landowner had falsely believed that the land would revert to his family on his father's demise, but he was mistaken. In a court of law the Abbot produced documents to conclusively disprove this belief and to confirm that the land had been transferred to the ownership of the Benedictine Order.

The son was not content and attacks on the abbey property by ungodly heathens in the employ of the new Lord of the Manor began. The initial attacks were minor in comparison to the present assault. Abbot Etienne now saw nothing but destruction. Fires burned in the fields and wooden outbuildings were ablaze. Some brothers had been ambushed and suffered a horrific end in their defence of the cross. Abbot Etienne knew he must protect the holy relics and the jewels held within the walls of the abbey and he must act quickly. He was usually so pleased with his life that he thanked God every day for his good fortune, but today he was distraught and his faith was sorely tested.

"I have seen enough," he confided to his Prior Tatwin and to two senior brothers, Tancred and Bernard, and turned away from the terrible scene. "We must now execute a plan passed down to me by my predecessor and friend, Abbot Laurent. We must, at all costs, get our religious holdings out of the abbey and hidden in prepared chambers, until we have law and order return to this godless part of the kingdom."

The attendant brothers were perplexed but did not comment. The small group descended the narrow stairway from the tower, with difficulty and near the ground the pounding of the outlaws axes, spears and battering rams against the stout door of the abbey was deafening.

"Follow me Brother Prior to the cellar," ordered Abbot Etienne, after he had given instruction to brothers Tancred and Bernard, who both simply bowed and scurried away. The Abbot continued, "We all have work to do and very little time to accomplish it."

Abbot Etienne did not see the heavy object as it arced towards him, but he did hear the cries of his holy brothers. The axe had gained entrance to the abbey through a small hole in the door and other instruments of death were following. He turned towards the cries and was hit on the head by the blunt side of the weapon. He fell onto the hard floor of the abbey and his fading sight became Stygian black for a few moments. He slowly recovered and simply whispered, "Brothers, may God be with you all at this terrible time, but I must go to the cellar to continue Gods work." He ordered his Prior to escort him. The Abbot stood and with blood streaming from a deep gash on his forehead, he stumbled forward and was guided by his Prior.

In the cellar, the Abbot and Prior were met by another elder member of the order, Brother Stephen, who had been waiting patiently for his Abbot by the old well.

"My lord Abbot," he simply said, noticing the Abbot's wound but ignoring the blood and making no comment.

The old well had been the original one of the abbey when it was founded and it had provided sufficient water for the few brothers and the animals housed in the confines of the abbey.

The well was still used but it could not fulfil the needs of the enlarged abbey and was used sparingly. The Abbot had brought with him from Normandy the knowledge of diverting streams to follow the line of the land and to overcome local drought. It was fortunate for the Abbot that his diminished eyesight had prevented him from seeing the destruction of the water channel and the associated holding chamber from the high tower. He would have been distraught and heartbroken.

"What I am informing you now," said the Abbot, "must not be divulged to anyone." He waited for both present to nod and kiss the crosses around their necks to confirm their obedience. He then continued, "There is a way out of the abbey." He waited for the news to be received and then said, "An underground tunnel was discovered when attempts were made to deepen this well to provide more water, but in this venture we failed." The Abbot waited for the information to be absorbed. The Prior and the brother stood motionless and were both speechless. "Down this well," he continued, but now gasping for breath, "there is a natural tunnel that leads out of the abbey and into a cave." The Abbot was panting now and again paused for breath. He eventually said, "The cave entrance is well hidden and is outside the encircling band of rogues attacking our beloved abbey."

The conversation was interrupted by the appearance of the two brothers, Tancred and Bernard, who had been with the Abbot and Prior earlier in the tower. They entered the cellar with three junior brothers and delivered ten packages. The two senior brothers presented papers to the Abbot, one a simple note scribbled earlier by the Abbot and the other presented a packet of papers from the library. The group then departed the cellar, and Brother Stephen and Prior Tatwin secured and bolted the cellar door. "And now," said the Abbot feebly, "I require you both to descend down the well and take the ten packages and papers and place them at the bottom of the well. Do not return to this room. Take the packages and papers to the cave and there stay concealed. In the dead of night, if it is safe, go to the coastal storeroom and deliver the papers and the packages to the brothers there."

Abbot Etienne knew his time on earth was near its end and he laboured to complete his orders. "It may require much work to convey all of the packages. The brothers at the coast will know what to do. On completion of the task go inland and seek sanctuary at the abbey there." With his life ebbing away the Abbot gave the Prior and Brother Stephen his blessing: "May our lord and the Holy Spirit be with you on your journey and bring you safely to your journey's end at our sister abbey inland."

Both brother Stephen and the Prior had difficulty hearing the last words of Abbot Etienne. They both knew he was in agony and kissed the ring on his finger, crossed themselves and descended the well.

Abbot Etienne, his strength gone, lay on the floor of the cellar and died a few hours later. He died listening to the screams of his brother monks, as they were tortured before slaughter. He also heard the battering against the cellar door and knew that it must eventually succumb to the onslaught. As he waited for the inevitable he lay on the floor pointing to a blank wall in the hope that this gesture would confuse his assailants. He had a smile on his face as he prepared to meet his Heavenly Lord.

CHAPTER 1

Wednesday 24th December

The sun went down over the far horizon, casting its bright orange glow into the waters of the small harbour. The seagulls screeched and swooped down towards a small boat, belatedly navigating the narrow entrance channel and seeking a safe haven from the expected high winds. The shop window displays were all lit up and encouraging customers into the stores to purchase their goods and the outer harbour lights began to flicker on as the afternoon light began to fade. It was Christmas Eve and the earlier snowfall had stopped only to be replaced by a serious drop in temperature.

Judas Wells looked out of the window of his company's Goods Reception Lodge, set on a small rise above the small town, and observed the winter scene. It was getting colder outside and the temperature in the lodge was also dropping. Judas switched on the heating system and the machine coughed into life. The small building in which he worked was a very compact unit with a small kitchen area, toilet facilities, store rooms, a goods reception area at one end and a home for the security staff at the other. In a separate shared alcove, a photocopier, shredding machine, computer and an old printer were housed. It was a very well designed unit and very functional. All of the guards got on well with each other and with Judas and there seemed to be no friction in the camp.

There were four guards that performed the day duties on the site, each twelve hour shift being performed for four consecutive days and then the guards had four days away from the lodge. There were also four guards that performed the night duties on the site, again using the same system.

Originally the guards performed day and night shifts, but when it was discovered that some preferred nights for working and others preferred day attendances, arrangements were put in hand to accommodate the preferences of the guards. The system worked well and was only a problem when annual leave or illness forced available staff to attend for day or night duty on their rota days off.

Outside snowfall was predicted for later and it was expected to be a white Christmas, at least for a few hours. The winding roads out of the small town of Beaufort St. Vincent were busy with vehicles carrying people who were all trying to get home ready for the festive celebrations. Judas did not celebrate the Christian holiday and had volunteered to work on each day of the Christmas break to answer any urgent telephone calls that may come in and deal with them accordingly. This work would normally be performed by the security staff, but at the moment they were required to do permanent patrols around the site because of a spate of local robberies. Construction work was in progress on the site to expand the production capacity and, because of the inclement weather, building work had stopped and some of the company workshops were open to the elements and therefore a magnet for thieves. Construction work would begin again in the New Year. The security guards in the lodge had cameras to assist in deterring crime, but so had other companies in this industrial area and they had still been targeted. The company closed tonight and would reopen on Monday 5th of January.

All of the expected goods deliveries had been received and the company delivery vehicles, visiting nearby towns, had nearly all returned. The factory Yuletide Party was in full swing. The receptionist had transferred the telephone system to Judas and he was surprised at the lack of callers. He looked around his work domain and was inwardly satisfied. He joined the small but ambitious model railway company three months ago, at the end of September, when he had been made redundant. He had been employed at his previous post for ten years and had volunteered for redundancy when the stationery, photocopying and shredding duties with which he was involved were relocated to the main office, about 13 miles inland from the satellite complex. In fact he was pleased to get away from the job as more and more work was being added to his duties and he often had to stay late to complete urgent work. A number of other staff were also made redundant.

On his release he had quickly applied for employment at his present situation, with Beaufort Models and after the necessary reference checks and a strenuous medical, he had been accepted, even though he was fifty nine years old. Judas was thoroughly enjoying the complete change of employment. Previously the goods reception work he was doing was performed by two part time employees on six hour shifts and on their retirement within a fortnight of each other, he had taken on the duties for the full day's work. He preferred working for this company and he thought he was appreciated for his performance and dedication to the work. However, on his final interview for the position, he had been advised that as the two staff he was replacing covered each other's annual leave, it was proposed to employ another member of staff to work in the goods reception lodge and for each person to cover each other's vacations. It had also been decided to change the attendances to four days on duty and four days off. Judas was happy with this suggestion and was looking forward to sharing his work with a new colleague, but with additional security patrols to account for, management had decided to put the new rotas on hold until the New Year.

A couple of employees walked out of the complex and shouted to him, "Merry Christmas."

He returned the greeting, "And may I wish you the same," as they strolled by. He again looked out of the window and viewed his recent employer's building, seeing the lights on the Christmas tree twinkling in the old office window. Some engineers were still to be seen at the site, but they were due to relocate to the main office after the Christmas Holiday. The festive mood seemed to be missing from the activities of his old colleagues and he guessed that they were not happy at their imminent departure from the building. He had been advised that most of the furniture and records had already been taken to the main office and only the engineering rearguard were left in the building. He had also been advised that the remaining furniture and current workloads of the engineering staff would be loaded into vehicles tonight and parked at the main office, ready for unloading after the festive break.

The last two delivery vehicles returned to the site and Judas booked them in and passed on some messages to the drivers. The barriers were opened and closed after the vehicles had passed through. The drivers were requested to park their vehicles in a designated area near to the security lodge, for added protection during the Christmas break. All eighteen vehicles were parked in three rows and security cameras were trained onto them. Judas locked the goods barriers but could see that a few private vehicles were still in the car park and he left the exit barrier operational for card use.

The night guards arrived early on foot as they both lived locally. All the security staff used the Goods Reception Office as their base, beginning work usually at six o'clock, but today, Christmas Eve, it was different and they had been asked to come in early. Judas wandered over to the guards section of the lodge and simply said to Gordon and Richard, the departing guards, "The compliments of the season to you both. Enjoy your time away." Both men thanked him and they left the lodge to do a final external patrol of the site before signing off duty for the festive break. The guarding schedules were not the normal ones because of the additional work and the guards all looked forward to their days off.

The new guards completed their paperwork and prepared the shift log ready for any pertinent entries during the shift. After twenty minutes the first guard left the lodge to begin his internal patrol and wished Judas the compliments of the season. Judas smiled and returned the greeting.

"I don't think he knows about you and Christmas," said Adrian as Colin, the other guard, closed the door, "I will enlighten him sometime."

"No problem," said Judas, "a lot of people just say it automatically."

The final cars left the car park and Judas mechanically locked the in and out barriers and activated the gate alarm system. The last store's pedestrians left the complex and a few said, "See you next year."

To one couple Judas replied, "Thank you. I look forward to seeing you then," and received a very frosty glance. The only working staff on site were the industrial cleaners. They had arrived early and had been told they could leave when their duties were complete. The Christmas party in the main office block had ended, and all clerical workers had left the site in various stages of intoxication.

"What time are you in tomorrow?" asked Adrian, looking up from his log book.

"The same time as usual," replied Judas, "why do you ask?"

"Oh I just want to get away in the morning as soon as possible," said Adrian. "My wife wants me to drive her to her sisters and it's an hour's drive there and back. I will spend a few minutes with my sister-in-law and her kids and see them open their presents and then get home to bed. Actually I should have been off work today, but I promised Keith I would cover this shift for him as he has visitors staying with him over Christmas and they return to Scotland on the 28th. In case I don't see you in the morning, enjoy the day."

"Okay," said Judas, "thanks."

At 6 o'clock Judas left the Goods Reception Lodge and said to Adrian, "Merry Christmas and a very pleasant journey tomorrow. By the way the cleaning staff are still on site but should be leaving early." Adrian just nodded.

Judas walked the two miles to his late Georgian residence and entered. On his walk he had seen numerous homes decorated for the Christmas festivities, but his abode was completely bare of such trimmings. He lived in an old property, full of character, which had been the home of a prosperous mill owner and built in 1800. It was simply called "The Miller's Retreat."

It was close to the ruin of the large Victorian church, close to the library, and nearby was the school which he often attended in the evenings for historical and geographical lectures. Most of the town service trades were available within walking distance. The old mill property overlooked woodland and a disused windmill. From his garden he could see the start of the still navigable canal and canal basin. Further on and in the middle distance, he could see the lighthouse and its flashing beacon.

The town also had a ruined mediaeval castle, built by Jean Beaufort. This minor noble and loyal lieutenant of William the Conqueror built the castle on a high promontory, which overlooked and defended the area. This upstart had demanded that any permanent settlement established near to the structure should proclaim his ownership, hence the town name. The St. Vincent part of the town name was insisted upon by his Portuguese wife. The magnificent structure was destroyed by the parliamentary forces of Oliver Cromwell in 1646 during the English Civil War and simply left to decay. At present, the building ruins were being excavated by various archaeological agencies and many exciting finds had been unearthed and were on display at the local museum. The town hugged the coast and seemed compressed by the surrounding hills.

The Miller's Retreat had at one time been converted into a guest house following the deaths of the mill owner's five unmarried daughters. Judas had bought the property as a development project and also because the building was in a prime location, overlooking the coast and the single track railway line and close to the marina and inner harbour of the small market town. The previous owner's private rooms were only a small part of the property. When they retired they moved inland and the guest house reverted to private use and was sold to Judas.

Judas was very pleased with the property he had bought and he was also very pleased with the work he had done since moving in. He lived in the rooms that the previous owners had used as this was all he needed. He had moved into the property just three years and two months ago and had loved the layout at first sight. It contained all of the rooms and requirements necessary to provide a guest house with a good return on his investment. One very interesting structure was a tower that had been added to the original plan by the miller so that he could see all three of his mills from the windows. The stairs to the tower were still in place but were unsafe so Judas had to use a ladder to gain access to the tower and enjoy the view.

Judas loved this property and had development plans for this building, which would eventually bring it back into use as a guest house. That, however, was a project for the distant future. Next to the building the old Georgian coach house had been converted into a triple garage. Behind this transformed building there were three large, empty storerooms and above these were the old servants' quarters of the original mill owner. One day Judas would try and sort out what to do with the rooms, but that was a priority for a later occasion. In his domain, his study was the nerve centre of his home. All the bookcases contained his evening class notes and records.

The large plot his property stood on was on a slight rise with a herringbone bricked driveway. The front garden had two large lawns and associated borders, separated by the driveway. There were two further lawns at the rear of the buildings plus rockeries and vegetable plots. Judas was a competent gardener and he was very pleased with the developments he had done to the whole garden.

When he moved in, he discovered that the previous owners had found it very difficult to keep on top of the gardening requirements and had arranged for a local garden service to sort out the site problems. For the inner household duties Judas had obtained the services of a middle-aged lady cleaner, Mrs Juliette Gilchrist, who had been highly recommended by the previous owner's wife and came twice a week to deal with the household requirements. Judas had never regretted retaining her services and was also very impressed by the activities of the gardeners. They were much more competent than he and they maintained the garden to a very high standard.

After dinner Judas settled down in his study. He took from his side table the copious notes he had made from numerous books and newspaper articles and also from historical magazines. The latest notes he had entered were from a very old Victorian book outlining the known facts concerning the long lost property of the local ruined priory. He had picked up the book belonging to one of the security guards on his second or third day on the reception work.

"It's a damn good read and a fascinating subject," said Roy, the senior man, "I found it a totally compelling read and so did my colleague Geoff. I bought it in a second hand bookshop last year whilst on vacation in Chester and I just couldn't put it down."

Judas had thumbed through a couple of pages and agreed that it looked a good read, whereupon Roy said he could borrow the book.

The book was absolutely superb and it put all the known historical facts concerning the ruined priory and its stolen relics and artefacts in chronological order. It then added other pieces of information that were possibly true, followed by information that had once been believed but had then later been discredited. Judas was so impressed by the book he had ordered a copy from the local bookshop.

Judas had been told of the story whilst at infant school and at junior school and had often wondered what had happened to the abbey property. Many people had dedicated much time and effort to discovering the lost property but to date no-one had been successful. Every year or so the local paper gave space to the story and to the various attempts to solve the mystery. However no new information had been unearthed for years and even later books had not contained any new revelations about the lost items but had only repeated the known information. Some of the later books had sensationalized the more lurid known events but had not furthered the paths of knowledge or discovery. In fact, the earlier Victorian book contained in one tome all the known knowledge relating to the circumstances of the time. There were a few minor facts that had been unearthed after the old book had been published but nothing earth shattering. When he had read the book, Judas had checked his notes against the information in the book and made a few minor alterations to his script. He had then returned the book to Roy.

Judas opened the folder and began to read the notes he had penned, which contained some information extracted from the Victorian book written in 1840. Judas knew the facts practically by heart but there was always something special about reading them anew. He had obtained various printouts on his computer about the missing property, but there was no new concrete information available, although there was still plenty of speculation going on as to its whereabouts. After reading for about forty minutes Judas packed the information into his small case and got everything ready for the morning. For once he was looking forward to Christmas Day.

CHAPTER 2

Thursday 25th December

Judas walked to his Goods Reception Lodge in a positive mood and was anticipating a quiet day at work, when he could hopefully find time to re-read the notes he had viewed last night and look at the other papers he had brought with him. He arrived at work quite early and was greeted by Colin with the news that the first day guard was John and he was already out on his initial patrol.

"He should be back in the lodge in about 30 minutes," said Colin, "after he's completed the perimeter fence check. When Geoff arrives, I'm off. For the first time in years the roster sequence lets me be off with my family at Christmas and I'm going to enjoy it."

He smiled smugly at Judas and then realized that attendance at work was no problem for him, as he did not celebrate the Christian Festival.

Geoff arrived and Colin left the lodge after the very brief handover. Judas called out, "Merry Christmas" and received the same from the guard. Geoff then settled down to his paperwork, after the office and factory intruder alarm, fire alarm and smoke alarm systems had been activated. After a few minutes both men sat back and just as they were about to talk Judas heard the bleeping of the fax machine. All such machines in the complex had been switched to the Goods Reception Lodge and he walked over to the instrument. Judas put the non urgent paperwork in an envelope addressed to the sales section and placed it in his out tray. Judas and Geoff then turned their attention to their own work.

Judas looked at the paperwork left in his incoming tray by one of the office staff who must have left for home very late on Christmas Eve. It was a list of expected receipts and deliveries on the day the complex opened next year. He filed the list in his folder ready for the start of the New Year. He turned to Geoff and was surprised to see he was on the telephone. He then saw John, the other day guard, walking back to the security part of the Goods Reception Lodge and as he opened the door to enter he wished him, "The compliments of the season."

John smiled, "And may I return the compliments to your good self," he said very eloquently.

John was then greeted by Geoff.

"Our annual leave requests for April have been agreed and cover is available."

Both guards were relieved at the news and Geoff went out onto his patrol with an enthusiastic walk.

"I'll do a full internal patrol of the office block and factory and I should be back by 8 o'clock," said Geoff as he left the room.

It began to snow and Judas looked out over the small outer harbour. It was still quite dark and it was now eerily quiet. He turned around and looked out of the rear windows at the railway line. Beaufort St. Vincent was still a terminus, but an unused private railway siding, the company having ceased trading many years ago, had been extended to serve the inner harbour development and the industries situated through the short tunnel and inland.

He then turned and sought out the signal cabin that had been the place of employment of the handyman at the orphanage before his retirement. Every time he saw the signal box he thought of Adam. He had known him for all his youth and he felt it more than anyone when the old man passed away. Adam had been the signalman at the station during the war and he often told stories that captivated all the children.

Adam did the maintenance and gardening work at the orphanage and was very content to be overworked and very busy. He had lost his wife and both daughters during the war and had busied himself in his work to the end of his days. It was his way of coping with his loss. Adam was the person who had taught Judas much about gardening and carpentry and had also instilled in Judas the necessity of keeping records. Judas then came out of his reverie and began work.

He had decided to amend the layout of some forms he used on his duty and to try and cut down on the paperwork that was generated. The two part time staff had set up the documentation system and it was very cumbersome. Judas put his thoughts down on paper and eventually produced a system that amalgamated various forms into one. He had never seen the logic in having all the forms separate when some could be combined. Those that could not be changed he just accepted. However, he neatly wrote out all the forms he used on his duty and he would get some photocopies of them before he left the site tonight. The forms were used by Judas to prepare a monthly statistical record for the Company Facilities Manager and the part timers forms were always attached to the record. Judas left his amended papers on a cabinet by the door, as a reminder to him.

Then on a whim, as no other entries would be made by him on most of the forms for the remainder of the year, the exceptions being for the incoming and outgoing telephone calls and fax messages, Judas decided to complete the December return for his Facilities Manager. He carefully took the scraps of paper and recorded the information contained thereon onto his new return. He completed it in all sections and, where telephone calls and faxes were concerned, he entered the current figures in pencil, ready for any future amendment.

Judas sat back in his chair, facing his tidy desk and looked for something to do. It was however difficult as he had no outstanding work to do and the telephone and fax machine were exceptionally quiet. He looked around the lodge. Everywhere he looked boxes and files were stacked neatly and all work surfaces were clean, neat and tidy. He then entered a very small store room at the rear of his desk. It contained six metal filing cabinets, set against the far wall and he gingerly opened the upper drawer of the first cabinet. He saw that the contents were all neatly filed in order, but to his dismay he noted that last year's records needed shredding to make space for the New Year's papers. He remembered being told during his training that the work needed to be done and the previous part time staff said they would do it one weekend. Apparently they had found other things to do and the job was now urgent.

Judas began to put the records for shredding into an old sack and had emptied the first drawer when he heard John call his name. Judas looked around the door and saw John pointing to two cups of coffee and a glass of orange juice.

"It's very early for a break, but it is appreciated," said Judas. "I'll be there in a moment."

John and Geoff both had mince pies and a piece of cake with their drink, but they knew Judas would not eat anything.

"I always overeat at Christmas," said John, "but I thoroughly enjoy this time of year."

"Likewise," confirmed Geoff, "but the festive break passes so very quickly."

After ten minutes of idle banter with the guards, Judas returned to his small store room, opened the second drawer of the cabinet and was pleasantly surprised to find that there were no papers for shredding. He meticulously checked the other two drawers of the first cabinet and still found no papers for shredding. He quickly checked the contents of the remaining five cabinets and found that all scrapping had been done. He then checked the contents of the sack to make sure he had not made a mistake. He hadn't. His trainers had just overlooked one drawer of papers.

Judas then went into the alcove next to the store room and began shredding the offending records, after extracting all of the paperclips, pins and staples. On completion of that task he obtained fifteen photocopies of the forms he had prepared and filed them in his folder. The mid morning break arrived and Judas opened his case and took out his private notes. The guards usually staggered their coffee breaks, but today was different and they had arranged to sit together and enjoy each other's company.

These new notes related to what Adam had told him when he had been at the orphanage. He opened the folder and began to read. He had hardly begun this task when he had to stop. Judas was physically shaking as he recalled the terrible day when the old man died. He could still hear the high pitched shrill of the young girl who had found him slouched on the floor and the running feet of the staff going down the narrow stair case to the basement where Adam had his room next to the furnace. Adam was still alive and the doctor was sent for and as Judas was available he was dispatched to the surgery. Judas had only just returned to the orphanage after completing his evening paper deliveries for the local newsagent and wondered what the commotion was about. On hearing the news his blood froze but he ran like the wind to summon the doctor. Unfortunately the doctor arrived too late to help and Adam, a devout Christian, was reunited with his beloved wife and children.

Judas forced himself to continue reading and he completed the task with great difficulty. However the next section was a list of the possessions of the old man, neatly kept in his room and documented after his death. This unenviable task had been foisted on Judas as no-one else wished to do it. Judas had meticulously gone through every cupboard, drawer and wardrobe and had listed every found item and entered it under the location of finding. It was a task he had to do and he did it with great sadness and accuracy. He had never heard Adam talk of any living relatives but, if there were any, they were entitled to the possessions of the old man. He passed this list to the orphanage secretary and kept a copy for himself.

The next task he was assigned to complete was to sort out the contents of the old garden shed, where he found Wellington boots and heavy duty boots. Both pairs had belonged to Adam. All other items found in the garden shed were the property of the orphanage. Also in the shed was a small wooden cabinet which seemed out of place in such an environment. It was by the door and pushed under a small protruding shelf. Judas had checked the inside of the shed for any personal effects and nearly missed the cabinet and when he opened it he found that it contained balls of twine, pegs and other small items for gardening use. It also contained a series of ground plans, all showing the orphanage gardens, written out in Adam's neat hand, with the location of the types of vegetable plants he had sown. There were seven years of plantings and all were meticulously folded and kept for future reference. Judas had listed the items belonging to Adam and now re-read the entries.

Under these plans there was an old, well-used note book. After a quick perusal to view the contents and to see if anything important was written in it, Judas had placed the book into his pocket. He just wanted something to remind him of Adam and he did not think this book would be missed. Therefore the book was not logged. The book did contain some notes written by the old man. Judas did not, at that moment, have the time or the inclination to study the texts but knew he would scan them later. Judas also took one copy of each of the station track arrangements for Beaufort St. Vincent and Beaufort St. Clement and also the track arrangements of the inner harbour system. Therefore these plans were logged as only one each and not correctly as two.

Judas then took the book and plans in his hand and thought deeply about his long time friend Adam. He still missed the old man, his stories of life on the railways and the help he had offered whenever it was needed. Judas looked at the book. He had, on many occasions, read it from cover to cover and remembered everything it said, but he could not decipher any of the information. There was a sketch of a cross and it showed various lines and symbols that he just could not understand. The more Judas looked at it the more confused he became. Adam had once told him that his great uncle had believed the symbols had related to the church slaughter and possibly gave coded information on the location of the hidden abbey artefacts.

Judas then looked again at the plan showing the station track arrangement for Beaufort St. Clement. The small town was about twelve miles away and was also on the coast but had nearly been washed away by a freak storm in 1881, when a high tide had been churned up by exceptionally high winds. The railway bridges into the town were swamped by the inrushing water and the railway line itself, the station and much of the goods yard, coal yard and engine servicing facilities were damaged beyond repair as much of the track bed was underwater. Attempts were made to re-lay the railway track bed at a higher level but the damage done by the freak conditions had caused the proposed new route to be unstable and the town did not recover its former importance after the loss of its railway terminus. It was still a pleasant place and a much admired holiday destination, but there was very little industry other than that associated with vacations. It did have a very short pier, but the builders had suffered financial restraints.

The population of the town had dwindled and some of the nearby villages were larger. Beaufort St. Vincent was saved from a similar fate because it was in a much better sheltered position when the storm hit, covered by a high headland. Beaufort St. Clement had always been considered the premier railway terminus in the region, ahead of Beaufort St. Vincent, even though the towns railways shared a common connection to the rest of the national system, about six miles out of the towns. After 1881 the town of Beaufort St. Vincent seemed to prosper more following the demise of its battered neighbour.

Judas was brought back to his work by the view of vehicle headlights arriving at the gate of the office car park. Judas recognised the vehicle as that of one of the senior Section Leaders and operated the automatic barrier to allow the vehicle and driver access. The driver stopped at the Lodge.

Judas opened a window and was about to pass on a Christmas greeting when the driver said, "I'll be back in about fifteen minutes. I'll just park and go to my office. Please knock off the office alarms," and with that Henry Brown was gone. John isolated the zone before Judas could get to it.

"I wonder what the problem is for him to be here on Christmas Day?" queried John and then called Geoff on the radio to advise him of the Facilities Manager's arrival.

The Facilities Manager, true to his word, returned a few minutes later and parked his vehicle outside the lodge. John reset the alarm. Geoff arrived back at the lodge and held the door open for the boss. Both Judas and John stood as the others arrived. They all mumbled a greeting to Mr Brown but they all seemed to know that seasonal greetings would be out of place.

"There is no problem," said Henry Brown, as he looked into the faces before him and reading in each one that they were expecting some bad news, "but I just thought that I would come in and say that the management and staff appreciate you all being here on this special day to continue your work.

"We realize that for those of you with families it must be a very difficult time, especially if you have small children, or grandchildren. I just wanted to say that your work is much appreciated by us all. Keep up the good work and please pass on my best wishes to the other guards and also to your families."

With that he held out his hand to all the men present and firmly shook theirs.

"One final point," said Henry Brown, "As you know management have decided to have two Goods Reception people working in the lodge and the new man will begin here in early January. From January we, as a company, will be open seven days a week and vehicles will be entering and leaving the site all over the weekends. Eventually our engineering workforce will be working three eight hour shift patterns, the same as on the continent. Therefore we will need Goods Reception personnel here for the whole week, from six o'clock in the morning until six o'clock at night. Judas will train him and when trained he will work four days in the lodge and have four days off. Judas will work the other days and then have his days away. We will have to sort out what happens at the time of annual leave, but at the moment we will just get the new man started.

"It has also been decided to have the office reception people here on weekends, as we are going to expand our production and output when the present building work and installation work is completed. The other office staff, including my department, will have to work one weekend every month. Hopefully the New Year will be a very good one for us all. When I return in early January I will let you know more details about the new man," said Henry Brown, addressing this last remark to Judas. He then continued, "I actually came in today to pick up some papers that should have been left on my desk by Richard Foote, but they are not there. I telephoned Richard before I came to the lodge, but there was no reply."

After a few moments Henry Brown left. "Oh, by the way" he said as he closed the door, "Merry Christmas."

With that he was gone and Judas opened the barrier for him to leave the site.

"Well that was a bit unexpected," said Geoff as he left the lodge to continue his patrol, "I was expecting something really horrendous, not thanks for our work during the Christmas festivities."

"I think we all were," said Judas, "but that was very pleasant and very much appreciated. I was also pleased to hear about the new man starting in early January. I'm looking forward to meeting him."

At about one fifteen the security guards had their lunch together. Normally they did not, as one guard would be out on patrol whilst the other was eating. Judas went over to them and had a cold drink whilst the other men consumed their vast amount of sandwiches, cakes and biscuits. During the break the men talked generally about the meeting with Henry Brown and how much they appreciated his attendance and his words.

At this point Judas thought of the day and of how little work he had done. However he had been requested to attend for all of the festive season and he would do so, but he hoped that the rest of the holiday would be busier. Judas then remembered that the internal telephone directory he had inherited was in a terrible state. It had crossings out and insertions and it looked a complete mess. He decided to visit the company receptionist's desk and photocopy her directory. He then asked the guard if he had any problems with him going to the reception area. The guard looked up puzzled.

"I just want to go over to the reception area to do some photocopying of the receptionists telephone directory, as this one is a complete mess. I should only be about thirty minutes. I do have a swipe card giving access to all parts of the complex as I am fully qualified at first aid and I am also a fire marshal. Will this be okay?"

No objections were raised and Judas went over to the office complex to produce the required paperwork, ready for work in January.

Judas returned to the lodge and entertained himself for the rest of the afternoon tidying up some folders, used by one of his predecessors, but which had not been used since their departure. Most of the contents were out of date and some files were just empty. Judas shredded the lot and where the files were reusable, he had stored them for future use. Judas was so preoccupied with his work he was startled to hear Roy and Adrian enter the lodge together, ready for the night shift.

"Merry Christmas," echoed both incoming guards to the men in the lodge and all returned the seasonal greeting. Judas then advised both of the incoming guards about the visit of Henry Brown and of the sentiments expressed by him. Both guards just smiled and said nothing. The day guards then came over and handed the guarding responsibility for the site to the incoming staff.

"Have a quiet and peaceful night," said Judas as he left the lodge and began his solitary walk home.

One day down and ten to go until normality returns and the factory opens, mused Judas. He entered his world and closed the door onto the outside world. His world was warm and cosy and he was slowly thawing out.

After a simple meal, he went into his study, opened his small case and began to read. As he was not overlooking Adam's old signal box, reading the information was much easier. Judas knew the information about the abbey by heart, but nothing fitted. In all of the various books he had read about the abbey and its lost artefacts, the authors had all indicated that nothing had ever been found that gave an indication of the whereabouts of the items. The only information Judas had read, concerning details of the items hidden by the two monks, was the list provided by Adam. He again looked at the page in Adam's book and began to ponder its meaning.

He still couldn't make sense of the markings and was beginning to feel that the copying of the original information from the actual cross might have been faulty. He persisted, but after an hour of fruitless endeavour, he decided to put away his papers. As he put down Adam's old notebook, open but with both covers flat to the small table, the pages parted and presented a page showing the drawing of an unknown object. This object was completely out of place in this book. It was in Adam's unmistakable hand although the wording on it was printed and could not be confirmed as Adam's.

The printed words simply said, "*NOTHING FITS. RIVERS IN WRONG PLACES, SETTLEMENTS IN WRONG PLACES and HILLS IN WRONG PLACES. NOTHING FITS.*"

However, it did have the arrow of a draughtsman pointing upwards next to the drawing and this was definitely Adam's work. The actual drawing was of an object and had nothing to do with geography. Judas looked at the page but could not figure out what the drawing represented.

He then yawned and realised he was tired, however he reflected that he had been busy all day although he didn't think he had achieved much at his employment. However he thought he had achieved less on his pet project whilst at home. He thought back to the page in the notebook, but decided that it would be better if he approached the subject with a fresh mind in the morning. He turned down his lighting and stared out of the window. The scene was very wintry and the Christmas tree lights were flickering on and off in the market square.

CHAPTER 3

Friday 26th December

Judas arrived early and was greeted by both Roy and Adrian, who were sitting at their desk ready for departure when their colleagues arrived.

"Any problems during the shift," asked Judas and both guards shook their heads. "Ah good," continued Judas, "hopefully the day will continue in a similar vein."

He went to his desk and pulled out a file with a few notes attached and began to read. He knew nothing contained on the file was urgent but he was reminding himself of the contents. Roy approached.

"Oh I nearly forgot," he said, "A lady telephoned early this morning, just after midnight and asked if you were working over Christmas. I said you were on the day shift and she said she would be here about ten o'clock to see you. Her name was Anita Wells. Your sister I presume. I hope this was okay?"

"Perfectly okay," said Judas, "but she is not my sister, and we are not related. It is just a coincidence that we have the same surname. The relevant authorities never gave either of us any additional information concerning this fact. Anita and I go back a long way. We were both born in the same orphanage and grew up together. She is my oldest and dearest friend. I told her in mid December that I had volunteered for extra work during the festive period and might be working over Christmas. Usually at weekends I visit her at the guest house called the Poacher's Retreat."

Roy was about to say something else, but at that moment the door opened and the first relief guard entered and Roy, after a speedy handover, headed for the exit door. A few moments later the other day guard arrived and Adrian left the building after a short conversation with his colleague.

Judas called "Good morning guys," over to John and Geoff, the incoming guards and they then all settled down to the events of the day. Judas looked for some work to do but could find none. Geoff left the security lodge after a few minutes to do his first patrol. Judas then had a thought. He had never been over to the main office, except the reception area, since he began work for the company and he was curious. He called to John.

"Would you have any objections to my going round the office block and the factory, just to acquaint myself with the layout of the site? I will take a radio set with me and if any problems turn up, contact me and I will return straight away."

After receiving no objections, Judas asked John to advise Geoff that he was going into the office and factory areas.

"Here, take these floor plans and keep them for your records" said John. "We have plenty of copies. We give them to new guards or relief guards to help them understand the building layouts."

Judas then advised John that he was expecting a visitor at about ten o'clock and then left the lodge and began his tour of exploration in the main company complex, beginning at the reception area.

For a mid range company dealing with model railway products, it was a well run organization with a very solid selection of sought after equipment. On his safari through the office complex, the drawing office, the production section and the transport department, Judas was very impressed by the cleanliness of the numerous sections. He was also impressed by the fact that all work in the clerical departments had been filed away, presumably in locked cupboards, for the sake of privacy. Judas thought back to his previous employment when he was the only person to file his current work away before leaving for the day and to unlock the cabinet when he entered his room in the morning, to retrieve his papers. Even his bosses left documents in their trays for anyone to view, unless the papers were of a private nature. He continued through the various corridors to numerous sections and departments and enjoyed his time as he learned much to put meat onto the bones of his present knowledge.

He entered a room off the drawing office and was surprised by its size. It was a second drawing office and was massive, but only seven positions were upright. The rest were evidently not used. He saw a sign on the wall, advising everyone to cover their work when they left the room and to file all of their papers and drawings when they vacated the building. He also saw photographs on walls and on boards showing various models they produced of locomotives, carriages, wagons and of associated railway buildings and structures. There were also diagrams of popular model railway layouts and Judas was fascinated by them, as Adam had often shown him drawings of various local station building designs and associated track formations. Judas was impressed by what he saw. The products and designs seemed to be of a very high quality and he knew, from his conversations with the security guards, that all the products were very popular in the retail shops.

After an hour of very fruitful exploration, Judas returned to his workplace.

Geoff asked, "Did you enjoy your trek around the office block?" and was happy to receive a positive reply.

"It was very helpful for me and a good time to explore when the buildings were empty. I thoroughly enjoyed it," beamed Judas.

He looked at the floor plans he had been given earlier by John and after a few moments he filed them at the front of the telephone directory folder, together with the plans he had photocopied from the receptionist's folder.

He then asked Geoff, "Has anyone telephoned the reception number?" and was relieved to receive a negative reply. It was now seven twenty and Judas could find nothing to do and was feeling surplus to requirements, when suddenly the intruder alarms sounded.

Geoff called John on the radio and directed him to the area of the factory that was flashing on the alarm console.

John replied "OK I'm investigating," and the radio channel was kept open. Judas went over to John's desk and waited. After what seemed an eternity John's voice came over the radio.

"Everything is okay, a bird has flown into a window and triggered the alarm. There is no problem. The alarms can be reset." Geoff chuckled into the radio.

"Thank God for that. I don't think the factory manager on call would be too keen to attend to any intruder incident today. Just think of the paperwork involved."

John laughed and went off air. However, to be on the safe side, Geoff left the office and joined John for a thorough search of the building interior, followed by a complex search of the site perimeter.

"We wouldn't normally both leave the security section," said Geoff as he closed the door, "but as you are with us for the Christmas period, it makes sense to do this. Any problems at all, contact us on the radio and we will come running. Well walking fast anyway," he joked.

Judas was on his own. He kept looking at the computer screens and at the intruder console. He had been trained on what to do in the unlikely event of one guard having to help the other, but he did not expect it to happen. His trainers had told him that they had never experienced any criminal incursions on the site during their involvement with the company.

Judas mused, "Just my luck."

After an hour both guards returned to the lodge and wrote in the guard report sheet. Geoff advised Judas that normally there were some people working in the factory or in the office block and the guards could count on them for assistance, but on Bank Holidays the whole complex was closed down. It was just unfortunate that today was the day the incident happened. However, no harm was done and everything was now back to normal. Both guards sat down and composed a report and then advised their security control. Judas went back to his section of the lodge and sat down at his desk. It was still only eight thirty and Anita was not due until ten o'clock. He then had a thought.

"Would you like me to do a thorough fence patrol? It will help me to understand the site better and will also give you both a bit of a break after the alarm problem?"

He addressed the question to no-one in particular but both guards nodded and it was Geoff who said, "We are both grateful. Many thanks Judas. We really need a rest after that incident. When alarms sound there is always an adrenaline rush, as you never know what to expect."

"Once more into the breach," said Judas and left the lodge. "Any problems, then you know the drill better than I."

He walked along the whole length of the perimeter fence, encompassing the complete site. He then walked around the various buildings, checking for any damage or security hazards, but could find none. He also checked various storage tanks and large containers and again could find no problem with the items. At nine fifty he returned to the lodge and was surprised to find Anita waiting for him.

John approached Judas and advised him, "Henry Brown telephoned a short time ago and said he would visit the lodge at about eleven o'clock. Before you ask, I have no idea why he will be here. He did not say," and with that John left.

Judas turned to Anita and smiled.

"It's good to see you" he said, "Have you enjoyed the break?"

Anita returned the smile and nodded.

"I only came in to see if there is anything you need. I know you don't celebrate this time of year, but I thought I would come in and see you anyway," she said.

"Thanks, but everything's okay," said Judas, "but I am still very pleased to see you." Anita then slipped an envelope and a notebook to Judas and he put the envelope in his pocket. He knew that it contained a payment of £200, which Anita gave him every month to pay off a debt. He signed the notebook next to the entry to say he had received the money.

A number of years ago Anita was having financial problems and was in danger of losing her guest house to the bank. Judas prevented this catastrophe and Anita was able to struggle on and the guest house became established and very successful. After a year Anita was able to begin repayments and the present sum was part of the process. Judas was not a registered usurer and did not expect or receive interest. However, he was always interested in any news concerning the guest house. He had also informed Anita that if the repayment money was getting to be a problem, then he was only too happy to stop the payments until business perked up. On signing the notebook he noticed that the amount outstanding was down to £4800.

Anita continued, "As I was going to be in the area, visiting one of our cleaners who has a very bad cold, I thought I would pop in and give you a verbal update."

She then outlined the bookings for the next few days and for the early part of the New Year. Judas listened intently and was very pleased that the guest house was such a great success.

"Oh by the way," continued Anita, "the girls working at the Retreat have asked me to thank you for their Christmas Cards and the boxes of chocolates and I would also like to thank you for my card and also for my perfume."

They looked at each other and laughed.

"However, tomorrow we will get back to normal and I will open up the place and switch on the sign saying 'Vacancies' and hopefully we will get some more customers."

Anita then continued, "Have you thought anymore about the Miller's Retreat being converted back to a guest house?"

His reply seemed to surprise Anita.

"Yes," said Judas, "I was going to give it some serious thought in the New Year, so I suppose I will now have to bring it forward."

Judas remembered back to the time when Anita had been given the guided tour of his property a couple of years ago. It was then that Anita had said that it would make a very fine guest house and she was certain that it would be a great success. She knew that Judas had bought the property with the intention of converting it back to a guest house, but not this quickly. However, he was seriously thinking of the idea and was also thinking that if he could turn the storerooms and the old servants' quarters into some sort of annexe it would create better living conditions for the resident housekeeper. When this was accomplished Anita and her accomplished deputy could then have another guest house to supervise. It was also in the mind of Judas that he could help with any chores at the guest house that might arise during his days away from his present work. Anita had known for a long time that the thought of developing the guest house interested him, but when she had first asked the question she believed it was just that: a thought. Anita, however, now knew that the thought was becoming a reality and she inwardly smiled as she realised that her mentioning about the development of the building every couple of months or so, had now triggered a reaction and the idea had gradually gained momentum in his mind.

"Oh! Great news," said Anita and was about to say something else, but at that moment the barrier began to raise and Judas looked out and saw the vehicle of Henry Brown.

He's early, thought Judas, as he saw Henry Brown manoeuvre his vehicle into a lodge parking bay.

"He needn't have bothered to be so precise," said John. "He's the only car in the whole of the car park!" and he laughed.

"Okay," said Anita smiling, "I will leave. I'll be in the guest house early tomorrow Judas. See you soon when hopefully we can discuss guest house developments."

With that she was gone. Judas took the £200 from the envelope and placed it into his wallet.

Henry Brown entered the lodge a few moments later. He was not smiling and he looked worried. He took off his trilby hat and overcoat and hung them on the coat hook behind the door.

"I have some bad news," he said, looking into the faces of all the men present. "Our chief layout designer for our model railway layout books, Richard Foote, has had a massive heart attack and has died." He waited for the news to sink in before continuing. "He was only fifty and we never suspected that he had any medical problems. Just before Christmas Richard said he was working on various layout plans that he hoped would be okay to go into the new book. These were the plans that should have been left on my desk. Tomorrow, a few of the draughtsmen working with him will be coming into the site to try and find the plans he was working on. Other staff will also be coming in to the complex to help. Hopefully, they will then get these plans and sketches into some semblance of order for us to try and deliver the new layout book. We promised the model railway press that we would have another book out early in the New Year and we have no option but to produce one." Henry Brown stopped speaking and let his words sink in further.

He then began again, "He did not have any family and his work was his life. He loved model railways and had a large layout in a special room he had built behind his garage. It was a superb layout and he had a plan of the system prepared for the book, plus great photographs showing the stations, line side industries and the harbour. He had begun the layout thirty years ago and had been slowly developing it.

"In the book it was hoped to show that layouts could start small and develop into larger complex layouts over a long period. He was trying to show that model railways were a great way of generating interest in the subject and adding to the project as and when the financial abilities permitted. We will have to work really hard to produce the required drawings for the publication but we will succeed. We will be here early in the morning, so could you please inform your colleagues, who will be coming in later, of the happenings, so there are no problems."

Both of the guards nodded and simply said "Okay."

Henry Brown then handed to the guards a sheet of paper showing the names of the staff arriving into work the next morning, from the drawing office, the graphics department, the publicity department, the design bureau and the illustrators.

Judas then asked, "Do you have any idea of the whereabouts of the papers required, or do they need to be unearthed?"

"Unearthed," said Mr Brown, "but I am sure we will find them locked away in his safe. It would be best if I could search for them now but I don't have a key for his safe. However, one of the drawing office staff has access to the safe and he has been contacted by telephone and he will drive back from his brother's tonight and be here with us in the morning. We will be able to get duplicate photographs of Richard's home layout, but if we cannot find his layout drawings I shudder to think what will happen. He was the sort of person who constantly dreamed up new layouts and just jotted them down on scraps of paper." He stopped again to catch his breath.

"You look very tired Mr Brown," said John. "We will let the night staff know what has happened, but I expect that Geoff and I will be on duty when staff arrive early in the morning. As you said you can't do anything now, so why not go home and relax for the rest of the day?"

Henry Brown agreed, "Yes I think I will." Then as an afterthought he said "Oh by the way, if any of you can think up some track ideas, it would not go unrewarded." With that he picked up his overcoat and hat and left the lodge. A few moments later he was off the site.

Judas congratulated John on saying what he had to Henry Brown.

"It hit the nail right on the head, he did look very tired and he certainly couldn't do anything today. Well done. You deserve Brownie points."

John smiled and seemed to blush.

"What did he mean about track ideas?" queried Judas.

John took a deep breath and replied, "A couple of years ago the then layout designer had a thought that people working on this site might have some ideas about track planning. A few of us thought up some plans for a small layout and three were published, although slightly altered and mine was one of them. I suppose I had better put my thinking cap on again. Although, in all honesty, it was my grandson who devised the plan, in reality in his train room and just copied down the track arrangement of his present layout. Most of the scheme was shown in the book."

Judas sat down at his desk and digested the information given by Henry Brown and the add-on by John. He thought back to Adam and of the copies of track layouts he had. He then realized that these plans were in his small case and he opened it up to retrieve the papers. He looked through all of the papers and knew that some of the stations had been closed during the Beeching exercise, but he thought that the other diagrams of rail formations might be of use.

He went over to the guard's desk and asked John, "Do you hold a copy of the last brochure for the company's products? I only ask as I am completely ignorant of anything to do with model railways, but as I have time on my hands at the moment, I thought I might try and develop my ignorance into something productive."

John looked up and smiled, "I can do better than that," he said. "The old guys on your job passed all of their model railway papers and accessories to us before they left and we just filed them with ours. I'll get them out for you later, plus the one eighth track planning package the drawing office gave out when they were eager to get layout ideas. After a good read of the paperwork and a few attempts at getting used to the track geometry, you should be okay. I'm no expert but I did do reasonably well, although my grandson did much better than I did."

Judas thanked him and sat down at his desk. True to his word, twenty minutes later John produced the box containing a load of papers and accessories and gave them to Judas.

"This is last year's sales brochure, showing photographs of all the products manufactured by the company," said John. "It will give you a good idea of the models produced and the latest two layout books will give you an insight into the level of track designs required. Have fun." He turned away but continued over his shoulder, "By the way, when you want to know about the one eighth board and the miniature track pieces just give me a shout and I will come over and explain it to you." And with that he retreated to his desk.

For the next two hours Judas diligently read the company literature and studied the track layout plan books and was thoroughly absorbed by the subjects. He then tentatively began to use the small track pieces to copy track formations in the layout book. He was going to ask for help, but John was out on his patrol and Geoff was in a deep conversation with his controller on the telephone. After a few trials with some simple designs, he ventured onto a more complex layout and was surprised how simple it was becoming. He continued scanning the track layout book and saw four plans that he liked parts of, but other sections of the designs did not seem to be of the same excellence. He therefore used the small track pieces to duplicate the parts of the plans that he liked and then joined the four parts to make two new layouts. He was beginning to see the light at the end of the tunnel!

Judas produced four plans in total and then entered them onto graph paper and then entered the rail code next to the item. He then looked up and saw both guards having lunch. He looked at the wall clock and was surprised to see it was two o'clock. He prepared himself an orange squash and went over to sit with John and Geoff. They both looked up and Judas showed them his efforts at the plans.

"I'm impressed," said John. "You seem to know what's required. Keep using the small track pieces and you can really make some complex track plans. Try using the board next time as this will give a scale area for you to plan your layout inside. It comes in handy, as it stops you trying to put track into spaces that it simply cannot fit into. However, very good."

"Yes, very good," added Geoff who had also looked at the plans and then again said, "Very good." Judas smiled as he downed his drink.

After half an hour Judas returned to his desk. As he sat down the telephone rang.

It was Anita. She simply said, "On my way back to the guest house, I decided that I needed some exercise so I made a long detour. I eventually circled back to the town and I passed the timber yard. I saw that a delivery of damaged poles had been made, presumably just before Christmas and had been placed neatly in the compound. It looks like Simon will have some exercise when he returns to work, getting them sawn up and bagged." She laughed. Anita knew that Judas had helped Martin and his wife Susan with money to keep the timber business going, after the banks had refused them a loan and she also knew that the business was now financially secure.

"Great," said Judas. "Hopefully next week Martin and Susan will have plenty of customers wanting wood, as the weather forecast for the rest of the year is not very good."

Anita then said, "It was good to hear that you are considering opening up the Miller's Retreat. This town urgently needs another good guest house and I am sure it would be a great success. Please keep me updated on your thoughts. I've got to go now. Speak to you soon," and with that she was gone.

For the rest of the afternoon Judas read and re-read the brochures and the track plan books. He sketched out some more layout thoughts onto paper and the small track pieces were then used to confirm that the track geometry was correct. He also used the scale board and was finding it to be a very useful tool as it gave a scale area for him to work to. He then produced some more drawings onto graph paper and entered the rail codes next to them. At five fifty he photocopied his plans and put the original ones in an envelope ready for Mr Brown. He then placed the brochures, the track plan book, the small scale track pieces and the scale board into his case and clicked it closed. His mind was still on layout planning and he had a few other track ideas that he would pursue later tonight.

At six o'clock Judas left the lodge as John and Geoff were outlining the day's happenings to the incoming guards Adrian and Roy.

"Goodnight everyone," said Judas as he left the lodge. He then walked to the timber yard. It was on his way home, with only a slight detour. On reaching it Judas looked into the compound and saw the damaged poles through the windows, sitting neatly by the wall in the compound. Martin would definitely have plenty of exercise on his return to work and hopefully Susan would be inundated with orders for firewood. He continued his walk home.

After his evening meal Judas entered his study and extracted from his case the items he had brought home from work. For the next hour he juggled various ideas around and eventually he had four new designs of layouts that he was very pleased with. He wrote out the plans in the usual way and was very satisfied with his evening's labours. After a few moments deliberation he telephoned Martin at his home, near to the Timber Yard and wished him and Susan a belated "Merry Christmas." Martin already knew about the poles being in the compound, as he had been on site when they had been delivered on Christmas Eve morning.

"On Monday we get back to normal," said Martin, "and I sincerely hope next year is as good and productive as this year."

CHAPTER 4

Saturday 27th December

On arrival at work Judas was surprised to see that the car park had a number of vehicles occupying the design bureau spaces. He was expecting various visitors during the day, but not this early. Judas opened the lodge door and was greeted by Adrian.

"The first person arrived at about five twenty and the rest came soon after," he said. "Roy is with them at the moment in the design section and should be back any moment now. I just hope they find the papers and drawings they are looking for."

At that moment Roy returned and nodded to Judas and then said "Some papers have been found, but not the most important ones. However they are still searching."

With that the lodge door opened and John and Geoff entered together, for their last but one day shift of the year and were apprised of the situation with the design staff. On completion of the handover Adrian and Roy left the site and after contacting their control to sign on duty, John and Geoff began to write up their logbook.

Judas sat at his desk and took out the plans he had laboured on the previous night. He still liked the look of them and inwardly congratulated himself on the designs. He would pass the plans to Mr Brown during the day and hopefully get some feedback on whether they were of any use to him, or not. He also carried in his case the notes he had on the lost property of the local ruined abbey.

He walked over to the guards and was about to speak when his duty telephone began to ring. He wandered back to his desk, answered the call and transferred Mrs Brown to the Design Bureau extension. Judas returned to the guards, who had finished preparing their report book and were watching the happenings in the car park outside the design section external door. Numerous people were carrying small personal cases and lunch boxes from their vehicles to the offices and the security doors were closed behind them.

"God I hope they find the papers they are searching for," said Geoff and then added, "It looks like being a very long day for them all." Judas agreed and walked back to his desk and again looked at his drawings.

The morning was quite busy, both in the main building and in the lodge. The men in the design bureau were searching in every conceivable nook and cranny, trying to find the missing paperwork of Richard Foote. After only a few minutes of fruitless search, Mr Brown telephoned Judas.

"I have some names and telephone numbers of personnel that need to be contacted," he said, "but as you know we have problems here at the moment. Would you please collect the list and phone the people, but do not phone before about eight thirty. When contacted, please transfer the call back to me in the design bureau."

Judas collected the list from Mr Brown's desk, but the bureau boss was nowhere to be seen. The bureau door had been left open and Judas commented, "Henry Brown really must have a lot on his mind to allow such a breach of security."

Judas busied himself at his desk and at the required hour he began his telephoning. All of the calls were to distant locations and only two of the eight failed to connect. Some people were not happy to have their Christmas vacation interrupted, but when Judas explained about Mr Foote's demise and the circumstances, their attitude changed. He transferred all six of the contacts to the design section and concentrated on the outstanding two numbers and called every fifteen minutes. On the second attempt he contacted both of the outstanding parties and he transferred the calls as requested. Judas then updated his statistics form to include the telephone calls.

Good job I only totalled this section in pencil he thought.

It was at about nine thirty that Henry Brown ran over to the security lodge and with a beaming smile announced that the "lost" papers had been found, together with some other papers that were associated with the plans and also the photographs of Richard Foote's superb model railway layout.

"Ironically it was the last person that you put through to me that sorted out the problem," he said to Judas. "Robert Grey was having coffee with his design colleague Richard just before Robert left the site to go away for his seasonal break. Richard showed him some plans and asked for his comments, which Robert duly gave. These comments were very positive and Richard seemed happy. Richard then wished Robert a Merry Christmas and put the papers in his A5 folder and slid this into his overall pocket. We found his overall hanging by his office chair and the folder, photos and papers were still in the pocket. Success!" He beamed.

"That is good news," said Judas and then looked over to the part of the car park holding the vehicles of the design staff. He saw some of the vehicles moving towards the exit gate.

"Some of the guys are leaving to return to their homes," said Henry Brown, "and the senior men are staying to get the drawings, photographs and notes into some semblance of order. Richard Foote was a very gifted man, but he was very untidy at his desk and we have found numerous drawings, sketches, notes, photographs and various scribbles in all sorts of places in his office. I suppose I had better return to the job in hand, but I thought I would give you the good news. Your colleague John already knows as he was with us during our search," concluded Henry Brown.

"Thanks for the information," said Judas, "I will pass the news to Geoff when he returns from his patrol."

Henry Brown was very relieved and Judas could see that a large weight had been lifted from his shoulders. Mr Brown then said, "My only involvement with this layout book was to take the plans from Richard Foote and take them to the Managing Director for his inspection and approval. I was actually going to see him tomorrow at his home and deliver the papers to him there. God knows what I would have done, or said to the MD if the papers were still lost. I am so relieved."

Judas then said, "This may not be the moment, but whilst you are here Mr Brown, I would like to show you some forms that I have amended, which will be easier to complete and use. The old forms were numerous and cumbersome and this revised form can be used to replace a number of the old forms. I must admit there are two forms it cannot replace so I have left these alone, except that I have written them out neatly and have photocopies. At the end of the year I will send the statistics over to you with the old forms and the new forms and you will see the benefits of the new system. That is I hope you do." Judas handed blank copies of the forms to Mr Brown, who in his relieved state seemed happy to receive them.

Judas then continued, "You asked us to prepare some layout drawings for you, in case the papers from Mr Foote could not be located. I obtained some literature from John, which I avidly read, and I also read the layout books supplied. I was also given the miniature track pieces and I have been quite busy. These are the layouts I have been trying to sort out and if they are of any use perhaps you would let me know. I believe John may have some plans also."

Henry Brown also accepted the layout folder from Judas and thanked him for his efforts. He seemed surprised at the number of pages in the folder and said "I will definitely look at them later, but at present I must get back to the office and to my colleagues."

Judas watched Henry Brown as he walked back towards the design bureau office and thought that he would hear nothing more about his track designs, as the papers of Richard Foote had been unearthed. He was therefore surprised when he saw Mr Brown go to his vehicle and place the folder onto his front passenger seat.

Judas returned to his desk as the telephone was ringing. It was Anita.

"Sorry to ring you at work," she said, "but I have been discussing with Stephanie Faulkner the prospect of having another guest house to run and we have a slight problem that could be proving very costly. I will come straight to the point. People are now telephoning me for vacation reservations for May, June, July and I have just had one for August. We are half booked already and I know some of our regulars would be disappointed if they could not stay with us, so I have pencilled in their names and will be contacting them in the next few days to get confirmation of their dates. This town is a very popular holiday destination and if we had either a larger guest house, with more rooms, or even another guest house, we could make more profit. Have you thought anymore about what you said yesterday? I am not trying to pressurise you but it is a good opportunity to make another sound investment and I am certain that you will not lose out financially."

Anita stopped to take breath. Judas was convinced that she had read the conversation from her note pad and was also very nervous. He then said, "I was going to ponder over the problems tonight and look at various plans for the property. I will telephone you tonight and we can discuss my thoughts."

For a good part of the morning, Judas doodled some plans for the conversion of the store rooms behind the triple garages and the old servants' quarters, into habitable quarters for the person running the guest house. He was determined that their rooms would be better than those used by him or the previous owners. There was no great amount of work to be done in the lodge, only a few telephone queries and for most of these calls he was able to satisfy the caller's queries. Also a few fax messages were received, which he posted to the correct department. Other telephone calls he put through to answering machines. He mused that he was busier today than yesterday, but he still hadn't done much actual work.

He had, however, already done scale drawings of the rooms involved in his home project and he was making reasonable progress. He wasn't too worried about the conversion of the main property to a guest house as it had already been done once, although he would have to comply with new fire and safety regulations and with health and safety standards. Judas mused that he was certain that Anita had possibly sorted out these problems already. He came up with a few ideas that he was pleased with concerning these proposed new living quarters, but nothing that gave him a real buzz.

The lunch break came and Judas sat with John and Geoff and had a cool drink with them as they consumed the contents of their bulging lunch boxes. The guards talked about the day's events and also of what they were planning to do whilst they were both away from work on their rest days.

"I'm off to see my sister Eileen, with my wife," said John, "and we will both definitely enjoy the gastronomic experience. Her husband Paul was a hotel chef and is a fantastic cook."

Geoff laughed and countered with, "I am under orders from 'she who must be obeyed' to take her to her favourite shop to buy her a birthday present. This is one of the problems when birthdays and Christmas Day follow each other."

Both John and Judas sympathised. Eventually the conversation turned to the complexities of the local football team, grandly called Beaufort Valley Rangers, and of its lack of success. Judas excused himself and returned to his desk.

When seated Judas pulled out his folder and began again to doodle various plans for the rooms behind the garage. The area was not excessive but he thought it would be adequate and much better that the rooms he was using at present. He knew when he bought the main building that it was a large development project for him and he also knew that the property would end up as a guest house, but he wasn't expecting it to be so soon. Judas kept sketching away and then suddenly he had the spark of an idea.

For the next thirty minutes Judas produced four plans that he enjoyed and was fully satisfied with their content, but still he wanted something better. He kept changing the layout of the plans but seemed stumped to find any improvement. He heard Geoff close the door as he left the lodge and knew the lunch break was over.

He put the plans away into his case and looked for some work to do. He looked into the car park and saw some of the staff in the car park having a cigarette break. Henry Brown was with them although he was a non-smoker. After a few minutes Mr Brown went to his vehicle and took out the papers from the front passenger seat. He pulled them from the envelope and after a detailed scan he walked to the lodge.

"Judas," said Henry Brown, "these new forms are very much better than the old ones, so please go ahead and use them for all future statistics." He then added "Well done."

Mr Brown then left the lodge and returned towards his colleagues enjoying their cigarettes. It was then that he saw the layout plans prepared by Judas and he stopped in mid stride. He rejoined the group and showed the plans to some of his colleagues. After a few moments four of the group, including Henry Brown, walked into the factory building. After fifteen minutes this group walked towards the lodge, each of them carrying a wad of papers.

"Oh hellfire," said Judas, under his breath, as he watched the group get closer.

As he entered the lodge, Henry Brown asked, "Judas, are these plans your handy work?" and he produced the papers he had been given earlier.

"Yes," replied Judas very defensively, "I did have an attempt at trying to sort out some simple plans as you requested. Is there a problem?" He then added, "Are they any good?"

"Good," said Henry Brown, "they are superb. Just what we needed. They are not in the same league as Richard Foote's complex designs, but they are perfect for the development of the basic train set to a layout that is operationally taxing for the youthful and enquiring mind of a young train enthusiast. Just what we needed. Can you do some more?"

Judas smiled, "I am so pleased that you like them." He looked into the faces of the group and was surprised to see them all smiling. He then reached into his case and extracted twelve more designs and handed them to Henry Brown. Mr

Brown placed them onto the table and was smiling from ear to ear. His colleagues were also smiling and one of them said, "These are absolutely brilliant. You look at some track plans and you just know that they will work. Believe me these will work," and with that he slapped Judas on the back.

The group returned to the main complex and after forty minutes, Judas was summoned to the Design Bureau. Henry Brown met him at the door, where the smokers had congregated and let him in.

"Don't look so worried," he said. "We thought you would like to see one of your plans laid out on a baseboard." He then guided Judas to the design workshop where a number of staff were busy constructing a model railway from one of the plans supplied by Judas. Some of the guys looked up and waved. Judas smiled back.

"You seem to be quite popular at the moment," said Henry Brown. "We've put a couple of your plans into a computer and put in the station building, the signal cabin, the goods shed, the cattle dock, the coal yard and the loading dock. This is a printout of the finished item. We are absolutely thrilled with the results. These plans are really good and the guys in the design section are adamant that they should go into the layout book. They are also pleased at the way you picked out the main point of the design, like the cross country station and just concentrated on that and left the rest of the layout for the builder to utilize the space he had left to complete the layout. Very well done. We are going to do this treatment to all of your plans and when we have finished I will bring over printouts of the computer graphics."

Henry Brown then handed over the computer printout and Judas was amazed at the amount of detail shown on the printed page.

"Thank you Mr Brown," he mumbled, slightly embarrassed, as he returned to his work place. He was really chuffed at the events of the day. He was greeted at the door of the lodge by John, who was excited because another plan of his grandson had been accepted for publication.

For the remainder of the afternoon, Judas was busy dealing with telephone calls from wives seeking times of their husbands' arrival at home and also dealing with various faxes from non-Christian countries that believed the factory to be operational. Judas was dealing with a fax request when Mr Brown came into the lodge and handed him the promised computer graphics.

"As promised," he said. "The design staff have asked me to thank you and to congratulate you on the work you have done with the track plans. They really are superb and we are all sure that the layout book we are working on will be a great success. Thank you once again." With that Henry Brown left the room and walked to his vehicle.

A few moments later both Adrian and Roy entered the lodge and John and Geoff began the handover procedure. Judas packed the information recently given to him into his small case and readied himself for exiting the lodge.

During his walk home he thought about the plans he had drawn of the rooms behind the garage. He then stopped in his tracks and discovered new thoughts racing through his mind. Stephanie Faulkner, Anita's deputy, would be in charge of the Poacher's Retreat when Anita, hopefully, took on the running of the Miller's Retreat. Stephanie lived with her husband, in the property at the rear of the guest house. There was even a garden gate adjoining the properties and in any emergencies Stephanie could be on site within minutes. Therefore, Anita's present, basic accommodation, consisting of a small bedroom, shower room and small sitting room, could be converted into another en- suite bedroom for guests when she took over the new guest house. That would mean Anita would need her own rooms and these should be located away from the guest house, but close to hand. Judas knew he had to give his dearest friend some excellent living accommodation and ideally the rooms behind the garage would be perfect and they could be converted into something special. This then gave Judas more problems than answers and he now had to sort out the requirements of Anita. He would ask her tonight for her input. He also had to sort out his own requirements for his own future home.

Judas was brought out of his thoughts when he entered his home and was surprised to see some post on his kitchenette table. It had been placed there by Juliette, his cleaning lady. There was also a thank you note from her, concerning his Christmas present of a bottle of her favourite perfume. Juliette always preferred to do this cleaning work on Fridays and Saturdays, as her husband was a sports fanatic and spent his weekends supporting his local football or rugby team in the winter, or his cricket team in the summer. Juliette always kept his small annexe spotless and the rest of the building was always clean, neat and tidy. Juliette was always paid cash and Judas always left the money under his tin mug in the kitchen.

Judas opened his other post, but as none of it was urgent, he put it on his computer desk for viewing later. An hour later he settled down to some serious thinking about the proposed guest house. He extracted the building layout plans from his file and studied them carefully. Most of the main building fell into place with only a couple of glitches and these could be sorted out with Anita's help. However, the storerooms behind the garages and the old servants' quarters above these rooms were causing problems. He thought Anita would like plenty of space for her accommodation, but he was having great difficulty in getting any resolution to the problems. Nothing was resolved and he failed miserably. He continued for an hour, but could not produce a plan that was acceptable to him.

He then stood up, walked round his desk and reached for the telephone to contact his friend. As he returned to his desk he saw the plan upside down and something clicked in his brain. He put down the telephone and began to think of new designs.

In addition to the three large storerooms and the old servants' quarters, he added in the two large bedrooms and shower room above the triple garage. Judas then doodled some new and even bigger plans, showing a kitchen, utility, dining room, lounge and toilet on the ground floor and two bedrooms, an en-suite, a bathroom, study and a sitting room, on the first floor. Judas thought to himself, *this is more like it*. He sketched a few more plans, but could not improve on the original one and so stopped. With this layout, glorious views were available from the study and sitting room windows, over the front garden and the distant railway line and shore line. Judas was pleased and relieved with the plan and he did not think he could improve on it, so he therefore telephoned Anita. After the pleasantries Judas got down to business. After a few moments Anita interrupted and said, "It sounds complicated, I had better come over."

Anita arrived and was guided into the study. All the plans were on the desk and Judas asked the all important question, "Do you want the running of this place as a guest house?" Without hesitation Anita replied in the affirmative.

"However," she continued, "there are a great number of hurdles to overcome and as I have surmounted them at the Poacher's Retreat, I am sure I can overcome them here. I must, however, be very frank with you. I hope to stop working when the last payment of the loan is made. I hope that is acceptable."

"Perfectly acceptable," said Judas, "that will not be a problem."

The evening then consisted of sorting out the accommodation behind and above the garages. Anita was happy with the proposed layout as it gave her plenty of space compared to the cramped quarters she had at present. There were also a few changes she suggested which would be of benefit to the main building.

At the end of the meeting and after a tray of biscuits and fruit and various cool drinks, both parties were happy. Judas had insisted on setting up generous financial arrangements for Anita for running the place and these would be set out in a contract with his lawyer. He also agreed to give the plans they had devised to his architect to prepare new exact drawings and to make sure the proposals were acceptable and complying with the various legal requirements, safety requirements and building regulations in force at present. Because of work commitments Judas could not see his solicitor or architect until early in the New Year and this was accepted by Anita.

"Just one question," said Anita, "where on earth are you going to live?"

"Nothing to worry about," Judas lied, "I have a few ideas." The remainder of the evening and night was spent in a pleasant atmosphere, where two very old and dear friends enjoyed each other's company. Anita left at about midnight.

CHAPTER 5

Sunday 28th December

Judas was ready for another hectic day when he arrived at work. Adrian and Roy were eagerly awaiting the arrival of both John and Geoff, so that they could go to their homes and enjoy their four days of festivities and relaxation.

"See you in the New Year," said Judas as he went to his desk. The incoming staff arrived soon afterwards and after a very quick handover, as there was nothing to report, the night shift staff left the lodge. Judas called over a greeting to the day guards and received a wave in reply. At six fifteen numerous members of staff began to arrive for more work in the design section. Judas saw that various faxes has arrived during the night and sorted them out and put them in envelopes ready for delivery. As very little was happening at the moment he took the envelopes over to the post room in the office block and placed them on the table. As he exited the office block by the side door, Judas met Mr Brown arriving.

"Oh, good morning," said a startled Mr Brown and regaining his composure he continued, "I've just come in to pick up the design papers and the layout plans and then I am going to see the Managing Director. He telephoned me last night and said he would have other board members with him, so I thought I would come in early today and go through the papers and plans before I drive over to see them. He only lives at Beaufort St. Clement, so I don't have far to go." He then walked past Judas and went up the stairs to his office.

Judas returned to the lodge and sat down at his desk. Nothing much was happening and the guard in the lodge was busy writing. John looked up from his report book and said,

"Henry Brown said he will go over to see the MD in a couple of hours and on his return he may contact some other members of staff to come in. It all depends on the meeting." He then returned to his entries in the book.

Judas reached into his case and extracted the plan of the station layout at Beaufort St. Clement and the proposed enlarged station complex. The station layout he had done for Beaufort St. Vincent had been liked by the design staff. It showed the essence of the layout design, but had to miss out a couple of sidings which he considered to be excessive to the plan, but was still able to keep the essential elements of the design. They also liked the much simpler Inner Harbour System extension which was practically an exact copy of the original layout plan. He had just opened his sketch book when he was interrupted by three telephone calls. He explained to the callers that the factory was closed and as the calls were not urgent he put them through to the extension for messages to be left on the voice mail.

Judas then looked at the old Beaufort St. Clement railway layout and marvelled at the size of the town. In 1880 it compared in size to Beaufort St. Vincent, but now it was just a shell of its former glory. It had a Victorian church in the town centre and a ruined mediaeval castle on the only high ground of the town. The original track arrangement however was very compressed as it was sited between two bridges, one a short bridge over a road and the other was a much longer bridge over the estuary. Judas began to sketch the station layout in his book and then became certain that he could use the miniature track pieces to better effect.

After twenty minutes of trial and error the scale rails had proved successful. Every pertinent track and structure was shown, including the station buildings, signal cabin, the goods shed and carriage sidings, the coal and cattle sidings, the loading bay and the engine shed and coaling line. The two private sidings were also included but slightly out of place from the actual location. Judas quickly drew the finished layout in his book and included the item numbers of the rails and structures.

Judas then began to look at the plan of the proposed new layout for the town and he was again able to use the miniature track pieces to show the design that had been agreed before the storm. He copied the station approach, the station building and the signal cabin from his previous effort as the details were the same and the rest of the plan seemed to fit very neatly into place. The engine shed and coaling line were also copied from the previous design as they had not moved. The new larger goods shed, with additional siding, side and end loading bays, cattle and additional coal and carriage sidings, were all shown in their new positions and the two private sidings were again shown slightly out of place. Judas again entered the layout in his book with the item numbers shown. Judas sat smugly at his desk and congratulated himself on his achievement.

He was interrupted from his smugness when Henry Brown came into the lodge.

"The coffee machines in the main building have taken a battering and are either empty or broken. The chocolate and snack machine in the canteen is also empty. Can I beg a cup of coffee from you guys?"

"Any time," said John and went to the kitchen area of the lodge and began preparing coffee for three. "Squash for you Judas?" he queried and received a nod.

Geoff returned from his patrol and complained that it was very cold and it was raining. John gave Henry Brown a small bar of chocolate from his lunch box, for which Mr Brown was very grateful.

"My wife says I must go on a diet, so I now have only two bars of chocolate for today," joked John.

Henry Brown strolled over to Judas and then sat down. His eyes fell onto the map showing the layout of Beaufort St. Clement and he seemed impressed by the plans that Judas had prepared using the track pieces and the entry in the layout book. His eyes then fell on the map showing the proposed new layout for the station complex and he seemed spellbound. He next saw the sketch done by Judas of the station complex and the prepared plan using the track pieces and had to sit down. After what seemed an eternity, speech returned.

"Good God!" exclaimed Henry Brown. "Where on earth did you get that map? I have been looking for one with that information on for years. It's priceless!" Without waiting for any reply Henry Brown continued, "When the Beaufort St. Clement station and complex were destroyed last century, the railway company was in financial difficulties and it was only the tourist industry, forestry and a couple of large local companies that kept the railway afloat. The directors of the railway were trying to bring in more trade to the town and had great plans for the future. However, this would mean enlarging the station complex and facilities and plans of these proposals were said to have been completed three days before the storm. It is definitely known that these plans of the enlarged station and facilities were produced and agreed because letters and notes confirm this, but after the storm the plans were never found."

Henry Brown sat down and John gave him a steaming mug of coffee.

"I ask again, where did you get this plan?" said Mr Brown.

Judas replied, "From the signalman who was employed in the cabin over there. When he retired he became the handyman at the orphanage where I was born. When he passed away I found some plans and this was one of them."

"I never, ever thought I would see a plan like that," said Henry Brown and continued, "I have been searching all over the place for anything to do with that station and here is the jewel in the crown. You have made my day. Could I please have a copy of the map and a copy of your scale plan to show the MD? He like me has been searching for any information he could get on the revised railway layout of the town. He will be overjoyed." He then added sheepishly, "That is if you don't mind."

"No problems," said Judas, "I hope you have a great meeting with the boss and the board members. I honestly didn't know the original plans were missing and I honestly do not know how the signalman obtained them." Henry Brown sat back and enjoyed his coffee and chocolate bar.

"I have a few photographs of the station, before it was decimated by the flood," continued Henry Brown, "and so does the MD. He and I have always been fascinated by the events of that terrible calamity and unfortunately not many photographs are available of the station as it was in 1881."

Henry Brown stood up and asked Judas if he could take the plans and get them photocopied. Judas raised no objection and reached into his case. He extracted Adam's photographs and quite casually said to Henry Brown, "I presume the photographs you have are the same as these?" and he handed them over. Judas continued "They are dated on the reverse 1880 and they are numbered from one to thirty six."

Henry Brown took the photographs and simply quizzed, "Thirty six? There are only six photographs known to exist of the 1881 station. I suppose there are a number of duplicates in here. Oh yes, I have seen..." and he then stopped speaking and after a few moments slumped back down into his chair. "I have never seen the majority of these photographs before," said an incredulous Henry Brown, after intently looking at the snaps for two minutes. "I presume these are also the work of the signalman?"

Judas nodded and then repeated, "There are thirty six photographs and they are all numbered on the reverse and dated 1880."

Mr Brown then added, "These photographs show various station buildings, signal box, coal bunkers, goods shed and cattle dock. They also show various locomotives, carriages and goods vehicles. I have only seen six of the snaps. Honestly the photographs you have are unique. They are priceless. Have you any more surprises for me?"

John and Geoff had been listening intently to the conversations of Mr Brown and Judas and when Henry Brown went to the main office to get photocopies of the maps and prints of the photographs, John said, "This time Judas you definitely deserve Brownie points. I have never seen anyone who works here happier than he is today."

After twenty minutes, Henry Brown returned to the reception lodge and handed the plans and drawings to Judas. He then said, "I have telephoned Paul Gibson and he will be here about two o'clock this afternoon. I hope to surprise him with the map and plans of Beaufort St. Clement, of 1880 and of the 'lost' plan of the proposed development. I also want his input on the track drawings you have done and hopefully we can then get them into the new book, as well as the others you have done. Paul is a very keen photographer and he will be very surprised and happy with copies of your friend Adam's photographs. I will be back for two o'clock."

With that Henry Brown walked to the door. As he left the lodge he turned to John and said, "Oh by the way John, please let your grandson know that both of his plans will also be in the layout book this year," and he laughed. As he left the lodge he had a sprightly spring in his step and walked briskly to his vehicle.

John smiled, "He told me earlier that one layout plan was going to be used, but now both. My grandson will be really chuffed."

After Henry Brown left the car park, Judas returned his plans, papers and photographs to his case. He also put away in his case all of the papers and drawings he had recently done for the new publication. John went out on his patrol later than normal, but it had been a very interesting and enjoyable interlude with Henry Brown and all of the men had inwardly smiled. After a few moments the telephone rang and this call seemed to open the floodgates. The next two hours were very hectic for Judas as he explained to callers that the complex was not yet open, but they could leave messages on the voice mail of the required department or send faxes. Then, as quickly as it started, the calls petered out and the normal tranquillity of the season returned. It then began to snow and in the car park the vehicle parking lines were soon obliterated by the settling flakes. Judas looked out of his side window and saw a diesel locomotive trundle by towards the station. He reflected that he had heard a locomotive yesterday but this was the first one he had seen since Christmas Eve. He mused that Adam would not have approved, he was an advocate of steam and in his eyes nothing could improve on his beloved steam locomotives.

Lunch time came and Judas sat with John and Geoff, who openly talked of their intentions during the next four days, when both of the men would be away from the lodge. Judas thought back to his previous job and looked out of the window at the unlit building of his previous employers. The building looked very uninviting; the blinds had been taken down, it was dark and the paint was beginning to flake; and as he looked away, slowly munching a health bar, he thought he saw something move in his old office. He stared and was about to look away again when he saw another movement. Someone was in the building. Judas knew that for the past few years he had always been the one who had volunteered to go into the building over the Christmas period, during the day and to set the alarms and secure the main door on his exiting the building. He volunteered because no-one else wanted the duty, even though the pay rates were triple the norm. He was certain that his old employers, having vacated the building and made it secure, would not have anyone on site. With the problems his present employers were having with additional security patrols, due to the spate of local robberies, Judas decided to act.

Judas said, "Excuse me guys, but could you look towards the building over to the left, first floor window, third from the right and say if you see anything move. Don't make it obvious you are looking." Both guards stopped talking and peered to the left, being very inquisitive, but also trying to look natural.

"What am I looking at?" queried John and then said, "Yes, something moved."

"I saw it too," confirmed Geoff, "It was a man."

"Thanks for the confirmation." said Judas, "Can you please keep an eye on the building whilst I contact the constabulary? It may be okay, but better safe than sorry."

Judas informed John and Geoff at every stage of the proceedings, when he had contacted the police on the emergency number. He gave the required information to the controller and then said, "There may be a good reason for someone to be in the building, but we are just playing safe. The building has been vacated by the staff and everyone has been relocated to the main office and I honestly do not think there is anything in the building worth stealing." The controller said a police vehicle was in an area nearby and would be diverted immediately and could Judas and the guards keep observing the building.

Fifteen minutes later four police cars screeched to a halt outside the building and a number of police officers sprinted to strategic points around the building. After another five minutes, two additional cars arrived, one had the security officer of the old company on board, who Judas recognised and access to the building was gained. Twenty minutes later four dishevelled young men were escorted from the building and put into another vehicle that had been parked nearby. One of the young men Judas recognised as being one of the canteen staff of the old company.

A few moments later one of the police cars pulled up at the lodge and a jubilant driver said the men they'd apprehended were thought to be the gang responsible for the spate of robberies in the area.

He continued, "The officers in the car, which had been cruising in the area nearby, observed a parked van close to the high wall, behind the building and the van driver had been recognised as a known criminal. The officers then radioed this information to our controller and a small team was hastily assembled for action. The gang had gained access to the building by breaking in on the ground floor at the back, and fire extinguishers, fire hoses and an abandoned clapped out generator had been stolen and put into the vehicle." The policeman laughed as he continued, "The driver of the vehicle was apprehended whilst lighting his cigar. However, it cannot be confirmed that this is the group responsible for the spate of local robberies, so please keep up the good work and remain vigilant. You security guards are to be congratulated on your awareness of the situation." Before John or Geoff could correct him he was driving off to his station. They both turned to Judas who just smiled smugly.

"I think this calls for a celebratory drink," joked Judas.

As the policeman left, John telephoned through to their Security Central Station to outline the happenings of the afternoon to a controller. The controller was very interested, but asked for a written report of the incident to be sent as soon as possible. John provided a very short report of the incident, containing all of the facts and placed it in the post tray. Geoff wrote an even shorter incident report in their log book.

"I sincerely hope they are the ones responsible for the robberies and I hope we can soon get back to normal. I think I'm shrinking due to the amount of walking I have to do. My feet are screaming for some respite," joked Geoff.

John was not in a joking mood and simply said, "I'm going to finish my sandwiches. If I don't eat something soon I may regret giving Henry Brown that chocolate bar." "There shouldn't be any change in our duties until all the building work has been completed," suggested Judas. "The buildings are quite open in parts and even if these thieves have been apprehended, others may be around awaiting their chance to get on site." Judas could practically hear John and Geoff groan. At this juncture all the men sat together and the guards continued with their lunches.

The silence was broken by Geoff, who said, "After the problems of the past few days, it was good to see Henry Brown smiling again. I suppose he will be even happier now that some of the local criminal element has been caught." John however was too busy eating to respond. Judas just smiled.

Henry Brown returned to the site at ten minutes to two. He parked his car and walked briskly over to the security lodge.

He walked up to Judas and happily said, "The MD was absolutely thrilled to see the photographs of the old station complex at Beaufort St. Clement and he was overwhelmingly thrilled to see the plan of the proposed development of the station. In fact he was practically in tears. The board members were also thrilled to see the photographs and have asked for copies of them. Will this be okay with you?" He looked at Judas and Judas nodded.

Henry Brown continued, "I have also shown the MD and the senior board members the drawings we are hoping to put into the new layout book. I must say, here and now, that they were all very impressed with the plans we already have and also they are very pleased with the computer graphics that we have generated. It was a very pleasant meeting and we did some good work. We then had a very enjoyable lunch, with the full Christmas fare, including delicious desserts, followed by mince pies and various cakes and I left all the board members and the MD having coffee and brandies."

Judas looked at both Geoff and John and inwardly smiled. He could practically hear their stomachs rumble.

"I am pleased they liked the paperwork and the photographs," said Judas, "but will there be a problem with the revised layout plan, considering it has been lost for such a long time?"

"I don't know," said Henry Brown, "I will have to pass that problem to our lawyers."

At that moment Paul Gibson arrived, the barrier was raised and Henry Brown went into the car park to greet his friend and colleague. Geoff was about to switch off the factory alarms, when the two men returned to the reception lodge.

"I have brought Paul in because when I show him these photographs and plans, he may have some questions that I cannot answer."

Paul Gibson sat down in the chair earlier used by Henry Brown and seemed very confused by the antics of his boss.

He was presented first with the photographs of Beaufort St. Clement station, including various buildings and various items of rolling stock. He slowly viewed each print, the first ones were those that he had seen before, but when he reached the seventh print, he became very surprised and completely speechless. He eventually began to say something, when he was interrupted by Henry Brown and given the revised track plan of the station complex. These were plans that he had never expected to see and he was even more surprised and speechless.

Paul Gibson eventually said, "Where in the name of all that is holy were these photographs found and is the plan genuine?"

Henry Brown was about to speak, when Judas said, "The photographs were the property of a signalman, who worked in the signal cabin over there and he also had in his possession the plans of the proposed station development for Beaufort St. Clement. Adam was a very devout Christian so we may assume everything is genuine. I honestly do not know how he obtained them or why they were never made public." Mr Gibson was about to ask if he could have copies of the photographs and of the station layout, when he was presented with a folder containing the required information, by Henry Brown.

For the next few minutes, Henry Brown showed Paul Gibson various layout plans that were to be used in the forthcoming book and some of the computer graphics that had already been generated.

"Richard Foote really did us proud with this collection," said Paul Gibson eventually and continued, "He was a great layout designer. It will be a very fitting epitaph."

Henry Brown seemed embarrassed, but had to admit that he was a very gifted layout designer and then added that only half of the plans were the work of Richard Foote.

"It was Judas here that did most of the rest, although the really complicated ones are Richard's. A couple are from John over there and a few more were devised by some of the other guys in the design section and in the rest of the factory." Henry Brown then took a plan out of another envelope and passed it to Paul.

"This is the plan of the proposed station revision at Beaufort St. Clement, as done by Judas, using our track geometry and you will see it is a superb plan catching all of the elements at the station."

After a few moments Paul simply said, "Absolutely brilliant." He walked over to Judas and shook him firmly by the hand and repeated, "Absolutely brilliant."

"I only saw the photographs myself this morning," said Henry Brown, "and I was as dumbstruck as you. I must admit that I never expected to see the proposed station development track diagram as it had not been seen again after the catastrophe at Beaufort St. Clement. I took the plan and photographs to the MD this morning at his home. All members of the board were also there and to put it bluntly they are all as chuffed as hell."

After a few minutes Henry Brown passed a sheet of paper to the guards, on which was a list naming six senior board members of the company, who were to arrive within the next half hour.

"Please let them in and advise them that Paul and I will be in the main conference room. I know it sounds grand but in this room we can spread out and it's also warmer than the board room. I will pass on to each member a copy of the photographs and the station revision plan of Beaufort St.

Clement. They all know that I have a surprise for them, as I told them that when I telephoned them from the MD's, but they don't know how big a surprise it is. Later I will give each member some layout plans and get them to write up the literature for the layouts that will appear in the publication we will be producing. Personally, I will be writing the article about the Beaufort St. Clement station, both past and proposed and also the Beaufort St. Vincent station. Some of the guys may be here for the rest of the holiday, as will Paul and I."

With that both men got up and walked to the door. Henry Brown then turned and said to Judas, John and Geoff:

"Can I please ask you all not to say anything to anyone about the photographs and layout plans you may have seen today? As a company we want the forthcoming track layout book we are producing to be a complete surprise to the model railway fraternity. We believe it will also be a complete surprise and eye opener to the general public of the two towns and we do not want any leak of information that will deflate the bombshell we will deliver to the modelling world."

All three men agreed to this request. Both managers then left the lodge and went into the office section of the complex. Geoff switched off the office alarms. Just as the two men disappeared through the door, the first of the listed members arrived and within ten minutes all had been advised of the venue of the meeting. Nothing more was seen of them all afternoon, although various lights could be seen in various parts of the office block. Even on their security patrols the guards did not see the men, as a sign had been placed on the door leading to the main conference room saying "*NO ADMITTANCE.*"

For the remainder of the afternoon the guards and Judas busied themselves with various jobs that had to be done. The guards toured round the site doing their regular patrols and checks and Judas amended his statistical records to accommodate the increase of manpower on site. He also obtained prints of the revised forms agreed by Henry Brown and filed them in his folder. As he had practically nothing else to do he cleaned out some unused cupboards and washed the shelving, just to give him some employment and to keep him active. Just as he began to put the cleaning equipment away the telephone began to sound and this heralded another bout of intense activity in the lodge. At five o'clock the calls were slowing down, but wives were still contacting their husbands in the conference room and trade outlets were requesting the supply of products to replenish their shelves after the festive rush. Judas answered the latest call and was relieved to hear the voice of Henry Brown.

"Judas, can you please come to the conference room? There is nothing to worry about, the board members on site just want to see you," and with that he hung up.

Judas advised Geoff of his summons and simply said "In case I don't get back before you and John leave, have a good time sorting out your wife's birthday present and please tell John to try and not overeat at his sisters." Geoff chuckled at this attempt at humour and thanked Judas for his comments.

At the conference room, Judas tentatively knocked on the door, which was opened by Henry Brown and he was ushered inside. All of the senior board members stood up and went forward to Judas and during the next forty minutes he was introduced to the whole of the assembled group. He was congratulated on the layouts he had developed, on the drawings he had done, on the photographs of the Beaufort St. Clement station and on the discovery of the lost proposed station development at Beaufort St. Clement. Judas had never before been so popular and it was completely foreign to him.

Judas answered all of the questions asked of him and the answers seemed to please the listeners. However, Henry

Brown sensed his unease and guided him to his own table where he showed him the work he had been doing with the labelling of the thirty 'unknown' photographs of the Beaufort St. Clement station.

"I hope you think I did a reasonable job on the photos?" he asked. Judas sat down to collect his thoughts and read the descriptions of the photographs on the cards. He thought they were exceptionally good and he could sense that Henry Brown was putting his heart and soul into the work, as the discovery of these plans and photographs were very significant for the company and its future.

Judas stayed with Henry Brown for ten minutes, looking at the various drafts of notes he had written concerning the stations and their various buildings, rolling stock and motive power. When Henry Brown was called away Judas did not like to look at his work with him not being present, so he just sat. He looked around the room. He liked the wood panelling on the walls and he also liked the ornate skirting board and the architrave around the doors. It was a beautiful room and it had superb lighting. Judas looked again at the skirting board and thought back to the orphanage and the basic skirting boards that adorned the rooms there. He then remembered that Adam had been so disgusted with the ones he had in his basement room, ill fitting and with three different heights of wood, he had taken them out and replaced them with ones he had installed himself.

Henry Brown returned.

"My sincere apologies for my absence, but I had to sort out a minor problem to stop it becoming a major one," he said.

"These things happen," said Judas and then queried, "Everything now okay?"

"Definitely okay," confirmed Henry Brown, who then looked at his wall clock. "Ye Gods Judas. I'm sorry but I seem to have kept you here after hours."

"No problem," said Judas as he walked towards the conference room exit. Some of the men present again thanked him for his input.

He returned to the lodge and was happy to see that Gordon and Richard were on duty. Judas spent about twenty minutes with the men and they talked about the tragedy of Richard Foote, the apprehension of the criminals and the absolute pleasure Gordon and Richard had suffered by having no security duties to perform during the festive season.

Gordon said, "I honestly enjoyed this Christmas more than any other. It was absolutely superb. Very relaxing and very pleasant."

Richard added, "Mine was also very relaxing and very pleasant. However, I really did overeat, but I did do some walking during the break."

Gordon countered, "I also did some walking, but only to the restaurants or to the pub."

Judas smiled at this attempt at humour. He was pleased that his colleagues had both enjoyed a very peaceful time with their respective families, but he could see that both were apparently not happy to return to work on the night shift. Judas then realised that it was six forty and he was very late going home. He bade the night guards a very pleasant and quiet evening, after making sure they were aware of the staff on site.

On his walk home he suddenly thought that neither he, Geoff or John had informed Henry Brown of the apprehension of the criminal gang and of his and the guards involvement in the action. He made a mental note to do it tomorrow. For some reason he then thought of the meeting he had attended that afternoon with Henry Brown. He was pleased that the work he had done was appreciated and one of the draughtsmen had even complimented him on his accuracy and his drawing expertise. He then reflected that Adam would have been proud of him for producing the drawings of the layouts he had designed for the book. Adam had always told the children in the orphanage to apply themselves to the task in hand and, even if it was a difficult task, dedication would make it easier. He still missed the old man and he was proud to have known him and to have been instilled with his work ethics.

Judas arrived home, picked up his post and followed his usual routine. Afterwards Judas took Adam's book from his case; the book he had liberated from the old garden shed at the orphanage. Judas sat in his armchair and made himself comfortable. He thumbed through the pages and realized that he was not gleaning any information from the book. He could practically recite the contents, but he decided to begin afresh and he started to read Adam's neat script. He concentrated hard on the page and his mind went into study mode. However, as he began to read he heard in his mind the old man's voice.

"Take heed my boy, the treasure is buried out there somewhere. I have told you all many times about it and also told you what is known about it, but as yet it is still hidden and is still a mystery. However, one day!"

Judas struggled back to reality and began to read, but he still kept hearing the old man and it was very disconcerting. He persevered and applied his mind to the task in hand and he was really thankful that Adam's script was so very easy to read and also to understand. However, as he read, he seemed to be reading the text in the style of Adam and inwardly he smiled:

BACKGROUND

1. *A small inland abbey, built in 1302, on solid foundations, still thrives in the local Christian community. Much of the building was destroyed at the time of the reformation but the remains of the abbey now serve as the parish church and the clergy is well respected.*

2. *A small church, satellite to the above abbey, was built in 1408, about twelve miles away and nearer to the coast. The church was built on high ground and in the far distant past had been surrounded by water because of sea incursions. This church and abbey had various holy relics in their possession. They also had gold and silver plate and other fine objects containing rubies, pearls and sapphires.*

3. *The land around the small church was rich soil, but in earlier times, because of sea incursions and the ensuing problems with salt deposits, the land was not productive. However, sheep and pigs thrived on the higher ground around the church.*

4. *However, there had been no sea incursions in the past twenty four years. Land had drained naturally and other areas had been reclaimed, and the soil was now rich and productive from 1432.*

5. *Four miles to the east of the small church was a small inlet with a jetty. The river by the small church flowed into the sea here. By the small bridge over the river, the monks built a storeroom and living quarters for four brothers. The storeroom was required to house wine casks, the wine being a major earner for the abbey and*

the church. This storeroom was built about 1450. Wool was also a valuable commodity and was also stored here, before shipment to market.

6. *By 1470 the church and abbey were growing wealthy from the sales of wine and wool and numerous landowners had given the church various areas of land, originally poor land, but now valuable assets to the church.*

7. *This wealth was coveted by numerous outlaw bands and they instigated various campaigns against the brothers of the church.*

A   *Cattle were killed or stolen*
B   *Haystacks were burned*
C   *Isolated huts were set on fire*
D   *Carts were smashed*
E   *Small boats were smashed*
F   *Horses were released and chased away*
G   *In an isolated incident two brothers were killed*

In pencil under the above notes Judas had written "Why?"

8. *An officer of the law and a small garrison of men, were sent out to be stationed at the nearby castle.*

9. *The outlaw bands were slowly driven from the area of the isolated church and its buildings and lands, by the determined actions of the sheriff and his men.*

10. *In 1475 the landowner, who had given whole parcels of land to the church, died in a riding accident. The land was not originally productive, but now was a great asset to the abbey, because there had been no sea incursions in the area for over 40 years.*

11. The landowner's son believed the land would revert to his family on the death of his father and was shocked when the church elders produced documents to support their ownership.

12. This son's inheritance was only one eighth of what he was expecting and he vowed to regain the lost lands from the church.

13. The attacks against church property and their animals begin again.

14. The local sheriff dies in an action against a marauding band of robbers, and his replacement is not worthy of the position. He is active in the abbey town, but not in the outlying districts.

15. The attacks against the church increase and some of the brothers are injured. At this point, with no help from the law the Abbot decides to protect the brothers, the gold and silver plate and the holy relics.

16. All the brothers are ordered to stay within one mile of the church and all animals, where possible, are housed within church grounds.

17. The church is attacked by the aggrieved son, his henchmen and his accomplices. The brothers retreat to the church and await developments. The Abbot is badly wounded.

18. The Abbot orders that the gold and silver plate be divided up into ten manageable packs. The holy relics are split into a further two equal packs.

19. The nearest settlement is the small inlet four miles to the

east. In addition to the storeroom and monks quarters, there are half a dozen   shacks. The local people are fishermen and farmers.

20.   The church is now surrounded and all outlying shacks and storerooms are burned. All animals are driven away or killed.

21.   The Abbot, on his deathbed, entrusts the gold and silver plate and the holy relics to a Prior and a long serving brother, to get through the encirclement and to put the items in a safe place. The plate and relics are put down a well and then into a tunnel on a ledge above the water line. The two men then enter the well and taking one load each, walk through the water chamber into a cave. The Prior and brother return and collect the remaining packs and take them to the cave and await nightfall. These two holy men and the Abbot are the only ones who know the whereabouts of the items.

22.   In the night the men leave the cave, the entrance being outside the encircling band. The brothers deliver the first two loads to the monks at the storeroom and deliver the note from the Abbot informing them that the items are to be hidden for safety. The Prior also gives them a bundle of papers from the Abbot for safe keeping.

23.   The brothers return to the cave, during the same night and on the next four nights delivered all the plate to the monks at the coast. Only two monks were at the coast at this time.

24.   On the following night the Prior and the brother leave the cave with the relics and deliver them to the brothers at the coast. The Prior and his helper then return to the cave, progress along the water chamber and to the ledge

at the bottom of the well. Below them, in the water, are the bodies of the Abbot and some of the brothers. The only sounds from above are the agitated voices of the intruders.

25. *They retire to the cave and pray for the souls of their murdered brethren.*

26. *All of the next day they are in the cave or at the bottom of the well shaft, on the ledge. The intruders are still above them, searching.*

27. *That night they leave the cave and return to the coastal retreat. As they follow the river they hear horsemen above them riding to the coast. A short time later the horsemen return on their way back to the abbey.*

28. *On nearing the coast, the Prior and the brother see that the storeroom has been burnt to the ground. The two monks were dead. There were no signs of the fishermen or farmers.*

29. *The Prior and the brother bury the two slain brothers and, taking what food they can salvage, they hide in the hills, not knowing if the papers, plate and relics have been found. The Prior swaps his simple wooden cross with that of the senior slain brother.*

30. *The next morning, the fishermen and farmers return to the settlement and at mid-day the aggrieved son and his accomplices arrive at the scene to interrogate and then murder the inhabitants. The Prior and the brother, still hidden in the hills, now know the papers, plate and holy relics have still not been found.*

31. *The Prior and the brother stay in the hills in an isolated sheep pen.*

32. *They return to the settlement and bury the dead inhabitants.*

33. *They return to the sheep pen and decide to try and reach the inland abbey, but to go by separate, circuitous routes. The brother returns to the cave after three days and then makes it back to the inland abbey, to report to the Abbot. The Abbot has heard of the atrocities committed at the church only two days ago.*

34. *The Prior returns to the coastal storehouse site and looks at the reverse of the cross he has taken from the deceased brother. The Prior believes the random markings on the cross are the directions to the buried parcels but he cannot understand the meaning. He resolves to investigate and when times are more settled he will retrieve the relics and the papers.*

35. *The relics, the papers and the treasure were never recovered.*

36. *The Prior spent many years looking for the lost items and on his deathbed he passed on his cross to his Abbot.*

37. *The Abbot made copies of the information onto parchment and placed some of these in the abbey library archives. When the Abbot died suddenly, the cross was buried with him.*

On completion of his reading of the above Judas was convinced that there was nothing he had read that he didn't know already. All of the above information was available in various books that had been written on the subject, but none of the publications contained any new revelations on the subject of the missing items. The notes were definitely Adam's and Adam had said, on many occasions, that the relics and the gold and silver plate were out there waiting to be unearthed. Inwardly Judas apologised to Adam for not furthering the knowledge of the whereabouts of the missing items. Judas was about to continue reading when he heard the telephone ring. He saw from the number on the screen that it was Anita.

"Hi Anita," he said, but before he could say anything else, Anita interrupted.

"Hi. I have just been given some news about the orphanage site. As you know it was closed two years ago and the property was put up for sale. I am now informed that the site has been bought by a developer and it may be demolished to make way for apartments, or even offices." She paused.

"I see," said Judas. "It was a lovely old building, but it had seen better days and, in all honesty, I don't think it can be converted to anything else. Who has bought the site?"

Anita told him and she continued, "I will ring them tomorrow and see if it would be possible for me to go and look at the place again, with one of their office staff, before it is demolished. I would like to get some photographs of my old room and the dining room and the kitchen and another one of the front garden. Also, I will take one of the main entrance hall. If you want me to, I will also take a photograph of your small room and any other places you want me to snap."

Judas thought back to his small room. It was right at the top of the building and had previously been a very small store room. He had been put in there on his own as he had to get up early each morning for his work at the newsagents and he therefore did not disturb anyone by his movements.

"I would really appreciate it if you could also get me a copy of the photographs you are taking, minus your room and a photograph of Adam's room and the boiler room," continued Judas, "and also a photo of the rear garden and another of the site of the old garden shed. The shed itself would have gone long ago. Unfortunately, I cannot get away during the day until the New Year, so when you telephone tomorrow, would you please advise them that I will also contact them and arrange a nostalgic visit. It will bring back many, many memories."

After the telephone call Judas could not concentrate on the notes he had been reading and he put them down. He thought back to the orphanage, his very small room, Adam's room, the boiler room and the garden and its shed. He retreated to the kitchen and prepared a refreshing drink. He then remembered that he had not opened his post for the past couple of days and he retrieved the envelopes from the study. One was from his local college, offering various weekend courses in January, including historical and geographical subjects, which would interest Judas. The other correspondence was completely unimportant and was shredded. Judas then idled away the rest of his evening, but his mind concentrated on the old orphanage.

CHAPTER 6

Monday 29th December

Judas arrived at work just in time to see Gordon and Richard leave the site after being relieved early by Keith and Colin. It had been an uneventful night on the site and the guards then advised Judas that the local radio station has reported the news about the apprehension of the gang responsible for the spate of the local robberies.

"In fact it appears to be the only news of any worth locally."

"Oh hell," said Judas, "I just remembered, I have to let Henry Brown know about the events of yesterday." Judas then asked the incoming guards how their Christmases had been and was pleased that both had enjoyed the festive holiday.

Colin announced, "Santa has been very good to me this year and my wife gave me a camera. It just shows that hinting for months definitely pays off."

Keith did not elaborate on his days away, but simply said, "I relaxed."

The day guards then settled down to the normal routines of the site and Judas looked around for something he could do. He then realised that he was running short of some forms, papers, pens and pencils and he advised Colin that he was off to the stationery room for the items. Colin then switched off the alarms for that section of the building and Judas left the lodge.

Twenty minutes later Judas returned with the items he required and filed them. A few cars were in the car park and a few people were having a cigarette before entering the building. The wind was howling and the temperature was falling. According to Colin snow was forecast for later in the day, although it was not expected to settle on the ground. Judas was about to speak to Colin when his telephone sounded. It was Anita.

After greeting her, Judas said, "You're an early bird today, is there a problem?"

"No problem," replied Anita, "but I will be out for most of the morning. When I have finished my meeting I will pop into the developer's office on my way back to the Poacher's and arrange a viewing of the old site. I will take my camera with me just in case they have someone available at the time to accompany me to the orphanage. If they have I will get the photos you require. Whilst there I will advise them that you will wish to see the building also and you will telephone them next week."

A few moments later Anita was gone. Judas then thought back to the old building and the memories, both good and bad, that he had. He looked into the car park and saw that more cars were arriving. Henry Brown walked by the lodge and waved to the guys inside.

"He seems happy," said Colin as he picked up his telephone. Judas walked quickly outside and told Mr Brown of yesterday's incident, concerning the police activity in apprehending the criminals and omitting his involvement.

All Henry Brown said was, "That is good news," and continued his journey.

After about ten minutes the reception telephone began to ring, to be followed by a constant volume of queries. Judas was busy for the rest of the morning; some calls were for the staff on site and other calls were forwarded to voice mail machines. A few calls were of a general nature and Judas answered them as best he could.

At about eight twenty five Judas looked out of his lodge window towards the building of his previous employers. He could see a small group of people standing around and he was perplexed. When a coach entered the site a few minutes later, all was revealed. This was the coach that had been temporarily provided by management to transport the staff from this satellite building, to their new offices in the company's main complex. He could see a number of people slowly trudging onto the coach and he could see that very few individuals had any enthusiasm for the journey. He then saw his old boss walking very slowly down to the entrance driveway and out of sight of the coach. He inwardly chuckled when the coach left the site, leaving her waving strenuously in its wake. He surmised that this would not be deemed a great start by her new colleagues, by her bosses, or by her own office staff. He saw her hurriedly exit the old site and scamper towards the bus station.

At eleven o'clock the calls slowed down and by midday they had practically stopped. Just as Judas was about to sit with Keith and Colin and have a well earned drink, the telephone sounded again. For the second time it was Anita.

"I am at the old orphanage site at the moment with a lady from the developers and I have taken the photographs I wanted and also the ones that you require. I wasn't sure how you wanted your snaps, so I took them from each side of the rooms. I hope they come out okay. I will get them printed this afternoon and bring them over."

"Oh you are an angel," said Judas and continued, "will they be okay with my contacting them and going over the building next week?"

"Actually, when I told the lady in the office why you wanted to get a last look at the property, she said she would be pleased to see you on site tonight from six o'clock, if that would suit you? So you could visit tonight if you want to. They have plans for some large development, which will replace the old orphanage when it is demolished."

Judas was quiet for a moment and then said, "Great, I will go there straight from work."

Judas sat with the guards during the lunch break and they told him of the pleasurable and enjoyable time they both had during the Christmas holiday. They had both eaten too much and consumed too much alcohol, but they both said that for the New Year, diets were a priority.

"However," said Keith, "that will be for the New Year. Until then it will be full steam ahead for sandwiches with turkey fillings, sausage rolls and numerous mince pies." "Hear, hear," echoed Colin, mimicking a Member of Parliament. Nothing however was said about cutting down on alcohol.

Some of the staff on site left the complex at about one o'clock and said they would return tomorrow, but there were still six vehicles in the car park. Judas went back to his desk and amended his statistics figures to reflect the staff on site. The rest of the afternoon was very lazy and only two telephone calls came in for staff on site. Judas thought about his visit tonight to the orphanage and he again thought of the wonderful times he had enjoyed with Adam.

At about four o'clock Anita entered the lodge. Judas introduced her to Keith and also to Colin when he returned from his patrol.

Eventually she said, "Here are the pictures you asked me to get, plus copies of the ones I required for myself. I hope they are good enough for you."

"I am sure they will be just like you..." said Judas, "...perfect."

Both Colin and Keith sniggered. Judas looked at the photographs and was amazed at the detail. He only had a quick scan, but was very pleased with all of them. Anita had taken four photographs of each of the rooms, from each side and also six photos of the very overgrown rear garden. Also she had taken four photographs of the jungle at the front of the building. He reflected that Adam would be disgusted and he offered up an apology to the old man. Anita had also taken four snaps of the old garden shed, one from each side, and Judas was surprised to see some panels from one end of the dilapidated shed defying gravity and fighting to stay upright. He felt a knot in his stomach.

"How much am I in your debt?" asked Judas.

Anita ignored the question and asked, "Are you going tonight?"

"Yes," answered Judas.

"Then I will come too," stated Anita. "I will be at the orphanage for six o'clock."

With that Anita left the lodge.

After a while Judas began to look at the photographs more closely, but then the telephone system began to interrupt his viewing. Again and again callers were wanting details of the opening date of the complex, as they were in urgent need of re-supply. Other callers wanted different information and were put through to the staff on site. A few callers requested to be put through to extensions where they could leave voice mails. During a lull in the calls, Judas went back to the photographs and scanned them all very carefully, especially those showing Adam's room and also those of the garden, which had been Adam's pride and joy. He looked again at the room photographs and saw the skirting boards that Adam put up after scrapping the old ones. He didn't know why but he kept looking at them and after a while he put them back into the folder.

Judas left the lodge punctually at six o'clock. Keith and Colin left the site at the same time, after handing over the security duties to Gordon and Richard. The leaving guards were relieved that their first day back at work after the Christmas break, had gone so well. The oncoming guards seemed happier tonight than they were last night.

Judas walked to the old orphanage site with very mixed feelings. He hadn't been on the site for many years but the memories came flooding back to him. Some were good memories, whilst others were not so good. Judas did not know what to expect and he tried to put all negative thoughts out of his mind. The night was very cold and as he neared his destination it began to snow. The snow was falling rapidly and it settled in silence.

Anita was waiting for him at the archway entrance and they walked together along the short driveway. They slowly approached the only vehicle on site, a white van with the developers logo boldly displayed, which was parked to the side of the main entrance to the orphanage. The sales assistant, Jennifer, greeted them and led them to the main building. She kindly assured Judas that she understood his reasons for visiting and, after she'd unlocked the sturdy door and switched on the lights, she and Anita walked to another part of the complex to give him some time alone.

Judas walked to the secondary stairwell and went up the narrow passageway to the room he once had. It was absolutely minute. There was a very rickety, wooden chair in one corner and Judas deigned to make use of it. He looked around the cramped quarters and felt very cold. He again looked at the photographs of Adam's room and still could not understand why he kept looking at them. He decided to go to see the room for himself.

Judas was very nervous as he descended the secondary stairs to ground level. The lighting was still as bad as it had been in his youth, but he remembered the route and reached the stairway to the basement without mishap. Judas descended and, as he did so, memories of that terrible day when Adam died came flooding back. He forced himself onwards and he was soon in the old man's room.

It was completely bare, devoid of any furniture and the door was off its hinges and lay on its side propped up against the flimsy wall. Judas looked around the room; something was bothering him but he did not know what. He walked up and down the small room. He stood in the doorway and paced in the corridor outside the room. He again looked at the photographs of the room, taken by Anita, and could see that some joins in the skirting board were not shown on them. Anita must have been standing off centre in the room. Judas applied his mind and could see no reason why the skirting board along this wall was using three pieces of wood and other walls used just one. He thought deeply about the old man and then suddenly remembered. Something clicked in his brain and it was an inspired revelation.

He recalled Adam's book and the draughtsman's arrow pointing upwards. The object in the book next to the arrow was an oblique projection drawing of the skirting board. After the thought had registered Judas looked out of the room into the corridor to see if anyone was coming. He was on his own, so he tentatively tapped each of the skirting board sections in the room. They were all solid, except the central one along the last wall. Judas tried to lift it as the arrow was pointing up in the book. It did not move. He tried more pressure, but it was still unmoving. He exerted a final muscular effort and there was a slight movement. He eventually got his fingers under the skirting board and this section lifted. He listened for any sound but could not hear anyone.

Judas saw a hole in the wall under the skirting board and inside was a metal box. It was a small box; about two inches high and about twelve inches long. Judas pulled the box from its prison and found it to be about nine inches wide. The box had a clasp at the front which Judas released and lifted the lid onto its hinges.

The box contained two slender note books and he quickly scanned them and saw that they included pages of various maps. The books also contained a variety of notes; some written in Adam's neat hand and others by an unknown hand. On impulse Judas decided that he would liberate the box and look at the contents later when he was at home. He opened his case and put the new found box inside it. He double checked to see if any other objects were left behind the skirting board, but there were none. He then forced down the open skirting board to meet the floor. He marvelled at Adam's ingenuity, the craftsmanship of the woodwork and the skilful construction of the sliding joint. He also double checked the other skirting boards to make sure they were solid and did not lift. They didn't. Judas then realised that the lifting skirting board was, at one time, behind and underneath Adam's bed; a perfect place for concealment.

Judas next went into the old boiler room. He shivered; it was very cold and bleak. The coal chute was still there but the ancient boiler must have been removed years ago. The walls were bare and in places they showed the marks of coal that had once graced the room. Judas looked at Anita's photographs and was content that they showed every detail. Judas made his way back along the corridors and the stairway to reach ground level. He returned to the main entrance hallway, making sure to switch off all lights to conceal his recent movements. Through the window he could see Jennifer and Anita in the entrance hall, in quiet conversation, and he went to them.

Anita turned and could see that Judas was troubled.

"Jennifer has some residential development plans available for various apartments in three stylish blocks, all of which are in prime locations within a mile or so of the town centre. I have taken the liberty of selecting six for you to look at. All are smallish, as you seem to like minimalist apartments. Jennifer says you can have the plans to scan at your leisure. I told her you may want a new home when your present one is redeveloped."

Judas smiled and said, "You are doing a lot of hinting at the moment, but you are right, I will soon need another home."

Jennifer then calmed the situation by asking Judas if he had seen all of the building he wished to see.

"If not you can just ring me on this number and I will sort out your access to the building," said Jennifer as she handed him her contact card.

"I have been to the bedroom I had as a boy," said Judas, "and to the basement. The rooms brought back many memories and I never thought I would ever say this, but I will miss this place when it is demolished. I have always looked at it as I passed by, but this is my first visit back for a number of years. What does your company plan to do with the site?"

Jennifer looked defensive and eventually said, "It is anticipated that when the building is demolished we will erect a Retirement Home on the site. I have seen the development model and it shows a beautiful building, containing everything that the select few residents could wish for.

"There will only be about twenty residents staying here at any one time and they will be catered for by a resident full time staff. The rear of the site will be landscaped, with wide walkways for wheelchair use and there will also be smaller garden features at the sides of the building. The area at the front of the building will be lawns, flower borders and driveway. As for the building itself, it will consist of self-contained units, for the residents, plus recreational rooms, a games room, a music room, a library, a computer room and a small swimming pool, with changing rooms. There will of course be a fully equipped medical centre and a reception area, but the main office, administration area and main storerooms will be on the first floor.

"Apparently the architects were hoping to use the front entrance of the orphanage and incorporate it into their plans for the building, but the Town Council vetoed the idea. That's about all I know on the subject and of course the details I have mentioned may change. However, in my humble opinion, that is what will happen."

Jennifer then stopped and apologised for waffling on about the site. Anita and Judas both said they had enjoyed the visit and thanked Jennifer for her time and patience. Judas was struck by the irony that the site started out as a Victorian orphanage, catering for penniless urchins and would be transformed into a twenty first century retirement home, for wealthy millionaires.

"Many thanks for allowing me to return to my old room and to put to bed a few demons," said Judas finally. "Also many thanks for your update on the development proposals for the old orphanage site. It has been most interesting. I must also thank you for the accommodation plans of the apartments in the new complexes near to the town centre."

He placed these plans into his case making sure that no-one could have sight of the contents. Jennifer gave Judas a photograph of the orphanage dated 1930 and another dated 1990.

"These are copies of photographs that we discovered in the matron's room when we came to view the site, prior to development. I hope the photographs will be a small treasure for you and I do hope that we can sort out an apartment for you when you require one."

The photographs were also placed into his case and Judas thanked Jennifer again for her thought and kindness.

Judas and Anita left the old orphanage and he walked her home to the Poacher's Retreat. They walked in silence as they were both remembering their youth and the people they had known at the orphanage. Judas declined a drink in the guest house kitchen and walked towards his home very briskly.

On arrival he quickly sorted out his normal chores and retired to his study. He took out the small box and withdrew both books. He decided to look at the maps and plans first, as he thought that if he looked at Adam's notes and the other notes, he would be depressed. Judas then discovered that the maps and notes were loose leaf sheets placed in the first book for protection.

The papers were a revelation. They showed a proposed railway line from the Beaufort St. Vincent harbour extension onward to a junction a few miles along the coast and then turning inland. Judas realised that if the other plans he had were dynamite, then these plans were definitely nuclear. There were nine plans with notes written on them and each showed a section of the line from the harbour extension to the junction with the main line. The line was single track and it doubled near the junction to give it easy access to and from the main railway system. Each map showed a section of the line and on map one, the line was marked A to B. On map two it was marked B to C. The following maps carried on with the same simple style of lettering. Judas laid out all of the maps on his table and he marvelled at the array of information. The maps with sidings and the station complex were followed by four large scale maps showing in greater detail the point work and in some cases the buildings.

A to B had no features except the single line.

B to C had a single siding midway along it for agricultural use.

Large scale map showing siding.

C to D had no features except the single line.

D to E had a station shown with the nearest village about a mile away. The station had a loop line, plus a bay, a coal siding, a goods siding and a cattle dock. The village was Beaufort St. Catherine.

Large scale map showing the station buildings, the siding structures and the track formation in greater detail.

E to F had no features except the single line.

F to G had no features except the single line.

G to H had a loop and some sidings going into a woodland area with associated industries.

Large scale map showing the loop and the sidings, plus the buildings.

H to I had no features except the single line.

I to J had the line furthest from the harbour complex being doubled to give access to the rest of the railway system.

Large scale map showing the single line being doubled to allow access to and from the main lines of the rail network.

The second book also contained loose leaf sheets and were in Adam's neat hand and also a "foreign" hand that was very hard to decipher. On initial inspection, the sheets did not seem to have any association with the maps or plans. Judas put them back in the box and would read them sometime soon.

Henry Brown would be speechless again, thought Judas. He then realised that he had the miniature track pieces in his case and he set about recreating the layouts of sections B to C, D to E, G to H and finally I to J. He began with map B to C as it was very easy to do. Next it was the turn of map G to H and this presented no difficulty for the standard track geometry of the company. This was followed by map I to J and again no difficulty was found in producing the plan. Plan D to E, however, was a bit more involved and Judas had difficulty getting the track pieces to work. After a few false starts he managed to succeed, although one of the sidings on the original plan was slightly out of place on the miniature plan. Still, he was pleased with his evenings work and produced the relevant drawings and entered the item numbers onto the pages. He then produced on his printer three sets of prints for each of the original maps and the model layout plans. He mused that Henry Brown was in for another shock. Judas ate a very late dinner.

CHAPTER 7

Tuesday 30th December

Judas walked to his lodge, contemplating what he would be saying to Henry Brown about his latest revelation. He was still deliberating what to say thirty minutes later and had reached no conclusion. He looked over to the day guards and simply announced, "I may have to go over to see Henry Brown again later and if I do I may be some time."

"Okay," said Keith nonchalantly, "no problem. We will look after the phones and any visitors, but keep the company mobile on you just in case we have an emergency."

Henry Brown arrived at about seven o'clock and again waved to the guards in the lodge. Judas gave him ten minutes to get himself settled into his office and then telephoned him.

"Mr Brown, Judas here. May I please come and see you as a matter of urgency?"

Henry Brown was taken aback for a moment and then regained his composure.

"Okay, you can come now, if you wish, before I start on my plans for the day."

Judas departed straight away and was soon facing Henry Brown. He placed his small case on the table and said, "Mr Brown, did you know that an extension of the railway line from the harbour sidings at Beaufort St. Vincent to a junction on the main line was at one time envisaged and planned?"

An incredulous Henry Brown looked up and simply said, "You jest of course."

"No, I never jest. I am told that I do not have a sense of humour," said an adamant Judas, "and I do have the papers to prove the line was proposed."

Judas reached into his case and took out the envelope that contained the copies of the maps and handed them over.

"The maps are signed by George William Robinson, who was responsible for the surveying of the route and I have the original maps. They are also signed by a couple of directors of the Great Western Railway and also initialled in capitals. The initials C ROFT are also shown, but I don't understand what these represent."

Henry Brown was not only speechless; he looked completely lost and bewildered. After an endless pause he reached over to his telephone and was thankful that Paul Gibson was in his office.

"Paul please come to my office and prepare yourself for the shock of the century, if not the shock of a lifetime."

Three minutes later a slightly panting Paul Gibson arrived and was invited to sit down by Henry Brown.

"This invitation seems menacing," suggested Paul. "What's the matter?"

Henry Brown was about to pass his set of plans to Paul Gibson when Judas gave him the second set of prints he had prepared last night. Paul slid the plans out of the envelope and just stared at each one. His face beamed wider with every plan he saw. "Are these genuine?" he eventually asked and Judas gave him his master copies to view.

"This is absolutely explosive information and it is also priceless. Who else knows about it?" demanded Henry Brown.

"Just you two and me and I will not say anything to anyone," answered Judas. "By the way, I have done the plans of the station, the agricultural siding, the woodland complex and the main junction using the company's templates and here they are. If they are any good, I hope they can also go into the publication. That is assuming of course that the information is released in the publication."

Judas handed over his work from the night before and also picked up the master copies from the desk in front of Paul Gibson. The two company men still seemed to be deeply pondering the enormity of the situation and Judas seemed to be surplus to requirements. He turned and was about to leave when Henry Brown said, "I presume these papers were the property of Adam and I ask again, will there be any more surprises?"

Judas shook his head.

"I very much doubt it, although I do have some more papers to read but they do not include any maps or plans."

Henry Brown and Paul Gibson both just nodded. With that Judas left the two men to ponder much and in very deep thought and concentration.

He returned to the lodge and was told by Keith that everything was okay and no-one had telephoned. After twenty minutes the telephone rang and by the ring tone Judas knew that it was an internal call. It was Henry Brown.

"Judas, I forgot to thank you for the plans, the ones from Adam and also the ones using our track geometry. They really are appreciated and Paul says the track designs you did are really good. However, we have to keep quiet about the discovery of the line extension from the harbour for the moment, until we have spoken to our lawyers and, hopefully, they will soon give us the green light to publish. We have also found out that George William Robinson was drowned in the

Beaufort St. Clement flood. I have not yet been able to find out anything about the two GWR directors or the capital initials. Anyway, many thanks and I will keep you informed of the developments." With that Henry Brown put down his telephone.

Judas opened his small case and was about to force himself to read the notes penned by Adam, when he saw the apartment plans selected by Anita. He took these out of his case and looked at them with a very critical eye. He saw the name of the architect on the bottom of the plans and smiled. It was the same one who he had engaged to do the outline plans of the Miller's Retreat. The layouts of all the apartments supplied by Jennifer were very well planned and he liked them all, but he did not like them enough to want any one of them. Anita had done a good job of selecting the plans, but unfortunately none of them had the zing effect on him and he put them back into his case.

On a sudden impulse, Judas rang the telephone number of the architect's office and after the introductions he was put through to Simon Lancaster, the named architect on the drawings.

"Hello Simon. It's Judas Wells and I would like to make use of your services again."

"Anytime," replied Simon, "what's the problem?"

"Anita has advised me that it would be a good idea to convert the Miller's Retreat back into a guest house. As you know it was my intention to do this, but at a much later date, but Anita thinks the time is now right for such action. I have doodled some designs for the rooms above the triple garage, which will be for Anita, who has already kindly agreed to be the resident manager of the place. I therefore need your constructive comments on the development of the site, on the

Health and Safety Certificate and the Fire Certificate for the building when converted."

"Hold on," complained Simon, "while I extract the property plans from my files." He put the handset down. After a while Simon returned.

"I knew this would happen one day, but I wasn't expecting it to be so soon. However, to continue with the project I must see you and presumably Anita, to sort out the room requirements and also to sort out the fire escape routes and external stairs and the placement of fire extinguishers and water hoses. And a few other things as well. Can I see you in the New Year?" and without waiting for a reply, continued, "How about Monday 5th January. I assume you are still working, so I could see you at about eight o'clock in the evening at my home if that is convenient. Helen would love to see you, and of course Miss Wells?" With that the arrangement was made.

Judas then telephoned Anita and, after the usual chatter, he advised her of the meeting with Simon Lancaster at his residence on Monday next. Anita was very excited at the prospect of the new guest house proposal being pursued with such vigour by Judas.

As there was no great amount of activity happening in the lodge, Judas decided to look at Adam's second note book and to view the pages contained therein. Judas, again, marvelled at the neat hand of Adam and re-read the old man's script about the known events connected with the lost gold and silver plate of the abbey. He also tried to read the other enclosed notes, written by another hand and found it very difficult, as it was a very bad scrawl. In some cases it was completely impossible to decipher and Judas put these pages to the back of the note book for investigation later. However, the notes he now began to read were Adam's personal notes about a relative of his and Judas felt very uncomfortable reading them. He felt it was like reading a friend's personal diary, but he forced himself to continue:

Recent Knowledge

A *In the late Victorian age, a highly respected historian and researcher was given permission to inspect the abbey library sources concerning the slaughter and ransacking of the church and coastal settlement.*

B *In his research the historian came across four copies of a paper showing a cross with unusual writing and markings on it. In the index of the library only three copies were listed. The researcher therefore kept one copy. All copies were checked and were found to be identical.*

C *The researcher was my great uncle, Albert, my grandfather's youngest brother. In his last will and testament Great Uncle Albert left to me all of his research papers, as I was his only living relative.*

D *A drawing of the cross was included in the papers and it showed a simple cross, with simple markings on it. It was assumed that the arrows pointing up and down represented north and south and the arrows pointing left and right represented east and west.*

E *It was also assumed that wavy lines on the cross represented rivers. However, the drawing also shows various lines and symbols that cannot be identified. It also showed figures next to the arrows.*

F *The drawing was very informative, but nothing fits. Rivers, hills, settlements and the coastline are in the wrong places.*

G *Great Uncle Albert once told me that he believed the*
   symbols related to the church slaughter and to the
   location of the church plate.

At this point Judas stopped reading. He already had a copy
of the drawing of the cross, as it was included in the book he
had taken from the garden shed of the orphanage. He could
recall all of the lines and letters on the drawing of the reverse
of the wooden cross, but as Adam had already written,
nothing fitted. Lines that were believed to be rivers and the
coastline just did not match the known geography of the time.

Judas then thought of the cross. From the drawing he could
remember that it was a very simple wooden cross and that
there were no embellishments on it, as they would not be
permitted by any of the mediaeval religious orders. However,
Judas had been convinced for a number of years that the
various markings on the reverse of the cross were the
directions to the hidden parcels of plate and other artefacts
from the abbey, but unfortunately, to date, no-one could
understand the markings.

At about ten o'clock Henry Brown walked to his vehicle
and left the car park. Just as he drove out of the car park, a call
came in for him from his wife and this call heralded a tsunami
of telephone activity. For the next two hours Judas was very
busy dealing with orders and queries from retail outlets and
with faxes requesting simple information. Other faxes were
put in envelopes and addressed to the correct department. At
about twelve o'clock the calls began to slow down and by one
o'clock Judas joined Keith and Colin for a well earned drink.
It was at this time that Henry Brown arrived back onto the
complex and waved to the guards and Judas as he passed.

Twenty minutes later the telephone sounded again and
Judas was summoned to Henry Brown's room.

"Nothing sinister," said the caller, "but I do need to speak to you urgently, so could you please come over to the design bureau in the next few minutes?"

"I will leave now and be with you shortly," said a worried Judas. He advised both guards of his destination and they agreed to take care of the switchboard. Judas got to the bureau door and entered. He was met by Henry Brown.

"I telephoned the MD this morning and told him that we had another bombshell that he should know about. As you know, I have only just returned and the MD was as shell shocked as Paul and I were, when you gave us the news. I told him that I had seen the original document and that everything is genuine. However, he says he needs to see the original document himself. If it is wrong and we release the information as genuine, our competitors would revel in our embarrassment and our company would not survive the ridicule or the scandal. Therefore, would you please allow me to take the original papers to him and let him pass them on to our lawyers and various experts to verify their authenticity?"

Judas could see that Henry Brown was very uncomfortable at having to ask the question raised by the MD and he therefore immediately agreed to the request.

"I have the papers in my case and I will fetch them for you now. I also have photocopies of them all." said Judas.

"I have to go back this afternoon to see the MD so, if I may, I will call into the lodge and pick them up on my way out?" said a relieved Henry Brown.

"No problem," said Judas as he left the bureau.

True to his word Henry Brown entered the lodge ten minutes later and received the papers from Judas.

"These are priceless," said Henry Brown, as he scanned the papers, "We will take very good care of them and I will make sure that everyone who handles them is also aware of their worth."

With that he left the lodge, walked to his vehicle and drove off. Judas returned to Keith and Colin to finish his drink, when his telephone rang. It was Anita.

"Simon Lancaster has just telephoned me to say that a person he was meant to be seeing tonight has a very bad cold and has cancelled their meeting. Simon will be available at his home tonight, at eight o'clock, for our meeting instead of Monday if you are also available? I have already said I can go."

"Yes I certainly am available and will be pleased to go," said Judas and then added, "Why didn't he contact me direct?"

Anita replied, "Simon told me he had been trying to contact you for over an hour, just after ten o'clock and had then given up. He then decided to try and contact me at the Poacher's Retreat, but, as I was out, he left a message with our receptionist. I have only just returned. I will now telephone his office and accept the appointment for tonight. By the way, what do you think of the apartment plans Jennifer gave you?"

It was a question Judas was dreading.

"They are good, but not for me," he replied defensively. "I looked at them all but there was not one that I could say that I really liked and would be happy to live in. Sorry."

"Oh don't apologise," said Anita, "I picked out the best plans in the file, but I wasn't really impressed with them either."

After reiterating that she would be at the meeting tonight at eight o'clock, she rang off.

The rest of the afternoon was fairly quiet, although there were about a dozen telephone calls. Most were put through to the design bureau staff or to voice mails. At about four o'clock many of the staff on site left early to go home. Snow was forecast and those that lived a fair distance away were going home before the expected snow settled and made driving more hazardous. By four thirty all staff had left the site and the guards were looking forward to a relaxing time, before being relieved by the night staff. Ten minutes later Henry Brown arrived back on site.

Henry Brown parked his car close to the security lodge and walked into the reception part of the lodge.

"The MD and the board members that were present, have asked me to thank you for allowing us to have the original papers and for your help in all matters associated with the plans," said Henry Brown.

He was trying to say very little in front of the guards, who were within earshot, but enough for Judas to understand the meaning.

"It was a pleasure and I sincerely hope the company lawyers and various experts will soon be able to substantiate the accuracy and genuineness of the documentation," replied Judas, trying to emulate the vagueness of Henry Brown's speech. Henry Brown smiled, nodded and went over to the design bureau.

As there was still an hour to go before the end of the shift, Judas pulled out his photocopies of the documentation he had given to Henry Brown for the MD. Judas looked at the maps and followed the railway lines from the harbour sidings to the proposed junction with the main lines. He then looked at the town plan of Beaufort St. Vincent as it was in 1880. It was, as he expected, much smaller than it is today, but it was still possible to see named streets that are on present day maps. He then looked at the coast and scanned along it to the north; to where the harbour extension line skirted the uplands, before being doubled and heading inland to the railway junction with the main line.

Judas retraced his steps to Beaufort St. Vincent along the coast but could not see anything unusual. He took out Adams second note book and quickly scanned the papers. He eventually came to the undecipherable pages and thumbed through them. These pages were written in bold strokes and by an educated hand, but there was no comparison with the neat hand of Adam. There were six pages that were written by this unknown person and Judas could make out a few words, but not enough to make sense of any sentence. These were followed by two pages that contained very rough diagrams of an area of land, including roads and rivers; these were not Adam's work either. The next six pages were in Adam's hand and Judas was relieved to see that the old man had attempted to unravel the mystery of the unknown script, by writing his decipherment of the words. When Judas compared some of the deciphered words with the original, he sometimes concurred with Adam's thoughts but, on other occasions, he had his reservations. Judas then photocopied all fourteen pages, with the intention of trying to do his own deciphering of the difficult script and detective work on the plans.

A few minutes before six o'clock, the night guards, Gordon and Richard, came into the lodge and, after the handover, Keith and Colin departed. As Judas was in no hurry to leave he kept reading the notes, but could not make any inroads into the decipherment of the paperwork. He again looked at the rough diagrams and was about to put them down when he noticed a very faint, partial signature at the bottom of the second page. It was signed Albert S. At this point he was hailed by Gordon:

"You seem to be on unpaid overtime Judas. It's time you were away home."

Judas waved, packed his papers into his case and put the work on his desk into his cupboard. After wishing the guards a peaceful shift, he left the lodge and began his walk home.

As he left the car park, it began to snow heavily and Judas wrapped his scarf tightly round his neck. He was also thankful that he had remembered his gloves. He heard a distant whistle from a locomotive and then it was silent again. Road traffic seemed non-existent and Judas concluded that most civilized people would be at home already. After all, it was very nearly the year's end. He arrived home, cold and weary, and thawed out by the radiator.

As he prepared to leave his home for the meeting with Simon Lancaster and Anita, Judas looked at the plans he had produced for the new guest house and was quite satisfied with his efforts. He hoped the forthcoming meeting would be constructive and that good progress could be made to get the project suitably launched. He also hoped to have time to see Simon Lancaster about a new home for himself, as he knew that this architect was responsible for some of the new residential developments in Beaufort St. Vincent and also in Beaufort St. Clement.

As he walked to his meeting it was still snowing and it was eerily quiet. There was very little wind and the only sounds seemed to be very distant. Judas arrived at the home of Simon Lancaster at seven fifty and was not surprised to see Anita waiting for him. Nothing was said and they walked up the long gravel drive together and were met at the entrance by Simon and his wife Helen.

"Season's greetings," said Helen, adding, "that is if it's not too late."

Anita responded with the usual reply. Susan, Simon's secretary, was also there in the background. She had been invited for dinner and to take notes of the meeting.

Susan also wished Anita, the complements of the season, although she knew Judas shunned Christmas festivities.

After these pleasantries, the meeting began in earnest.

"These are copies of the drawings that you have Simon," began Judas, "and I have indicated the various functions of the rooms."

Simon and Anita proposed various amendments to the drawings to comply with numerous legal architectural requirements and building regulations. It was then down to business concerning the legal contracts, the fire regulations and certificates, and the safety regulations and certificates. Anita raised a number of questions and queries during the evening and was content with the responses and she also contributed to the success of the meeting.

After an hour, a hospitality break was gratefully accepted by all parties and, at ten fifteen, agreement was achieved and all parties were happy with the outcome. The only remaining problem was for the installation of a lift servicing the cellar, the ground floor, the first and second floors, and the tower. Simon said he would arrange for an engineer to visit the property and to do a structural survey for the required installation.

Judas then casually asked Simon, "Have you designed any new residential developments in the town?" and was surprised at the response.

"Yes," replied Simon, "I have a few new apartment designs in the pipeline at the moment, but at present they are only in the planning stage. Anita told me about your going to the old orphanage for a look around before it is demolished and developed. The finished retirement apartments will really be expensive and very special.

"However, back in our world, I was not surprised when Anita told me that you did not enjoy any of the apartment plans that Jennifer gave you for the new complexes located near to the town centre. They were very standard, but that was what the developer required and in fact demanded."

"What are the locations of the local apartments you are presently working on?" queried Judas and then continued, "I will need somewhere to rest my weary bones in the town when the Miller's Retreat is returned to operating as a guest house. However, my requirements are very basic and simple as I am a minimalist."

Simon replied, "They will be in, or very near to, the town centre, but at present the developers are having difficulties in getting the locations they require. However, when they do get the legal, financial, engineering and construction issues all sorted out, plus the location problems also all sorted out, then I can promise you some really spectacular designs for the apartments. They will also have a purchase price to match."

"Oh well," said Judas, "I will just have to keep looking, after all a small apartment will fulfil all of my needs."

Judas and Anita left soon afterwards, after thanking Simon for his diligent work and patience.

"Thank you also Susan," continued Judas, "for giving up your evening to take the notes required. It was very much appreciated by both Anita and myself. Also many thanks to you Helen for the drinks, cakes and biscuits. Again many thanks to you all."

Judas walked Anita home, arm in arm, along deserted streets and it was still eerily quiet, although it had stopped snowing.

"I really can't believe that we have just begun the process of getting another guest house in the town. I really can't believe it," said Anita. She then talked endlessly about the meeting. "I'm really happy and excited about the new guest house and am really looking forward to the new challenges ahead. I am especially looking forward to my new abode above the garages. For me this will be absolute luxury."

At the Poacher's Retreat, Judas left Anita and was pleased to see that she was beaming and very happy. On reaching home he sat down and pondered the happenings of the meeting and read the notes he had written down. He then thought of his own situation. He still had to find himself a new home when his present abode was returned to its former use.

CHAPTER 8

Wednesday 31st December

The snow had stopped, but it was bitterly cold as Judas entered his workplace car park. A strong breeze was coming in from the sea and storm clouds were gathering. On his walk he thought about last night's meeting and he hoped that Simon's company would soon have the drawings ready for inspection. He was pleased that Anita had been there last night. She had been a great support and had been an asset during the meeting, and afterwards, on the way home, Judas reflected that he had never seen her happier or as talkative.

As he entered the security lodge, the night guards were preparing for the handover. Judas went straight to his desk and settled down to begin work. Judas greeted both Keith and Colin as they arrived and received a very chirpy "Good morning" in reply.

At six twenty Henry Brown arrived with Paul Gibson and they both waved towards the lodge as they passed. On seeing Judas, Henry Brown altered course and walked towards the lodge and entered.

"Good morning," he said to Judas, who echoed the same in reply. Mr Brown then continued, "Last night I had a telephone call, just before I left for home. It was from the guy who will be working here in the lodge, so you and he can work four days on duty and four days off duty, as I explained. He will be here for the two day induction course on company safety and first aid procedures etc, on Monday 5th January and he can start training with you in the lodge on Wednesday 7th January, unless you have any objections?"

"None at all Mr Brown," said Judas, "I look forward to meeting him and to training him. What's his name?"

"He is Martin Holland," answered Henry Brown and then continued, "I have some more news that you may have heard people whispering about on the works grapevine. Because of our working seven days a week, beginning on the 5th January, and also the fact that we will be taking on more staff when the contractors have finished the building and installation work, it had been decided that Richard Foote needed a layout design assistant and he was duly appointed and was to begin work here when the factory re-opens.

"With Richard's untimely demise, Stephen Lindsey will take over Richard's duties and we will have to get Stephen an assistant. Stephen is a very gifted layout designer and has done splendid work for a rival model railway company for a number of years. He only left the company because the production of the model locomotives and rolling stock was outsourced abroad and this produced unforeseen problems which led to a financial collapse. Also the fact that the items the company produced were for a specialist market did not help and the company suffered accordingly. The company is struggling to survive and it decided to cut its workforce. Therefore, Stephen was compulsorily made redundant. His old firm's loss is definitely our gain."

Henry Brown stopped talking to let the news be absorbed. He then continued, "I have shown him some of the layouts that we will be putting into our new book and he was suitably impressed. There was however, one thing he did suggest and I must admit it was something that I had not thought about. He suggested that, in the layout section of the book, we show a fairly simple layout design, possibly only a few points, with a simple station and then add to the layout in possibly six stages, to show what can be achieved ultimately from very humble and basic beginnings. I thought this was a very good idea and I gave Stephen the okay to design some layouts in that genre. I also showed him some of your plans Judas and he has asked if you could have a go at this exercise also. Therefore, may I ask you to have a go at developing this type of layout please?"

Judas thought he could hear the pleading in the voice and agreed. With that a relieved Henry Brown left the lodge and walked over to the factory entrance.

"Sounds like good news," said Colin to Judas, "and it looks like you are going to be busy designing again."

"True," agreed Judas, "but I haven't a clue for a layout yet. Hopefully something will come to mind, I just hope it is soon."

Judas need not have worried. He vaguely recalled that when he was learning about the track geometry of the company's products he had looked at a series of track designs in an old layout book and had copied parts of designs that he had liked using the small scale pieces of track. He decided to do the same again, only this time the designs were his and he had to select finished parts of layouts and lessen the track content for the initial layout plan. The final plan would contain all of the track in the sections chosen.

Judas was about to start when he was interrupted by the telephone and he was kept busy for the next three hours by numerous calls and by various faxes .He worked through this busy time and at about nine thirty he was able to return to his layout project for Henry Brown. Judas extracted the photocopies of the plans he had presented to Henry Brown and just looked at them very intently. He then drew a simplified country station plan he had designed earlier. He then drew a simplified industrial complex from another plan. Next he sketched another simplified quarrying complex and finally he penned a very simplified harbour section.

The telephone calls began again and it was another hour before Judas could continue his work for Henry Brown. At this point he took the track geometry pieces out of his drawer and began to construct the four different sections of layout. He knew that the sections did work with the track geometry and he soon had all four of the designs completed. Judas then juggled the four sections around until he had a basis for a model railway layout plan that he considered acceptable. His final attempt was for an "L" shaped layout and he joined all four separate sections with a linking track and placed them down onto the layout board. On completion of the design using the track geometry pack, he drew out the plan on graph paper and added the track geometry item numbers. Judas then added one point to each of the four sections on the board to show layout development and then drew out this plan on graph paper and added the item numbers. This exercise continued a number of times until all four sections were as they had been when in their original plans.

Judas then looked at other plans he had produced and took further sections and again simplified them. He continued as he had done on his first attempt, only this plan was for a high level terminus, with quarries and low level storage loops. After two hours, interrupted with numerous telephone calls, Judas had developed eight complete plans, each starting very basically with minimal track and developing into a very complex and workable layout. He photocopied all of the plans and papers he had prepared, in triplicate, and put one set in an envelope for Henry Brown. Judas then reached for the telephone and rang his boss.

"May I see you Mr Brown?" asked Judas.

After the initial surprise, Judas was invited to the office block and Colin agreed to deal with any telephone calls during his absence.

Henry Brown was seated at his desk when Judas entered his office and was invited to take a seat. At that moment the telephone rang with an internal call and Mr Brown answered it. When the telephone conversation was over, Judas handed the envelope to Henry Brown. The contents were extracted and Henry Brown seemed amazed at the contents.

"I recognise various parts of these plans," he said and when he had seen all of the pages he continued, "These are very good and you have even shown the presentation of the layouts from the basic level to the final development of the layout plans. I must show these to Paul Gibson straight away."

Paul Gibson was summoned by telephone to Henry Brown's office and entered a few moments later.

"Have a look at these Paul," said Henry Brown as his colleague entered the room.

Paul was handed the papers and sat down to view them.

After a few moments he simply said, "Wow, these are damn good."

When he had viewed all of the papers Henry Brown said, "I also think they are damn good and with your input, my input and Stephen Lindsey's input, we should have a solid base for layout developments in our new publication."

Paul agreed and asked if the present plans were all the work of Judas. On receiving confirmation from Henry Brown, Paul turned to Judas.

"I took two hours last night to come up with one plan and to develop it and you did eight simple plans with numerous developments into complex track layouts today. All of the plans are much better than mine. That's just incredible. Well done."

"They are also better than my two efforts," said Henry Brown and then added, "also well done from me."

Judas could feel himself blush. Henry Brown then informed Judas that, as it was New Years Eve, all the staff in the complex would be leaving the site at about four o'clock and would not return until the complex opened in early January. Judas was asked to inform the guards and to request vigilance until the return of the workforce. Judas nodded.

Back at the lodge Judas told both Keith and Colin of the message from Henry Brown and this was greeted by a grunt from both men. They were seated at their desk, having a late and very large lunch. Mugs of steaming coffee were also set down on the desk.

Judas continued, "On the 7th January I shall be training a new man in this lodge and when he is fully trained we will be sharing the work. The roster will be for duties of four days at work and four days away. I am definitely looking forward to getting some days away from here, but unfortunately I can't have any time off until Monday 19th."

Judas waited for the news to be absorbed and eventually Colin turned, swallowed a piece of cake and said, "Good. It's about time you had some time off. We were all beginning to think you were a permanent fixture in the lodge."

Keith chuckled at this attempt at humour, but continued eating.

The afternoon continued with all the lodge personnel doing their duties, although Judas thought his input was lacking in content. However, at four o'clock prompt, all of the factory staff and management left the buildings and various groups congregated together to wish their colleagues their best wishes for the New Year. At ten minutes past four, all the staff and vehicles had left the complex, with the exception of Henry Brown and Paul Gibson. Both were standing by their vehicles, which were parked close to each other and both men were in deep conversation. They both suddenly looked towards the lodge and seeing Judas looking at them, they beckoned him over to join them.

"Oh God," said Judas as he got up and walked to the door, "Now what have I done?"

As he approached the men he could see them both smiling and he relaxed slightly. Henry Brown spoke as Judas joined them.

"We just wanted to say a big thank you for all the work that you have done, in designing various layouts and also for the wonderful information and photographs of Beaufort St. Clement. Please believe us when we say that these revelations will be absolutely dynamite when the publication is released, which we hope will be in the next few months. Everyone in the company is sworn to secrecy and I am sure no one in the lodge will reveal any information to any outside sources. The MD has also asked me to convey to you his sincere thanks for your work on this project and for the plans and photographs of Beaufort St. Clement and he looks forward to thanking you in person in the New Year."

With his speech over Henry Brown shook Judas' hand, as did Paul Gibson, who added, "When I was contacted and told the terrible news about Richard Foote's untimely demise, I honestly believed we had a very difficult New Year ahead of us. However, with your plans and with the additional information about Beaufort St. Clement and Beaufort St. Catherine, I really am looking forward to next year. In fact I sincerely wish we were not going home now as I honestly could carry on working. Originally when we were called into work, it was thought that none of us would get any time off during the company's break. However, as we are fairly advanced in our preparation and as my dear wife deserves a short vacation, we are off to Norfolk for a few days break."

Both men smiled and wished Judas a very pleasant New Year and walked to their vehicles. Judas returned to the lodge and joined Keith. Colin was out of the lodge on an internal patrol around the complex.

"It looks like tomorrow will be a very quiet day," said Keith and added, "After working the day shift tomorrow I really will be looking forward to a few days of relaxation."

"I certainly wish you and Colin a very pleasant few days off and on your return the complex will be back to normal. Enjoy the days away and recharge your batteries," replied Judas.

The day began to drag and both guards did fairly quick patrols. On completion, Colin and Keith activated the intruder alarms and confirmed that the infra red alarms were automatically connected and that the smoke alarms and fire alarms were operational. The guards and Judas then sat together and talked about the happenings of the past few weeks and of their ambitions for the New Year. Both Keith and Colin had decided that their New Year resolutions would be to begin a diet and this time they would succeed in keeping to the diet. However, this gesture was apparently an annual event as neither man had the mental discipline to keep to a strict food intake regime.

The hands of the wall clock crawled up to the top of the dial and Gordon and Richard entered into the lodge together.

After the handover, Keith said, "The complex is now closed until Monday 5th January, according to Henry Brown, so may I wish you all a very pleasant New Year."

Judas was about to wish the guards a very pleasant and peaceful shift, when Gordon said, "The recent incident at the neighbouring property is in the local weekly gazette. I'll read it out to you."

However, before he could begin the telephone rang and Judas automatically answered it. He was very surprised to discover that the caller was Simon Lancaster.

"Oh thank God I have contacted you before you left for home," said a relieved Simon and then asked urgently, "Can we talk?"

"Of course," said Judas, "fire away. What's the problem?"

Simon Lancaster then began, "I only have a few minutes, as I have to go out, but this is the problem. I have been engaged in a conversion project for a well known and very well respected building contractor. My task was to convert an old industrial warehouse building for use to a business conference centre. This building would then be used to stage numerous courses and events required by some very well known and very select multi-national corporations. The facilities will be first class and the owners of the complex, who wish to remain nameless at the moment, believe they have spotted an ideal opening for this type of requirement. The building work is nearing completion and the property in question is located near to the port area of the town and is fairly close to the town centre. All that remains is for the building to be inspected, accepted and given the various safety and fire certificates etcetera and then it can be filled with the necessary furniture and soft fittings."

Judas could not think how this conversation could involve him but manners dictated that he should continue listening.

Simon continued, "The developer had also been tasked with finding and developing a site nearby to construct a small hotel to accommodate the participants at the conferences. This hotel was to be owned and run by the same nameless individuals. Two adjacent sites were originally targeted for this hotel development and the actual structures on the sites were dismantled. I had designed a small hotel for the site and foundation building work had just started when several skeletons were found. The local museum staff went on site and, to cut a long story short, it was discovered that the bones were Roman and according to my old history teacher, the Romans were not supposed to have come to this place. Therefore, work stopped and the Town Council and the Local Museum, plus the Archaeological Society, are adamant that the site had to be excavated. The archaeologists went on site and found a number of artefacts that confirm that there was a Roman fort here and it was of such importance that the site and numerous buildings had to be excavated. In view of this and the fact that all the other available sites close to the conference centre were considered too small or otherwise unsuitable, I now come to the crunch. The developer is desperate. If there is no suitable hotel near to the centre, then the centre will not be a success."

Judas could sense that Simon was building himself up for the finale, but when it came it was a complete bombshell.

"Would you be willing to sell the Miller's Retreat?"

Judas was speechless and there followed what is commonly referred to as a pregnant pause.

After what seemed an eternity, Simon Lancaster asked sheepishly, "Are you still there?"

Judas recovered from his shock and simply replied, "Yes."

After a few more seconds he had regained some composure and asked Simon, "Who volunteered my property?"

Simon answered fairly defensively, "No-one has volunteered your property, the developers just asked me if I could help them with the search and I thought of the Miller's Retreat. It is in the right location, not too far from the conference centre. It is a perfect size and when it is developed how we recently agreed, it would be ideal. Also the rooms are spacious and some existing rooms can be used for small gatherings in the evenings for the participants. It also has plenty of space at the front of the property for car parking. It was just a question that I asked. Are you interested? If you are, I can guarantee a fantastic price for the property."

Simon Lancaster then mentioned a figure that Judas found to be staggering and he had to sit down. Simon also added that the company would be prepared to let him have a quality apartment at one of their complexes in Beaufort St. Catherine, when they were completed in the next few days, as part of the deal. Judas just looked shocked.

After a few more seconds Simon said, "I'm sorry if it was a bolt from the blue, but I was just thinking it would be a marvellous financial opportunity for you. After all you are not getting any younger and, at sixty next birthday, you should be getting your plans made for your retirement. Could you give it some thought tonight please, as a matter of urgency? If you do contact Anita, by all means outline to her the contents of this call, but please do not inform anyone else of the conversation. It is not general knowledge about the Roman fort, the conference centre or the proposed hotel. If I may, I will call you tomorrow, for a reply? Sorry but I have to go now as I have a very important and urgent meeting with another client."

With that Simon Lancaster put down his handset. Judas put his telephone down and was conscious that Gordon and Richard were looking at him.

"Bad news?" enquired Richard.

"No, not bad news," replied Judas, "just a bit of a shock."

After a few moments Judas got up from his desk and, regaining some composure, wished them a pleasant and peaceful shift.

"Oh, I nearly forgot, both Keith and Colin are making a New Year resolution and both guards are going on diets."

"So are we," said Gordon and laughed as he snapped off a corner from a large bar of chocolate. Judas just smiled.

As he left the lodge Judas needed fresh air and walked down to the harbour to clear his brain. A few small boats had been marooned and left lying on their sides as the tide had receded and he could see the lighthouse beacon flashing as it revolved. It was unusually quiet and he could only just hear the rippling sea. He found a seat by an embankment and settled down to do some serious thinking.

He recalled everything Simon Lancaster had said and as he was keen on history he tried to figure out where the site of the Roman fort could be. He had no success and forced himself to concentrate on the matter of the hotel development. The one thing that kept returning to his thoughts was the comment by Simon about him becoming sixty next birthday. That really hurt. But it was true. On 29th February he would be sixty. He thought very seriously about his future. What did he want to do? Did he want to develop his property into a guest house with the associated problems? Where was he going to live? He finally thought of Anita and what would become of her if he sold the Miller's Retreat? Eventually Judas retreated towards his home.

After he had entered through his garden gate, he unlocked his post box and was surprised to see it was half full. He carried the contents inside and was relieved to see that none of it was important, and most of it was simply junk mail. Tonight he had much on his mind and did not want to be distracted by trivialities.

Judas sat down. He was still very disturbed by the earlier telephone call he had received from Simon Lancaster. He wrote down all of the pertinent facts that Simon had spoken about. He was still in shock at the price the company were willing to pay. He was also pleased at the prospect of a quality apartment at Beaufort St. Catherine. He decided to telephone Anita. His call was answered by a male voice that Judas did not recognise and he was passed on to Anita.

"Hello," she said defensively, "this is an unexpected pleasure."

After the pleasantries Judas asked her if she had seen Simon since the meeting and received a negative reply.

"Why do you ask?" she queried.

"He telephoned me just as I was leaving the lodge," replied Judas, "and he told me some confidential information about his work and he also asked me some profound questions about my future plans. This confidential information and these plans involve you, so would you mind if I came over tonight to get your input? I know it's New Years Eve, but it is important."

"Come on over, I could use the company," invited Anita, "John, who you just spoke to, has just left with his wife Stephanie Faulkner and I am all on my own. We have no guests until Tuesday and from then on we are solidly booked for all of January. See you soon."

Judas walked quickly to the Poacher's Retreat, pressed the bell button and entered.

Anita looked up and gasped, "Oh God, you look awful. Whatever is the matter?"

Anita invited Judas to sit and passed him a tray she had prepared containing a cold drink and some savoury biscuits. "You look as though you need this," she commented.

"I have some awkward news," said Judas, "and I would like your opinion on how to proceed. Your future is involved in this important decision as well as mine."

"This sounds ominous and interesting," said Anita as she settled down in a comfortable chair, stole one of his biscuits and listened intently.

Judas outlined what had been said by Simon Lancaster, missing out nothing, not even the staggering figure or the offer of an apartment and he covered every aspect of the conversation in complete detail. When he had finished he invited Anita to comment. Anita sat there speechless.

"That's how it affected me," said Judas eventually.

After what seemed an eternity Anita said, "You must accept this offer with both hands Judas and set yourself up for the remainder of your life. After all you will soon be sixty."

"Thanks for that," said Judas, "That's what Simon said. Are you sure you haven't seen him?"

Anita smiled and simply shook her head.

"But what about you?" asked Judas in a very serious tone, "What will happen to you?"

Anita took a long, deep breath and after a few moments said, "A few days after your birthday I will also be sixty. I only accepted to go to the Miller's Retreat because you asked me and I thought I owed you some loyalty for the loan. There was also the prospect that I would have a decent home for a few years, until I stopped working. However, I will be quiet content to stay here and when I have paid off the money I owe you, I will stop working. The rooms I have here are not much but I will get something better when I eventually retire. After all, I, like you, only need something basic. You must look to your future and stop worrying about others."

With that Anita fell silent.

Judas was also silent for a long time and then eventually said, "Okay, when Simon contacts me tomorrow I will accept, but only if you will allow me to help you to get a property that you really want. Believe me when I say that, according to Simon, the properties at Beaufort St. Catherine will be very plush and I do assure you that the property you are going to have, wherever it is, will not be basic. When we find something that you want, whatever the monetary shortfall is, I will pay it."

"But you can't..." began Anita, but Judas interrupted her.

"These terms are final. You are my oldest and dearest friend and you deserve a long and happy retirement, starting soon, in comfortable surroundings."

Judas munched on his biscuits and drank from his glass. Anita sat in her easy chair and had tears flowing down her cheeks.

Judas stayed for only another twenty minutes and then left. Anita was still tearful and was trying to come to terms with the fact that she would soon be able to stop working and leave the running of her guest house to Stephanie Faulkner. As Judas walked back to his home it began to snow heavily. It was eerily quiet and bitterly cold, but he had a spring in his step. Judas realized that he was really looking forward to tomorrow and also to his conversation with Simon Lancaster. Reality then struck as he realized that, as his property was required urgently, he would have to leave it soon and he had nowhere to go. He was in a sombre mood as he entered his annexe.

CHAPTER 9

Thursday 1st January

When Judas walked to work it had stopped snowing, although there was a thick mist and he was glad to be wrapped up in a thick overcoat. As it was the first day of the year and no staff were on site at the company, the guards and Judas expected it to be a quiet day at work. According to Gordon it had been exceptionally cold during the night. Gordon placed the weekly gazette on Judas's table, folded to the page relating to the robbery and smiled. Judas wished both Gordon and Richard a very pleasant four days away and when the day guards arrived they both left the site.

"Happy New Year to you both," said Judas to the day guards as they began their shifts. They were about to return the greeting when the telephone on their desk rang and Keith began talking to his base manager. Judas sat in his office chair and shuffled some papers on his desk. He saw the grandly named weekly paper, *The Beaufort Gazette*, which Gordon had placed onto his desk. Judas read the report of the attempted robbery and the apprehension of the villains. He was pleased that the constabulary had not provided the reporters with definite information on the arrests and he hoped they would not release any details. As both guards were still busy dealing with their controller, Judas turned his attention to the matter in hand. After the conversation last night with Simon Lancaster and his meeting with Anita, he was anxious to agree to the sale and to get everything down in writing. He contemplated telephoning Simon at home, but decided not to because of the very early hour and he replaced the receiver.

Judas then took out of his case the notes he had written last night about Simon's conversation and re-read them. He read them a second time to make sure he had not omitted, or even misread, any information. He was still staggered by the amount of money he was being offered and he kept looking at the figure on the paper. It then began to concern him that Anita was beaming when she left Simon's home two nights ago, presumably at the thought of running a new guest house and was now telling him to look to his future and to sell his property. He resolved to telephone her later to see if she was still okay with the decision.

At that moment the guards finished their telephone conversation with their controller and both turned to Judas.

"Happy New Year," they said in unison.

Judas stood, smiled and returned the sentiments to the guards.

After a few seconds, Keith said, "We have just been advised by our security controllers that Beaufort Models will be needing more security guards when the present extensive building programme is completed. Apparently we guards are to be moved into a larger purpose built structure close to a new car park entrance and quite close to the main office and engineering entrances. There will be three day guards and three night guards on duty each shift and the rosters will be amended accordingly."

Keith and Colin waited for the news to be absorbed by Judas, who eventually just said, "Did your controllers say when this change would come into force?"

Colin said, "No, but they did say that the changeover would be at a weekend, as this would cause less upheaval to this company."

The guards then talked together about the changes and wrote legible notes, from their earlier scribbled efforts, for their colleagues. Judas returned to his desk and again read his own notes from his conversation last evening with Simon Lancaster. After a few minutes, Colin went out to do a quick patrol and Keith settled down to sort out some unfinished paperwork. Ten minutes later Judas was still mulling over what he was going to say to Anita, when he heard the guards' radio bleep. It was Colin, informing Keith that a vehicle was approaching. Both Judas and Keith looked up and eventually made out that the vehicle belonged to Henry Brown.

"Now what?" said Keith as he opened the barrier.

Henry Brown parked his car as expertly as usual and entered the lodge.

"A very happy New Year to you both and my very best wishes to you and your families."

"Thank you Mr Brown," said Keith, "and may we wish you also a very pleasant and enjoyable New Year."

Before Judas could speak, Henry Brown continued, "I feel sure that this year is going to be a very good one for the company and the management and directors have asked me to tell you that they have very high hopes of a healthy and profitable future."

At that moment Colin arrived. He had not completed his patrol but he was just curious. Henry Brown went over to see him and passed on his best wishes for the New Year and told him of the company's hopes and aspirations.

After a few minutes Henry Brown asked Judas to join him outside. Colin returned to his patrol, leaving Keith in the lodge.

Standing next to his car, Henry Brown began, "This is very difficult, so I won't dress it up in any way. The company are very grateful to you and the guards for your contribution to the contents of our design book, due for publication next year... err, sorry... this year. Your contribution has been exceptional; fantastic track designs and also the previously unseen photographs and unknown layout plans of the station development at Beaufort St. Clement were absolutely sensational. Added to that the previously unknown plans for the extension line to Beaufort St. Catherine and the line then going on to join the main line were equally sensational."

Before Judas could say anything, Henry Brown continued but in a more serious tone.

"As you know our lawyers have been tasked to see if there would be any problems with our publishing these facts to the media. They are adamant there will be no problem, so would you mind if we attributed the discovery of the photographs and the lost track plans and station layout to Adam and could we also add the name of Richard Foote to the credit."

Judas's face beamed with sheer delight.

Henry Brown continued, "As both men are no longer on this mortal coil, if there are any legal problems it will be easier to deflect them."

Judas had tears in his eyes as he said, "Go ahead. Adam would be absolutely thrilled."

Henry Brown seemed very relieved and shook Judas by the hand and thanked him for agreeing.

"I know it's New Years Day," said Henry Brown, "but I have to go and see the MD today and he will be very relieved at the outcome of our talk. We can now go ahead with the long process of getting our design book ready for the publishers and hopefully it will be available to the model railway fraternity on time." He then changed tack. "As I told you recently the new man will be here for you to train on

Wednesday 7th January for nearly two weeks. His name, as you know, is Martin Holland. He was made redundant from his previous employers after thirty five years and he is a keen model railway enthusiast. If the guards ask anything of what we have been talking about, just say we discussed the new man and his training. There is a slight problem however. On the weekends, the 10th and 11th January and the 17th and 18th January he has commitments and will be unavailable to work so can you please carry on as usual?"

Judas nodded. Henry Brown continued, "Ironically, he is showing his own model railway clubs layout at a minor exhibition in Thornton Beamish on the first weekend and at another exhibition on the following weekend. During the second week of training you can just sit with him and he will do the work whilst you just keep an eye on him. After that you will be working four days on and four days off. Is that okay with you?"

Judas raised no objections and Henry Brown went to his vehicle a very relieved man. He then called back to Judas and returned to speak with him.

"Silly me," said Henry Brown and continued, "What was Adam's surname?"

"His surname was Stonehaven," said Judas and he watched Henry Brown enter it into his notebook. Judas then watched him leave the car park and saw the barrier clang into its support. He looked up to the heavens and felt snowflakes fall onto his face.

The temperature was dropping and Judas realized that he was very cold. He walked briskly to the lodge and entered. Not waiting to be quizzed by Keith, Judas told him that a new man would be starting in the lodge on Wednesday 7th and he would be training him for a period of eight days and after that they would be working a four day shift. He also mentioned that the new man was a model railway enthusiast. Judas could practically hear Keith grown.

"Did Henry Brown say anything about the new staffing requirements, or anything about the new gate house?"

"Absolutely nothing," said Judas and continued, "He also said nothing about the completion of the present extensive construction work or anything about the installation of the manufacturing machinery. In fact Mr Brown took a very long time to say very little."

Keith was about to say something when Colin entered the lodge.

"Ye Gods," said Colin, "It's freezing again. I am very, very cold so I only did a short patrol and I'm hungry."

Judas smiled. Today was the day both guards began their diets and it was already getting difficult for Colin to continue. Keith outlined to Colin the contents of the talk between Mr Brown and Judas and when advised that the new man was a model railway enthusiast, Colin groaned.

"Oh hellfire. Not another one. Is nothing sacred?"

Both guards laughed and as they were feeling peckish they decided to have a mug of steaming coffee and invited Judas over to sit with them. As Judas left his chair his telephone rang. It was Anita.

"Can you talk?"

"No problems," replied Judas and she continued:

"Were you really serious last night about accepting the developer's proposals as outlined by Simon Lancaster?"

"Yes," replied Judas and before he could say anything else, Anita continued.

"And were you serious about me stopping work?"

"Again yes," said Judas and this time Anita paused before continuing.

"Were you also serious about helping me with the financing of my new home?"

"Of course I was and am, serious about all of these points raised," said Judas, "Why do you ask?"

Anita was silent for what seemed an eternity and Judas felt that he could hear faint whimpering down the telephone.

Eventually she responded, "I didn't sleep much last night as I think I was in shock. I have always had plans for when I retire but these plans seem to be always getting further and further away. Recently it has been a question of going forward one step and being pushed back three. Now I can make definite plans, if you are sure about what you said?"

Judas, not wishing to say anything in front of the guards that could be taken out of context, simply said, "Everything is okay. When Simon calls me and we finalize our details I will call you and we can arrange to meet. I really will look forward to that. Do not worry about anything. Oh, and by the way, may I wish you a very healthy, happy, peaceful and prosperous New Year."

Anita was openly sobbing as she replaced the receiver.

Judas went to the guards and sat with them. When Keith went from the lodge to begin his patrol Judas returned to his own desk. He got out his notes again concerning the proposals of Simon Lancaster and studied them. He was still impressed by what he saw, although he found it extremely hard to believe what he was reading. He then thought about Anita and was hopeful that her sobbing had stopped. He was thinking about telephoning Simon when the instrument rang. Judas snatched the receiver and the caller was Simon. There were no pleasantries from Simon.

"Yes or no?"

Judas theatrically waited a few seconds before answering, "Yes."

"Oh that is exceptionally good news. Thank you for that. What a relief," said a thankful Simon Lancaster. "Before you say anything else, let me speak for a while. When the developers contacted me and explained about their archaeological nightmare and asked if I could help with their problem, I had the plans for the Miller's Retreat right there on my desk. I put your property forward only because it is in the right location and fulfils their needs. I went to their main office and I even showed them the plans and they were impressed. They were so impressed that they wanted to see the property, so I took it upon myself to take them to it, whilst you were at work, to view the outside of the buildings and the gardens. They were even more impressed and they even wanted to know the name of the gardening contractor that you use. In fact they were so impressed by what they saw that they have given me this additional information as an inducement."

Judas was beginning to have a sinking feeling, but did not interrupt.

Simon continued, "They are prepared to offer an additional sum if you will leave your property within three weeks. They are prepared to double this extra sum if you will leave your property within a fortnight. And if you leave your property within one week they will triple this offer."

Judas was very silent and eventually said, "I presume the apartment offer is still open?"

Simon responded instantly, "Yes, the apartment at Beaufort St. Catherine, including all kitchen and utility fittings and bathroom fittings and the figure I mentioned yesterday is still an open offer. The only thing that is different is the additional money available if you leave your property in three, two or one week."

Simon had finished and Judas was silent and shocked. He was absolutely staggered by the amount of money that was being offered.

Simon began again, "I'm sorry if you thought it was wrong to go onto your property, but they needed to see it and it definitely impressed them. Before you ask, yes I have been paid well for this solution to their problems, but the outcome benefits you very handsomely and you can retire at sixty if you want to."

Judas was silent for a moment longer and then said, "I have no issues with you and the developers being on the property. After all it did help them with their problem and it definitely has helped me. However, I have to make some arrangements about when I shall leave and I will contact you again later this morning. When I sort out my leaving day I shall require everything in writing, signed, sealed and the cheque in my hand before I move out. I will definitely not be retiring from work as I really do enjoy my employment. I also have to contact Anita, as she will definitely be retiring and I have promised to help her to find a suitable apartment."

A relieved Simon accepted these conditions and said the developers would also accept these conditions and concluded that it was a vast weight off his mind and he looked forward to speaking to Judas later.

Judas was about to replace the receiver when he realized that he had not given the name of the garden contractor and duly passed over to Simon the required information.

"The men and girls employed by the company are all exceptional and very hard working people and I have never had any problems with any of them. I thoroughly recommend the people and gardening company to the new owners."

He was about to end the call when another thought hit him and he posed a question to Simon, "Would you like to take the developers into the property, for them to see what they will be buying?"

A stunned Simon was taken aback.

"Yes," I am sure they would love to go inside. Are you sure you don't mind?"

"No problem," said Judas, "the emergency access key to the rear door is in a coded metal box hidden behind the triple garage. The furthest away window was bricked up by the previous owners, but the matching brickwork was countersunk and the metal box is on the left hand side. The access code for the key is four digits, the date of my birth, followed by the month of my birth. You have that information in your files. When you enter my home the alarm system is the same model as yours and the code is still my birth date.

"Everything in the property is included in the sale with the exception of the items in the annexe. All of the equipment in the kitchen, the bathrooms, the en-suite bathrooms, in fact everything in the main home and garage complex, including all upper floors, are included. The keys to the garage and the three roller door mechanisms are in the top drawer of the annexe hall table. The annexe items are personal and I will get them sorted and, if I do not want any item, I will arrange for its removal. I think that covers everything." Judas then remembered about the tower. "Oh one more thing," he said, "the tower stairs are unsafe so there is a ladder close-by, so if they want to go up into the tower, then use the ladder."

"Okay," responded Simon, "I will contact the office and get the guys to meet me at the property. I will make sure they respect everything there. Thanks again for this," and with that he hung up.

Judas telephoned Anita and the receiver was quickly picked up. Immediately Judas outlined the conversation he had just had with Simon. At the conclusion the silence from Anita was deafening.

She eventually said, "Oh my God" and broke down in floods of tears. After about a minute Anita had recovered her composure.

"Is there anything I can do to help?"

"Nothing at the moment, thanks," said Judas, "I am just going to contact Juliette Gilchrist to see if she wants any of the furniture. It is good quality but it is also very basic. I also have to telephone my gardener to apprise him of the events and to say that I believe he will be contacted by the new owners and requested to continue on the site. Oh, by the way, I will be training a Martin Holland on my duties in a few days time and I will then be able to get a few days off. We can then meet and look at some homes for you."

After a few more minutes of chatter between two very dear friends, the conversation ended. While the thought was in his mind, Judas telephoned his gardening contractor and his call was answered immediately. Judas wished him a Happy New Year and then went on to advise him of the changes to the ownership of the property.

"Also," said Judas, "may I thank you and your company for the work you have done on the site, to transform a wild jungle into an oasis of peace and tranquillity. I have recommended your company to the new owners and they will be contacting you in due course and arranging for you to continue with the maintenance of the grounds. Because of the shortness of the notice of termination I will not cancel the direct debit until the January payment has been made."

The gardening contractor, lost for words, simply thanked Judas and wished him a very Happy New Year.

After another couple of minutes Judas telephoned Juliette's number and was about to leave a message on her voice mail, when she answered. After the pleasantries and further thanks for his gift of a bottle of her favourite perfume, Judas outlined what was about to happen with the Miller's Retreat. He explained that developers were buying the property and why and he said he would be leaving in a few days.

"I hope you will still be able to 'look after me' when I get my new place at Beaufort St. Catherine and in the meantime I will continue to pay you, as the notice is so short," stated Judas.

Juliette objected, but her protestations were not accepted.

"Also," said Judas, "the developers will be at my property very soon today to look around. Everything will go except a few basic things in my annexe and of course I will be keeping everything in my study, plus the television and recording machines etcetera in the lounge. If there is anything in the rest of the annexe that you want for your home or for the charity, then just place a sticky note on the items and they are yours to do with as you wish."

For some years, Juliette had been involved with a charity that supported the local school for the blind, and Judas hoped the furniture might be a welcome contribution.

"Are you sure about the furniture?" asked Juliette. "Some of it is very good, although more functional than stylish."

"If you want it, it's yours," said Judas. "I hope to be out in the next few days."

Juliette was dying to ask why he was leaving so very quickly, but decided it was none of her concern and just thanked him.

She thought deeply and finally said, "May I have the two easy chairs in the lounge room for my daughters' bedrooms and all of the bedroom furniture for our spare bedroom. And may I also have the small coffee table for the lounge?"

Judas immediately agreed. It was then that Juliette suggested that the items be collected this afternoon and he was pleasantly surprised, although slightly concerned.

"All of the items you have requested are full of my possessions," said Judas defensively.

"I will extract all of your clothes from the wardrobe and put them in the bathroom, together with any items from the bedside cabinets." Juliette continued, "My husband Andrew has gone to town with his sister. When he arrives home we will collect the items in his works van. If there is any furniture left in the property, would you like us to empty it and take it to the charity warehouse for sale?"

Judas was again surprised and readily agreed, knowing that his personal papers and documents were in a secret safe in the garage complex.

Juliette finally said, "I assume the empty storage crates in your garage will be used to hold all of your books, folders, files, tapes and CDs when you empty your bookcases? Apart from the items in your study there shouldn't be anything left apart from your clothes, which can be put into the case you have on top of the wardrobe. No offence intended but you should be able to fit all your clothes into the one case. I assume the study furniture that you are keeping will have to be put into storage until your new home is available. We have a lockable double garage and only one car. The van is too high to go into the other side of the garage, so if you want to make use of it you are most welcome. When you are ready to leave your present home, we will collect all of the furniture and crates in the van and store them until you move into your new apartment. I'm sure it will be okay with Andrew."

Judas was amazed and delighted at the suggestion and instantly agreed, with the proviso that if it was not convenient with her husband then it would not proceed. Judas advised that he hoped to leave the property on Sunday morning.

"By the way," said Judas, "when you collect the bed and mattress, if you want the duvet, duvet cover, linen, pillow cases and fitted sheets then you are more than welcome to take them as well. Spare sets are in the drawer below the bed."

A few seconds later Juliette asked, "Where will you sleep tonight?"

"Oh that's taken care of," lied Judas.

"Okay then," said Juliette. "Thanks again for all of the items. You really are a very generous person. I will bring home all of your clothes that need washing and return the items in the morning when I start at your property. After all, tomorrow is Friday and I will be there bright and early. On Saturday, when I have finished, I will leave the key in the annexe hall table." After a few seconds Juliette said, "Ah no, I will leave the key on the floor. Can I also have the table?"

Judas laughed and agreed. After a few more minutes idle chatter Judas thanked Juliette for her work and said he looked forward to her joining him at his new home. After this long interlude of doing personal business, Judas felt guilty and looked for something to do.

He suddenly remembered the new statistics format he had developed, and extracted them from his top drawer and photocopied them. He would give the main copy to Henry Brown on his return from the MD. Judas was interrupted from his work by Keith who beckoned Judas to join him and Colin for a drink. Judas sat with the guards and had just finished his drink when he noticed that both guards were munching some savoury biscuits.

So much for the diets thought Judas.

After chatting generally for a few minutes, Judas returned to his desk and was stumped for anything to do. Apart from the two personal incoming telephone calls, the instrument was silent.

"Would you guys have any objection to my going out and doing an external fence check, just to get more acquainted with the site and its layout?"

The offer was gratefully accepted.

"Ye Gods you're as keen as mustard Judas," joked Keith.

"Must be a New Years' Resolution," chided Colin.

Judas left the lodge and set off around the perimeter of the site. He tested his radio with the lodge after about two minutes to confirm it was working. He then wandered slowly around the site, not doing much checking, but doing a considerable amount of thinking. He decided that when he returned to the lodge he would have to notify the utilities of his moving date and also notify the Insurance Company. The list was getting endless so he jotted down the organizations he would have to advise. He sedately continued his walk around the fence and then did an inspection of the building exterior. At the furthest point from the lodge Judas began to shiver. He realized that it was getting colder and the wind was getting blustery.

Time to return, thought Judas and he quickened his step as he continued his patrol. The temperature was definitely dropping and Judas was relieved to see the lights of the lodge as he rounded the final corner.

"Nothing to report," said Judas mimicking the guards. They smiled and entered in the report that a patrol had been completed.

"Any telephone calls?" queried Judas and was disappointed to learn that no calls had been received.

The rest of the morning was quiet and not much work was done. In fact there was very little to do and the guards talked endlessly about the local football team and its lack of success. Judas re-wrote his notes about his dealings with Simon Lancaster, not because they were wrong, but because he could put them into order.

At eleven thirty, the guards sat together for an early lunch and Judas could see that it was a painful affair for both men. No sandwiches, no sausage rolls and no cakes. Both men had salads, fruit and yogurts. Judas could see that it was not going to be a very happy lunch break and he was certain that the afternoon was going to be a very arduous one. However, he joined them for a drink. After ten minutes the telephone rang and Judas was pleased to get away. It was Simon Lancaster.

Judas said, "I was going to call you in a few minutes to see how things went. Was everything okay?"

"To quote you Judas, it was perfect," said Simon. "The guys were in the office when I rang them, as I knew they would be and they jumped at the chance to see the inside of the property. In short they were very impressed. They couldn't believe the kitchen and the gadgets therein, they were very impressed by the bathrooms. They thought the en-suites were fantastic and they liked the bedrooms and the fitted wardrobes. In fact all of the rooms were pleasing to them.

"I showed them the annexe, the rooms above the garages, the various store rooms and the tower and they are very pleased with the property and they are happy to go ahead. I did show them the plans that you prepared for the apartment above the triple garages and they may proceed with them for their manager of the property. In fact, because they will not have to do too much with the property except furnish it, put stairs up to the tower, sort out the accommodation over the garages and sort out the cellar, they have decided to buy the new equipment that has been installed and have revised their offer upwards."

"You jest of course," said Judas. After a few seconds he said, "Tell me Simon, you are joking?"

Simon countered, saying, "No, I am not joking. I have a cheque in my hand, made payable to you and you can collect it tonight if you wish. There will be another cheque made payable to you and the amount will be determined by the number of days you stay there."

Judas regained his composure and informed Simon "Much of the annexe furniture that I will not be keeping is being collected this afternoon and I hope to get the rest put into storage on Saturday. I also will, if things go to plan, finally leave the Miller's Retreat early on Sunday morning."

Simon was impressed and said he would notify the developers that they might have ownership of the property on Sunday, if events go to plan.

Judas then sheepishly asked, "What will the revised price be, assuming that I leave on Sunday?"

Simon, being very dramatic and theatrical, waited about ten seconds before he spoke. The figure was whispered and Judas was pleased that he was sitting down. He also quickly wrote the figure down.

To end, Simon said, "I have placed the various building keys back into the locations where I found them. Thanks again for everything Judas. You really should consider retiring."

When the conversation had finished, Judas realized that he had not said anything about collecting the cheque. However, he had other worries for the rest of his working day and tonight. Judas added to the list of the things he had to do when he got home and was surprised that he was now on the second page. He was meticulous and wrote down everything that needed doing. For a few moments his mind turned to Adam who had instilled in him the need to be accurate and to be methodical.

He was brought out of his thoughts by Keith saying, "Henry Brown is driving into the car park."

Judas looked up as the barrier closed and saw Mr Brown park his car next to the lodge.

"Hello again," said Henry Brown, as he entered the lodge, "I have just returned from another meeting with the MD. It went well and the MD sends his best wishes for the New Year. I am just off to my office for a few minutes to drop off some papers and then I am going home and that is where I shall remain for the remainder of the holiday. I really am looking forward to the New Year."

"Before you go Mr Brown," said Judas, "here are the statistics for December. They are in the old format and the new."

Henry Brown smiled as he took the forms and left the lodge. He walked briskly to the rear door of the complex, the alarm having been isolated, and he entered. After five minutes he retraced his steps to his vehicle and left the car park with a final wave to the guards. The alarms were reset and Judas returned to his list.

It began to snow and there was a quietness about the area. Judas looked out of the window, over the car park and towards the main office building. It was early afternoon, it was getting dark and it was definitely getting colder. Colin entered the lodge, after a perimeter fence patrol, and complained that the temperature was rapidly falling and he was freezing. Keith prepared coffees for the guards but Judas declined a drink. Both guards seemed to be struggling with their diets and on one occasion Judas thought he heard a stomach rumble. The afternoon was a very quiet affair and both guards seemed to have a reluctance to go out on normal patrols, but truncated them to shortened outings.

At four o'clock Judas asked, "Guys, would you mind if I went out and did a perimeter patrol? I have some important things to think over, I need the solitude and I need the exercise."

Keith and Colin looked at each other and gratefully accepted the offer, as neither guard was relishing the cold tour around the site.

As Judas left the lodge Colin said, "He's too eager. It definitely must be a New Year resolution."

When Judas closed the lodge door, Keith answered, "I doubt it. I think he's had some bad news."

Judas started his patrol around the external fence and did the required radio check. It really was very cold and he could feel that it was getting colder. He walked briskly all the way round the site and then checked the exterior of the buildings. Everything was as it should be and he stood by an out building to get protection from the very cold wind. Apart from the noise of the wind it was very quiet. Judas began to think about the work he had to do tonight and it began to worry him. There was so much to sort out and so little time to do it. He was, however, determined to leave his property on Sunday morning. He took, from his pocket, his notebook containing the list he had prepared. He read it through and wondered if he had missed anything off.

Judas was interrupted in his thoughts by a radio call. It was Colin.

"Judas, is everything okay?"

Judas realized that he should have been back in the lodge about twenty minutes ago, as full patrols only take about an hour.

"Nothing to report," answered Judas, "I will be back in about five minutes."

Judas closed his book and walked very quickly back to the lodge. He hadn't realized that he had been standing for so long, sorting out his list of priorities for this evening at his home.

"Sorry guys, I just got sidetracked," said Judas as he entered the lodge. "Everything was in order, although it is very cold outside and I think it is going to get colder."

The rest of the afternoon was a very long affair. No telephone calls and very little work to do. Judas always liked to be busy and when he wasn't it always worried him. However he again got out his note book and re-read the list he had prepared. He couldn't think of anything to add to the list, so he sat there in deep thought. The night guards, Adrian and Roy, arrived together and the relieved guards did a very quick handover and by six o'clock they had left the site.

Judas, as a matter of courtesy, said to the new guards, "I presume that you both enjoyed your days away," and both nodded.

Roy continued, "I can definitely recommend time off at Christmas. I ate and drank too much, but I thoroughly enjoyed my time away."

Adrian added, "Same here" and continued with his paperwork.

Judas left them after about five minutes. The walk home was a very quick one for Judas. As he trudged through the streets he thought long and hard about the work that he had to do tonight. It was still worrying him as he turned into his drive and he quickly marched up the slope to his annexe.

Judas entered his home and was surprised to find that Juliette and Andrew had collected the crates from the garage and stacked some of them in the hall. However, in one crate there was a bin liner containing his clothes from the wardrobe and in another there was a second bin liner containing all of the items from the bedside cabinets. He also noticed immediately that the annexe hall table had been taken. He entered his small bedroom and saw that all of the furniture items had been removed and he was very relieved. He went into his lounge and saw that the radio, TV and recording equipment were still there, but all other items of furniture had been taken away.

He entered his bathroom and saw a note on the wash basin from Juliette, asking if she could have both of the wall cabinets. Judas smiled, emptied the items from both cabinets into a small carrier bag and simply printed "*Yes*" on the note. He next emptied his small airing cupboard and placed the sheets, towels and assorted cloths and flannels into another black bag and placed it in a crate. When he entered his study he realized that in this room there was a lot of work to be completed tonight.

Judas retreated to the hall and extracted, from the clothes bag, the items he would require in the morning and also some old clothes for use tonight and changed. He re-entered the study, carrying some crates, and placed his books in two of them. He placed his audio tapes, videos, CDs and DVDs in another two crates and placed his various files and project papers in another two crates. He next took his printer, shredder and various machines required for listening to audio tapes and CDs and wrapped them in towels and placed them in another three crates. Lastly, he went to the lounge and placed the radio, small television and recording equipment, suitably wrapped, separately in another two bins. He was very pleased with his work so far and then realized that he was hungry. Everything was going well and all he had to do now was to sort out the kitchen, but he decided he had to eat first.

After his very simple meal the telephone rang. It was Juliette, who thanked him most sincerely for the furniture and Judas thanked her most sincerely for the work she and Andrew had done to make his evening task much simpler.

"There is one thing I want to ask and I hope you won't think this wrong of me to do so," said a reluctant Juliette.

"Don't worry," said Judas, "later tonight I will take down the bathroom cabinets and you can take them with you tomorrow. I will also put your money in one of them. Then on Saturday I will leave my clothes etcetera in a case, which will be kept here with me for the night and the crates and the bare furniture that are left can be put into your garage, if that is still okay?"

"Err, it wasn't that, but thank you for the cabinets and yes we will collect the items for storage on Saturday afternoon," said a hesitant Juliette and then she spurted out very quickly, "What I was going to ask was about the white goods in the kitchenette. Are they also available?"

"Of course they are," replied a very relieved Judas, "If you want them they are yours."

The rest of the conversation revolved around the fact that Andrew's sister Mary had just gone through a very difficult and hurtful divorce and was not financially secure.

"Mary's ex-husband had massive debts and he also trashed the family home in an act of vandalism," said Juliette, "and Andrew is doing his best to look after her interests. Her ex-husband is now living abroad. Mary has sold her old home and now has a very small but pleasant cottage nearby and needs some items for her kitchen."

At the end of the conversation Judas simply said, "Help yourself to the items on Saturday, they are Mary's. I am sorry for her circumstances but please give her my best wishes for the future."

As Judas was walking away from the telephone, it began to ring again. This time it was Simon.

After the pleasantries Simon asked, "Can you please confirm when you will be leaving the property?"

"I am spending Saturday night here and will leave about five twenty on Sunday morning. Why do you ask?" requested Judas.

Simon went on to describe in detail how the developers would require the gas, water and electricity services to be left on and the property to be functional for Monday when they would be on site.

"If you can notify the County Council of your departure and the Insurance Company of your change of residence and any other notification that affects you personally, then the developers will prepare letters to advise the mentioned utilities of the change, plus the telephone company. These will require your signature to terminate the contracts and I will bring them to you for you to sign. I will also bring the cheque for the agreed sale price of the property, plus the additional cheque for the early departure date. The developers will also pay the final accounts for the property. Will that be acceptable?"

"Ye Gods yes," said a very surprised and even shocked Judas, "I have no objections whatever, but you do realize that I will be working until six o'clock on Saturday."

Simon simply said "Yes."

During the conversation Judas had written down what was required of him and read it back to Simon. He also advised Simon that he would leave the numerous blocks of salt for use in the water softeners.

Simon continued, "The developers know that they have to get permission for the change of occupancy etcetera and this process has been initiated. They also want to check the area of the site and draw up plans in anticipation of the acceptance of the change."

Simon then went onto the subject of the apartments at Beaufort St. Catherine. He advised that they were expected to be completed and ready for viewing by the general public by 5th January. Some of the plush apartments had already gone to favoured clients, but there were still plenty to choose from and Judas was advised to go there at the earliest opportunity to view them.

"The sales office in the foyer of the complex is open until ten o'clock at night," said Simon, "and the lady in charge of the people on the late shifts is Jennifer, whom you have already met. Jennifer has been told to give you every assistance."

Judas smiled and remembered that it was Jennifer who had given him some plans of smaller apartments near the town centre and also two photographs of the orphanage.

Simon ended the conversation and said he would advise the company about his Sunday departure and again thanked Judas for all he had done to make the transition go smoothly.

As a parting shot Simon said, "When you see Jennifer, ask her about the facilities in the lower ground floor," and he then put the receiver down.

Judas was puzzled but decided to let the comment pass. He returned to the job in hand and ticked all the items that he or Andrew and Juliette had completed off the list. Those that were left to complete were only minor items and he felt very relieved. He then took the cabinets off the bathroom wall, put them in the hall and put the promised money for Juliette into the smaller one.

Since his agreement to sell his property, Judas had not bought many food items and his fridge was completely under worked. In a cupboard he had some cracker biscuits, a few cans of fruit and a few energy bars. That was it. It was a fairly frugal meal, but he did enjoy it. Judas then decided that he would finish off his packing tomorrow and, as it was late, he prepared for bed and slumped onto the floor under a travel blanket.

CHAPTER 10

Friday 2nd January

Considering he had just spent the night on the floor of his bedroom, Judas awoke happy and refreshed. He walked to his workplace, with a sprightly spring in his step.

He entered his working environment at about five forty and was informed that the night had been exceptionally cold and both guards were looking forward to curling up in their beds. It was their first shift back at work after an enjoyable few days away and they were feeling weary. They did not converse much and when John and Geoff arrived, the handover was short, sweet, uneventful and to the point.

Judas sat at his desk and wrote out a letter to the County Council, advising them of his departure from his property and if they wished to contact him they should forward any correspondence to the Poacher's Retreat. He also prepared a similar letter to other organizations that had to be made aware of the change of ownership. He photocopied the letters, addressed the envelopes and got the mail ready for posting.

Judas then turned to John and Geoff and asked, "How was your time away from the lodge?"

The answers from both were disappointing.

"I have a flaming cold," croaked Geoff and John simply said "Snap."

As he did not wish to venture too close to his colleagues, Judas took out his notebook and looked at the list of items that required completing at his home.

Judas kept himself busy and prepared the forms he would need when the complex opened on Monday. The Christmas break should have been a fairly relaxing time, but circumstances had conspired to complicate the Festive Season. However, it had been enjoyable and eventful thought Judas and also very tragic. He really was looking forward to training his new colleague and was also eagerly anticipating a very good year for the company.

At seven o'clock, as no guard had done a patrol, Judas called over to John and Geoff:

"As you guys are a bit under the weather, would you like me to go out and do an internal patrol of the main office complex, and then check the perimeter fence and the building exterior?"

"As you can see," said a relieved Geoff, "we are both suffering at the moment and we would be very pleased if you would do the first patrol."

"I think I can remember the internal patrol drill from when you took me around the site during my induction course," said Judas as he left the guards.

After a few steps outside the lodge he did the obligatory radio test and continued the patrol. The walk did him good and cleared his brain. He wandered slowly around every nook and cranny near the fence and on completion of this task he checked the windows and doors of the office building and workshops. He also investigated inside the newly built rooms that were open to the elements and satisfied his curiosity. His final patrol was a simple walk through the clerical complex, after requesting the guards on his radio to switch off the alarm system. After an hour and ten minutes, Judas returned to the lodge.

"Nothing to report, everything in order," he said casually.

"While you were out," said Geoff, "we had a phone call from a Simon Lancaster, who said he will be here at about nine o'clock."

"Oh great," answered Judas, "I am really looking forward to seeing him again. We have a little bit of business to sort out."

Judas then got everything placed on his desk that he needed to resolve with Simon. He read and re-read the entries in his notebook, but could not think of anything that he had missed. He kept himself occupied for a few minutes and then looked over to the guards. They were both very quiet and he could see that they were both suffering. Judas decided that they needed a coffee and prepared the drinks. As he placed the steaming mugs on their desk, both guards sneezed in unison and seemed relieved at his action. Both looked ill, but were not admitting that the ailment was anything other than a minor irritation. Judas prepared for himself his usual drink.

They all sat for a few minutes and Geoff eventually croaked, "I had a very enjoyable New Year at home relaxing. Then my better half decided that she wanted to visit the shops for the end of year clothes sales. That's when I began to suffer, both medically and financially."

John then countered, "I also spent New Year at home, but I simply had no energy and just didn't feel too good. I now feel worse."

Judas listened with interest and sympathy, but when the topic of football arose, he was pleased to see a vehicle arrive at the barrier and he recognised Simon.

Judas greeted Simon and took him to his end of the lodge, after introducing him to the guards, who just waved.

"I have here the various pages of paperwork requiring your signature," said Simon when he and Judas were seated. "I assure you that everything is correct and there are no hidden clauses. My own lawyer has read it and has confirmed that everything is as I explained to him. Believe me, if there were any problems with the paperwork, then I would lose a great commission fee."

Judas took the papers and read each one quickly and signed each as he finished scanning it, plus initialling the under copy. When he had finished signing he gave Simon four keys. Simon looked puzzled.

Judas explained, "The paperwork I have just signed says the developer has all of the property, except the contents of the annexe. The keys are for the brick buildings in the garden: the summerhouse, containing garden and patio furniture; the tool store, with the maintenance equipment; the potting shed structure, containing gardening tools; and the small store, containing the lawn mower, power washer and bush trimmer etcetera. The gardener also has a key to the structures and makes use of the equipment. I also have another set of spare keys. On the site there is also a dilapidated greenhouse, but this is not locked. When I leave the property on Sunday, it is my present intention to leave the key fob press button mechanism for the garage doors in a safe and secure place and I will let you know where later."

"I don't think the developer had it in mind for the outbuilding contents to be included, but for the sake of accuracy, I will advise the guys of the details," said Simon.

Simon then reached into his brief case and extracted a dozen plans of apartments at the developer's complex at Beaufort St. Catherine and also a site plan of the complete development. There were also artist's representations of the furnished rooms of some of the residences. There were three blocks of apartments, all in a crescent and in a beautifully manicured environment. Judas was impressed.

"These are for you and were given to me by Jennifer. She hopes to see you in the very near future and she will be delighted to show you around any of the apartments that you wish to see," said Simon.

Judas took the plans and had a quick look and was impressed by the beautiful designs of the apartments and the spaciousness of the rooms, which in some cases seemed enormous after his annexe.

"Now for the finale," said Simon and reached into his wallet. "I am pleased that you are sitting down, because believe me, you need to be." He then looked round to make sure the guards were not within earshot. "The first cheque is for the amount I said the developers were prepared to pay for the property, plus their offer to purchase the new equipment that you had installed in the kitchen and the bathrooms and shower rooms," said Simon and placed it on the desk in front of Judas.

Judas was spellbound.

"The second cheque is for the agreed amount for vacating the property within one week," continued Simon and placed it next to the first cheque. "The final part will be for you to go to the development at Beaufort St. Catherine and to choose your new home. The completion of the work will be in about a fortnight," concluded Simon.

Judas was speechless and practically in shock. He began to thank Simon, but Simon simply said, "It has been a pleasure to be of service. You really owe me nothing. It was just a fluke that when the developers contacted me, your property plans were on my desk and the rest, as they say, is history. Believe me when I say I have been paid handsomely for my contribution to this project and without your contribution and agreement, I would be much worse off. Therefore I suppose I should be thanking you."

With that Simon held out his hand and firmly shook the hand of Judas.

The guards looked round and could see that Judas was practically white.

"Coffee and biscuits anyone?" asked Geoff and got up to prepare the drinks.

Judas had his normal drink and Simon enjoyed a mug of steaming white coffee, some biscuits and a small wedge of cake, supplied by John. The guards sat together, still not looking well, but seeming better than earlier in the day. Simon was about to ask Judas when he might go to see Jennifer, but could see that his friend was troubled, so he just sat there and enjoyed his drink and his snack.

Judas eventually said, "Sorry I am not a very good host today, but I really am in shock. I have seen these figures written down and they are just figures, but when you get the actual cheques, it is a completely different matter."

When he had finished his coffee, Simon withdrew and after thanking Judas once again for his agreement and the guards for the drink and refreshments, he left the lodge and drove out of the car park.

After a while Judas thanked the guards for the drinks and Geoff asked Judas if he was okay.

"Yes I'm okay," said Judas, "I have just had a bit of a shock. However, I need to clear my head, so if it's alright with you guys I will go and do another patrol and you two can stay in and keep warm."

Both guards were relieved at the offer and were grateful for the attention Judas was showing. Judas left the lodge and after making his radio confirmation call, he began his check of the perimeter fence. He walked slowly and deliberately until he was out of sight of the lodge and then he stood next to a partly built wall and contemplated just what had happened. He took the cheques from his wallet and still could not believe that the money was his. He had expected Simon to see him in his annexe tonight, not this morning and he had not brought his bank book from his safe in the garage complex.

He suddenly felt vulnerable. He continued his patrol and, as earlier, on completion of the fence check, he inspected the building. He reported back to the guards.

"All in order as usual," stated Judas and they entered the patrol times of departure and return in the log book. Judas then stated, "If you turn off the office and factory alarms, I will do an internal patrol of the buildings."

Both guards practically agreed in unison and both reached for the off switch for the alarm system.

Geoff said feebly, "Many thanks for helping, we'll take care of any phone calls."

Judas did a thorough check of the offices, the design bureau and the planning office and inspected numerous other departments, to confirm their safety. He then retreated to the reception area in the office, checked Henry Brown's home telephone number and dialled. The telephone was answered very quickly.

"Mr Brown, it's Judas here, sorry to bother you at home but I have a request."

"Fire away," said an intrigued Henry, "What's the problem?"

Judas began, "As I will be training Martin Holland next week and as the trainee cannot be left on his own without supervision, could I please have time off today to get a banking problem sorted out. I haven't had any time off since I started working for the company and the problem is urgent. I won't be long and I'll return when the problem is sorted. The guards will take care of any telephone calls and I will take a radio with me in case of any emergency."

Judas waited for a response. No objections were raised by Henry Brown and Judas returned to the lodge.

"Everything still in order," he said as he opened the door and continued, "I have just spoken to Mr Brown and he has agreed that I can leave the site to go into town. Would you mind looking after the switchboard please? It hasn't bleeped all day so you shouldn't be overworked."

The guards raised no objections. The alarms were reset and Judas left the site and walked briskly to the town centre. It was very cold and the temperature was definitely dropping. There did not seem to be too many people wandering around the shops, even though the New Year sales were in full swing. He posted the various letters he had written this morning and was pleased that they were now on their way.

He eventually entered his bank and waited in the queue. It was a short queue and he was at the counter fairly quickly. He explained that he did not have his bank book with him and just wanted to put two cheques into his account. No problems were encountered until the counter assistant saw the amounts and called over her supervisor.

"You really should see our investment consultant," the lady said, "as this amount of money in this type of account is not financial sense."

Judas resisted all attempts by the bank staff to get him to see an investment consultant immediately, but he did make an appointment to see one on the 19th January, when he would have finished training Martin Holland.

Judas marched swiftly back to the lodge, after making a small detour to a family bakery and buying two cakes and a small box of chocolate and ginger biscuits, to thank John and

Geoff for looking after Simon earlier. These were gratefully received and eagerly devoured, during their lunch break. Their colds had not dimmed their appetites.

Judas was relieved the money was now in his bank and was safe. All he had to do tonight was to clear the kitchen. It shouldn't take long as there was very little in there, except cleaning utensils and those could go in a crate. He would also have to get his personal papers out of the garage safe. He would clear the fridge on Sunday morning when he left, together with the few cans of fruit.

He ran his mind over the contents of the kitchen and for some idiotic reason he thought of the refuse bin. He determined to put a sticker on it tonight and leave it for Juliette's sister-in-law, Mary. Judas began to smile. He thought about the tin mug, the tin plate and the tin bowl that he had in his cupboard. These items reminded him of his time in the orphanage and he cherished them. When he was at the orphanage, they were the only possessions, besides clothes and toiletries, that he had. His few pieces of cutlery and crockery he would also put in the crate, suitably wrapped up.

Judas suddenly thought that he had to get some accommodation organized for Sunday night. He remembered there was a very pleasant and well appointed guest house near the centre of the village, which was about half a mile from the apartment complex. He checked in the Yellow Pages and found the telephone number. After a few minutes he was all booked up.

Judas explained, "I have to be at work very early each day and therefore will not require breakfast."

"In that case," the lady suggested, "I will provide you with a packed lunch instead."

"That may be a problem," suggested Judas, "as I have a stomach problem and can only eat cold food and I am also a vegetarian."

After a few moments dealing with questions and answers, the two were able to agree the contents of a compromise lunch pack. Judas was suitably impressed. Judas was even more impressed when the lady said she was also a vegetarian.

"I have been a vegetarian since my twenties," said the lady, "and I have never had problems with any of the allowed food, but I definitely could never just eat cold food. It must be difficult."

"It is at times," said Judas, "but I survive."

Judas could sense that the lady wanted to ask what his problem was, but manners prevented her asking.

"However," Judas continued, "I eat cold food because hot food hurts my stomach. It always has and I have no idea why it does. However, I am told that as a baby I could only have milk at room temperature and if it was hotter I would spit it out. Whenever I have tried to eat hot or even warm food, my senses rebel and I dutifully now accept the problem. As for being a vegetarian, I simply cannot eat meat or fish. It's as simple as that."

Oh you poor dear," ventured the lady and continued, "Never fear, I will make sure you have plenty of food in your cold packed lunch. I look forward to seeing you when you arrive."

Judas booked accommodation for one week, beginning on Sunday night, but said that it might be for longer depending upon circumstances.

From country walks in the area he knew that the village had grown considerably since the Victorian era and met with all the requirements needed by the vacation industry and its users. It was originally a coastal village with a small, working harbour, but because of a silting problem in the river mouth and the reclamation of some marsh land for agriculture use, in the Victorian era, the village was now two miles inland. The river was still used by small cargo boats and there was also a small marina, which catered mainly for the yachting fraternity and for the high influx of weekend sailors.

The village was also the proud possessor of the remnants of a ruined mediaeval castle and a very attractive fourteenth century church with a solid attendance of worshipers. Added to this, there were the usual services and facilities required to provide the daily needs of a bustling and thriving community. There was also a good coach service to nearby coastal towns and inland communities as well as an information centre for the visitors.

Importantly the village also had a bank, the one used by Judas, and, because of the popularity of the area, an estate agent's office had just opened. The area had a good selection of pathways for walking into the nearby nature reserve and surrounding area and was a bird watchers paradise. Judas was looking forward to living in the community. He then reflected that the only thing the village lacked was a railway station and he then accepted that, even if the village had a railway connection, it would have been a victim of the Dr Beeching axe.

Judas took out the plans that Jennifer had given to Simon and studied them all very intently. They were all magnificent with an expensive price tag to match. All of the apartments were allocated two enclosed parking bays, sited under the towers and accessed from the rear of the buildings. All of the apartments, in all of the tower blocks, were on three levels and the designs in all were stunning. In the central tower the apartments were evidently for parents with children and had the space required to support a young family. In the right hand tower, again, the apartments were for married couples, but did not provide excessive space for offspring. The representations of the furnished rooms were very impressive and Judas admired the art work. However, he could never see himself in any of these designs as they were simply too lavish and enormous for his needs. The left hand tower, however, was completely different. It was designed for the confirmed bachelor, or female equivalent, and contained various apartment plans that simply took his breath away. They were all magnificent and breathtaking, but there were three that he especially liked and he kept reading the literature and looking at the representations of the furnished rooms. He resolved to involve Anita in this selection and decision.

At this point Judas realized that the guards were still suffering from their colds. They were both wrapped in their overcoats and looked worse than they did this morning.

"Okay guys," he said, "I'm off to do another site patrol," and then added, "That is if you have no objection."

Both guards mumbled, "No."

After a short stroll his radio burst into life and he confirmed to Geoff that it was working. Judas slowly walked around the perimeter fence and was very deep in thought. He mused on the fact that he only had two more nights to spend at his home and that he would be away early on Sunday morning. He'd had great plans for the property, but now they were just broken dreams. However, he had been paid exceptionally well for the property and he must now move on.

His thoughts returned to the security check and he completed the fence patrol. He continued his walk and did the external patrol of the building, waving to the guards as he passed by the lodge. He walked around the complex but could find no security problems and retraced his steps towards the lodge. The sky was overcast and it was very cold. It was also very quiet, serene and peaceful.

Judas entered the lodge and, mimicking the guards, said "All in order, nothing to report," and returned to his desk.

The rest of the afternoon was a very quiet affair. The guards were not very communicative and Judas stayed as far from them as he could. He looked at the three apartment plans again and was fascinated by all of them. He wondered what Anita would make of the plans and whether she would approve of his selection. He basically knew in his own mind that he would select one of these plans, but as yet he was undecided on which apartment catered for his needs the best.

He was still studying the plans when he was interrupted by a loud sneeze from John, followed by a loud groan. Both guards were suffering and Judas decided that it was time for the day's final patrol. He volunteered for this task and completed it without incident. The icy conditions forecast were present, but Judas was deep in thought and was not feeling the cold. He was very surprised when he saw the lodge lights as he turned the final corner. He could see that the guards were still in their overcoats, as he entered the lodge.

"Everything okay," said Judas and returned to his desk.

It was then that Judas realized that he must prepare some instruction notes for Martin Holland and he extracted, from a drawer, the file he had prepared for himself when he was under training. He spent the next twenty five minutes reading through the pertinent pages, amending the text to reflect the recent changes that he had made and including the revised forms. He then photocopied each sheet and placed them in a folder ready for Martin's arrival. As he put the folders away he was interrupted by the arrival of Adrian and Roy, the guarding team for the night shift. After a hasty handover,

John and Geoff vacated the lodge. As Judas was leaving the lodge, Roy, the senior guard on the complex, approached him.

"The guards told me that you had done the patrols today, so many thanks for that. It is very much appreciated by us all. Geoff did telephone our central control to say that he and John were ill, but all the other guards trained on the site were covering their own assignments, or were un-contactable. Unfortunately, this is a very difficult time of the year for the guarding industry. I hope that tomorrow the men feel well enough to attend. If they are here and still feeling and looking poorly, would you mind just doing some of the patrols please?"

Judas agreed, saying "No problem. I enjoyed doing the patrols today and tomorrow, if necessary, I will again enjoy doing the patrols."

He could see that Roy was relieved. Judas left the lodge and walked briskly away and reached his home without incident.

As he entered his gate he opened the post box and was relieved to find it empty. He then went to the rear of his garage and extracted his private papers from the safe, including a copy of his last will and testament and a few lesser items, and placed them all in his small work case. He entered his annexe and saw that Juliette had placed his clean laundry in a plastic carrier bag in the hall. Judas changed and got his clothes ready for the morning. He then began sorting out the work he had to do tonight.

He packed his clothes and, Juliette was correct, the items did fit into a single case. He then remembered the swing lid rubbish bin in the kitchen. It was clean and empty and so he stuck a note on it simply stating, "A present for Mary." He then thought of the bathroom scales, retrieved them and placed them with the bin. He finally put the few pieces of cutlery in a small carrier bag and placed them with other items in a crate. He placed all the cleaning material in the same crate, together with a few bathroom items. Other miscellaneous items he simply wrapped up and placed in another crate, leaving a little space for anything else he found that needed transporting.

That was basically it apart from the contents of the fridge, a few food items in a cupboard and his personal papers from the safe. Judas wasn't hungry, but he recognised that he must eat to feed the inner man and prepared himself a very frugal meal. Afterwards he realised that the biscuit cupboard was also surplus to requirements, took it off the wall and placed it with the others for Mary. He resolved that in the morning he would take any food left to the lodge and if necessary, he would "dump" it there. He then had a shallow sleep.

CHAPTER 11

Saturday 3ʳᵈ January

Judas was up very early, after a very troubled sleep. He had much on his mind and he kept thinking of the work he had done to ease the move and trying to think of anything he had missed doing. He made sure the furniture and items for storage in Andrew's garage were all in his study, plus the items for Mary. The other items, that he would require tonight, he left in the kitchen in carrier bags and in his case. Judas skipped breakfast and set off for work feeling tired and apprehensive. He resolved to contact Simon Lancaster about the garage safe access number and to confirm that he would leave the Miller's Retreat tomorrow morning.

At work Adrian and Roy were all ready for a quick departure and cheerily greeted Judas on his arrival.

Roy said, "John and Geoff will be in today. I telephoned them both at home last night and they both said they were feeling much better."

"That is good news," replied Judas and continued, "If they are not fully fit and need me to do any patrols I will willingly go round the site."

Roy was about to speak as both of the day guards entered the lodge, swathed in heavy overcoats, scarves and gloves. After a quick handover the night crew left the lodge. John walked over to Judas.

"Thanks Judas for the patrols you performed yesterday, we are both grateful," said John and continued, "We are both much better today."

Judas just nodded, but he inwardly thought that John looked much worse than he did yesterday.

"Unfortunately you both still look full of cold symptoms," ventured Judas and eventually Geoff agreed.

The guards entered all of the relevant clerical requirements into their report book and Geoff prepared himself for the initial patrol. Judas went to the kitchen area and put his drink in his section of the cupboard. He then looked up and could see that Geoff looked dreadful. His eyes were running and his speech was hardly recognisable.

Judas said, "Let me do the first patrol and you both can stay here in the warm. I need the exercise."

Neither of the guards raised an objection and Judas could see that they were both relieved to be staying in the lodge. He made his radio check call after a few moments and began the patrol. The patrol was done quickly and Judas was about to return to the lodge when the radio crackled into life.

"Base to mobile, please go to rear door of office block, to allow entry for the staff to fill the vending machines. Over."

"Will comply. Out." answered Judas and hurried to the required door.

He had been so totally absorbed by his work and private problems, that he had forgotten that the drinks and food machines throughout the site were serviced by the providing company every Saturday, except bank holidays.

Judas arrived at the door and wished Allison a "Happy New Year" and slid his entrance access card through the door slide. The door lock clicked and Judas opened the heavy door for Allison to enter. She expertly manoeuvred her long trolley through the opening. Allison would be on site for about two hours and could get to the corridor, foyer and restaurant machines that she needed to clean, service and fill ready for the opening of the complex in the coming week. Exit from the building was by a simple push pad.

Judas had a thought and radioed the lodge, "As I am in the building, I will do an internal patrol of the whole complex. Out."

Judas wandered around the building for the next hour. Everything was in order and on his way back to the lodge he passed Allison and purchased some energy bars and some bottles of drink. These items he would take home with him tonight to compliment his last meal at the Miller's Retreat.

Back at the lodge, the guards entered the patrol details and prepared a drink. It was eight minutes past eight and Judas settled down to read his notes on what was left to do at his home. He then reflected that this time tomorrow it would not be *his* home. He then thought of Anita and realized that he had not spoken to her for a few days. He resolved to contact her later in the morning.

Judas did another two complete external patrols of the site during the morning, much to the relief of both guards, who were still battling with severe cold symptoms. In fact it was quite a relief for Judas to escape the heat of the lodge, as the radiators had been put into overdrive by the suffering guards. However, at eleven o'clock Judas telephoned Simon at his home and confirmed that he would vacate the Miller's Retreat, at five o'clock in the morning.

"However, there is one more important piece of information that I have to tell you," said Judas.

"Sounds interesting," answered a bemused Simon. "What important information would that be?"

"The safe at the rear of the central garage," continued Judas, "I presume you would like the combination?"

"I had no idea there was a safe on the premises, where is it?" requested Simon.

Judas then explained, "On the rear walls of all three garages, in the centre of the wall, there is a square of wood and on each of the squares is a small wooden representation of an old cart wheel. The wooden square in the central garage is much lighter than the other two and lifts off quite easily. Behind this wooden square is a wall safe with push buttons for access to the contents of the safe. I will not give the actual code over the telephone, but you can definitely work it out from the following. It is four digits. The first is my birth date plus two days, the second is my birth month plus one and the third and fourth are the last two digits of my birth year."

After about twenty seconds Simon said, "Okay, I think I have worked it out and sometime on Monday I will pass the information to the new owners. In case I have got it wrong, will you be at work on Monday?"

Judas answered:

"I am here until the 18th January and then I will get four days away. I really am looking forward to that. However, to continue, the key for the post box, next to the walkway entrance and the spare garden structure keys will be in the recessed box behind the garages, plus the garages press buttons for the roller door mechanisms. Finally when I leave the property for the last time, I will place the external door keys in the same box.

"One final point – I have notified numerous organizations of my move from the property and requested all future correspondence to be forwarded to Anita at her guest house, until advised otherwise. In case any post goes into the post box at the old address, would you get it to Anita, please?"

Simon agreed and after a few more moments of idle chatter the conversation ended. Simon was going to ask Judas why he was still going to carry on working, especially now that he was a very wealthy man, but decided that it was none of his concern.

Judas then realized that he had still not contacted Anita and he immediately telephoned her. It was Anita that answered. After the pleasantries the two friends settled down to talking about their dreams for the current year.

"Simon gave me some more plans from Jennifer, for my new home and there were three that I especially liked," ventured Judas. "They are located in the left hand tower of the development at Beaufort St. Catherine."

Anita countered, "I am looking in the local press for properties in my price range, but unfortunately I have not seen any that I particularly like. However, I will keep looking." Anita then hesitantly asked, "You really are certain that you will help me with the finances?"

"Yes, I am certain," said Judas. "As I keep telling you, you are my oldest and dearest friend. We have been through a lot together, both at the orphanage and also afterwards, in the real world. God willing, we will now, thankfully, have a much better and more secure future ahead of us. When the apartment development is complete I will need your expertise and input in selecting my new abode and I will do anything and everything in my power to make your new home the residence you want it to be."

Judas was quite surprised at the eloquence of his speech and was more surprised to hear the crying of Anita at the end of the phone.

After regaining her composure Anita said, "I look forward to helping you in any way I can to select your new home."

Judas looked up at the guards and saw that they were still huddled around the radiators, so he volunteered to do another internal patrol. Judas left the lodge, made his radio call to the guards and entered the office and factory complex to do a thorough check. Judas was very happy as he wandered into every room just to make sure that everything was still as it should be. He actually enjoyed the work as it gave him something to do. After an hour, he was on his way back to the reception area, when it registered with him that if he returned to the lodge the guards would still be sneezing and spluttering, so he called them on the radio.

"Everything is as it should be, so I will now do another external patrol. Out."

The guards did not reply, but they were very surprised and grateful. The external building patrol contained no surprises and Judas returned to the lodge and was again met by a blast of very hot air.

"Everything is still in order. Just a pleasant jaunt around the complex."

Geoff said, "Many thanks Judas" and suitable entries were made in the report book.

Both guards then continued with their lunch.

Judas inwardly thought: *their illnesses certainly do not have any adverse effect on their insatiable appetites*.

Judas returned to his side of the lodge and got out his check list for leaving his property. He prepared himself a cold drink and sat at his desk. The more he read the list the more he was convinced that he had covered all aspects of his leaving the premises. He looked out of the window and saw that it was getting darker. There were thick clouds blocking out any light and it was definitely getting colder. John and Geoff were still trying to fight the good fight, but unfortunately, both had lost the contest. Judas volunteered to do another full external patrol and a fence patrol for the guards and both were relieved at his generosity with his time.

The fence patrol was conducted in a very methodical manner and was uneventful. The external building patrol was conducted in the same manner with the same uneventful conclusion.

Judas radioed the lodge and asked, "Is another internal patrol necessary? If required I will do one."

The pleading in John's voice convinced Judas that his services were required. The building alarms were switched off and Judas entered the complex.

The pre-set heating for the building had raised its dormant head and was getting the offices and design bureaus ready for the arrival of staff on Monday. Judas looked outside and could see that it was quickly getting very dark. He looked in the other direction and observed the signal box, once the working home of Adam, and he thought of his old friend. The lights were on and the present signalman could be seen at the far end of the box. Funnily Judas had not heard any movement of passengers or freight during the day. He thought of his friend once again and he then resolved to read the notes he had on Adam, when he was settled into his new home, to see if he could decipher the information he had amassed on the mediaeval tragedy.

Judas returned to the lodge and could see that the guards were fidgeting and getting ready for a quick departure when their replacements arrived.

"Nothing to report, everything in order," said Judas, as he retreated to his desk.

He read through his notes again and waited for the incoming guards to arrive. Adrian and Roy arrived within minutes of each other and, after a very quick handover, Geoff and John left the site. Judas was about to leave the site when he was stopped by Roy.

"Many thanks again for your help with the patrols. John and Geoff told me about what you have done today and it is very much appreciated by us all."

Judas was embarrassed and again just nodded.

Judas walked home and realised, quite suddenly, that this was the last time he would venture this way again to return to the Miller's Retreat, whilst he owned it. It was a sobering thought and it helped him to focus his mind on the work that had to be done tonight.

At home Judas checked his post box for the last time. It was empty. He then decided that when he had entered his annexe and switched off the alarm system, he would then take the three garage roller door mechanisms, the post box key, the spare garden structure keys and the external door keys and place them in the recessed box behind the garage. It would save him time in the morning.

He entered his annexe and could see that all of his furniture had been collected by Juliette and Andrew. Also the furniture left for Mary had also gone and there was a "Thank you" note from Andrew. Juliette had done wonders with the annexe and it sparkled. Judas went outside and took the keys and door mechanisms and placed them in the garage recessed box, with the assistance of a small torch he had in his annexe.

He sorted out his clothes ready for morning and finished packing things into his case. The few items left he would put into his case in the morning. Judas did not wear a watch but carried a small alarm clock in his pocket. He amended his wake up time to half an hour earlier, to give him plenty of time in the morning to get to work with his small and large case. He prepared his last meal at this address and was content. After supper he slowly walked around his property and thought deeply about the improvements that he had made. He was inwardly satisfied and he was content. Everything had been done and, although it was early, he changed and settled down for the night.

CHAPTER 12

Sunday 4th January

Judas had a very stressful night. He kept wondering about his actions and he found sleep very difficult. Eventually he had a very shallow sleep, but woke up at about four o'clock and decided to get up. He showered for the last time and packed away everything into his only suit case. He looked at his list. Everything was ticked off and he began to relax. He ate his last breakfast at the property, without enthusiasm, as he was not hungry. After a last sad look around his annexe he took his cases and carrier bag outside onto the pathway. He dropped the latch, put on the alarm, switched off the light, closed the door and walked down the pathway to the street.

The walk into work was a longer affair than usual, but Judas still accomplished it in fairly good time. It was a very quiet morning, even for a Sunday. There was a heavy mist and it was very cold and icy underfoot. Although he had no problems with pulling the case, Judas was very relieved to see the welcoming flicker of street lights above the security lodge. He had left for work ten minutes earlier than normal and had arrived for duty at his normal time. The guards were surprised to see Judas with a large case, but said nothing.

As Judas entered the lodge Roy again thanked him for all of the patrols he had done yesterday and said he hoped that the guards today would do the guarding work themselves.

Judas modestly acknowledged his thanks and replied, "If John and Geoff are still ill, I will willingly help out again with patrols."

Roy was about to thank him again for this gesture when Geoff arrived complaining about the very cold weather and followed into the lodge by John who was complaining about the icy conditions. Both of the day guards were still not very well, but were definitely a little better than yesterday. After the handover, the night guards quickly left the assignment, not wishing to stay any longer than necessary in a germ ridden environment. The incoming guards completed their log book entries, contacted their control office and huddled next to the radiator. Judas reflected that today was going to be a repeat of yesterday.

"Would you guys like me to do the initial patrol?" asked Judas and his suggestion was, again, gratefully accepted by both men.

John even croaked "Thank you."

He left the lodge and he could feel that it was going to be a very long day. He slowly did the fence and external patrols and had no problems. As he entered the office reception area he stopped and the silence was deafening. He was about to begin his patrol when the radio burst into life.

"Base to mobile, message, over," said Geoff.

"Receiving, over," replied Judas.

"Please telephone a Miss A. Wells at her home ASAP. Out." requested Geoff.

Judas went to the receptionist's desk and immediately telephoned the number for the Poacher's Retreat. Anita answered.

Without any opening pleasantries Anita said, "I really am sorry to ask again but are you still serious about my stopping work and being able to retire before repaying your debt?"

"Yes I am still serious," replied a stunned Judas, "why on earth would you think otherwise?"

Anita replied, "I just had to be sure, because Stephanie Faulkner and her husband would like to buy the Poacher's Retreat. Stephanie is an excellent deputy and practically runs the place anyway. She and John have always wanted a guest house of their own and when I mentioned that I might be able to stop work very soon, they asked if I would consider letting them purchase it. If, or when, the sale goes through, Stephanie and John would like to eventually extend the guest house to provide more bedroom accommodation. If you are sure then I will put in motion all of the things that have to be done to sell places like this and we have already agreed that they will make a part payment to me and the remainder will be paid monthly. This is of course dependant on surveys and valuations etcetera. We will get this agreement and financial arrangement sorted out eventually with our lawyers. You really are happy for me to stop?"

"Of course I am," said Judas and continued, "and I would be extremely happy if you sold the place to Stephanie. She is a wonderful and very caring person. The Poacher's Retreat will remain in very capable hands. Also you, Anita, will be able to take a very well earned break and take it easy for a while."

At this point Judas thought he could hear a change in Anita's speech as she tried to hold back the tears.

"If you really are sure, I will go ahead. Will it be okay if I still keep paying you monthly until the debt is paid off?"

Before Judas could say anything, Anita burst into floods of tears and hung up.

Judas continued on his internal patrol of the building. After about an hour he returned to the lodge so that he could contact Anita again.

"Everything is okay, nothing to report" said Judas.

The guards thanked him for his help and entered the times of the patrol into the report book. It was eight minutes past eight and Judas decided he needed to contact Anita. He telephoned her again and she answered straight away.

"You have nothing to worry about Anita," said Judas, "just look after yourself and plan for your future. How are you feeling now?"

"Not too bad now, thanks," said Anita, "but earlier it really hit me that I can soon retire and do some of the things I want to do. In the past, others seemed to get all of the favourable breaks and I didn't get any. Others had holidays whilst I ploughed any surplus money I had into the business. Now I can plan for my future."

"Whilst on the subject of futures," said Judas, "I left the Miller's Retreat this morning for the last time and I am staying at a guest house in Beaufort St. Catherine, from tonight until I can sort out an apartment in one of the towers there. As I told you yesterday Jennifer gave Simon some plans for me to peruse and I like three of them in the left hand tower. After I have booked into my lodgings, I will go to see Jennifer and have a look at the three properties. The place is open until ten o'clock tonight."

"Oh God, I forgot about you leaving today. Sorry and I'm sorry that we had no vacancies here for you to stay until your move, although tomorrow we are completely empty because our guests cancelled due to illness, so Stephanie and I will go to our lawyers, accountants and to an estate agent to start proceedings for the transfer of ownership of the Poacher's Retreat to her and John. I do not expect any great problems to develop and I hope to soon be free and retired. In fact I want to be away from here by my sixtieth birthday at the beginning of March."

Anita continued: "Stephanie's legal people are at Beaufort St. Clement and mine are at Beaufort St. Catherine. After we have sorted out things with our lawyers etcetera, I think we might have lunch and a girl's afternoon out. In fact, whilst I am in the area, I will visit Jennifer at the tower complex and see if she has anything in the local areas that I might be able to afford."

Judas was happy to hear Anita being so positive about her future and he wished her well.

He then added, "I am going over to see Jennifer tonight after work and will be looking at the three apartments I mentioned earlier. I really like the one overlooking the coast, but the other two are also magnificent. Your comments would be appreciated."

Anita agreed to view the apartments tomorrow and to give him her honest opinion about which one would suit him best.

Both of the guards were still huddled next to the radiator, so Judas elected to do another quick patrol of the perimeter fence and the external patrol of the building. When he had done the radio call and was out of sight of the guards, he looked at the plans of the three apartments he had brought out with him to study. He still liked them all, but he was being pulled towards one in particular. He resolved there and then to telephone Jennifer after lunch and to check if his preferred apartment was still available.

He continued his patrol with a spring in his step, which he put down to the fact that he was soon to be in his own apartment. Mid-way through the patrol he quickened his step even more, as the temperature was dropping and it had begun to snow again. Only a few flakes at first and then it got worse. After twenty minutes, as he was about to enter the lodge, the ground had a light, white covering. John and Geoff were not impressed, but prepared a steaming mug of coffee for themselves and gave Judas a glass of his preferred drink.

"Still nothing amiss out there," said Judas, "apart from the weather".

After half an hour, the snow stopped as suddenly as it had begun. Whilst it was clear, Judas did another external patrol of both the fence and building and returned after an hour. For the rest of the morning Judas read his duty notes to make sure they were correct. At ten minutes past noon he telephoned Jennifer. The contact telephone number of the tower block sales office was shown on the various plans and it was she that answered. Judas introduced himself and Jennifer remembered him from their meeting at the orphanage development.

"Hello again." answered Jennifer. "Did you like the plans I gave to Mr Lancaster?"

"They were absolutely superb." answered Judas. "Many thanks for them all. I especially like three of the apartment plans and the artist's impressions of the finished premises." He then quoted the apartment references and casually asked, "Are they still available?"

Jennifer responded immediately, "Yes they are all still available."

Judas was inwardly relieved and said, "Oh good, may I visit tonight for a guided tour?"

"I look forward to seeing you then," said Jennifer and was preparing to hang up when Judas continued:

"Anita Wells will visit the complex tomorrow and hopefully give her approval of my selection. Unfortunately, Anita may have a different opinion to mine. Also, may I ask a favour? If Anita wishes to look at any of the apartments for herself, would you please allow her to do so? Then if Anita says she likes one but cannot afford the apartment, would you please advise her that arrangements could be made to make it affordable. I will explain when I see you tonight."

Jennifer was a little bemused but simply agreed.

Judas then said "Simon Lancaster, the last time that I saw him, told me to ask you about the facilities on the lower ground floor. Please may I be enlightened later?"

Jennifer chuckled and again agreed.

During the afternoon, both John and Geoff did a very quick perimeter fence check and an even quicker external patrol of the building. Both complained that the temperature was dropping, but Judas put this down to the fact that both guards were cradled over a radiator for most of the morning. Judas again busied himself with making sure the duty notes for his trainee were concise and accurate.

When Geoff returned from his solitary patrol, both guards prepared drinks with biscuits and cakes. They croaked that their wives were trying to get rid of the surplus food they had bought for Christmas and the New Year and they were both the sacrificial lambs. However, they did seem to enjoy the drinks and the food much more than the patrols they had done during the afternoon. As the guards were definitely not feeling too well, Judas volunteered again to do the final patrol of the day.

The guards were relieved and Geoff said, "We really are grateful for your help. However, I think we are both slowly returning to the land of the living. Thanks again."

The fence and external building patrols were carried out quickly. The guards were correct, it was getting colder and Judas hurried back to the lodge. After warming his being for ten minutes, he had the office alarms de-activated and entered the main complex.

The building was very dark. It was still eerily quiet and it was quite cold. He hadn't noticed it before, but it did seem much colder than when he did his previous patrol. He switched on the corridor lights and the various office and bureau lights as required and did a very thorough final patrol of the day shift. It took him over an hour as he was delving into every corner of the complex. When he had finished his inspection, he was still feeling very cold and as he exited the building, the icy conditions were not appreciated.

"Nothing to report, all in order," said Judas to the guards, who again thanked him for his work, after resetting the alarm system. Judas smiled and returned to his desk.

"Oh by the way," he said over his shoulder to the guards, "it is devilishly cold in the office complex. Will the heating be put on for the incoming staff in the morning?"

"It's on a computer programme and will come on automatically," said Geoff as he huddled ever closer to the overworked radiator.

For the remainder of the Sunday shift Judas busied himself with tidying up his desk and making sure he had his duty notes all in order. He was about to put the notes away when the fax machine, that had been dormant for most of the festive break, burst into action. Judas took the pages and placed them in an envelope and addressed it to the design bureau. He mused that very little had been received since Christmas Eve and he wondered if the floodgates were now about to open. As Judas looked at the clock, Adrian and Roy both entered the lodge together and after a very quick handover with nothing to report, the day guards departed the site. After a few minutes Adrian left the lodge to do the first night patrol.

At this point Judas unzipped his large case, extracted the clothes he would require in the morning and his change of clothes for tonight and put them in a sturdy carrier bag. He then placed his night clothes and toilet bag in his small case and re-zipped his large case. He waited until Roy, the senior guard on the complex, had done his entries in the report book and then said:

"I will be leaving the large case here for the night and will arrange for one of our drivers to deliver it to a guest house in the morning. As of this morning, I no longer live at the Miller's Retreat, but I have no permanent address at the moment, so I am staying in a guest house for a few days."

Judas waited for the news to be absorbed.

Eventually Roy simply said, "Okay, thanks" and started writing again.

Judas was convinced that the information given had not registered and he resolved to repeat it to Roy in the morning.

Judas left the lodge with his two packages and walked along streets that he knew, but they looked strange in the darkness. They seemed dimly lit and it was getting foggy. He met no-one on the pavement and traffic on the roads was minimal. After half a mile he turned left through an elaborate archway, onto a footpath leading towards a Victorian church and began to climb. Before reaching the church, he turned right onto a well maintained footpath. It was the beginning of the coastal path to Beaufort St. Catherine. It was not a steep climb, but it was constant. Judas knew the path well, but he had never walked to Beaufort St. Catherine in the dark before. This pedestrian route was over two miles distance, but the road route was about six miles.

Judas had a torch and after a short while he was comfortable with his progress. Well positioned markers with reflectors enabled all walkers to know their exact position on the footpath in relation to the coastal edge. The whole of the walkway was very well maintained; the local council knew that walkers, bird watchers and even those seeking solitude, made great use of the numerous public footpaths in the area and contributed greatly to the local economy. Judas laboured on and, after a while, he could see the beckoning lights of his village destination. It still took him fifteen minutes to reach the end of the coastal path, which brought him onto another lane and this released him onto the pedestrian walkway over the old canal and then onto the main road opposite the local library.

As he emerged from the gloom, he saw the three blocks of apartments across the main road. He was surprised to see that the architecture embraced the Victorian style, but it did add to the magnificence and power of the structure. Judas was impressed by what he saw. He decided to go to the guest house first and make himself known to the proprietor, to sign in and to get his meagre belongings into his room.

The Ivy Lodge Guest House was a very well lit establishment, with a welcoming sign and an exceptionally pleasing appearance. It had been an early Victorian attempt at a simple country hotel and had initially been successful, but this success had not lasted. Some of the rooms had been closed off and only the first floor had accommodation for guests. Judas could see from various photographs on the walls that it had been a magnificent building, but was now only a mere shadow of its former glory. Judas was greeted eagerly by the lady of the house, who had been in the kitchen baking.

"Good evening sir," she said, "and welcome to our humble establishment."

Judas explained that his main case would be delivered tomorrow with his clothes and other items. The lady smiled and, after the usual formalities, he was shown to his pleasant and spacious room and given keys to the front door and to his room door.

"After I have settled in," said Judas, "I have to go out to sort out some business, but I will not be late returning."

"There's about four very good places to eat around here," said his host, as she was leaving his room, "just turn right at the pavement and go to the village centre. However, it being Sunday, they close early."

After fifteen minutes, Judas returned downstairs and his nostrils were filled with the gorgeous smell of freshly baked bread. He lingered for a few moments and then left the building and walked back to the apartment blocks. In the darkness they seemed very imposing. Towers two and three were larger than tower one, although they were all of the same height. He had noticed from the plans that Jennifer had given him that two of the blocks were larger than the other, but in the pitch black backcloth of the night, it was very evident. Judas also noticed that the main access roadway to towers two and three passed between them and curved round at the rear of each block into the underground car parks. The access roadway to the first apartment block passed it on the right hand side of the tower and round into its rear car park. All towers had a central entrance and seemed very dimly lit. Judas could also see that there was a pathway leading to the smaller tower, through an area of raised flower beds and winding past a very small man made pond. Even in the very dim light it looked stunning.

Judas could see the sales office caravan and walked towards it. He was about to enter when Jennifer came out to meet him. She greeted him.

"Hello Mr Wells. Very nice to see you again. I have been expecting you."

"The name is Judas," he replied, "and I am very pleased to be here."

Jennifer knew the three apartments Judas was interested in and took him to the main entrance of the smaller tower block.

"Most people go to look at the properties available in tower blocks two and three, as they are the larger apartments," said Jennifer and continued, "but I personally prefer these properties as they are, in a word, cosier. I hope you agree."

As they entered, Jennifer switched on the lights and the glare was blinding. They passed the counter and office of the receptionist and Jennifer advised that the counter would be staffed from six o'clock in the morning until ten o'clock at night. After that access was only available by access code or swipe card.

They entered the elevator and at floor five, they reached the top foyer. The first apartment Jennifer showed him was absolutely stunning and Judas was completely mesmerised by its compactness and beauty.

"This apartment is absolutely brilliant. It has everything any mere mortal bachelor could want," said Judas and he immediately thought that this was the new home for him.

However, out of politeness, he determined to view the other properties he had told her about, before telling her. The second apartment Jennifer showed him was equally stunning and Judas was very pleased that he had decided to continue with the viewings.

"I thought the first apartment was great but having seen this one, I'm now seriously reconsidering," said Judas.

Jennifer laughed and confirmed that other customers that she had shown around the apartments had the same problem.

The third property was absolutely out of this world, in Judas' view, and he could not conceal his pleasure and enjoyment on being guided around it.

On completion of the tour around the property, Judas said, "I am now completely confused. I thought apartment one was superb and could not be bettered. Then you showed me apartment two and I then thought that this apartment could not be bettered. Next you showed me apartment three and this last apartment is absolutely out of this world. It is magnificent. Thank you for your time and expertise. It is very much appreciated."

Judas had to openly admit that Jennifer had done a wonderful job in showing him all of the properties he had requested. She delved into every nook and cranny of the apartments and showed him all of the gadgets available. However, this last apartment had everything he needed or would ever need and, according to the handout given to him by Jennifer, this apartment overlooked the distant coast and the cliffs, the inland harbour, a yachting marina, a park area, a wood and in the opposite direction there were the inland hills. The flashing light of the distant lighthouse to the south was also a comforting sight. To the left of the tower block there was a wildlife haven, a treasure for walkers and lovers of the countryside, which conveniently meant that no future developments would be allowed on the land. This clinched it for Judas and the monthly maintenance expenses were also very reasonable.

Although the rooms were slightly smaller than the other two apartments he had viewed, this was for him. It was a property on three levels. The kitchen was superb, with every conceivable piece of equipment he could want. There was a lounge, a dining room and a sitting room. Upstairs, there was a master bedroom and guest bedroom, both with en-suite bathroom and two further bedrooms with a main bathroom between them. Up another flight of stairs, there were small storage rooms and a study. This study area consisted of two rooms and was enormous compared to the small space Judas was accustomed to at his annexe and the larger room had a small balcony. Judas was absolutely thrilled and advised Jennifer to pencil his name down for the apartment, with the proviso that tomorrow, Anita Wells would visit the sales office and request a tour and, if she approved the selection, then he would definitely have the apartment.

It was then that Jennifer dropped another bombshell.

"This property is among the cheapest in all of the tower blocks. I suppose it's because most people have families and need the larger spaces provided in the other buildings. Because of this, our company will not be building any more of these smaller apartments, so if you want any of the furniture, it is available for sale."

Judas was surprised and pleased.

He said, "Tomorrow, when my friend Anita and Stephanie Faulkner, arrive to view the apartment I have selected, and if Anita gives her approval of the apartment and also her approval of the furniture in situ, then yes I will have the apartment and buy the furniture." Judas then went on. "Also tomorrow, as I mentioned on the telephone earlier, if Anita wants to look at any of the apartments, could you please let her see what she wants. If she sees a property she would like to have, but says it is too expensive for her, just tell her she can afford it."

Jennifer looked baffled and was more bemused than ever.

Judas continued, "If she wants a property and says it is out of her price range, please just say you can work out a plan for her to own it. Then please take the apartment off the market."

"Okay," said Jennifer and after a slight pause continued, "I will do as you ask, but I will need your telephone number to advise you of her choice and to see how we continue."

Judas and Jennifer then left the building and Judas escorted a still confused Jennifer back to her sales office caravan.

"Oh, I nearly forgot. With the apartment you also get two parking spaces allocated to you in the basement. Your allocation will be numbers thirty nine and forty." This time Judas smiled and remembered what Simon Lancaster had told him to ask Jennifer.

"What is on the lower ground floor?" he asked inquisitively.

"Ah yes," said Jennifer, "let's go and have a look."

They returned to the main entrance, entered the lift and, at the first level down, the doors opened at the car parking area and Jennifer pointed to the spaces allocated to Judas. The area was well lit and spacious, with security cameras. He saw a lighted office in the far corner of the car park and could make out the word "Security" above it.

"Guards are always on duty," confirmed Jennifer.

The lift then descended to the lower level and the doors opened. Judas had an open mind on what to expect, but he had not expected this. There was a large swimming pool, with showers, sauna and changing rooms. There was also a well stocked gymnasium, with all kinds of equipment and finally, there was a fully stocked games room. On the end wall of the games room there was a large television screen. Judas was pleasantly surprised.

He escorted Jennifer back, once again, to her sales office caravan and to her colleague who was awaiting her return. This time Jennifer was smiling. Judas gave Jennifer his lodge telephone number.

As he left, she said, "I will work out the cost of the furniture in the apartment, if your selection is approved by Miss Wells, and send you an account."

Judas returned to the main road and walked back towards the guest house. It being Sunday, he believed there would be no shops open and he realized that he was hungry. As he neared the guest house, he saw about two hundred yards ahead and on the opposite side of the road, some lights. He decided to investigate and was pleasantly surprised and relieved to find an arcade open. He bought himself some food items and returned to his guest house.

His host was busy with some chores. She greeted him cheerily and offered him a cool drink and some biscuits, which he eagerly accepted. She informally introduced herself as Amanda Bailey and said her husband was Stephen. It was a rewarding time for Judas, as he was able to learn from this lady about the village and the present situation regarding the local economy.

"Everyone in trade seems to be feeling the pinch," said Amanda, "and this guest house is no exception. However, we remain very positive and believe that the guest house is a viable enterprise." After a few moments Amanda continued:

"Me and Steve did have plans for an extensive development and to utilise the six unused bedrooms and to convert them to four bedrooms with en-suite bathrooms. We also hoped to create a pleasing tea room and cake shop by utilising another part of the property and extending it. Unfortunately, the banks, after listening positively to our proposals, ultimately decided to refuse us a loan. We are now waiting for an upturn of fortunes. Steve, bless him, was forced to take a job as a delivery driver, during the day and, at nights and weekends, he works here doing maintenance and general repairs. He's outside at the moment, getting things sorted out for the morning. There's no peace for the wicked. Times are very hard at the moment for us both, but if we can stick together and keep going until the end of the summer, we should be able to survive.

"By the way," said Amanda, changing the subject, "I have put a mini fridge on the table in your room with your packed lunch for tomorrow inside."

Judas thanked her for her kindness and retired to his room. He reflected on what the lady had said and then settled down to a mini feast of health bars and fruit.

Before retiring for the night, Judas took out the A5 notes he had prepared for Martin Holland and re-read all of them to make certain that they were correct. He was feeling tired, as he reached the last page and was then surprised to see a sketch of a rail layout he had done for Henry Brown. It was a composite plan, taking parts of numerous other layouts he had designed and putting them together to make a completely different layout. This layout plan was a terminus at high level, descending down in two loops to the upper main baseboard. Each loop had sidings leading to industries. Judas could remember designing it and could remember using the miniature track pieces. He could even remember putting down the track item numbers, but he was fairly certain that he had not given the plan and papers to Henry Brown. He was suddenly very tired and retired for the night.

CHAPTER 13

Monday 5th January

Judas had another troubled sleep, even though he was very tired. He arose very early, collected his packed lunch from the fridge and set off for work. His mind was a blur as he hurried to his employment and he eventually reached the security lodge.

As he entered Roy looked up from his desk and said "Good morning."

After Judas had settled down at his desk, Roy came over.

"I just want to thank you for all the patrols you did for the guards, over the past few days. I know it can't have been easy, but it is very much appreciated by us all." Roy then continued, "Last night, when you left work, I was trying to sort out some new attendance rosters for the revised security loading on the site. You said something about the Miller's Retreat and I'm afraid I didn't pay much attention to it. What was it you said?"

"I didn't think it had registered with you," laughed Judas and then advised the senior site guard, "I no longer reside at the Miller's Retreat, as the property has now been sold and for the next few days I will be staying at the Ivy Lodge Guest House, in Beaufort St. Catherine."

Roy nodded and made a note on his pad.

He then said, "Many of the workforce are already on site and some are looking eagerly forward to the New Year challenges, when the company will be working a seven day system." Roy continued, "Other employees, however, said they were not enthusiastic about the new system and were not looking eager at all to the new working conditions."

Judas just nodded and wished Roy and Adrian a pleasant four days break, just as John and Geoff came into the lodge. The handover was brief and both of the night guards left. Judas prepared his forms for the day's action and checked his list for the five expected deliveries during the day. He was about to ask the guards if they were feeling any better, when the first delivery vehicle arrived.

This delivery vehicle was followed by various large vehicles belonging to the site contractors, carrying staff and equipment required for the extension work at the complex. The guards raised the barriers and waved the vehicles through, after receiving a staff list from the foreman. As all incoming staff had been on the site before the festive break, no-one needed to attend an induction course. Also they all knew the site safety procedures, the first aid procedures and the location of fire hydrants and extinguishers. It was good to see the men back on site again and this heralded the beginning of some internal work in the factory. It was still very cold outside and external building work would have to wait.

These vehicles heralded a very busy period and all five incoming vehicles were received, documented and logged in the gatehouse, unloaded by the stores staff and logged off site by eight o'clock. The company's transport fleet were involved with deliveries to the local towns and villages and to a couple of inland cities and all had to be logged out on a list, against their vehicle number with the time of departure and logged in with the time of return.

It was about ten o'clock, after a very hectic four hours, that Judas received a drink from Geoff.

"Thanks again Judas for doing the patrols during my and John's illness. We are both beginning to feel a little better, so best foot forward."

Judas smiled and nodded, inwardly thinking that they were both still coughing at regular intervals and looked really ill. To confirm his suspicions, during the morning, both guards only did two external patrols each.

The morning then began to settle down and, at eleven o'clock, Judas requested a driver who was making a delivery to a regular customer in Beaufort St. Catherine, to take his case and deliver it to his guest house. On his return to the site just before lunch, the driver gave Judas the thumbs up sign and Judas waived. At noon the guards reverted to their usual practice of one guard working, whilst the other was eating and then changed over. Judas then remembered his packed lunch and, as he extracted it from the fridge, both guards looked at him very quizzically. After twenty minutes Judas had finished his lunch and had enjoyed every mouthful. He thought that cracker biscuits and various salad items had never tasted this good before and then he remembered that this was his first meal of the day.

At about one o'clock, Henry Brown brought Martin Holland into the lodge and introduced him to the guards and then to Judas.

After handshakes all round, Martin said, "I have definitely enjoyed my first morning at the company and I wholeheartedly approve of induction courses for new entrants at any company. Safety procedures, first aid procedures and a thorough knowledge of the complexities of the site are of paramount importance to every person on the site."

Judas nodded in thorough agreement.

Martin then said, "I must apologise to you for not being able to do either of the first two weekends during my training as I unfortunately have commitments and will be displaying my own club's model railway at two exhibitions. I'm really sorry."

Judas smiled and said it caused him no problems.

Judas then said to Martin, "I have prepared a folder of notes for you, covering all aspects of the goods reception work," and he took it out of his case and presented it to him.

As he opened the folder some papers fell onto the floor and were picked up by Henry Brown. Judas continued speaking to Martin.

"I will go through every aspect of the duties required by the company and I look forward to seeing you on Wednesday for the start of the training."

With that Martin left the lodge, clutching his folder and walked swiftly to the works canteen for lunch.

Henry Brown approached Judas and queried, "I presume these are your plans as they fell out of your case?"

Judas replied, "Yes they are. I tried to produce a composite plan, featuring a terminus at high level with the main line spiralling down past industrial complexes and then going over a valley to another siding complex, leading to a country station and ending up going into the fiddle yard staging area with a reverse loop located under the terminus. As you can see it proved difficult to get the incline correct and the clearances correct, hence the meandering main line after the lower industrial site. Do you like it?"

"Like it?" questioned Henry Brown, "It's superb. It shows what can be achieved by a modeller, starting in a restricted space with a terminus and developing the layout by adding to it, when time, space and resources permit, and ending up with a complex medium to large layout. This has to go in the book."

Henry Brown then photocopied the papers and on his way out of the lodge told the guards and Judas that he would bring Stephen Lindsey over to be introduced to them later. With that he returned to his office.

The afternoon's work was not as hectic as the morning's work, but there were still fifteen delivery trips made by the company's vehicle fleet. After the last vehicle had left the complex, the afternoon seemed to settle down to its normal routine and Judas and the guards were relieved when Henry Brown, true to his word, brought Stephen Lindsey over to the lodge. The guards were introduced to him first and, after a few minutes of introductory chatter, he was introduced to Judas. His handshake was warm and friendly.

"I am told that you are the man who has contributed most of the smaller and medium sized plans to the book that is being produced. I am also told that you had a hand in finding out some new information about the station at Beaufort St. Catherine. The plans of yours, that I have been shown, are very good and are of a very high standard. Keep up the good work."

Judas thanked him for his kind words and was about to continue when his telephone rang. Henry Brown and Stephen Lindsey took the opportunity to escape from the lodge.

The telephone call was from Anita and she was happy and in a very jubilant mood.

"Can you talk?"

"Yes," replied Judas, "but some vehicles may come back in a few minutes and then things might get hectic. Have you had a good day?"

"Absolutely brilliant," confirmed Anita and then went on to inform Judas of her and Stephanie Faulkner's day out. "We have arranged with our estate agent for a building survey to be completed at the Poacher's Retreat and have arranged for the property and business to be valued. We have also been to a lawyer's to begin the process of transferring the property and have also sorted out the financial arrangements, with everything dependent upon the outcome of the surveyor's report and the valuation."

"We also had lunch," continued Anita, "and afterwards we went to see Jennifer, the sales office lady. She said she was expecting me and showed us both around the apartment you liked. You really have got taste."

She laughed, before continuing:

"And the furniture is absolutely superb. Stephanie also agrees that the place is magnificent. The views from the windows to the nature reserve, the superb gardens, the distant coastal cliffs and the marina are also stunning. We also had a trip down to the basement and that is fantastic. At the end Stephanie was absolutely drooling.

"It was then that Jennifer suggested that we go and look at some other apartments. She led, we just followed and we looked at five absolutely stunning properties. We eventually got to an apartment that I thought was also fantastic. I also enjoyed the view, but this time I was looking inland, over the village and to the hills. Stephanie also thought the apartment was fantastic. Foolishly I asked the price but it was way over the limit I am willing to pay. Apparently it was your second choice, Judas, before you saw your dream home. Jennifer said I could afford it as she would work something out, but I declined. I asked if she had any in my price range and she said she would check her files and advise me. Oh, by the way, Jennifer asked me to let you know that she has worked out the price of the furniture."

Anita was about to continue when Judas said, "Sorry but vehicles approaching. Glad you had a good day. I will telephone you before I leave tonight to get the rest of your news."

Judas was really happy that Anita had liked the apartment and the furniture and he determined to go to the sales office tonight and sort out the money he owed. Whilst there, he would also telephone Anita and tell her that the apartment she liked was hers, if she still wanted it. Judas was really happy that Anita was embracing her imminent retirement with such enthusiasm. He then realized that he had never seen any of the views from the apartment windows, but if Anita liked them then he was certain that he would. The rest of the afternoon was fairly hectic, but the time passed quickly. The guards did another two external patrols each and seemed to struggle to complete these. Before he left the lodge Judas prepared the forms he would need in the morning.

Judas said to John and Geoff, "I hope you have some pleasant days away and I hope your health problems will soon be over."

Judas greeted Gordon and Richard as they entered and wished them a peaceful night. After a speedy handover the day guards left.

Judas telephoned the Poacher's Retreat and the receiver was picked up quickly by Anita.

"You really have got a beautiful home," she said after the pleasantries and continued, "it is really stunning and I am sure you will be very happy there. The views are fantastic. I am very pleased for you."

"Thank you for your approval of the apartment. I am very pleased that you like my taste in both home and furniture," said Judas. "Have you received any information from Jennifer concerning other properties?"

He received a negative reply.

Anita continued," I saw an apartment that I thought was perfect for me, but not at that price. However, I will call Jennifer tomorrow to see if she has any other properties available in my price range."

After a few more minutes of innocent banter between two very close friends, the conversation ended. Judas was in deep thought as he walked through the streets and onto the coastal path leading to Beaufort St. Catherine. He knew what he wanted to do, but he didn't want to anger or embarrass anyone. The temperature was definitely dropping and Judas felt himself shiver. He just hoped he was not going to suffer like the guards John and Geoff. He was still in deep and confused thought as he walked to the sales office and was pleased to see Jennifer.

"Hello again," she said as Judas entered the sales office caravan, "I have been expecting you. I saw Miss Wells and her friend this afternoon and they both gave the thumbs up to your choice of apartment and also they loved the furniture. This, by the way, is the account for the said furniture. Miss Wells also liked the second apartment that I showed you yesterday, but she said she could not afford it. Like you asked, I told her I could arrange something, but she still said no. I have however taken it off the market as per your instructions."

"Thank you for all you have done for me today," said Judas, as he looked at the paper Jennifer had given him and sat down opposite her to write out a cheque. He passed the paperwork to her and she acknowledged receipt of the document.

"This is a bit delicate," said Judas to Jennifer, keeping his voice low so that her colleague could not hear, "but as you know Anita and I have known each other since our days at the orphanage. You also know that she is my oldest and dearest friend and I do want her to have the property for her retirement that she really wants. I once promised her that I would help her to find a property and I guaranteed her that the property she obtained would not be basic. Is the price of the property Anita likes still the same as on the sales literature you sent me?"

Jennifer nodded and said, "The prices have not changed for over three months."

To confirm her statement she got up slowly and walked to a cupboard behind her desk and took out a copy of the sales literature for the apartment Anita liked and passed it to Judas. This paperwork had the sale price printed on it.

Judas thanked Jennifer sincerely for the information and asked, "May I telephone her now?"

A confused Jennifer then pushed the telephone on her desk towards Judas, who then began dialling.

The telephone was answered by Stephanie Faulkner, who, after the usual opening chatter, said, "Judas, you have a very pleasant and impressive property and I am completely jealous. I sincerely hope you enjoy your new home and have a wonderful future."

After a few moments she passed the phone to Anita, who was still happy with the day's events. Judas said he was with Jennifer at the sales office caravan, sorting out the cheque for the furniture and he had been talking to her about Anita's visit.

Judas then asked, "Were you really impressed with the apartment Jennifer showed you and Stephanie this morning, overlooking the village and the hills?"

"Of course I was impressed," said Anita, "who wouldn't be impressed by such an apartment, but unfortunately it was over my price limit by thirty five thousand pounds. I could have dipped into my retirement fund, but I honestly couldn't justify it. Besides I have to keep some money in reserve for furniture. Please do not worry yourself, I will find something soon."

"You have just found it," said Judas, "The apartment has been taken off the sales market and is now yours. I once told you the property you would have would not be basic and this is definitely not basic. I will pass the telephone over to Jennifer."

With that Jennifer confirmed that the property had been taken off the market and Judas was writing out a cheque for the excess amount as she was speaking. Judas could hear Anita openly weeping and he hoped Stephanie was close at hand to comfort her.

After a few moments, Jennifer was able to advise Anita of the technical requirements involving the purchase of the apartment.

"The outstanding payment for the apartment will be expected in the next month. I look forward to seeing you again soon Miss Wells. I am sure you will be very happy here."

Jennifer passed the telephone back to Judas, who could still hear a tearful Anita on the end of the line.

She slowly regained her composure and said, "Judas you can't do this," but he interrupted her.

"I just did it. You deserve it. I once promised you a plush home and you definitely now have one. I also look forward to being with you in the shallow end of the swimming pool. All I have to do now is to learn to swim."

He heard Anita cry again and she replaced the handset.

Judas left a very happy Jennifer, who could now expect a bonus to her salary for the sale of another apartment and headed back towards The Ivory Lodge Guest House. It was now bitterly cold and it began to snow. However, he was very happy, knowing he had a new home and his dearest friend was about to retire and also had a new home. He walked briskly towards the guest house and went to his room. He unpacked his case and had an untroubled night.

CHAPTER 14

Tuesday 6ᵗʰ January

Judas left the guest house in a very positive mood and was soon on the coastal path. He was still happy and content, with the knowledge that very soon his lifelong friend Anita would be retired and established in her new apartment. The thought gave him a very warm glow inside, which was helpful as it had continued snowing during the night and the footpath was very icy. It was also bitterly cold and he was pleased that he was wearing gloves and a thick scarf. He saw the welcoming outline of the church spire and eventually reached the pavement. He met no-one, he could hear no traffic and it was eerily quiet. After a few minutes the lodge came into view and a few seconds later he entered.

Gordon and Richard were seated at their desk, finishing some paperwork and awaiting the arrival of the day guards. Both guards looked up and greeted Judas as he went to his desk. There had been no problems during their shift, but it had been very cold and icy underfoot and both men were eager to go home and get to bed. Five minutes later, the incoming guards, Keith and Colin, arrived and a few moments later the outgoing guards departed. The new guards nodded to Judas and began their preparations for the imminent security patrols. Judas settled down for the expected onslaught of incoming and outgoing traffic. He looked at the list on his desk, collected from reception by the night guards and was surprised to see that the expected delivery vehicle movements for the day, compared to yesterday, were minimal.

At six thirty Anita telephoned and had now recovered her composure. However she was still slightly tearful, but was beginning to believe what was actually happening.

"Are you really sure I can have the apartment?" she eventually asked.

"Of course I am sure." said Judas, "The apartment is yours and I have given Jennifer the cheque for the outstanding amount. As soon as the rest is paid you can start sorting out furniture and then move in. I am really looking forward to seeing you exercising in the gymnasium."

Anita laughed and then said, "When I have sorted out the furniture and moved in, I will be able to pay off the rest of the loan for the Poacher's Retreat. Stephanie and her husband have agreed to pay me three quarters of the valuation price when it is transferred and the rest in annual instalments. This has already been sorted out with our solicitors."

Judas was pleased that everything seemed to be going smoothly, but said, "You don't have to pay the loan back in full if it will be a problem. You can continue with monthly payments."

However, this time Anita was adamant and when the call finished she was composed and elated.

The outgoing vehicles left the site just before seven o'clock and three of the five delivery vehicles had arrived by nine o'clock. The guards had done the external fence patrol and the external building inspection by ten o'clock and Judas thought that both men were looking tired and drained. In fact both seemed to be suffering from the cold weather conditions and were complaining openly about the icy conditions underfoot. At about ten o'clock it began to snow again. The guards huddled around the radiator, in their section of the lodge and put off the next patrol for as long as they could. However,

Keith eventually ventured outside and completed his patrol in half the normal time.

"It's really cold out there and it's also very icy underfoot," he said when he returned, "so take care when you do your patrol."

This last remark was directed to Colin, who just nodded and then loudly sneezed.

"Oh God," thought Judas, "not more invalids in the gatehouse".

The morning drifted on slowly and the two remaining delivery vehicles arrived before noon. Each was directed to its unloading bay and released from site on completion of its delivery. As the receptionist was now on duty, Judas had no company telephone calls to deal with and at times he was desperate for something to do. He re-read the notes he had prepared for Martin Holland and was content with the information he had prepared. He then wondered if Martin had read his copy of the notes.

It was pleasing to see the factory lights shining through the windows of the engineering section, the design section, the office complex and the conference rooms. The general workforce of the company had been away for too long over the festive interval and attempts were now in motion to get the factory back on track. Judas mused that since the company had returned to work yesterday, he had only seen Henry Brown and Paul Gibson as they parked their vehicles in the car park.

By one o'clock, most delivery vehicles had returned to the site and Judas settled down for lunch. It had stopped snowing but the ground and car park were still covered in white. Just as he had packed away his lunch box, a loud noise from the station area made Judas look up and he saw the upper part of a single unit slowly pull out of the station. He then looked at the signal box and again thought of Adam. For the last few days he had been completely absorbed with the sale of his own property, the sorting out of his new property and the designs of various model railway track plans for the company and had not looked at any of the other notes from Adam's room. He determined to rectify this oversight tonight. He still had the papers at the guest house and he would re-read Adam's notes and try to do some more deciphering of the "foreign hand". He would also have another look at the plans of the proposed extension lines.

For the rest of the afternoon Judas sat at his desk, with very little happening on his duty, or on the duties of the guards. Keith and Colin both completed one fence patrol and one external building patrol each during the afternoon, but each patrol seemed to be of shorter duration than the last one. By the time the office staff were departing the complex for their homeward journey, there was a biting wind blowing shoreward and it was beginning to snow again. Judas looked again at the guards and noticed that they were both seated very close to the radiator and both were shivering and occasionally were also sneezing. At the end of their shift both day guards were ready for a quick departure, overcoats were on and everything was ready for a speedy getaway. Gordon and Richard arrived practically together and, after an exceptionally fast handover, Colin and Keith left the lodge. The incoming guards nodded to Judas and settled down to their duties.

As he was about to telephone Anita, Judas looked out through the lodge window and saw Henry Brown and Paul Gibson in deep conversation before exiting the site. He also saw the frame of Simon Lancaster marching purposely towards the lodge and Judas opened the door for him to enter.

"Sorry to be so late, but I am pleased that I contacted you before you left the site," said a panting Simon. "I have something for you, from the the Miller's Retreat post box."

He then handed Judas an envelope and he immediately recognised the slanting writing of Susan at the timber yard. Judas then realized that he had forgotten to advise Susan and Martin of his change of residence and he resolved to correct this omission at the earliest opportunity. He opened the envelope and extracted a cheque, which he put into his wallet.

Judas then apologised to Simon, saying, "In the rush to be away from my old home, I omitted to notify Martin and Susan of my change of address. I will telephone them tonight."

Simon Lancaster simply smiled and gave Judas another envelope. This second envelope contained a note from the Beaufort St. Vincent College, where Judas took courses in historical and geographical subjects, informing him of upcoming evening classes in January and weekend courses available in February. The enclosed note also advised that the college reception area would be open until nine o'clock each weeknight until the 9th January for enrolments.

The final envelope was handed to Judas by a smiling Simon and when he opened it and took out the cheque, Judas was bewildered. It was the cheque he had given to Jennifer for the furniture.

Before Judas could ask, "Why? The cheque is definitely good for payment." Simon said, "The apartment you selected was among the lowest priced in the whole of the three towers and the developers had incorrectly assumed that you would possibly select the most expensive apartment and had allowed for this in their calculations. But when you made your choice and selected one of the lowest value apartments, they decided to waive the cost of the furniture, hence the return of the cheque."

Judas protested, "I honestly did not know that my selection was one of the cheapest apartments, but I chose the one I most wanted. Are you sure about this?"

"I am completely sure," said a chuckling Simon Lancaster, "and your protestations are completely dismissed."

After a few minutes of further bickering, Judas requested Simon to sincerely thank the developers for their generosity and said he would also write to them personally in the morning to thank them. Simon left after a few minutes as he had another evening meeting. Before doing anything else, Judas shredded the unwanted cheque and he then entered the details of Martin and Susan's cheque into his record book and initialled the entry.

Judas then began to telephone Martin, but suddenly realized that he did not know the number of his apartment, or indeed the name of the tower block, so he replaced the receiver. Next Judas telephoned Anita and was pleased to find her in a non tearful mood.

"Thanks again for your wonderful generosity," she said, "and for your actions in securing for me the home of my dreams." Before Judas could say anything, Anita continued, "The surveyors have contacted me and confirmed that they will complete their survey work at the Poacher's Retreat by the 9th of January. Also Stephanie has confirmed that her finances are in place to complete the agreed transfer arrangements, dependent upon the surveyors report and the valuation figure."

Judas was very happy for his friend and it was good to hear her being so positive.

Anita then asked, "How has your day been? It can't have been better than mine." Judas skimmed over the work details of his day and his meeting with Simon Lancaster, but did say that at one stage, when he heard a traction noise from the station, he looked up at the signal box used by Adam and thought again about the old man.

"I still miss Adam," he said, "although he has been gone these many years. He taught me a lot, especially he told me to apply myself to everything I attempt."

"I miss him too," said Anita.

This fact surprised Judas, as he'd never thought that the death of Adam had affected anyone else at the orphanage but him. After all, he was the only one that openly wept at Adam's funeral. Anita then went on to describe the way that she developed her handwriting and composition style with the help of Adam's very interesting stories.

"I would write down the stories in sketchy note form and I would neatly write up the notes afterwards."

Judas never knew this about Anita. He had always listened to Adam and written up his stories from memory.

Anita then said, "I still have the stories written down somewhere. I last saw them about three years ago and when I read them I had tears in my eyes."

Judas then advised Anita that he also wrote down the old man's stories.

He then said, "When you pack up your belongings at your present home ready for your move to Beaufort St. Catherine, if you re-discover the papers, could I please have a photocopy of the sheets? Sometimes, I was out working at the newsagents, or running errands, when Adam was entertaining in the evening and I would love to read some of the stories I missed."

Anita agreed to his request, saying, "I have no idea at present where to look for them, but no doubt I will find them soon."

The conversation continued for a few more minutes and, when it was finished, Judas was really pleased to hear Anita being happy and positive.

Judas left the lodge and, on reaching the main road in Beaufort St. Catherine, he walked briskly to the Ivy Lodge Guest House. As he entered, Amanda invited him into the kitchen for a drink. She had remembered that Judas could only drink cold fluids and gave him a tankard of lemon barley with ice. Her husband, Stephen, then entered the kitchen and he and Judas were formally introduced. He was a man of medium height, very slim build, bearded and with a full head of black hair and his handshake was welcoming. He told Judas that he had been at work all day and had just done some maintenance work in an upstairs bedroom.

"Onward and upward," he said as he excused himself and returned upstairs.

After thanking Amanda for the drink, Judas retired to his room and after a few minutes walked out to the development sales caravan to see Jennifer. It was colder than earlier and the expected high winds were beginning to arrive. Jennifer was surprised to see him, yet laughed when he asked her the number of his apartment and the name of the tower block.

"It's Bournebrooke Garden Apartments and it's number fifty six. Thornegraves Boulevard, Beaufort St. Catherine, Beaufort St. Vincent."

Jennifer laughed again when she saw the look of incredulity on Judas's face.

"Ye Gods," he said as he wrote the address details into his notebook.

Jennifer also provided the postcode and, on searching her records, she said, "Telephone service will be connected when required, but you will have to sort this out with your provider when you have moved into your apartment."

He thanked her for all the information and left the office.

As he walked towards the main road, Judas telephoned Martin from his mobile, but was transferred to the answering machine. He apologised for his forgetfulness, gave his new address, thanked Martin and Susan for the cheque and said he hoped to see them again soon. When he reached the main road Judas walked to the village. It was a very pleasing early Victorian village that depended on the tourist industry for its existence. It had a small but busy marina and a small working harbour. It also had a nature reserve and was a haven for bird watchers and it also had numerous public footpaths for the walking fraternity. Judas wanted to explore more, but it was getting much colder and he needed to return to the guest house and get some food.

On returning to his room, he ate a simple meal. He then extracted from his case the small box containing the notes he had taken from Adam's room and began to read. He was completely absorbed by the notes he was reading. Judas found all of the notes to be fascinating, especially those including the maps and those in the second note book, including the undecipherable pages of the foreign hand. He also read Adam's attempted unravelling of the unknown script. Judas was still baffled and his lack of progress began to worry him. He then decided that he would take the maps and notes he had taken from Adam's room to work in the morning and photocopy them. This would allow him to leave the main papers in his room and to look at the copies obtained when opportunity permitted.

Tomorrow, Judas would begin training Martin Holland on his goods reception duties and he was certain that after the first week of intense working with his trainee, Judas would be able to sit back and see his new colleague working perfectly in the lodge. Judas mused that it might then be possible to read the notes and hopefully make some progress. He packed the paperwork away and placed the box into his case. He was looking forward immensely to tomorrow.

CHAPTER 15

Wednesday 7th January

Judas was getting accustomed to the walk into work and, as he entered the lodge, he was greeted by both Gordon and Richard, each with a croaking voice. Both had succumbed to the cold weather and were shivering. They were both looking forward to getting home and to bed.

Judas stayed away from the guards and said loudly, "Hopefully you will both feel better after a good sleep."

He went through his usual routines and then went to the photocopier to copy the papers he was looking at last night. After about ten minutes Keith and Colin entered the lodge and after a practically non-existent and silent handover, the night guards left the site. The on-duty guards looked at the report book for the night shift and were surprised to see that only one fence patrol and one external building patrol had been carried out by each of the outgoing guards. Judas reflected that this was the same patrol pattern as performed by the day guards yesterday.

Judas completed his photocopying task, filed the papers into his case and prepared his files and folders for his trainee. He also scanned the Receipt and Delivery list on his desk and was pleased to see that it was not excessive and would let his trainee slide easily into the factory procedures for these tasks. Whilst he waited for Martin Holland to arrive, Judas began a letter of grateful thanks to the developers for their generous gift of the furniture in his apartment and for the return of his cheque.

He was half way through the letter when Martin Holland arrived at the lodge and was met by Judas. He was introduced to the day guards, Keith and Colin, who both shook him by the hand and welcomed him to the lodge. Judas then took Martin to the section of the lodge where he would be working. Initially, Judas showed him the various rooms of the lodge, the welfare facilities, the first aid cabinets and the fire extinguisher positions, the photocopying machine and the shredding machine.

Judas then continued, "You have already met John and Geoff and tonight I will introduce you to Gordon and Richard. We are a happy group and you will be introduced to Adrian and the senior guard, Roy, on Friday at the changeover of shifts."

Martin then apologised again to Judas, "I really am sorry for not being able to cover any of the Saturday or Sunday work for the next two weekends. As I explained on Monday, our group is committed to exhibiting our model railway at two national exhibitions, on these dates. Sorry."

Judas smiled and said, "No problem."

"Yesterday, Mr Brown showed me some of the layout plans you prepared for him and they were absolutely magnificent. He asked me for my opinion, due to my belonging to a model railway club and I told him that they were first class," said a jubilant Martin.

Judas was embarrassed but thanked him for his kind words.

"You really are gifted," said Martin, but, before he could continue, a vehicle appeared at the reception window and Martin's training began.

Martin was a very capable and attentive person; he was eager to learn and seemed to pick up information very easily and quickly. During a lull in the morning work, Martin began to read the folder Judas had prepared and presented to him. During this time, Judas took care of any vehicles movements.

When Martin had finished reading, he said, "These notes are very well written, they are very clear and concise. So far I have no problems understanding them."

During the morning coffee break Judas asked the guards, "Will you please take Martin out on your next perimeter patrol and also on your next external building patrol, to acquaint him with the site? This will help him to relate to the various buildings used by incoming and departing vehicles."

Both guards agreed. It was only at this point that Judas realized that he had not asked either of the guards if they were feeling any better than they were yesterday. This omission was duly rectified.

"Ye gods, I'm so sorry, but I haven't asked you both about your colds."

Both said they were on the mend and were now feeling a little better, although they still did not seem to have any enthusiasm or energy.

Martin sat with the day guards for coffee and learned in brief what their duties involved. Judas sat at his desk and continued working on his letter to the developers, when not involved with incoming or exiting vehicles to or from the site. The morning passed slowly and Judas eventually finished his letter to the developers. He re-read the letter and was very pleased with his work. He photocopied the papers and prepared the envelope for posting.

At one o'clock Martin returned to the lodge with Colin and seemed impressed with the external characteristics of the complex. He had been taken on a tour of the offices, the design bureau, the drawing office and the planning department by Henry Brown and Paul Gibson during his induction attendance. However, he had not been shown into the sections of the complex undergoing building alteration because of the safety problems, but Colin had allowed him to squint through some holes in the shielding tarpaulin to gain a better knowledge of the site layout. Judas thanked the guards for their help, as did Martin. Martin then had lunch whilst Judas attended to the lodge duties and then the roles were reversed.

During the afternoon, Martin read and re-read the notes Judas had given him earlier and when he'd finished, he said he understood the procedures. Judas was pleased with the training; it had gone well and Martin was a very able and competent student. As the day progressed Martin took on more and more of the work and Judas just sat back and supervised. The day to day work had been picked up very well and everything was running like clockwork. The complex month-end returns would be shown to Martin next week, but Judas was confident that he would have no problems.

It was mid afternoon when Judas realized that both guards were in the lodge and were huddled around the radiator. They were shivering again and had both been sneezing. Judas went over to them and could see immediately that both men were suffering from very severe cold symptoms; their desk was strewn with packets of pills and peppermints, both were taking tablets and bottles of cough mixture were openly on display.

The remainder of the afternoon went well and Martin confidently dealt with all of the work that he had been trained on during the day. The goods reception duty had not been busy during the day and Judas was relieved that this gave him the opportunity to give a solid base to Martin's training. Tomorrow Judas would outline to Martin some of the more brain teasing aspects of the work, but he was certain that these difficulties would present no problems to his trainee. Judas was really feeling happy with life at the moment and he even went into the small kitchen and prepared coffees for the guards and Martin. These beverages were gratefully received by all, although the guards croaked their gratitude and were still huddled around the overworked radiator. Both day guards were wrapped in their scarves, gloves and overcoats when the night guards arrived and after a hasty handover, Keith and Colin left the assignment.

Gordon and Richard were still looking unwell, but both said they were feeling better than they were yesterday. Judas took Martin over to the incoming guards and introduced him to them. After the introductions, Martin said he was enjoying the work and was looking forward to tomorrow.

He then said to Judas, "If I may, I would like to take the folder home ready for some bedtime reading?"

Judas just nodded. Shortly afterwards Martin left the lodge and wished everyone a very enjoyable evening.

"You're training him too well," said Gordon, "he's too eager."

Judas and Richard smiled.

Judas then said, "I suppose you have seen from the guard report book that only a few fence patrols and external building patrols have been done by Keith and Colin during the day. They really were not well during their shift and I don't think you two are much healthier than they were. Would you like me to do the first fence patrol and first external building patrol on your shift?"

"Oh God, yes please," said a relieved Gordon and then added, "I now see where Martin is getting his eagerness from."

Both guards chuckled.

Judas prepared himself for his security patrol and put on his overcoat, scarf and gloves.

"Once more unto the breach, dear friends etcetera," he said as he left the lodge.

As he stepped outside, he realized why the guards were so pleased at his volunteering. It was freezing and the temperature was definitely dropping. He did the radio check and received acknowledgement from the lodge. Judas then gingerly made his way around the perimeter fence and was slow and thorough in his progress. He could hear the humming of the factory machinery but saw no-one during his patrol. After forty minutes, he began the external building check of the complex. He checked every external door to confirm that it was fully locked and, after another forty minutes, Judas returned to the lodge and was greeted by the grateful guards. After a few minutes, Gordon left the lodge to do an internal examination of the complex. As the factory was now working full time and the canteen was open all night, Judas suspected that Gordon's enthusiastic willingness to go on the internal patrol was driven by an ulterior motive.

After five minutes, Judas left the lodge and walked into Beaufort St. Vincent and after twenty minutes entered the college reception area. On his way to the college he posted the letter he had written earlier. The college foyer was deserted except for a young secretary and he went to her desk. Judas produced his college identification card and enrolled onto two evening classes. The first was "The History of Maps" and the second was "Roman Britain." The classes were to be held on Thursday and Friday evenings, the first class beginning on January 15th. Judas also advised the young lady of his new address and the details were entered into the records. Just as he was leaving the foyer, he met his history teacher, with whom he had attended many wonderful classes, on numerous historical subjects.

"Hello there," said Gavin Melbourne, "I just knew that you would be here for the course on the Romans. It's just my luck that as soon as I had completed my notes on the course saying that the Roman's never settled in this area, then evidence is uncovered to prove me a liar."

Both men shook hands and wished each other well for the coming year. Judas pleaded ignorance of the Roman presence, as he was not certain of how Gavin knew of the local fort.

Gavin Melbourne could detect the query in the face of Judas and asked, "Have you not seen the article in the *Beaufort Gazette*, about the local discovery?"

Judas answered truthfully that he had not. Gavin was about to go into details when his mobile telephone sounded and he was called away to collect his wife from her lecture at the museum.

As they parted Judas said, "I am really looking forward to the course on Roman Britain and still wondering how you will square the circle concerning the Roman presence in this area of the country."

Gavin shrugged and smiled.

Judas walked back towards the security lodge and wondered how the local weekly paper had discovered details about the unearthing of a Roman fort in the town. He had been requested by Simon Lancaster to inform no-one and he had not said a word to anyone. As he passed the lodge he could see both guards huddled over their desk. He continued his journey along deserted streets and eventually reached Beaufort St. Catherine. He spotted the glowing street lamps and navigated his way to the guest house.

As he entered his room, Judas saw an envelope on the table. He recognised Anita's handwriting and opened the packet. Inside were photocopies of the notes that she had written after Adam's evening talks. In total there were twenty six sheets of paper and all were written in Anita's youthful, neat handwriting. Judas looked for a covering note in Anita's adult hand, but there was none. He left the papers on the table and determined to read them later, after he had showered and eaten.

An hour later Judas began to read the notes presented by Anita and could remember most of them, as he must have been present at the talks given by Adam. All of the pages had been dated and he placed those that corresponded with his notes next to his writings in transparent sheets in his clip file. He also re-read his notes to confirm that Anita's writings did not contain any new information. Judas was relieved to confirm that all duplicated pages written by Anita corresponded to those he had written.

There were six other sheets presented by Anita, outlining Adam's talks that Judas had no information on. He checked the dates to confirm that he had no notes on the subjects. He placed the pages into transparent sleeves, but did not file them and determined to re-read the new material again in the morning at work. On one of these pages from Anita, there was a reference to an area, which developed centuries later into the large village of Beaufort St. Catherine. The entry simply stated that in Roman times their naval vessels skirted along the very treacherous coast. Judas had never known of this fact and he had no idea of how Adam had obtained the information.

Judas reckoned that he and Anita were usually working at the same time in the evenings whilst at the orphanage, which accounted for their being only six occasions when Anita was present and not him. Then he mused that there must have been innumerable occasions when neither party were present at Adam's talks. On reflection he believed that between them they had missed about eighty per cent of Adam's evening stories. He then realized that he was completely drained, mentally and physically, and he also decided that training duties were exhausting work.

CHAPTER 16

Thursday 8th January

Judas walked to work not feeling one hundred per cent fit. He had a sore throat, but he put this down to yesterday's training programme and all the talking he had done explaining the necessary duty activities to Martin. Thankfully he did not have any other symptoms of a cold or flu. However, he did feel the cold weather as he walked to work and he was looking forward to reaching the warmth of the lodge. The heat in the lodge was stifling and both guards were suitably dressed ready for a fast exit from the lodge. They both croaked a greeting to Judas and complained that the night had seemed never ending.

"The building contractors have returned to the site," said Gordon, "and are busy in various places around the complex."

Judas went to his desk to view the expected vehicle movements during the shift. He was relieved that there would be plenty of activity, with incoming and outgoing vehicles on site throughout the day. This activity would allow Martin to see what a normal day in the lodge would be like. At that moment Martin arrived on site, closely followed by Keith and Colin. The outgoing guards hastily performed the security handover and vacated the site.

Martin placed his instruction notes on the table and scanned the list of expected vehicle movements.

He greeted his instructor with good humour and said, "Last night, I read the notes you provided, from cover to cover and I enjoyed reading them."

Judas looked over to the guards and saw them both smile. However, they had very little to smile about, as Judas could see that they were both still suffering from the cold and were again huddled over the radiators. Judas was about to speak to them when the first delivery vehicle arrived on site and this heralded a very busy morning for him and for Martin.

At ten o'clock, Judas prepared beverages for the guards and for his trainee. He felt very guilty just sitting there supervising the activities of Martin, who seemed to have mastered the complexities of the day-to-day running of the site very easily. Judas reflected that it took him longer to learn the work, but he put this down to the fact that he was trained by two completely different people. As Martin was so competent, Judas decided to take out the papers in the transparent sleeves written by Anita to photocopy them and to carefully read them.

He scanned all of the six sheets very methodically and enjoyed reading the stories, especially the one concerning the Roman navy and its association with the coastline near to the area which became Beaufort St. Catherine. He could picture Adam reciting the events and he still had fond memories of the old man. He was still busy reading the notes for a second time, when Simon Lancaster came into the lodge.

Simon explained, after the initial greeting, "I have just been to the developers for a site meeting at the Miller's Retreat and they have instructed me to give to you, Judas, the ownership papers for the apartment. And here they are."

Simon was acting very dramatically and he waved the papers before presenting them to Judas. Judas could feel himself blush as he accepted the documents and he quickly signed the required paperwork to cover his embarrassment and to legalize the transaction.

"The property, with all of its contents, is now yours. You can pick up the access cards from Jennifer, you can put your own access numbers into the machine by the door and you can move into the apartment as soon as you like," said Simon, as he was about to leave.

"Thank you for taking the time to bring this paperwork to me," said Judas and continued, "Do you have a few moments to spare?"

Simon nodded and said he had a meeting in town in half an hour, so he was okay for about ten minutes.

Judas then put on his coat and walked out of the lodge with Simon and told him about the Ivy Lodge Guest House.

He added, "The owners were hoping to extend their guest house to make it more profitable. However, their requests for a loan by their bank and other financial institutions, have fallen on unsympathetic, financial ears. They are working like demons at present to get the finances into place, but I fear it will be a very long process. I would like to help the owners financially to achieve their dream. They want to modernise the six unused bedrooms they have by converting them into four bedrooms with en-suite shower rooms which will give them a greater financial return. They also want to establish and develop a tea and cake shop in another part of their property, for use by the general public. I will speak to them soon and hopefully get the monetary agreement sorted out with them and their lawyer. If everything is okay would you have any objection to them contacting your company and having the proposed plans produced for the extension?"

When Judas had finished talking Simon said, "It's already been done by my company. They have already been given the plans for the bedrooms, the en-suites and the tea room annexe. Alan, one of my guys, did the measurements and drawings for the upgrade about three years ago."

Judas was very surprised, and also relieved, that the owners had their dreams down on paper and were working very hard to achieve their objective. Judas thanked Simon again for his time and for the documents.

As he left Simon said, "Good luck with the guest house people. According to Alan, the couple are both grafters and deserve to have success."

Judas returned to his work, wondering how Simon could remember such details from three years ago.

As he re-entered the lodge Judas realized that he had not contacted Anita to thank her for the photocopies of her notes. He resolved to telephone her at the earliest opportunity and this opportunity presented itself after about ten minutes. There was a sudden lull in the traffic and he contacted the Poacher's Retreat. His call was picked up quickly by Anita, who was pleased to hear from him.

After the usual greetings Judas thanked her for the sheets and then asked, "How are the various agents progressing with the surveying and the valuation of the property?"

"The surveyors and the valuation agents are here tomorrow and, if there are no problems with their findings and figures, we should be able to proceed very quickly," said a very excited Anita. "Stephanie and John are also happy at the progress being made and are both keen for the complete transfer to take place. When this changeover happens, I will book into a guest house and sort out various purchases for my new home. I have already seen some furniture I like."

Judas laughed and was very pleased that his dear friend was now very happy and contented. She was her old self again.

Anita then said, "As you have been allowed to retain all of the furniture that was on display at your new apartment, what are you going to do with your old furniture from the Miller's Retreat annexe?"

Judas explained that it was at Juliette's, being stored in her garage, until required.

"Why do you ask?" said an inquisitive Judas.

Anita replied, "Because I would love to have the two small bookcases in my new apartment. I know they are not considered modern, but they are really functional. And anyway, I like them."

Judas agreed that Anita could have the items and the call ended a few moments later. Judas went back to supervising.

During another lull in the movement of traffic, Judas contacted Jennifer and asked when it would be convenient to move his meagre contents, contained in various crates, into his new apartment.

Jennifer just said, "The apartment is yours, but I have asked the company cleaners to give it a thorough clean, ready for your occupation. Would it be convenient to move in on Monday?"

"Certainly," said Judas and added, "As I do not have the access cards, would there be any objections if I arranged for the crates to be delivered on Monday and then advise the delivery driver to contact you for access."

Judas was about to continue when Jennifer replied, "There will be no objections and I look forward to seeing the delivery driver. By the way," she continued, "there are various rooms here, on the ground floor of the main complex, where the items and furniture could be stored, if you wish, until claimed by yourself."

Judas decided to make use of this offer and thanked Jennifer accordingly.

After another hour Judas decided that it was time for him to contact Juliette and make arrangements to collect the two small bookcases and the crates from her garage. He also decided that he would donate the three medium sized bookcases to Juliette's charity, raising money for the blind, if she wanted them. He telephoned and the voice mail machine blurted out its message. Judas was about to speak when Juliette stopped the recording machine and answered. After the initial greetings Judas advised Juliette that he would be moving into his new home very soon and was looking forward to living in Beaufort St. Catherine.

He also told Juliette, "My friend Anita, will soon be living in the same apartment block and has indicated that she would like the two smaller bookcases. Would your charity like the three larger bookcases?"

Juliette took a while to answer and Judas began to feel uneasy, when she said, "Would you mind if I had them instead and I will make a donation to the charity?"

"They are yours," said a relieved Judas.

Juliette continued, "Our study has been taken over by our daughters, for homework and revision and Andrew has been squeezed out of his 'Domain'. We are in the process of planning a second study, hobby and games room at the rear of our garages and these will be Andrew's new recreational retreats. The building work should begin in the spring. He has a large collection of books, CDs, Videos, etcetera and he would love to have these items stored in bookcases. He also has a half size snooker table and his pride and joy is his model railway. At present the snooker table has its legs off and is propped up against a wall together with the model railway baseboard and the model railway equipment is packed away in various boxes. Are you sure it's okay if we have the bookcases?"

"As I work for a model railway company, I could never come between a man and his model railway," joked Judas. "The items are yours and I sincerely hope you enjoy them."

"Would you like us to bring the bookcases and the crates to your new address? We could deliver the items on Saturday."

Judas was shocked and delighted at the suggestion and immediately agreed, with the proviso that he would only accept the offer if it was okay with Andrew.

"He will be only too willing to help, considering the goods you have given to his sister Mary, the furniture you have given to me and my daughters and now the bookcases you have released to Andrew. They are just the sort of bookcases he wanted."

"It was a pleasure," said Judas, "to help a lady in distress and to help your daughters and I sincerely hope Andrew finds the bookcases to be of use to him. I was about to contact a delivery firm to organize the removal of the crates and the small bookcases from your garage, but if you are sure you can manage the crates and furniture it will be much appreciated."

Judas then gave Juliette the very long address and she thought it was as amusing as Judas had when he had first heard it.

Judas continued, "You will have to contact Jennifer in the sales office caravan for access to the building. Jennifer has also allowed me to have the items stored in some ground floor rooms until Anita and I need them."

After his telephone call to Juliette ended, Judas was very relieved and content with the outcome. He telephoned Jennifer again to say the items would be delivered on Saturday and not Monday as he had said earlier.

While all this was going on, Martin was diligently working away at the job and doing sterling work. Judas congratulated him on the work he had done and advised him that tomorrow he would instruct him on the month-end procedures and monthly statistics and quarterly returns. Martin smiled. Judas then telephoned Anita and left a message on the voice mail.

"Your bookcases will be delivered to the tower block on Saturday and will be stored on the ground floor until you require them. As for me, I shall be moving into my new apartment on Monday night."

At one o'clock, Judas had lunch and again enjoyed it. He then prepared drinks for Martin and the guards. The guards had only done one perimeter fence check and one external building check during the morning. Both men were now huddled next to the radiator and were looking completely drained. Judas got himself a drink and sat with Martin. After a very hectic morning, the traffic seemed to stop arriving or departing and, for the next two hours, very little vehicular activity took place.

Judas decided to begin the training with Martin for the monthly and quarterly returns and other various statistics required by the company. For the remainder of the afternoon, Judas went through every aspect of the returns, using copies of the last month's statistics to clarify the information. Martin was very attentive and the training went very well. At the conclusion of the talk, Martin asked for clarification on two points and when these had been covered by Judas in more detail, Martin was content. For the next hour Judas took over the work in the lodge and Martin went through the notes he had been given to cement the knowledge into place.

At five o'clock, Martin took over again and the final rush of the day began. By six o'clock, all company vehicles had returned to site and only one delivery vehicle was on site being unloaded. Gordon and Richard entered the lodge within two minutes of each other and the day guards croaked their handover instructions to them and hurriedly left the building.

Judas said to the departing guards, "I hope you have an enjoyable evening and also hope that, on your return in the morning, you are both feeling much better."

Both guards just waved. Martin again took his notes home with him and the night guards settled down to do their required paperwork. Judas reflected that both incoming guards seemed to be suffering the same affliction as the day guards and, on completion of the book entries, both men huddled next to the overworked radiator. The final vehicle left the complex and Judas completed his ledger and filed all of his work in the cabinet. He then also bade the guards a very pleasant evening and left the site.

Judas finally reached his guest house after what seemed a longer than usual walk. He checked his pocket watch, but he was not late. He entered his room and after a few minutes Amanda knocked on his door and delivered his lunch packet.

"I'm pleased you like the packed lunches," she said, "but if there is anything specific you like just let me know. By the way, would you like me to do any washing?"

Judas gratefully accepted the offer. He was then invited down to the kitchen for a drink and a few moments later took the laundry down with him.

Judas sat talking with Amanda and Stephen and had a very pleasurable time with them. They were a very happily married couple who had suffered numerous setbacks in their working life at the guest house, but these tragedies had been overcome with great determination and energy. Their openness and frankness about their plans and aspirations for the future were refreshing to Judas and he resolved to help them make their dreams a reality. However, he did not want to get involved with his plans until he was settled in his new home and therefore decided to bide his time. He had a very enjoyable hour with his hosts and prepared to return to his room.

Amanda said, as he departed, "I will finish the washing and get the items ironed and put them on your bed in the morning."

Judas thanked her and left the kitchen.

In his room Judas took out Adam's papers and re-read them, but he could not get his mind to concentrate on the contents. He decided to read the papers again, but he still could not concentrate on the subject. Therefore, Judas decided on an early night.

CHAPTER 17

Friday 9th January

Judas woke early and left the guest house in a very positive frame of mind. He was very confident that Martin would make a fine colleague for him at the lodge. He also looked forward to having a working schedule of four days in the lodge, followed by four days away from work. He then reflected that he had not had any days away from work since he began employment at the company. He also reflected that he had enjoyed the work and also had a very good relationship with his colleagues in the security lodge. It was a cold morning, but a brisk walk to work heated up his body and he soon entered the security lodge.

He was greeted by both guards spluttering germs, as they sneezed in unison. The room was stifling and the radiator was still working overtime, blasting out heat. Judas did his chores and stayed out of the way of the guards. The day guards arrived on site within minutes of each other and both were still suffering from very severe colds. The security handover was non-existent. Judas wished the departing guards a relaxing few days away and hoped they would be able to recover their health. Gordon and Richard both smiled and thanked him as they left the lodge. Martin arrived full of enthusiasm for the day ahead.

"Good morning all, let the fun begin," he said before settling down to work.

The guards looked up in complete disbelief and Judas could not help but smile. Martin scanned the vehicle movement sheets and waited for the first delivery and departure. When the work began Judas felt very guilty as he just sat there supervising.

The morning was a long affair and it was very busy. There was an unusually high number of incoming vehicles bringing items to the factory stores and an equally high number of vehicles delivering items to the numerous retail outlets and regional logistics establishments. Martin took everything in his stride and competently and efficiently dealt with the very busy workload.

At ten o'clock, Judas prepared drinks for Martin and the guards, just for something to do. Both guards had been out and each had completed a very quick fence patrol. Keith and Colin were still looking very ill, but they were both soldiering on manfully under the strain of their affliction. However, both guards complained bitterly that it was getting colder and by mid-morning it was snowing. At about ten minutes before noon, the traffic eased and Martin took a well earned break for lunch. Judas took over the duties and was very relieved to be eventually doing some effective work.

After his break Martin was back at the helm of the lodge and continued with the good work he had been performing during the morning. Judas then had lunch. Keith and Colin both did another quick fence patrol during the afternoon and both were relieved that, after this shift, they would be away from the lodge for four whole days. The incoming and outgoing traffic eased by mid afternoon and Judas showed Martin again the monthly returns and statistics. Martin had remembered all that Judas had said yesterday on the subject, but Judas had to be sure that Martin had understood the complexities of the required documentation. Judas then carried on with his duties whilst Martin read and re-read his notes to cement the information into his memory. At five o'clock, Judas again relinquished his seat and went back to his supervising.

After ten minutes, the last delivery vehicles were off site and all company vehicles and vans had returned. Martin then began to outline to Judas the activities of the model railway club to which he belonged.

"I have been involved with my model railway club for a number of years and I have produced a number of layouts. Initially, I was not very good at modelling structures, but I did reasonable layout designs. Members of the club helped me to improve my modelling skills and eventually I was asked to accompany them to an exhibition, but only as an observer.

"I got better at modelling techniques and eventually I produced a layout, with a good standard of structural work and a good operating potential. I have now been exhibiting our various layouts for six years and I have thoroughly enjoyed the atmosphere and the buzz of the exhibition circuit. Our present layout is the best one I have ever designed and built and is of a small country terminus, leading to forestry sidings and a fiddle yard. In fact this is the small, compact layout we shall be exhibiting at Thornton Beamish this weekend and next weekend the layout will be at Cranston Market. I will be accompanied at the exhibitions by two club members, who will assist with the setting up and operating of the layout."

Martin paused for a drink before continuing.

"I really must apologise again for not being able to do any weekend work at the lodge, for the next two weeks, but I have already confirmed with the event organizers that we will attend the exhibition."

Judas could see that Martin was genuinely apologetic.

"Martin do not worry, it presents no problems for me. I honestly wish you and your colleagues a safe journey and I sincerely hope the exhibition goes well for you all."

"Thanks for that," said Martin and then asked Judas, "What type of model railway do you operate?"

"Sorry, but I haven't got one," replied Judas. Martin was completely astonished at this news and was even more astonished to learn that, until recently, Judas had never designed a layout.

Martin regained his composure and said, "You have a superb gift for designing model railway layout plans. I have been shown some of your drawings by Mr Brown and Mr Gibson and they both instinctively knew the designs were absolutely first class."

Judas was embarrassed and stood up to hide his emotions.

At five fifty, the day guards were ready for the handover to Adrian and Roy, the incoming guards, who duly arrived two minutes later. The handover was formal, as Roy was the senior guard and the day guards left after five minutes. Judas wished the departing guards a speedy return to health.

"I hope to see you both fully fit on your return to duty," he said.

He then took Martin over to see Roy and Adrian and formally introduce him to both. The guards welcomed Martin to the team.

"Now Judas will soon be able to have some days off work," said Roy.

After a few minutes of chatter, Martin left the lodge and departed for home. Judas was about to leave the lodge when he remembered that the Poacher's Retreat was to be valued today and the surveying of the site and the building would be taking place. He returned to his desk and telephoned his friend. The receiver was picked up very quickly by Anita and she confirmed that the estate agents and others had been on site and had performed their tasks with patience and enthusiasm.

"They spent a long time investigating the building and the grounds," said Anita," and they seemed content with the information they had. They also indicated that they would check their findings on their return to their offices and write up a report. This report, they said, would be forwarded at the earliest opportunity.

"Stephanie and John were at the property during the inspection and both seemed very happy at the conclusion of the investigations."

"That's great news and a relief for us all," said Judas. The call ended after about five minutes of friendly chatter and Judas was very pleased that everything was progressing well for Anita. She seemed very happy at the end of the telephone call. Judas stayed for a few minutes and wished Adrian and Roy a pleasant and peaceful shift. Then he left the heat of the security lodge for the icy conditions outside.

Judas arrived at the Ivy Lodge Guest House and went straight to his room. Amanda had placed his washed clothes on the bed, all neatly ironed and pressed. Judas did a few chores and went downstairs to the kitchen. Stephen was seated on a bar stool, at the centrally raised breakfast table of the well appointed kitchen. He had a cool drink ready as Judas opened the door.

"I was about to call you," said Stephen, as Judas entered, and placed the full glass on the table top. "Mandy will be here in a few moments," continued Stephen as Judas settled down on a stool. "She has only gone out to collect a few items of groceries."

Stephen began to tell Judas of his day's work and Judas responded by telling him of his training Martin. Both men listened intently to the other and were surprised when

Amanda entered the kitchen. Both husband and Judas greeted her and she placed her bag of purchases on the floor and sat with the men.

Judas then thanked Amanda for sorting out his laundry and also for the superb job of ironing it. He then began to thank them both for making his stay at the guest house such a pleasurable experience.

"I will be leaving your lovely guest house on Monday and I will pack my meagre possessions into my case and collect the case on Monday night after my return from work, if that was acceptable?"

Both Stephen and Amanda nodded.

Judas continued "I will be moving into my new residence at Bournebrooke Garden Apartments on Monday night."

Both Stephen and Amanda seemed impressed by the information.

"Would you please put the account into my room and I will present payment by cheque when I collect my case on Monday night."

Judas then began to speak more seriously to them both.

"I saw Simon Lancaster yesterday and Simon said that it was Alan, one of his company men, that had done the drawings for the proposed extensions of the bedrooms and the tea rooms at the Ivy Lodge Guest House."

Both Amanda and Stephen looked at each other and then looked back at Judas and nodded.

Judas could feel their unease and continued, "Please, there is nothing to worry about. I would just love to see the drawings of the proposed extension, as you have told me so much about it."

Judas could see the relief in their faces and Amanda again nodded and left the room. Judas continued with his drink. After a few moments, Amanda returned and placed the drawings onto the breakfast table. The drawings were opened and Judas could see that Alan was a very fine draughtsman. The plans were very neat and showed the extensive alterations required to convert the six unused bedrooms into four bedrooms with adjoining en-suite bathrooms. The tearoom was to be created by utilising two large store rooms at the side of the guest house and extending them rearwards with a separate kitchen and baking area solely for its use. Fitted tables had been shown on the plans for the customers and the seating was for twenty four persons. Amanda then spoke.

"It is our earnest desire to open up the guest house to its full potential, with another four large bedrooms with en-suites and also to provide the local community with a pleasing tea room. I just know that it is what is wanted locally and we are certain it would be a great success.

"Our banks both declined us a loan, even though we had saved over a quarter of the money required for the extension. These bankers then suggested that if there was an appreciable upturn in the economy, then the banks might possibly reconsider their position."

Amanda practically spat out the end of the sentence and Judas inwardly smiled. Judas now realized that both people genuinely believed that they could have a much better guest house and a much better future if they could develop the property to its former grandeur. Judas also realized that although their dreams had been dashed, their enthusiasm was still high, but their expectations of achieving their dream were floundering in a turbulent sea of doubt and uncertainty. However, they soldiered on, hoping for a miracle cure to their problem.

Judas retired to his room and put on his jacket and overcoat. He then went out into the very cold and icy wind and made his way to the sales caravan in front of the tower blocks. He was relieved to see Jennifer with her colleague and went into the caravan. Jennifer was surprised to see him, but greeted him with pleasure.

"I have here the access swipe cards for your apartment and also the code numbers for your digit box entry system." She handed over a small brown envelope. "Would you sign here please to acknowledge receipt?"

Judas read the paper, signed in the appropriate place and handed back the sheet to Jennifer.

Jennifer then continued, "Earlier today, a lady telephoned to say that she and her husband would be delivering some containers tomorrow, housing some of your equipment and belongings and also some bookcases, and asked in which room they were to be stored. I gave her the information and she indicated that they would be here in the morning. Therefore, as the cleaning of your apartment has already been completed, if you want to get the items to your rooms tomorrow, you can. In this caravan we have a set of sack wheels you can borrow to get your bookcases into the elevator and wheel them to your apartment."

"That lady was Juliette," said Judas, "and she was my cleaner at my old address and will continue to do sterling work here." Judas thought for a moment and then continued, "Jennifer, would you please allow Juliette access to my apartment, as she will wish to view the rooms, to get an idea of what will be involved and the financial consideration she will be able to calculate."

Jennifer willingly agreed and then gave Judas the room number where the items would be stored and he was relieved to discover that it was very close to the elevator.

Then, on impulse, Judas said he would like to go to his apartment and Jennifer just nodded and smiled. He made his way past the elevator and walked up the five flights of stairs. He then used his new swipe card and access code to gain entry to his new apartment. It looked better than ever, absolutely perfect, and he marvelled at his good fortune at being allowed such a beautiful home. He wandered into every room and was filled with pride and happiness. He simply could not believe it. He determined that tomorrow he would bring his containers up from the ground floor room and deposit them roughly where he wanted them to go.

Judas then looked out of the windows. He could see that it was still icy and he could hear the wind howling. He looked towards the coast, but could see no lights on land although he could see two lights on a ship at sea. He looked inland and could see numerous street lights and well lit residences, but there seemed to be only nominal vehicular activity. He next looked over the nature reserve and this seemed to be in Stygian darkness. Judas then reflected that he had only ever seen his apartment during the evenings and he had never seen any of the views from his windows during daylight. He definitely hoped that Anita's opinion of his outlook would be shared by him.

Judas left his apartment, secured the door and walked down the stairs and exited the building. He was going to enter the sales office, but saw that Jennifer was on a telephone call, so he just waved and received an acknowledging wave in return. He walked briskly back to his room at the guest house.

CHAPTER 18

Saturday 10th January

Judas put a few items into his large suitcase before leaving the guest house and placed other requirements into his small work case. He made a quick scan of his room and quietly left the building. On his walk to work, he began to think about his apartment and then he thought about the numerous crates being delivered by Juliette and Andrew during the day. He also knew that he would have the dubious pleasure of transporting them all up to his new home.

Judas entered the lodge and was again met by a wall of very hot air. It was absolutely stifling and Judas began to cough and clear his throat. He quickly performed his chores and went to his desk. He searched for the sheet showing the vehicle movements in and out of the factory, but could not find it.

He queried the absence of the papers with Roy, who simply answered, "No papers were left on the reception desk for collection by the guards."

Before the festive break there were never any deliveries or collections made by company vehicles on a weekend, but now the factory was working a seven day week, Judas expected Saturdays and Sundays to be the same as normal work days. His telephone then rang and he transferred the caller to his required extension. He then remembered that the reception staff were only in on weekends during office hours and he would have the telephone transferred to him until eight thirty. The day guards arrived and, after a routine handover, Adrian and Roy departed just after six o'clock.

John and Geoff both seemed to have recovered from their illness and both again thanked Judas for the security work he had performed on their behalf, during their period of inactivity.

"No problem," said Judas, "pleased to be of service."

Geoff left the lodge on patrol and John continued with his clerical work. From his time of arrival to the transfer of the telephones to the receptionist, Judas dealt with four calls, all for the design bureau. It was after he had been contacted by a sleepy sounding receptionist, saying she was taking back the switchboard, that Judas suddenly realized that he still had the box of original papers from Adam's room in his small case. When he had transferred the switchboard, he retrieved the box. Underneath the box he saw the original book from Adam that he had found in the old garden shed at the orphanage. It was at this point that Judas realized that, in this small case, he was carrying all of the information he had from Adam concerning the railway extension and also all of the notes Adam had written on the lost plate. The revelation frightened him.

Judas resolved there and then to photocopy all of the information he was carrying and, when in his apartment tonight, he would put the original documents into his study safe for the sake of security. Judas began this task of duplicating his records and was relieved that he had completed the task without interruption by any incoming or outgoing vehicles. He placed all of the duplicated records into transparent sheets and put them all into a folder. Then he returned the original papers and the book from Adam to the box and put the box and his folder into his small case. As he closed the case the telephone rang.

It was the receptionist, who said, "I am ill, coughing and sneezing and suffering from some sort of bug and I am going home. The telephone system is being transferred to you as of now. However, one of the other office girls will take over the reception duties in about an hour, but she is on an urgent job at the moment. Is this okay?"

Judas took a deep breath and said, "Okay, no problems. Go home and keep warm and hopefully you will soon be your normal self." Judas then had a thought and continued, "While you are on the line, can you please check to see if any vehicle movement sheets have been left out for us?"

Judas could hear the girl opening drawers and eventually she said, "Yes, I have it here. I will bring it over as I go to my car. Sorry for not leaving the sheet out for collection by the guards, but I really wasn't very well yesterday. Anyway thanks for taking on the reception work."

As promised the receptionist delivered the required paperwork to Judas and he could see that the girl was definitely unwell. He scanned the sheet and was dismayed to see that there were eight outgoing deliveries scheduled for the company vans and eight incoming vehicles bringing in stores to the workshops. As the girl drove out of the car park the first delivery vehicle arrived.

For the next two hours Judas was very busy with telephone calls and incoming and outgoing vehicle movements. At eleven o'clock the relief receptionist telephoned and apologised profusely to Judas for not relieving him from the switchboard duty at the due time. Other work problems in the Accounts Section were harder to sort out than originally thought and had taken up too much time complained the new girl. Judas was pleased that the reception duties had been taken off him and he could now concentrate solely on the vehicular movements into and out of the site.

The security guards were very enthusiastic doing their duties, both internal and external and Judas initially put this down to guilt, for them not doing the required patrols when they were ill. However, he dismissed this thought when John arrived from the works canteen with hot sausage rolls, cakes, chocolate bars and two large steaming cartons of coffee for himself and for Geoff. Judas just smiled, as the guards devoured their lunches brought from home and then began on the canteen's supplement.

At one o'clock, Henry Brown and Paul Gibson entered the lodge.

The senior man said, "We are both going to attend the model railway exhibition being held in the town of Thornton Beamish to see how our publicity stand is coping. It was a last minute attendance for Beaufort Models, as the local model shop, which should have attended the show, has ceased trading, due to the sudden death of its owner.

"If the information stand and sales kiosk, which were speedily prepared for the show, are a success, then the company will consider attending future exhibitions. Next time, however, assuming the board members agree to continue exhibiting, they will have the time to prepare a professional trade display stand of our company products and also they will have a large selection of information books and model items available for purchase at the model exhibition venue."

As they left the lodge, Henry Brown said, "We will not be back on site again today, but we will both be here very early in the morning. We are travelling to the exhibition in my car and Paul's car is being left on site overnight."

As they departed the car park, Judas began his lunch. During the afternoon the guards kept up their patrols and on each occasion of an internal patrol, the incoming guard was well stocked with canteen provisions.

By three o'clock, all of the incoming and outgoing vehicle movements had been completed and Judas took a well earned break. The guards also seemed to be taking a break from patrols, as it had started to rain and puddles were forming in the car park. Dark clouds were gathering and this added to the gloom of the afternoon. The car park lights flickered on and Judas could see from the number of vehicles that the afternoon and evening shift was fully staffed. Judas was reluctant to do some of the month-end work, as he wanted Martin to see how and from where the figures were obtained. Therefore, he telephoned Anita, but when the voice mail cut in, he put the instrument back into its cradle. He next telephoned Jennifer and asked if the crates had been delivered by Juliette and Andrew and was relieved to hear that they had.

"That's great news," said Judas. "Now when I get there tonight I can get them upstairs and into my new abode."

"Well, actually," continued Jennifer, "I have some people here at the moment doing various clearing up jobs ready for the official opening of the tower. Would you like me to get them to take the crates up to your apartment and just leave them in the hallway? I do still have a master access card and I do know the code. I will also get them to put the bookcases just inside the door of your study."

"Absolutely, I was really looking forward to lugging my humble possessions up to my rooms, but you have deprived me of that pleasure," joked a relieved Judas.

Out of politeness Jennifer chuckled. Judas was a little concerned that Jennifer could still get into his new home, but he then reflected that it was a security requirement and he did trust her implicitly.

Jennifer then confirmed that Juliette and Andrew had been into his new apartment.

"Both commented very favourably on your selection of a wonderful new home. They also congratulated you on your taste of furniture and they were very impressed with the views that you have out of your windows, seaward, inland and over the nature sanctuary," said Jennifer. "By the way, Juliette gave me an envelope for you and you can collect it at anytime from the sales office. If I am not on duty, one of the other girls will know where it has been placed for safe keeping."

Judas thanked her and said he would collect the envelope tonight. He surmised that it was the figure Juliette would charge to continue his cleaning duties.

At four o'clock, the relief receptionist contacted Judas and asked him if she could transfer the switchboard to him thereby allowing her to return to an urgent problem in the Accounts Section. Judas was pleased to be able to do something and readily agreed.

The girl then added, "In the morning I will be back on the reception duties and this may be for the whole day."

The numerous telephone calls kept Judas fairly busy for the remainder of his shift and he was relieved to see Adrian and Roy enter the lodge just before six o'clock. The guards did the necessary transfer and the day guards left the lodge. After a few minutes, Judas also left the lodge.

The walk back to the Ivy Lodge Guest House was a fairly miserable affair. It was raining and water was running down his neck. He was pleased that he was wearing gloves and a scarf, but he was still very cold. After what seemed an eternity, Beaufort St. Catherine came into view through the gloom. Judas walked quickly to the guest house and seeing nothing of his hosts, he went straight to his room. After fifteen minutes, he left and had a brisk walk to his new apartment.

He looked into the sales office, but could not see Jennifer, so he walked to the entrance of his tower block and walked up the stairs. He entered his apartment, using the swipe card and the security code, and was still trying to come to terms with his good fortune. He saw all of the crates had been neatly stacked, in four blocks, on the hall floor and he took out his notebook to check that none of the crates were missing. The tally was correct. His first task, however, was to place the small box taken from Adam's room into his upstairs study safe and, on completion of this task, Judas felt relieved.

Whilst in the study area, he placed his various sized bookcases and computer table along the walls of the room furthest from the balcony. In the other study room were the computer table and bookcases donated by the developers. For the next two hours, he laboured putting his meagre possessions onto tables and into the various cupboards, wardrobes, dressing tables, bedside cabinets, bathroom cabinets, kitchen cupboards, study bookcases, hall cabinet and also filling up a few other places.

He was half way through the task of unloading the crates, when he surmised that for a person with meagre possessions, he had a lot of goods! He inwardly smiled as he saw on his breakfast bar, prominently displayed, his tin mug, his tin plate and his tin bowl. The items reminded him of the orphanage and of his origins. He was very pleased with his evening's work and he looked around his new domain with glowing satisfaction. Judas then decided that he would go to the sales office and get the envelope Juliette had left for him and he exited his apartment and walked down the stairs.

Jennifer was sitting at her desk and warmly greeted Judas as he arrived.

Judas replied, "Many thanks for arranging to get the numerous crates into my new home. It is very much appreciated."

Jennifer just smiled and then handed Judas the envelope. After a few minutes of idle chatter, Judas left the sales office and went to the arcade to stock up on some food items for the security lodge. Judas returned towards the guest house and, on passing a newsagent's, he saw in the display window a small book outlining the historical development of Beaufort St. Catherine. He purchased a copy. On reaching his lodgings, Judas entered and was pleased to hear his hosts in the kitchen. He silently went to his room and placed his shopping into his case. He then returned downstairs. He reflected that the next few minutes might be very difficult, for both himself and his hosts.

He entered the kitchen and was warmly greeted by Amanda.

"You must have heard the kettle boiling."

"I honestly didn't hear the whistling of the kettle, but if I had, I would have been here sooner," said Judas. "Is Stephen anywhere around?"

Amanda advised that he would be back in a moment, when he had fetched something from his shed.

"At the moment the shed seems to be his second home," said Amanda as Stephen entered the kitchen. Amanda placed a hot mug of tea for Stephen and a cool drink for Judas onto the breakfast bar and pulled up a stool to join them. After the chatter about the day's events, the conversation stalled and Judas saw his opportunity to begin his difficult talk. Judas began and quickly got into a good rhythm.

"I know from your good selves," he said, "that plans have been drawn up for the guest house extension, but various banks declined to advance a loan to cover the building expenses. You showed me the plans and they are very comprehensive and show your dreams perfectly." Judas saw both smile and nod and he continued. "I also have been in contact with Simon Lancaster on an entirely different matter and, through very good fortune, my outcome has been very successful. Simon and his wife Helen are very dear friends of mine and I have known them for many years. In fact, it was

Simon's company that I engaged to draw up the architectural plans for my last property, to convert it back into a guest house from a simple residential dwelling. Circumstances changed and this good fortune is the reason I am here at your guest house, waiting to go into my brand new apartment in the town."

Judas could see he had a captive audience and decided to put meat onto the bone and into the conversation.

"You are both hardworking and honourable people and you deserve the opportunity to follow your dream and reach the end of your rainbow. Would you therefore allow me to provide the funds to fulfil your dreams and to extend the guest house and to provide a tea shop? I can draw up an agreement for repayment and you can take it to your lawyer to put it into legal jargon, but, as I am not a licensed usurer, no interest will be charged. You will have the first year, from the completion of the building work, completely free of repayment and after that repayment can begin. The figure of the monthly repayment will have to be agreed between us."

Judas stopped talking to take a few breaths and to take a drink from his tankard and he then looked up at his hosts. Both Stephen and Amanda looked shocked and said nothing for a few seconds. They both looked at each other and it was Stephen who spoke first.

He simply asked, "Why?"

"Many years ago, when I was at an orphanage," began Judas, "the handyman was a person called Adam. He was a wonderful man and the children of the orphanage absolutely enjoyed being with him. We all willingly worked the chores and labours that he gave us and afterwards we listened to the wonderful stories that he told. His working life was spent on the railway and he was employed as a signalman. His wife and daughters were killed in the war and, on retirement from the railways, he dedicated his life to the orphanage as a gardener and handyman. When he died, life was unbearable at the orphanage, as the only human light in the establishment had been extinguished.

"Adam instilled in me the belief that if a job was worth doing, it was worth doing not just well, but exceptionally well. He also instilled in me the fact that money is not to be squandered, but put to good use. His wife apparently said that 'Money was made round to go round, not made flat to stack'. I have been fortunate and I have the capital available, but it is only in a bank and, if you need it, then it can be made available for you. As I said earlier, I have seen the plans and I think I know how much extra cash you need to complete your extension and the tea room. If you wish to contact your lawyers and discuss the proposition with them, I will fully understand. I will willingly write out the things I have said, so that, if you wish to proceed, the lawyer can provide you with a legal, watertight agreement, which I will be pleased to sign."

Judas sat back on his chair and his hosts just sat there.

"One more thing," continued Judas. "If we go ahead, no mention of the transaction must be made public. The agreement will be between us and your lawyer. Also, if in future I enter your tea room, or stay at your guest house, I am not to receive any preferential treatment or waving of any charges. That is no way to run a business."

Judas could see that both Stephen and Amanda were still in shock.

"I know I've given you a lot to think about, so I'll give you some time to mull it all over."

He finished his drink and retired to his room. At this point Judas decided he needed nourishment and he opened a packet of biscuits. He then wrote himself a note to remind him to notify various companies and others of his new address for future correspondence and he also jotted down the essential points of his recent proposition with his hosts.

It was still early and, in an attempt to stop himself worrying about the evening's events, Judas decided to relax by drawing out another layout plan. He hadn't thought out many recently and decided to try out one of his more successful designs with an L-shaped layout. He doodled around for about half an hour and, when satisfied with the rough sketch, he extracted the miniature track segments and constructed the layout to make sure the track geometry would work. It did work and he was relieved. He then attempted to design a medium sized terminus, in an "Out and back" configuration and it was only after an hour's toil that he was finally satisfied with his labours. He drew both of the layouts onto graph paper and entered the item code of the track next to the corresponding part of the diagram. Lastly, he packed the used miniature track segments flat into his case, separated by a large towel and both layout representations weighed down by folders to prevent movement. Satisfied with his efforts he was about to retire for the night, when he remembered the book he had purchased earlier. However, he was very tired and he resolved to read it tomorrow.

CHAPTER 19

Sunday 11th January

It was a strange night for Judas. He lay in bed worrying about the evening's events. He was pleased that he had spoken to his hosts about the guest house extension and the tea room, but their reaction to his proposal worried him. He was hopeful that it was only the suddenness of the proposal that had taken them by surprise, rather than outright indignation at the suggestion. However, he eventually fell asleep and woke up startled by the alarm. He quickly prepared himself for the day and departed the guest house for work.

After a successful battle against the blustery elements, Judas reached the sanctuary of the lodge and greeted Adrian and Roy. Both guards were eagerly awaiting the arrival of John and Geoff. After the usual banter, Judas placed some biscuits into the cupboard and went to his desk. He saw the vehicle sheet by the telephone and was surprised to see only four departures from the site to inland distribution centres and no incoming vehicles. He was even more surprised when Adrian advised him that two of the vans had already left the site and passed him a note showing the vehicle numbers and times of departure. Judas wrote down the information onto the sheet and, as he finished writing, the other two vehicles departed the site. Judas knew that it was going to be a long day, with very little to do except the early reception work and the expected calls would only be from wives to husbands etcetera in the factory.

The guards quickly completed their paperwork and Geoff exited the lodge to do an external fence patrol. John sat at his desk, surveying the camera screens and munching a biscuit.

Judas therefore typed on his computer screen various letters to the utilities, confirming his date of ownership of the apartment and printing the documents. He also wrote to other organizations giving similar details. He then prepared envelopes for the information to be sent and applied postage stamps. Next he took the miniature track segments of the two layouts he had designed last night from his case and carefully opened out the towel. Both had survived the trip into work and Judas took them to the photocopier to obtain prints and also copied his graph paperwork. He placed the paperwork on his desk and, after a few minutes, he had completed the filing. He then extracted from his case the recently purchased information book, relating to the development of his new village home.

The book was very informative. It contained a host of information on the development of the village, including copies of early maps of the local area. It also showed, on these maps, various areas of land that had been reclaimed from the sea. Numerous influential and prominent individuals had passed through the settlement, according to book, but the only prominent persons that had resided in the village were the two Beaufort's, after whom the settlement was named. There was, however, one piece of information that he was happy to read and this simply stated that "Roman vessels were known to skirt along the very treacherous coast and to frequent the area." This proved that Adam's information was correct, although this was the only published confirmation Judas had ever seen to confirm this event.

On completion of this task, he extracted from his case the notes he had photocopied from Adam's originals and tried to read them. He recalled the day he had been into Adam's old garden shed and found the papers and he again thought of his old friend. He put these hurtful and negative thoughts to the back of his mind and he pressed on with his task. He practically knew the information by heart, but he hoped and prayed that he would discover something that he had missed earlier or have some inspired revelation whilst reading. He forced himself to continue and he re-read Adam's neat writing.

BACKGROUND

1   A small inland abbey, built in 1302, on solid foundations, still thrives in the local Christian community. Much of the building was destroyed at the time of the reformation but the remains of the abbey now serves as the parish church and the clergy is well respected.

His brain was in turmoil as he continued to read the script, but he forced himself to go on. Half way through Judas was relieved to receive a telephone call, but the caller only wanted to leave a message on a voice mail and was put through to the required extension.

Finally, Judas could see the end of the background notes from Adam, but so far he had not furthered his knowledge on the subject. He ploughed on and was relieved to reach the last piece of information on the list.

37   The Abbot made copies of the information onto parchment and placed some of these in the abbey library archives. When the Abbot died suddenly the cross was buried with him.

When he had finished reading, Judas knew he had gained no new information from this task and he put the folder down. However, a few moments later, he thought about what Adam had discovered concerning Roman vessels skirting along the very treacherous coast and frequenting the area. This, Judas decided, was important and he added this information at the end of Adam's list.

Geoff returned to the lodge from his patrol and, after a few moments, John went into the office complex to do an internal check of the premises. Judas suddenly remembered the envelope in his pocket from Juliette and he opened it. It was the information concerning his apartment cleaning and the figure quoted for continuing to look after his property was less than he thought it would be. Judas was very pleased and he returned to his file.

Judas was about to look at the next set of notes, when two delivery vehicles returned to the site and, after a cheery wave, the drivers parked the vans in the compound. Judas completed the entries in the folder and was about to return to his reading when he realized that he had not received any confirmation from the receptionist of her arrival. He pressed the telephone intercom button and the receptionist answered after a few seconds.

"Oh Christ," she croaked, "my profuse apologies for not informing you of my arrival. Please transfer the switchboard over to me. Sorry again."

Judas obliged and said, "If you have still got the urgent work to complete from yesterday, then I will be pleased to continue with the telephones."

The girl declined the offer, as the urgent work was now completed.

Judas continued reading the notes, but these failed to make any impression on his brain and, after a few minutes of uneventful research, Judas filed his papers. As he did so, he saw the layout plans and the information he had on the Beaufort St. Clement station prior to its destruction in the raging storm. Judas extracted these and he also took out the enlarged photocopies of the photographs that had so enthralled Henry Brown, Paul Gibson, the MD and the Board Members. Judas inwardly chuckled as he recalled the surprise on the faces of Henry Brown and Paul Gibson, as they discovered the information and saw the unknown photographs for the first time. Judas looked quickly at the information, but it did not help with the mediaeval problem at hand.

Judas then continued with his reading and extracted the plans of the proposed railway line from the Beaufort St. Vincent harbour extension to the main line. These plans were the next papers in his folder and he did not expect to glean any information from them, but he looked at them anyway. Judas then had a thought. It was a profound thought and he wondered why he had never thought of it before. As these papers were filed by Adam with the notes about the lost abbey artefacts, could they be connected? It was a blind act of faith, but he pursued the notion vigorously. He then recalled how Henry Brown and Paul Gibson were both spellbound and speechless when he showed them the drawings. He continued looking at the plans and carefully read all of the information written on them.

A to B had no features except the single line.

B to C had a single siding midway along it for agricultural use.

Judas continued reading the notes, although he was getting no feedback from them that he did not already know. This fact disturbed him. He was also disgusted with himself, as he thought he was letting Adam down by not understanding why his old friend had kept these plans. Judas continued and soon reached the final map.

I to J had the line furthest from the harbour complex being doubled to give access to the rest of the railway system.

Large scale map showing the single line being doubled to allow access to and from the main lines of the rail network.

Under the final map of the proposed rail network, there was a photocopy of an additional map dated 1784, but there was no indication of its location. The map itself had no connection to the above railway line, although it did show a small settlement and it did have a coastline. The map was a very faint photocopy.

Judas scanned the maps and drawings but there was absolutely nothing that jumped out at him that could be classed as unusual. He went over the maps and drawings again, this time with a magnifying glass, but again with no striking revelation. He studied the coastline on the maps very intently, but there was absolutely nothing that seemed out of place. Judas began to despair, but he then thought again of Adam and concentrated even harder.

His next task was to read all of the fourteen photocopied sheets of Adam's second note book. These sheets contained the six pages of text written by an unknown and undecipherable hand. There were also two pages of rough diagrams of an unknown area that included roads and rivers and were also written by the unknown hand. The final six pages were written by Adam and appeared to be his attempt to decipher the unknown and difficult script.

Following this, Judas forced himself to read the personal notes of Adam, relating to his uncle, Albert Stonehaven.

Recent Knowledge

A   *In the late Victorian age, a highly respected historian and researcher was given permission to inspect the abbey library sources concerning the slaughter and ransacking of the church and coastal settlement.*

B   *In his research the historian came across four copies of a paper showing a cross with unusual writing and markings on it. In the index of the library only three copies were listed. The researcher therefore kept one copy. All copies were checked and were found to be identical.*

Judas was still getting no feedback from the text, but he dutifully continued reading and was pleased when he neared the end.

F   *The drawing was very informative, but nothing fits. Rivers, hills, settlements and the coastline are in the wrong places.*

G   *Great Uncle Albert once told me that he believed the symbols related to the church slaughter and to the location of the church plate.*

The next section of paperwork Judas came to brought him up with a jolt. It was his own outline of the life of his friend,

Adam, and he had written it many years ago. The notes also contained copies of the list of Adam's belongings at the time of his death. Judas had been asked to do this duty by the head lady at the orphanage. He sorted out the requirements of the orphanage and he kept a copy of the list for himself. He re-read the paperwork and it brought back many pleasant memories of a wonderful man, but it also gave him great pain as he still felt the loss of his only true, male friend.

Notes on Adam

1   *Adam was a signalman at the station of Beaufort St. Vincent.*

2   *His wife and both daughters had been killed during the war when a lone enemy bomber had been hit by anti-aircraft fire and crashed into a group of railway properties.*

3   *On retirement, Adam came to the orphanage and was a great asset to the establishment.*

4   *He told the children stories, including the treasure stories, but left out the many gory details.*

5   *These stories were wonderful for the children, especially for me, and I always seemed to be more attentive than anyone else.*

6   *Adam the handyman died at the age of 88, having spent 23 years at the orphanage.*

The next papers were a list of the belongings of Adam, found in his room at the time of his death. Judas began to read, but had to stop. He just couldn't do it and he filed the notes. He comforted himself with the knowledge that these notes were private and added no pertinent information to his present investigations. However, he had to put the folder onto his desk and walk away. After a few minutes he returned and continued.

The next papers to read were photocopies of a printed map of the local area and also photocopies of the street layouts of Beaufort St. Clement, Beaufort St. Catherine and Beaufort St. Vincent. The original book of street plans only had these three places in it. The other sheets were never seen by Judas. The information was for the early nineteenth century and the original map and remnants of the book had belonged to Adam. Judas had not included it on the list as he thought it would not be missed and he just wanted something as a keepsake. Judas had thumbed through it many years ago and had seen that some areas had been marked by someone, but he did not know the identity of the originator. He decided he would have another look at the sheets, but first he went to the kitchen area for a drink.

As both guards were in the lodge, Judas prepared a hot drink for them and placed it on their desk and received thanks from both. Judas was feeling very guilty, as very little work for the company was being done by him and over half of the morning had gone already. However, there was very little work he could do and if he did anything, then it would deprive Martin of the experience in the morning.

"Are you guys now fighting fit?" asked Judas and the guards both nodded as they were busy eating. Judas returned to his desk. He was pleased that all the guards were now feeling fit and full of life and not huddling over radiators and trying to keep warm.

At his desk Judas again looked at the sheets showing the street layouts of the three local Beaufort communities. All three showed the old coastline as it would have been in the early nineteenth century. Judas marvelled at how much land had been reclaimed by the early drainage engineers. All of the maps had a line drawn on them and Judas recognised that it was the actual proposed route of the railway. He was about to turn the page, when he noticed that the proposed line from Beaufort St. Vincent to near Beaufort St. Catherine was shown in a different location to the approved plans he had in his possession. This worried him. It worried him even more when he noticed *C ROFT* written in Adam's neat hand on the Beaufort St. Catherine map. He recalled that these were the initials written on the plans of the selected proposed route, which was to have passed further to the west of Beaufort St. Catherine.

The next photocopy was of a surveyor's report and when he had read it, Judas understood why the proposed route had been moved further west from Beaufort St. Catherine, although the line returned to the approved route on the other maps and did not deviate. The western route had firmer foundations and would be safer. However, it didn't explain anything about the initials *C ROFT*. Judas surmised that Henry Brown and Paul Gibson would be amazed at this revelation of the surveyor's report. His mind began to race. He looked in the index of a present day atlas for places beginning with the word Croft that were not too distant. He found only two contenders, Crofters Bridge and Crofton Market. However Crofters Bridge was about twenty miles away and Crofton Market was just over the border and located in the adjoining county. Judas dismissed them both as being too far away.

Judas sat at his desk and stared at the papers and then he had a Eureka moment and chastised himself for being so stupid and blind. He had just noticed something about the initials that he had completely overlooked previously. There was a space between the capital *C* and the capital *R*. The other capitals had no spaces in between. He again looked in the atlas index, this time looking for places beginning with the letters *ROFT* that were not too distant. He was disappointed to find that no-where in the country were there any places beginning with these letters. Judas seemed stumped for a moment, but then reached for the local printed map of the area and scanned it very intently. He looked at it for fifteen minutes, even using a magnifying glass from his drawer, but again could not see any reason for the initials *C ROFT*.

He was in the process of putting the papers away into his case, when he decided to obtain two further photocopies of the Beaufort St. Catherine map and also two copies of the surveyor's report for the rejected route. He would hand these to Henry Brown and to Paul Gibson, the next time that he saw them. He then reflected that they would again be very surprised. As he put the papers away into his case, he again thought of how little actual work he had done for the company and he felt very guilty. However, he could think of nothing to do and, as it was one o'clock, he decided to have his lunch.

John and Geoff were both seated at their desk and both were eagerly devouring their packed lunch from home and both were looking forward to tackling additional food provided by the factory canteen.

Judas joined them and said, "It's good to see you both back to your normal selves, after the colds you suffered recently. Everyone was getting very worried about you."

John looked up.

"We were getting very worried about ourselves. Ye Gods I have never felt that ill before. However, I am now about seventy per cent normal."

Geoff joined in.

"About the same for me. Oh, and thanks again for all your help Judas during our period of inactivity," he said, before asking, "How has your day been? You seem to have been very busy at your desk."

"I don't seem to have done a lot of company work," answered Judas, "as if I did there would not be anything to show Martin on Monday. However, I kept myself active with some bookwork that needed doing. How about you guys, have you been busy?"

John ignored the question and simply asked, "Have you had any time off since you joined the company? Since your arrival you seem to have been a permanent fixture."

"Actually no," replied Judas, "I have not had any days off since I joined the company. As soon as I arrived, the additional security patrols and attendances were implemented to combat the spate of local thefts. However, I will be away on the 19th of January for four days and I am really looking forward to the break from work."

After the lunch break, Judas telephoned Henry Brown and was about to leave a message on his voice mail, when he answered.

Judas asked, "When you are passing the lodge Mr Brown, would you please call, as I have a couple of additional photocopies for you and also two for Mr Gibson."

Henry Brown seemed to be intrigued at the request and entered the lodge two minutes later. Judas handed him the two sheets of paper and Henry Brown began to read. On completion of reading the surveyor's report, he continued and looked at the map of Beaufort St. Catherine, showing the initial route of the line, further to the east of the actual selected proposed route.

Henry Brown, at the conclusion of reading both of the papers, just looked at Judas and then reached out for the telephone and called Paul Gibson, requesting him to see him in the security lodge.

As he replaced the receiver, Henry Brown smiled and said, "Adam's work again I suppose?" and Judas just smiled.

"I only have photocopies of the surveyor's report, but I do have Adam's original map showing the route, but I am not certain if it was drawn by Adam."

Paul Gibson then entered the lodge. Without ceremony Henry Brown handed the photocopies to him and waited for his reaction.

Eventually he said, "Ye Gods. Where on earth did you get this? Is it genuine?"

"I got it from Adam and I honestly believe it to be genuine," said Judas and continued, "Adam was a very devout Christian, as I told you once before, and a very honourable person and I am sure he would never do anything that was dubious."

Both men sat at the desk and Judas was left standing.

Judas then said, "The copies are yours, that is, if you want them."

Henry Brown looked up.

"Want them? God yes. It will stop me from begging for them. I will have to let the MD have a copy and he will be as chuffed as hell."

With that, Judas went to the photocopier and duplicated the two documents and presented them to Henry Brown. It was then that Paul Gibson saw the two track plans and picked them up. After a few moments he looked up at Judas.

"Yours, I presume?"

Judas nodded as the plans were passed to Henry Brown, who just looked at them and smiled.

"Can I have copies of each please?" he said eventually and Judas went to the photocopier and produced copies of the required paperwork and gave copies to both men. After a few minutes, both men returned to the main building and Judas returned to his desk.

Judas then turned to the local printed map and again used his magnifying glass on the sheet, but this did not help. He next pulled out from his drawer a modern ordnance survey map and looked at the local area, but again could not discover any reason for the initials *C ROFT*. Judas decided to give himself a break from this task and he began to put the photocopies of the local printed map and the photocopies of the street layouts for the three local settlements back into his folder. Whilst in the process of this filing exercise Judas noticed a photocopy of the cover of the original book of street plans. Underneath this cover was another photocopy, this time of the symbols used for the land features on the maps. Judas quickly scanned the information and was intrigued by the amount and diversity of the information it gave. He was about to put all of the paperwork into order, when his eyes became glued to the page. In black and white and underlined in faint pencil, were the important entries Judas was looking for. He could hardly believe his eyes as he read in the index:-

RO Roman

FT Fort

Judas could not believe his luck. His being meticulous had paid off handsomely this time and he was so relieved. However, there was no mention in the index for *C*, although Judas did know that in the Roman world *C* meant century or centurion. Judas was very relieved to have discovered some information given by Adam, but he decided that he had done enough research during the day and put his papers away. He also realized that he was getting tired. It was only just past four o'clock and the darkness was practically complete. Hopefully, he could do some more work tomorrow on this riveting subject.

For the remainder of the shift, Judas read the duty notes he had given to Martin, just to make sure he had covered every aspect of his duties and, having confirmed that the paperwork was correct, he put the folder back onto his desk. He then wondered how Martin and his club members had fared at the model railway exhibition, but he knew that tomorrow he would get the information first hand. He then turned his attention to Stephen and Amanda at the Ivy Lodge Guest House and he hoped that they would give him a decision tonight concerning the monetary proposition.

At ten minutes to six, Adrian and Roy entered the lodge to take over the guarding duties and, after a fairly quick handover, the day guards departed the building. It was pitch black outside and the car park lights were barely illuminating the vehicles. Judas could see from the puddles that it had been raining and he suddenly realized that he hadn't noticed it, as he had been so intent on researching his project. Adrian and Roy were busy dealing with their report book entries and

Judas tidied up his desk, filed away his paperwork and locked his cabinets.

As he left the lodge he said to the guards, "Have a very peaceful evening," and they both nodded.

On arrival at the Ivy Lodge Guest House Judas went straight into the hall. Inside it was a different world, warm and welcoming. Judas was about to go upstairs to his room, when Amanda invited him into the kitchen for a drink. Amanda prepared herself a mug of steaming tea.

"It will keep the inner person lubricated and warm and I'm sure it is the nectar of the gods," she said as Judas sat down.

His glass was placed on the table and Amanda sat opposite Judas with her drink and began to speak.

"Yesterday you spoke to me and Steve about our plans for this guest house and made certain proposals concerning money. Sorry if we seemed distant, but it was a lot to take in and, in all honesty, we were a bit shell shocked. The banks had rejected our request for a loan and we thought that our plans were doomed to failure. However, we kept our dream alive and we kept working on our ambition, but it seemed to be a case of a slowly disappearing dream."

Amanda paused to take a breath and to build herself up for the next sentence, but before she could continue the rear door opened and in walked Stephen. He wasn't expecting to see Judas and he seemed flummoxed for a moment.

"Oh hello," he said eventually, "I wasn't expecting to see you."

Amanda then spoke to her husband.

"I've just been telling Judas that last night we were a bit shell shocked at the information he gave us and we had difficulty taking it all in."

By this time Stephen had regained his composure.

"After the banks slaughtered our dreams, we kept believing," he said, "but it was getting harder and harder to keep the faith. But we kept dreaming."

Looking seriously at Judas, Amanda then asked, "What you said last night, were you serious?"

"Completely serious," said Judas, "The money is there if you want it. The repayment figure will only be the loan with no interest and repayment will begin one year after the completion of the building work. The repayment figure to be agreed between us. Your lawyer can draw up the agreement to make it legal and watertight."

Judas could see that his hosts were still in shock and yet they also seemed relieved that they could now go forward to develop their business and provide themselves with a more profitable future.

Amanda said, "My prayers have been answered, God bless you," and she had tears rolling down her face.

Stephen put his arm around his wife and nodded to Judas. Judas nodded in return, finished his drink and went to his room.

Waiting for him on his bed was an envelope containing his account from the guest house. Included in it was a short note from Amanda advising Judas to leave any items requiring washing on his chair in the morning and he could collect it at night when he returned for his case. After a few minutes, he changed and did a few chores. He left the guest house and walked to his new apartment and began unloading the remainder of the crates. Eventually, all of the items were placed in their correct location and hidden away in drawers, cabinets and wardrobes or placed on shelves. After about two hours, Judas had completed his task and stacked the empty crates against his study wall. It gave him a deep glow of satisfaction to know that tomorrow night he would collect his case from the guest house, enter his apartment, raise the drawbridge and settle into his own private castle.

On his way back to the guest house, he called into the sales office and was pleased to see Jennifer. It had been a slack afternoon for her and she was reading a book. She looked up and was pleased to see Judas.

"Hello Judas, good to see you again. Do you still like the apartment?"

Judas smiled and nodded.

"I just called in to thank you for all your help during the past couple of hectic weeks. I have just taken two nights to unload all of the crates and tomorrow night I officially move in. I really am looking forward to living here, although I have never seen out of the windows during daylight. Anita tells me the views are spectacular."

"The good lady is not wrong," said Jennifer and added, "Every time I go on the upper levels, to show people around the building, I always look out at the panoramic view and hope that one day I will be able to live in a place with such a view. All I have to do is marry a millionaire!"

Both Judas and Jennifer laughed.

Jennifer then said, "If the crates are empty, do you want them brought down from your rooms?"

For a moment Judas was stumped.

Eventually he said, "Yes please, but unfortunately I have no-where to put them, so I suppose they will have to go on one of my parking spots."

"If you don't want them I can get them taken back to our main stores," said Jennifer. "We are always having to beg, borrow or steal crates to carry our sales literature and equipment for the times we have to go onto new sites to set up sales offices, so it would help us if we could have them."

Judas readily agreed and again thanked Jennifer for her help. After a few minutes of idle chatter with Jennifer, Judas returned to the guest house. He saw nothing of his hosts and went straight to his room. He felt a little peckish and attacked a small packet of biscuits, followed by a drink. Judas then packed his case with the clothes he would not need again whilst at the guest house and prepared himself for an early night. He placed the clothes that required washing onto his chair, as instructed by his host. He felt contented and happy and had a long and deep sleep.

CHAPTER 20

Monday 12th January

As Judas entered the lodge, he was greeted by Roy and Adrian, who were both patiently awaiting the arrival of the day guards. Judas went to his desk, via the kitchen area, and saw that the vehicle list consisted of two full pages. He mused that Martin would have a very busy day ahead. A few moments later, John and Geoff entered the lodge and, after a couple of minutes, the night guards departed. Martin arrived full of enthusiasm and, after greeting the guards and Judas, settled down to his duties at the goods reception desk. Martin also arrived with a slight cold, but was manfully fighting it with pills, peppermints and a refusal to acknowledge that he was in any way ill.

Martin was about to tell Judas of his weekend exhibiting his club's model railway layout at the exhibition in Thornton Beamish, when the first vehicle exited the site and was closely followed by the second. Judas sat back and let Martin do all the work.

"If you need me for anything at all Martin, all you have to do is ask," said Judas.

The morning went very smoothly and Martin was proving very efficient and effective on the lodge work. Judas definitely felt very surplus to requirements, so he took out his notebook and began to write a list of jobs that he had to do once he was installed into his new apartment. The list seemed to be a fairly long one. After a quick read to make certain of his facts, Judas began to write out numerous letters, and was absorbed in the work. On completion of the task, Judas realized that Martin had been working diligently for two hours and had not called for any assistance. Judas was impressed. He then printed out address labels for his envelopes and stamped them ready for posting.

After another ten minutes, there was a complete break in the number of vehicles entering or leaving the complex, and Martin sat back and relaxed. He then outlined to Judas the happenings at the model railway exhibition over the weekend.

"Everything went well for the club and the layout we were operating worked perfectly, with only two minor glitches. There were numerous types of layout at the venue, some had solo operators on the smaller layouts and some had groups of operators on the much larger and more complex layouts. Some layouts were multi level in mountainous scenery and others depicted lowland areas and harbours. Also there were many varieties of the different styles of layouts available. Some were 'tail chasers' and just going around complete circuits of the layout. Some were models of a terminus and others were models of cross country stations, both styles having the associated staging areas or loops. Also, there were a couple of larger displays that were modelled on exact locations of city-sized station complexes. All of the popular gauges of present day railway modelling were on show and all members of our group were very complimentary on the high standard of workmanship on display.

"By the way," continued Martin, "I saw Mr Brown and Mr Gibson at the venue. They were at the stand inherited by Beaufort Models, and were near to the main entrance of the exhibition, and they and the other office staff were doing very good work publicising the vast amount of products the company produce. There was also a company sales stand there, and this was also doing a roaring trade selling company items and taking orders for later shipment to customers. From what I could judge," said Martin, "it was a very successful weekend for the company, considering the short notice the company had been given to produce a sales stand".

After a few minutes, more vehicles began to arrive or exit the complex and Martin returned to his work. Judas then returned to his computer and wrote out the terms he had outlined to Stephen and Amanda for the loan. He would present it to them tonight, so they could give it to their solicitor to prepare a binding legal document. All that had to be agreed was the actual sum to be borrowed and the amount of monthly repayment to be made, beginning one year after the completion of the building work. Judas read the typed list and printed off two copies.

Judas could see that the guards seemed to be back to their normal healthy selves and the patrols seemed to be of the correct duration. Both men, however, were feeling the cold, and Judas decided to prepare a steaming mug of coffee for them and for Martin. Judas mused that it was about the only work that he had done during the day that was associated with the company. However, both guards were grateful for the drink and Martin also nodded his gratitude.

Judas was pondering what work he could do, when the door opened and in walked Henry Brown. After the opening greeting, he placed onto the guards' desk the architects design for the new security building for the guards, which included a section allocated to the goods reception staff. Judas was called over to view the design and, compared to the existing lodge, the replacement building was massive. The section allocated to Judas and Martin for the vehicular activities was slightly larger than the present building and, in addition, specific rooms were allocated for photocopying, for shredding and for the copious volume of filing. The guarding side of the new building, however, had to cope with three guards, both day and night, and was massively larger than the present arrangement. Also, the new design had a larger kitchen area, better welfare facilities and it even had a rest room. Both of the present guards were nodding their approval.

"Judas, would you please photocopy the various plans so John and Geoff can show the incoming guards their proposed new working areas this evening?"

Judas took the pile of papers to the machine but was thwarted, as the ink cartridge needed replacing. Afterwards, he complied, placing the architect's papers in the machine. He produced three copies of the pertinent paperwork, one for his duty, one for himself and the other for the guards, and was about to return to the group, when he saw other papers.

The first showed the relationship of the new security lodge to the main buildings of the Beaufort Models company. The following paper showed the relationship of the whole of the Beaufort Models complex to the town of Beaufort St. Vincent. He photocopied this paperwork and also the next four sheets: two sheets showing the relationship of the town to Beaufort St. Clement and two sheets showing the relationship of the town to Beaufort St. Catherine. He had seen, on the Beaufort St. Catherine sheet, something that puzzled him. It simply stated "Ancient Stone" and its location was indicated by a jagged half circle on the page. During his various evening class courses on geography, he had never seen any indication of this feature on any local map and it puzzled him. He didn't know how or why it puzzled him, but it did, so he photocopied it.

Judas returned to the group and presented the original plans to Henry Brown and gave Geoff the photocopies to show his guarding colleagues this evening. Judas apologised for the delay and gave the reason. Soon afterwards, Henry Brown left the guards, with a parting request.

"Please look at the plans to make sure they fulfil the needs of the security staff. Judas, Martin, will you do the same to make sure your requirements are catered for?"

He then walked over to the reception side of the building and asked Martin, "How is your training progressing? Do you have any problems?" and was very pleased with the reply.

"Everything is going very well and I am enjoying the work immensely."

Judas nodded and added that there were no problems with the training whatsoever. Henry Brown left the lodge, and Judas placed the sheet showing the plan of the new security lodge onto his desk. He then filed his photocopies into his case and he would look at them again later.

It was still early and Judas asked Martin if he had any questions. He was relieved to receive a negative reply. Judas looked at the wall clock. It was only ten o'clock and Judas was again feeling completely surplus. His eyes then fell onto the wall calendar and his brow tightened as he had a serious thought. He wrote down his initials by the dates he would be on duty and then he entered Martin's initials by the dates he would be in attendance. Judas than saw that at the January month end, a Saturday, he would be in the lodge on the first day of his four day rota. Monthly returns would be due on that Saturday and Judas was hoping that Martin would be the person on duty to complete the required documentation. He knew that he had trained Martin on all aspects of the returns, but the first ones were always daunting. He therefore decided to come into the lodge on the Friday afternoon to sit with Martin whilst he wrestled with the statistical exercise. The documentation would be correct as of Friday afternoon and, if anything significant happened on the Saturday to drastically change the figures, Judas would add them in. If only minor amendments would be involved then these figures would be included in the February return.

There was another lull in the lodge and Judas was about to speak to Martin, when the telephone rang. Martin answered it and after a few moments he handed the instrument to Judas, whilst mouthing, "Anita."

After the pleasantries, Anita said, "I have just completed sorting out various items and old records, ready for my move, and I have discovered some more paperwork from Adam. This time, I have a photocopy of a very old map dated 1784, but there is no indication of the map's location. On the reverse of the map, Adam has written down some information that you may like to have. I am going into town this afternoon, so I will bring it to you. Sorry I missed it before."

After a few more moments of idle chatter Anita hung up. Judas was intrigued and baffled. It was unlike Adam to give out to anyone paperwork that he had written on, and it was unlike Anita to overlook anything. However, 1784 was a date that he remembered seeing and he was sure it was one of the papers he already had in his possession. He checked in his file and found the document, although there was nothing written on the reverse of the plan in his possession. He looked at the plan again, but it was very faint and he could not decipher any of the information contained on it. Judas re-filed the sheet into his filing system.

He then looked around the lodge for some company work to do and, not seeing any on his duty, he approached the security staff to see if they had any scrapping or photocopying that required attention. After a few seconds, the grateful guards presented Judas with two sacks of old paperwork that required shredding. Judas retreated to the machine and for the next hour he was busily engaged on this destructive mission. On completion of the task he cleaned and oiled the machine, ready for any future employment. Judas returned to see Martin and was pleased to see that he was coping well with the goods reception work.

Judas took over the work while Martin had his lunch and sat with the guards. He was actually pleased to be sitting at his desk and doing something on his own job rather than chasing around looking for work to do. He was just getting back into the joy of the job, when Martin returned from a quick lunch and Judas was once again made redundant. He therefore collected his packed meal from the kitchen fridge and sat with the guards who were still eating their lunches.

"I wonder when the new staffing arrangements will begin," questioned John, "I really am looking forward to getting another colleague into this working relationship." "Henry Brown didn't give a date for the new staff, but at least the proverbial ball is rolling," countered Geoff.

After a few more minutes of discussion about the new building, the guards returned their attention to the relegation battle of the local football team and how the match at the weekend against the league leaders would be a very difficult game. Judas excused himself from the guards company and re-joined Martin.

Twenty minutes later, Anita arrived and was welcomed into the lodge by Judas.

"Just a quick stop," said Anita, as she took off her gloves, "I'm on my way into town to look for some curtains, some furniture and I might even look for some clothes. According to Stephanie the sales are in full swing and I definitely do not want to miss out."

"You sound just like my wife," said Geoff and chuckled.

Anita smiled and handed Judas the promised paperwork.

"I have been thinking about how I got the paperwork," explained Anita, "and the only thing I can think of is that I must have asked Adam for some writing paper, to take notes during one of his talks and the photocopy was included with the pages that he gave me. That is the only explanation I can think of that makes any sense. Sorry."

"Please don't apologise," said Judas, as he opened the envelope, "I will get three photocopies of each side of the paper and put them with the other paperwork that I have. Thanks for bringing the information in. It's much appreciated. Do you still like the apartment?"

"Do I still like the apartment? What a question! No, I don't like the apartment; I absolutely love it and I can't wait to move in and try to sort out everything and to make it my home," said Anita. "I am just waiting for the survey and valuation reports for the Poacher's Retreat before I invest in anything for the apartment, but I will still enjoy window shopping. However, I will definitely buy some clothes in the sales. Now I must dash. See you soon Judas."

She seemed very happy as she retreated through the door.

"She also sounds just like my wife," said John, "Well she does, especially concerning clothes."

The guards again chuckled. Judas watched Anita as she walked to the main road. He then looked at the sheet of paper she had given him.

The writing was definitely Adam's, it was very neat, clear and to the point and it was a report of a conversation between himself and his uncle Albert. Judas always admired Adam's writing. He always used a fountain pen and black ink. Judas went to the photocopier and produced three copies of each side of the paper. He then began to look at the map in detail.

As Anita had told him this morning by telephone, it was dated 1784 and it was bereft of any location marker. However, Judas could make out some of the street names on the drawing, as it was a much clearer photocopy than the one in his files and he was able to deduce that it was an early attempt at a plan of the Beaufort St. Catherine village. The old map showed the village at about half the land area of the present settlement. Judas reflected that some parts of the old village had disappeared completely, buried under new developments, whilst other areas had expanded and prospered.

The one thing that really drew him to the page and excited him, was a large black cross mark on the sheet and penned by Adam, but this mark was in a different location to the one shown on Henry Brown's paperwork and was labelled "Standing Stone." This intrigued Judas, as Adam's symbol was indicated in the present nature reserve. Judas surmised that he should be able to see the exact spot that the cross was representing from his apartment balcony. Judas then took, from his office drawer, the Ordnance Survey Map, showing Beaufort St. Catherine and the surrounding area and confirmed that Henry Brown's map was correct, although the item was marked as "Ancient Standing Stone," with no jagged half circle symbol. This confusion of the location troubled Judas and he turned over the paperwork. He was about to continue reading Adam's notes when he heard Martin speak.

"That's all of the delivery vehicles for the day off site and all of our vans have returned to base. I think the day went well and I have thoroughly enjoyed it. I think I deserve a drink," said Martin as he got up and walked to the refreshment part of the lodge.

Judas smiled and said to Martin, "Well done, I am pleased that you enjoyed the day's events."

He put Adam's notes away and went over to look at Martin's work. It was neat, methodical and accurate, and Judas went to the kitchen area and congratulated Martin on his contribution to the working day. Martin prepared drinks for himself and for both guards, but Judas declined to join them. Both Martin and Judas then returned to their section of the lodge, and Martin began to talk about his model railway group and about their next layout project.

"After the next show at Cranston Market, the present exhibition layout will be put into the store room and our group members will begin designing and building a new one," said Martin. "For Christmas, one of our group received a railway track layout book from his sister in Vancouver, and shown in the book was a track formation that could be 'Anglicised' by mirror imaging and also changing the freight yard and engine house to British design standards. We have decided to use this layout plan as a basis for our new project and we will begin designing in earnest after the exhibition."

"What do you mean by imaging?" queried Judas.

"Oh, sorry," began Martin and continued, "It's when you have a railway system that has right hand running on the rails, for example, and you need to change it to the British system of left hand running. Canadian railways adopted the American system, so the plan in the book is right hand running. If you have difficulty swapping things over simply hold the layout page in front of a mirror and draw the reflection. That's mirror imaging."

Judas nodded as Martin continued:

"We also liked the plan because it fitted onto the baseboard of one of our earlier dismantled layouts and we did not have to prepare another new baseboard. In addition we all wanted the new layout to be multi level, and this plan had the gradient, elevation and height clearances calculated for us, in the design details. All we have to do is to design a reasonably sized goods yard, with all of the required facilities and locomotive facilities for steam engines and diesel units. The clinching factor, however, was the fact that the layout had a branch line with simple forestry and mining complexes. For this added bonus all that was left for us to do was to design a typical British terminal station, and we are all busy at the moment trying to do this."

Again Judas nodded and was about to speak, when Martin reached over to answer the ringing telephone. As Martin was dealing with the call, Judas walked over to his seat and again began reading. He soon discovered that he was reading Adam's script of the known events concerning the lost plate, gold, holy relics and other treasures from the church at Beaufort St. Vincent. It was written in Adam's neat hand and was his attempt to condense the information, to extract the meat and just leave the bare bone information. He still found it fascinating reading.

As Judas read Adam's script, he realized that his old friend had done great justice to his task and he was impressed. The facts were still retained and the surplus information was eliminated. He had read it numerous times, but he was still baffled as to why Adam had left some of the numbered points in full and had not condensed them. In fact Adam had written out the unaltered parts of the list and then filed them behind his own script. On conclusion of his reading Adam's work, Judas read his additional paper, concerning the events leading up to the burial of the treasure. It was titled "Background."

Items numbered *21* and *22*, were written in full. Judas checked the original version and again confirmed that the above were exactly the same as the original.

He continued reading the next two points, numbered *23* and *24*, which were also unaltered from the original. He again concluded that Adam must have had a good reason to leave the text whole, but he couldn't think of a reason at the moment.

The next two entries, numbers *31* and *32* were also the same as the original, but Judas reasoned that it was only because the original entries were so brief. The entry numbered *34* was also unchanged from the original, but this time Judas reasoned that it was so important to Adam, that he deemed it necessary to leave it unaltered.

Judas put the papers down and was in deep thought about what he had been reading. It was a shortened version of the original paperwork, but covered everything that was known about the events. He had also re-read his own papers, concerning the non-condensed parts of Adam's work. He was still baffled and sat for a few moments in deep thought, but he did not have any revelations.

Judas called over to Martin, "Any problems, just yell."

Martin looked up, smiled and shook his head. Martin was enjoying his work and Judas was sorry that there was nothing that his new colleague found troublesome. Judas sighed and returned to the task in hand.

He progressed to the next sheet in his file and this was also fascinating reading. It was Adam's attempt to show, in one section, the known contents of the missing items and the directional information relating to the burial of the plate. Again, it was shown in truncated form and was a direct copy from Adam's original shortened script. Judas began and, as he read each section of Adam's work, he checked it against the copy that he had and found them all to be the same.

It was at this point that Judas searched back through his notes and found the paper titled "Recent Knowledge" and photocopied it. He replaced the original in its correct place and put the copy under the recently read notes from Adam. He looked at the clock and saw that it was late. The guards were getting themselves ready for a quick getaway and Martin was eagerly scribbling on a notepad. Judas went over to him and Martin looked up.

"Sorry" said Martin, "but there was nothing to do so I tried to sort out a terminus station for the new layout. It isn't going well, so I hope the others have more success."

"What space do you have for the terminus?" enquired Judas, "And what direction is the lead in track, left or right? Also I presume the usual facilities will be required, such as a coal siding, goods shed, cattle dock, parcels bay, carriage siding, end loading etcetera?"

Martin nodded, gave the space available for the terminus and said, "If you can manage to provide all of those facilities in the space available, it will be a miracle. And the lead track is from the left."

Judas retreated to his chair and put pencil to paper. After five minutes, Adrian and Roy entered the lodge and, after a short handover, John and Geoff left the lodge. Martin stood up and followed the guards outside. After five minutes of doodling, Judas left.

His walk back to the Ivy Lodge Guest House was without incident and Judas reached the guest house and entered. He received a very warm welcome from Amanda and an invitation to join her in the kitchen. As he sat at the kitchen table, he took, from his case, the note he had typed earlier outlining his financial suggestion and passed it to his host.

"Here is a paper for your lawyer, outlining the details of the proposed loan. If you and Stephen would both read it and, if agreed, your lawyer can draw up the legal agreement and I will willingly sign it in his office," said Judas.

Amanda placed a tankard of squash on the table in front of Judas and picked up the paper.

As she began to read, Amanda said, "Stephen and I still can't believe our good fortune. We can't thank you enough for your generosity, especially after the banks declined to support us. Bless you again."

Judas then began to blush and excused himself for a moment to go upstairs to his room and collect his case and belongings.

Amanda had washed his clothes and they were neatly folded on his bed. Judas packed his case and after a quick check of the room he returned downstairs to the kitchen.

"That's just like you said," said Amanda, as Judas entered, and she placed the paper onto the table, "so we will go to the lawyer's in the morning, if that's okay with you?"

"No problem," replied Judas and added, "I'm sure everything will be fine. Now, if I may, could I ask how much I am in your debt and I will then settle up."

Remembering what Judas had said about not receiving preferential treatment, Amanda sheepishly presented the account and Judas took out his cheque book and presented payment. After a few moments he left the property and thanked Amanda for a very enjoyable stay.

Judas was sorry not to have seen Stephen, but he was certain that he would see him again soon. He quickly walked to his new apartment block and as he passed the sales office he looked to see if Jennifer was there, but he did not see her. He entered his apartment, put his case on the bed and returned to the ground floor. He realized during the afternoon that he needed some food items and he walked to the shopping mall and enthusiastically went about this exercise. After twenty five minutes, he had purchased enough items to keep the inner man from starvation for a few days, and he was pleased with his selection.

As he left the complex Judas decided to walk back to his apartment block by a different route, just for a change of scenery. As he passed the nearby church, he was surprised to see it fully lit up and he decided to investigate. He was met by the vicar, who said he had just completed a meeting with "Friends of the Church" and introduced himself as the Reverend Oliver Winchester. The reverend gentleman was completely unimpressed by the Christian name of his visitor.

"May I show you around our small church?" asked Reverend Winchester and Judas eagerly accepted. "It is a beautiful early fourteenth century church," stated the vicar, "and it has numerous stained glass windows and various holy relics which are on open display in locked glass cabinets. Also, in this wall niche there is a casket holding a small Roman urn, found locally three centuries ago. The urn, as you can see, is still whole, although it is very cracked."

"I thought the Romans did not come to this area," said Judas, "My history teacher has often said that fact."

"That is true," confirmed the vicar, "but the fact remains that the urn was found locally. However, the exact location of the find has been lost."

On departing the church, Judas thanked the vicar: "Thank you for a very interesting tour of your beautiful church. I have only just moved here to the village and unfortunately I sometimes have to work on Sundays. However, I look forward to seeing you soon preaching in the pulpit."

In view of his Christian name, this statement surprised Oliver Winchester.

Judas arrived back at his apartment, stored his purchases and went into the main bedroom to prepare his bed. He then saw a note on the pillow. It was from Anita, simply saying that she was just passing and thought she would do a good deed for him for a change. The note continued: "*Jennifer let me into your apartment, as I was doing a good deed for a very generous friend.*"

Judas smiled and telephoned the Poacher's Retreat. Anita answered.

"You really are a great girl," said Judas, "and many thanks for your most welcome kindness."

"Actually," explained Anita, "I was in my apartment doing some measuring for my curtains and blinds and I also took some measurements of the wall lengths and alcoves, to see what furniture would fit and also where it would fit."

She seemed so happy and content and it made Judas inwardly pleased to hear her laugh again. Anita then continued on a different tack:

"The surveying and valuation reports of the Poacher's Retreat should soon be completed and I will then sort out my finances for my beautiful apartment with Jennifer and also with you. I can then begin to move into my new home."

Judas could hear the excitement in her voice and it made him happier still. Anita was laughing as she replaced the receiver.

Judas retreated to his kitchen and prepared his first meal in his new home. It felt strange to be living on his own again, but he felt certain that normality would soon return. After his simple feast, he went into his study and opened his case. On top of his folder were the doodled track plan efforts he had tried to sort out for Martin. He had not been successful and it dented his pride. He tried even harder to squeeze all of the requirements for the model railway terminus into the available area, using the miniature track pieces from work, but he was having no success. Judas then had an inspired idea and looked at some copies of the plans he had presented to Henry Brown. After a few minutes of searching and thumbing through numerous pages, he came across a plan that, with a little compressing and a complete reversal in the direction of the lead in track, might suffice.

Judas drew out the plan in reverse onto graph paper, omitting one siding and compressing the country station to one platform face, although it did retain the bay platform and the engine release road. When he had completed the exercise, he looked on the plan for a place where a siding could be squeezed in and, after a few attempts, a space was found and a short siding was added. Judas was pleased with his work and, just to prove that mirror imaging worked, he took both plans to the bathroom and held the original to the mirror. From the reflection, Judas could see the mirror image of most of the original layout, minus the departure platform, and also one siding which was in a different location to the original. Judas was impressed.

It was getting late and Judas prepared tomorrow's lunch. It was not as elaborate as Amanda's packed lunches, but it would suffice for him. He looked around his new kitchen, liked what he saw, patted his tin mug as he left the kitchen area and went to his bedroom. He was content, but for some reason he could not sleep. Every moment in bed he was thinking of Adam's notes and of the markings on the cross. He delved into his memory and could picture the cross and its markings. He knew that the strange arrow and figure markings on the cross were placed among wavy lines that were thought to represent water. Other marks, thought to represent grass and land, also did not marry up to the nearby known coastline of the period in question. Judas had his mind working overtime, but he failed to penetrate the mysterious mediaeval mind of the unknown monk. It was a complete no-go area. Eventually, his thoughts were stilled and he drifted into deep slumber.

CHAPTER 21

Tuesday 13th January

Judas awoke and looked at his alarm clock. It was two thirty seven, he had been asleep for less than two hours and he realized that he was not tired. He did not have anything on his mind to disturb his sleep, except the markings on the cross and he simply put his present state down to this. However, he was now wide awake, so he went to his study and opened his work case. He retrieved his papers relating to the markings on the monk's wooden cross and just stared at it. The same thoughts he'd had on numerous occasions ran through his mind:

Nothing fits, where it should be land, wavy lines are shown depicting water and where it should be water, land features are shown.

He was afraid that he had hit the proverbial brick wall and he was not at all happy. He kept looking at the details shown on the cross and was then hit by a thought. He had no idea of the scale of the details on the cross and, therefore, it would be very difficult to judge the part of the mediaeval coastline that the cross details might be representing. This idea made Judas think even more deeply about the markings on the cross. However, he could reach no conclusion, so he decided to visit the kitchen and have a drink to clear his mind.

Judas returned to his study and approached his office desk. As he passed by a small bookcase he saw a local map and he remembered about the lack of knowledge concerning the scale of the details on the cross. He then had an inspired thought and placed the paper showing the cross in his printer and magnified the page three hundred per cent. He randomly chose this figure as he believed the actual information on the original cross would not be very large and the copying would be in the same vein. He was surprised at the clarity of the enlarged duplicate and he looked for any clue that he might recognise on the paper. He was disappointed to see that there were no identifiable landmarks that he could make out.

However, there was one piece of information on the larger print that he could not discern on the smaller print. On the ends of five of the wavy lines, originally thought to represent water, there was a black filled circle incorporated onto the right hand side of the line. These five circles were the only ones attached to the wavy lines, shown on the page and Judas pondered the significance. The remaining wavy lines were unembellished. Judas realized that the original cross must have had indentations pushed into it and the copyist had shown these as circles on his drawing. He could not arrive at any specific conclusion and put the papers down on his desk. After a few minutes, he retreated to his kitchen and had another cool drink. He sat and pondered his next course of action.

After ten minutes, Judas returned to his study and, as he approached his chair, he saw the papers on his desk were upside down. Another Eureka moment and he then turned the paper with the cross details through one hundred and eighty degrees. This now showed the water depiction on the cross over the land reclaimed from the sea and the land features on the cross were shown on land that had once been by the coast. It also meant that the arrows and figure markings were now upside down.

Judas then placed the enlarged photocopy upside down on the ordnance survey map, with the wavy lines over the land and his heart began to race. Three of the circles made up a triangle and the positioning of the circles matched the relative positions of the settlements of Beaufort St. Vincent, Beaufort

St. Clement and Beaufort St. Catherine, although not exactly as the scale was different. Judas realized that this was purely hit and miss on his part, but it was definitely a start and he hoped that three of the holes were meant to represent the local town and villages. The other circles went slightly further inland, but did not indicate any specific location. Judas, however, did realize that the nearest circle to the triangle would be very close to Beaufort St. Catherine. Judas was really excited about his findings and he jotted down some notes for him to pursue in the morning. He retreated back to bed in a very happy state of mind and slept soundly.

The alarm sounded and Judas cursed the machine, but got up and prepared himself for the day ahead. After a simple breakfast, he walked down the stairs and thought how pleasant it was to be in a warm and cosy environment. His thoughts were shattered as he left the building, as it was very cold outside. During the walk into work Judas thought deeply about his discoveries during the night. Eventually, he determined to try and sort out the correct scale of the paper containing the circles and to see if three of the circles did in fact represent the local three settlements. He was very excited at the prospect and was looking forward to the day, even though he was a little tired.

Judas arrived at work and was greeted by the departing guards, who were getting ready for their handover to the day shift. Judas went to his desk and was pleased to see that the sheets for collections and deliveries were both fairly long and would keep Martin fully employed for most of the day. It would be very good experience for him, and Judas knew that he would cope with the workload with his usual attention and good humour.

John and Geoff entered the lodge and were followed a few minutes later by Martin. The guards completed the handover and the night guards left the lodge to begin their days away from the company. The day guards then greeted Judas and Martin and settled down for the day's work. Martin sat at his desk and, on scanning the paperwork for the deliveries and collections, he seemed happy and content with what he had read. Judas was about to speak to Martin and to show him the track layout plan he had prepared, when the first vehicle arrived and Martin began his day's exertions.

Judas put the plan back into his case, sat at his chair and then thought through the actions he would take to give him answers to the problems he had created concerning his decipherment. He took from his case the photocopy containing the enlarged black circles and he measured the distance of each circle forming the triangle from its neighbour. He then looked at the ordnance survey map and measured the distance from each of the local settlements to its neighbour. The ordnance survey distances were less than the photocopy distances and so Judas went to the office photocopier and slightly amended the magnification of the original document to a lower figure. After four attempts he had the distances in agreement, so he pierced holes through the circles. He next photocopied the section of the ordnance survey map, dealing with the areas around Beaufort St. Vincent, Beaufort St. Clement and Beaufort St. Catherine. On completion of this task, he placed the pierced sheet over the ordnance survey photocopy, making sure that the holes in the triangle were over the mediaeval parts of the settlements. He then marked in pencil, through the five holes in the paper, the relative positions on the photocopy of the ordnance survey map.

The result was discouraging. One of the single holes, one of the two not involved with the triangle, was in the nature reserve and the other was a little further inland and in the middle of no-where and about two miles from habitation and about one mile from a minor road. Judas was puzzled. To sort out his mind Judas went over to the kitchen area and prepared drinks for everyone, including Geoff, who had just returned from his first patrol. Judas took Martin his drink and returned to his desk. Martin had been very busy, but the morning rush had slowed down and he was having a few minutes break. Judas therefore extracted from his case the track plan he had prepared and took it over to Martin and simply placed it onto his desk. Martin stared at the plan and after nearly a minute he looked up at Judas, smiled and nodded and was about to speak when an incoming vehicle arrived and Martin returned to his labours.

Judas returned to his seat and for a few minutes he was in deep thought. He was about to return to his project when Martin came over to him.

"Thanks for the track plan Judas. It really ticks all of the boxes we required and I am sure the other members of the club will be as pleased as I am for the layout and for its operational potential. It really is good."

Judas smiled and was relieved that his efforts were appreciated. However, Judas was slightly flushed and was pleased that another vehicle arrived at the lodge requiring Martin's attention and relieving his embarrassment.

Judas then returned to his papers and applied his mind to the problem. It was at this point that Judas had an inspired thought. From what he could remember, from his readings, Adam had already written down, that on the reverse of the original wooden cross, the lines and letters did not relate to anything. Everything seemed to be in the wrong place. So who placed the small circles at the edge of the lines thought to represent water? There must have been holes in the original cross, but did the copyist of the parchment show them? Judas was initially stumped, and he thought deeply about the question. Then he suddenly remembered that Adam's Great Uncle Albert had done some research on the subject. Judas went to his case and rummaged through his papers and extracted the one headed "Recent Knowledge", written by Adam, and began to read.

Judas eagerly read the list again. He'd read it only last Sunday, but today he read it with greater interest and enthusiasm. On Sunday he was trying to fathom something out. Today he thought he had something to go on. He carefully read every section of the list, from *A* to *G* and then re-read it again. On completion of his reading, Judas concluded that it must have been Albert that had been responsible for the circular markings, but he had no idea how he obtained the information or from where. Adam certainly did not know, as he'd already written that none of the symbols fitted any of the known geographical information.

It was then that Judas had another inspired guess. Were the undecipherable texts, written by an unknown hand, and the rough diagrams by the same author, the work of Adam's great uncle, Albert Stonehaven? Judas again went to his case and extracted all of the papers. He photocopied all fourteen sheets and replaced the originals back in his case. Judas studied the pages on his desk with the eye of an eagle, but was still baffled by the horrific writing style of the originator.

Judas then extracted from the papers on his desk, the six pages of the attempted decipherment done by Adam, followed by the two pages of basic diagrams. He concurred with most of the decipherment, but still found the original text very baffling. He also found the diagrams extremely bewildering. Judas then had another thought and cursed himself for not thinking of it before. If the work done by Adam was the translation of the unknown hand and also the decipherment of the plan, then there was no need to look at the papers and try to understand them. Adam had done the work. All he had to do was to follow the paperwork trail and hopefully solve the mystery.

Judas sat back relieved. He also then thought that the various lines on the back of the original wooden cross, that did not relate to anything, were simply placed there to create confusion. Everything was in the wrong place and when the paper was turned through one hundred and eighty degrees, the lines could not represent anything beneath the waves. Also, when the coastal brother buried the items, it was anticipated that the contents would be retrieved in the near future. The brother did not know that the Abbot was dead, or about to be killed.

After a few moments of reflection and contemplation, Judas went over to see Martin and to see if everything was okay.

Martin smiled, "No problems at all. Everything has gone smoothly and I am pleased with the morning's work. Over half of the incoming receipts and outgoing deliveries have been concluded."

Judas was about to speak when his telephone shrilled.

It was answered by Martin, who after a few moments informed Judas, "You are wanted in Henry Brown's office."

Judas left the lodge and headed for the main office complex. On reaching the bureau, Judas knocked on the door and entered. He was greeted by Henry Brown and Paul Gibson.

"Hello," they said in unison and Henry Brown continued, "These are the pages we have prepared that are going into the company's new book and we thought you would like to see them, as you have been so involved with the publication, both with the previously unknown material and with the track layout designs. We still have a lot of work to do and a lot of layout diagrams and associated operational suggestions to compile, but we are slowly getting there. We both hope you like the work that we have done so far and we hope that it meets with your approval."

Judas was about to speak when both men got up and left the room, saying they would be back in about an hour. Judas was directed to a table and chair by the far wall, where he settled down and began to read.

The pages consisted mainly of track layout diagrams, with associated operating scenarios. Judas saw a lot of his own drawings and was impressed by the way the design bureau had presented them on the page, showing the various stations, signal cabins, goods sheds and associated buildings in the same way on all of the designs. The layouts were also drawn to the same scale, and it was evident from the outset that the book would be successful. Judas read a couple of the operating scenarios and was mesmerised by the content, clarity and vision of the writers. When he came to the unfinished section containing the information about the devastating sea incursion at Beaufort St. Clement, he was pleased with the included detail and also with the simple note form used as a reminder for later enlargement, before the papers were sent for publication. The section on the extension line from Beaufort St. Vincent to the main line, passing near to Beaufort St. Catherine, was also in simple note form and all of the information was put down ready for later expansion. In short Judas was impressed at this work and would definitely be waiting impatiently for the finished article.

Henry Brown and Paul Gibson returned to the office at the appointed time and were pleased to see Judas diligently reading the texts.

They were even more impressed when Judas said, "I have thoroughly enjoyed reading the contents of the publication and I am eagerly awaiting the finished article."

Henry Brown then asked Judas about his trainee.

"How is Martin progressing with his training? Will he be okay on the reception work?"

Judas was pleased to reply, "Yes he is very competent and his training is going well. Martin is very confident and assured. However, and this is something I was going to bring to your attention later today..."

"Oh God what?" interrupted Henry Brown.

"Nothing to worry about," said Judas, "but Martin won't be on duty at the month end. So, if you agree, I will get him to do the required monthly returns on the 30th January. I will visit the lodge on that Friday afternoon and be with Martin to make sure the returns are accurate, up to and including the Friday. If there are any significant changes to the figures on the Saturday, the actual last day of the month, when I am on duty, I will add them in."

"No objections at all," said a relieved Henry Brown, "and many thanks for your conscientiousness. It will not go unrewarded."

As Judas was about to leave the design bureau, he realised that Henry Brown and the staff group of the company were unaware of his new address details. Judas advised Henry Brown that he had moved to a new property in Beaufort St. Catherine.

Henry Brown simply replied, "Write down the address and I will pass the information to the staff group after I have amended my records."

Judas quickly took a note book and pen from his pocket and neatly wrote down the very long address of his new residence. After what seemed an eternity, Judas tore out the page and handed it to Henry Brown, who simply said the same as Judas when he had heard it for the first time.

"Ye Gods."

"My sentiments exactly, when I first heard the address," said Judas and he smiled.

Henry Brown continued, "Is this block the one overlooking the nature reserve and the coast, with views over the town and inland?"

"I believe so," Judas replied, "but I have never been there in daylight, so I honestly cannot say. However, Jennifer, the sales lady for the developers and my friend Anita both agree that the views from the apartment are magnificent."

Henry Brown looked at Paul Gibson, smiled and said, "We are definitely paying him too much," and then laughed.

Judas left the office and returned to the lodge.

As Judas entered the lodge, he was pleased to see that Martin was still at his desk. He had received all of the incoming vehicles shown on the list, and the three company vehicles out on deliveries were not due to return to the site until later on. Judas asked Martin if he had any problems with the work and was pleased to hear that there were none. Judas took over the work whilst Martin sat with the guards and had his lunch. The conversation quickly turned to the local football team and the forthcoming relegation battle with the league leaders. Judas just ignored the conversation.

Nothing happened whilst Judas sat at the desk, and he was relieved when Martin proffered a cool drink.

"The morning went well," said Martin, "and the afternoon should have no problems either."

Martin then went on to tell Judas about his model railway club and how it had kept him sane after his wife's tragic vehicle accident.

"The club meets every Tuesday night and every new member is encouraged to join with others to learn the techniques required to plan and construct the layout and to electrify the system. If difficulties are encountered, there is always someone on hand to help solve the problem. Those members that have developed their modelling skills and are considered competent are invited to join a select band to plan and construct a club layout that will be taken to local exhibitions for display. Every fourth Tuesday, these senior members dedicate their evening to a running session of the exhibition layout, to make sure it is running smoothly and will operate effectively at the exhibition. Also these members will test the exhibition layout on the evening before transporting the baseboards and equipment to the exhibition venue."

Martin was in full flow, but at this point a private vehicle approached the lodge and he had to return to his reception duties.

Judas returned to his seat and ate his lunch. He then opened his case and took out the information book he had recently purchased and began to read. It was a very interesting and informative publication. Judas again smiled as he read the part about the Roman vessels skirting the treacherous coast and frequenting the area, and he again thought of his friend Adam. Judas continued to look at old photographs in the book and he avidly read the details relating to the diagrams in the book. He turned a page and just sat transfixed and stared at the two old maps. He had seen them before, but he then did not have the information he now had and his heart missed a beat.

The maps in the book were of a larger scale to the other maps he had been using and one map represented the present nature reserve and the other represented the inland area. These were the areas he had toiled over with the two single circles and the three other circles forming a triangle. Both of the maps in the book had details on them that the other plans he held did not contain. The nature reserve map simply stated "Stone" near to the centre of the reserve and the other map now showed the habitation as a manor house. Judas was pleased with the map information about the stone, but was disappointed with the other map as there was no discernible feature anywhere near to the position he had marked by pencil: the manor house being two miles away and a minor road being one mile away. The manor house was classed as a fifteenth century building in the book.

At this point Judas stopped reading and took stock of his present knowledge about the plans, maps and the buried abbey items. It seemed that a lot of information had been gained, but he needed a break to let the information be absorbed and understood. He sat for a few moments and came to the conclusion that he would be best advised to go to the nature reserve and to look for the stone and see if it existed. If it did exist, or even if it didn't, he could then think very seriously about his next course of action.

Judas, however, very quickly decided that if there was a stone in the nature reserve and it was positioned where it was indicated on the map, then he should inform the county archaeological society of his discoveries. This would allow professional archaeologists to continue with the delicate work of unravelling the morass of the decipherment and hopefully unearth the lost holy paraphernalia. He was, however, at a loss as to what action he would take if the stone did not exist. At this point, Judas decided to put all of his private paperwork away and went to sit with Martin.

The afternoon was going well for Martin. Two of the three company vehicles out on deliveries had returned and the third was expected to return within the hour. The vehicle movement list for the day would then be completed.

Judas asked Martin, "Are you okay with the information I gave about the month-end returns and do you think you will be able to do the required paperwork?"

"I am certain everything will be okay," said Martin, "but as we seem to have a bit of a break from vehicular activities, would you please go over the procedures again?"

Judas smiled, took out his training notes and began. Martin was attentive and Judas got the impression that Martin knew the month-end work well, but just wanted to cement his knowledge on the information required. Judas covered all aspects of the complex procedures and, on completion of the training, Martin thanked him profoundly.

At four o'clock, Henry Brown telephoned the lodge and Martin answered.

He passed the instrument to Judas and mouthed, "Henry Brown."

Judas was about to speak into the mouthpiece when Henry Brown spoke first.

"Judas, if it's convenient, would you please come to my office?" and then he added as an afterthought, "There's no problem so don't worry."

Judas went over to the office, after making sure that the guards were aware of his departure, and was greeted by Henry Brown.

"I have just been looking at the annual leave cards for members of my staff," said Henry Brown, "and I notice that, since you began working with us, you have had no days off. I'm sorry, but it just hadn't registered with me that you were the only one trained to do the work and it was a complete and inexcusable oversight on my part. You will have twelve days due to you for this financial year, ending in March. If Martin is okay with the duties and the work and he's happy with this suggestion, we think you need to take a couple of days off, to recharge your depleted batteries, returning on Friday to clear up any outstanding problems?"

Judas was relieved that it was nothing serious and thanked Mr Brown for the offer.

"I am sure Martin will be able to cope admirably with the work and I am also sure there will be no objections, so I would love to be away for two days," confirmed Judas.

Henry Brown passed Judas his leave card to complete.

"On Friday you can let me and Paul know if the views from your windows are as spectacular as they are reported to be." He laughed.

Judas completed his leave card, handed it back to Henry Brown and said, "I will give my mobile telephone number to Martin in case of any problems during my days away."

Judas returned to the lodge and casually enquired, "Martin, would you be happy to be working on your own for two days?"

Martin looked up.

"Yes, I will be okay. There should be no problems. Why do you ask?" he queried.

"Because I have been told to take two days off to chill out, and I will return on Friday. I will leave my mobile telephone number just in case any unusual problems arise," said Judas.

At this juncture Judas heard applause from the guards and Geoff even cheered.

"About time you had a bit of a break," said John. "I suppose you will be jetting down to Biarritz again?"

They all chuckled.

The rest of the afternoon was quiet. In fact, it was so quiet that after an hour of general talk about the lodge work and the new security lodge, Martin took out from his case some photographs of his model railway layout and some photographs of his club's layout and handed them to Judas for inspection. The modelling was of a very high standard and both of the layouts were exceptionally detailed. Martin also showed Judas a very detailed plan of his personal layout and also some more photographs, but this time of the various express and goods locomotives he had in his collection. Judas was very impressed and Martin said it was a labour of love for both him and his late wife. At this point Judas could see that Martin was near to tears and he went to the kitchen area to prepare coffees for the guards and Martin. As he presented the coffee to Martin, Judas could see that he had regained his composure.

Gordon and Richard arrived at five fifty and the handover procedure commenced. As there were no specific details to pass on to the incoming staff, the handover was completed fairly quickly.

As John left the lodge, he said to Judas, "Have a good break from the lodge."

Geoff added, "Just relax on the ski slopes."

Judas smiled and then confirmed with Martin that he would be okay if he took the time off.

"No problems," came the reply, "and I also hope you have a very pleasurable and enjoyable break. See you on Friday."

With that, Martin left the site.

Gordon wished Judas a relaxing break and Richard, not to be outdone, made the same comment. Judas left the lodge after a few minutes and the night guards settled down to do their required paperwork before beginning their patrols.

The walk back to his apartment was bitterly cold and Judas was pleased that he was wrapped up. It seemed a strange thing to say, but Beaufort St. Catherine was now his home village and he was thoroughly enjoying being there. As he entered the apartment building, he was pleased to feel the heat and he checked in the post room to see if he had any correspondence. There were two letters. Judas recognised, by the style of the print on his name and address, that one was from his bank and the other envelope brazenly advertised his insurance company.

Judas walked up the stairs and entered his castle and was eagerly looking forward to a very pleasant evening. He had a long hot shower and changed, and then went to his utility room and studied the instructions for the use of the washing machine. After a few minutes the machine was in full operation, although only half full with coloured items. Next, Judas took his papers from his case and carefully read all of the pages he held. In some cases, he penned additional notes to the ones he held, just to clarify the content. He then took, from his safe, the other papers he held on the subject of the missing items and compared the two sets. Where they differed, corrections were made and photocopies produced, to complete the exercise.

Judas then went to his kitchen and prepared dinner. Afterwards, he relaxed and began listening to a historical novel being read on a CD. Judas sat and listened very intently to this novel, which involved an archaeological excavation in the Holy Land during the last century. Although it was fiction, it outlined the problems encountered by excavators finding desecrated burials by ancient grave robbers in their quest for valuable buried artefacts. This made Judas think very deeply about his present situation, concerning the deciphering he had done and the conclusions he had reached. He did not want to do any prodding or digging which might cause damage to any structure he might locate. This might cause problems for future seekers if his present actions caused widespread damage. Judas switched off the CD and sat in silence pondering the problem.

After a few minutes of profound thought, Judas concluded that he must seek assistance with his project. He determined to go to the museum in Beaufort St. Vincent in the morning, after his visit to the bank, to hand in his monthly cheque from Martin and Susan at the timber yard. However, he was still of the opinion that before he involved anyone else in the problem, he must visit the nature reserve and try to locate the stone. At least if it was there it might prove to whoever he contacted that he was on the road of discovery and he would not be dismissed as a bit of a crackpot.

The thought that someone *might* think of him as a crackpot irritated him. This irritation prompted Judas to look at his papers again and recalculate his figures and the geographical locations he had earlier determined. He did not find any fault with his earlier effort and was now more content. He then took a break from his labours and looked out of his windows.

He could see the lights of his village and the lights of the various vehicles using the winding streets. He could see the dim lights in the carriages of a passenger train as it hurried south in the distance. He could also see some lights on numerous ships plying their trade on the ocean and he began to shudder as he recalled how cold it was on his walk home. Judas then thought that it must be even colder on the high seas. He next looked over the nature reserve and it was pitch black. He knew what he had to do in the morning and he was looking forward to it.

Judas then went to his washing machine and took out the clothes and placed them in the tumble dryer. This machine was much easier to use than his tumble dryer at the Miller's Retreat and he was relieved. He prepared the ironing board and the iron, ready for the upcoming task. Judas was quite "house-trained" and was quite proficient at most household chores.

Judas retired to his study and continued to listen to his CD. He enjoyed it and he was relieved that he had been made aware of the pitfalls of blind excavation in pursuance of a theory. At the end of the disc, Judas made out a list of the work he had to do tomorrow.

The top priority was for him to search and see if there was a stone in the nature reserve where marked on the map. He smiled as he read the entry and he thought of the map of Long John Silver. The list then included putting the timber yard cheque into his bank and then going to the museum to arrange a meeting with an archaeologist. On completion of these tasks, he would casually pop into the lodge gatehouse to see how Martin was coping with the work and he would then be free to explore his new village. Finally, he noted that he had to see if the views from his windows were as breathtaking as Anita and Stephanie had said. It looked like being a very entertaining and enjoyable day. The last work to be done was the ironing and Judas completed the task in his own methodical way.

CHAPTER 22

Wednesday 14th January

Judas woke early, before his alarm sounded, and got out of his bed. He had always been an early riser and when he was awake, after a reasonable sleep, he simply could not stay in bed. He went to the kitchen and prepared a cool drink. As he looked into his large fridge, he was shocked to see how little food he had in it and he decided that he must rectify the omission at the earliest opportunity. Judas then made his way to the lounge. He sat and looked at the daylight unfurling in front of him. It was a magnificent feeling to know that the day ahead was not at a working environment and he was certain that he was going to enjoy every precious moment of it.

Judas then remembered the envelopes from the bank and from his insurance company and retrieved them from his jacket pocket. He scanned the pages of the bank statement and was pleased to see the wealth that he had in the account. The insurance company acknowledged his departure from the Miller's Retreat and requested that he complete the enclosed form for insuring his new property.

On completion of his reading and filling in the insurance form, Judas wandered around his new home and marvelled at the perfection of his domain. He wandered onto his lower balcony and was pleased that the external doors were shut tight against the high wind. The light was slowly replacing the darkness and Judas could see some of the flickering lights in the village being extinguished. Some vehicles still had headlights on as they left the village and a few other drivers deemed the illumination unnecessary. Judas looked through numerous windows of his apartment and was stunned at the amount of scenery he had at his fingertips. He could see the distant inland hills and he had a beautiful view of the coast, the lighthouse, the harbour, the marina, and the old canal and associated basin. He also had a wonderful view of the village, the beautiful church and the magnificent ruins of the mediaeval castle.

Also, as he wandered around his new apartment, he at last espied the nature reserve. It was much larger than he had expected and there were several pathways crossing it. All pathways seemed to be signposted and all had numerous hides placed at strategic locations along them. Beyond the reserve, on two sides, were two large woodlands and, towards the coast, was an area of reclaimed dunes. The woodlands and dunes also had sign-posted pathways passing through and across them. Judas could now inform Henry Brown that the views from his windows, inland and seawards, were stupendous.

He next went up to his study areas and looked out of the windows onto the surrounding land. He looked down at the manicured gardens of the apartment block and he was very pleased at the attention to detail that the gardeners were showing. Even in winter, there was plenty of colour in the flower beds and the borders. He again viewed the mediaeval church and it looked even more beautiful than it had before. He did not know why, but he was looking forward to his next meeting with the Reverend Oliver Winchester. Judas then looked towards the distant inland hills and was again pleased to see a locomotive hauling freight on a southward journey. From this vantage point, Judas thought that the village of Beaufort St. Catherine looked stunning and beautiful and he was feeling pride in being a resident of this community.

Hurriedly, he got himself ready for the day and retreated to his kitchen. He had another cool drink and a simple breakfast. He collected his bank book from his wall safe and locked the door as he exited his apartment. As he descended the main staircase, he marvelled at the outside view. Outside the building, it was cold and he quickly walked to the shopping mall and acquired a fairly sizeable shopping trolley of goods. He was very happy with his purchases and, after payment, Judas entered the nearby garden centre and, after a short search, bought a small hand trowel. He then retreated back to his apartment and stored his food purchases in the fridge and the cupboards. The large fridge still looked fairly empty, but not as empty as earlier on. Judas then left again and headed for the nature reserve.

It was still cold, but the inshore wind had decreased in strength and the temperature was slowly rising. Judas took the hand trowel with him in a shoulder bag. He also carried a spare copy of the map, that he had deciphered earlier, containing the pencil mark where he believed Adam, or his uncle, had indicated the possible location of the stone. He also carried a complete set of his notes on the subject of the lost items. He walked to the nature reserve in a positive frame of mind and, on arrival at the main gate of the fenced compound, was confronted with a choice of four different routes, each of different lengths and each with its own special content. He was also confronted by a large notice board stating that all those entering must not in any way deviate from the wooden planked routes, as this could prove dangerous.

One route was evidently for birdwatchers, and various hides were available for different breeding birds. Herons and kingfishers were plentiful in the area and were apparently local attractions. A second route was for the use of anglers, who paid handsomely for the use of numerous angling positions and also for the pleasure of catching and then releasing their trophy. Another route was used by the walking fraternity, and allowed passage through the nature reserve fairly quickly, as the walkers sought the coastal path to the river mouth. The final route was for the non-specializing individual, who simply wanted to look around the whole of the fenced-in site. They also wanted to enjoy the solitude and leisure of a simple walk: to view from afar, various colonies of birds and to see the numerous types of fish in the pools and the lake.

Judas selected the last option. He chose it because it contained most of the high ground in the nature reserve and also because there was a pathway close to the position of where he thought the pencil mark on the map would be located. He was then at a loss as to what to do next. Judas walked along the meandering path and was searching for any indication of any stone or rock protruding from the ground. He saw nothing. He retraced his steps and still saw nothing. He kept looking at the map, but all it showed was the outline of the nature reserve, which bore no relationship to the representation of the nature reserve on the map at the entrance to the site. Judas was stumped and he sat on one of the numerous seats placed along the pathway to contemplate his next move. After twenty minutes, he was no nearer to a solution, so he exited the reserve, walked into the village, posted his letter to the insurance company and then walked into his bank.

There was no queue at the bank and Judas walked to the counter, presented his book and cheque and asked if the bank had details of his new address. The cashier looked on the computer screen and read out the address and Judas nodded. The lady then updated the book with the timber yard cheque and then looked at the total figure. She was amazed and asked Judas to wait a moment.

Judas thought, *here we go again*, but before he could say anything the girl had left her position.

After about a minute, a lady approached and Judas was about to speak when she said, "Mr Wells, I believe we have an appointment to have a chat about your finances on Monday in

Beaufort St. Vincent? Wednesday is my day for travelling around the local area and here I am, so if you are free now we can look at the options available and get you the best rates for your investments."

Judas was taken aback for a few moments, but then agreed to the request and was shown into a small interview room. The Financial Adviser was called Chrystal and she was a credit to her profession.

When Judas said he had to keep a certain amount in his bank book for an impending payment, no questions were asked. Chrystal simply said the remainder could be a very successful nest egg if invested correctly and she outlined the investing options available and the timescales of the investments. Judas listened intently to the suggestions made by Chrystal and he thanked her for her expertise and patience. He invested his money as she suggested and he was very happy with the annual returns projected.

After nearly an hour, Judas was out in the cold, although the sun was making a great effort to break through the cloud. He was very happy that the financial meeting at the Beaufort St. Vincent bank on Monday had been cancelled, as this left him four clear days to try and resolve his problem with the nature reserve. The problem, however, still remained and he had no idea on how to proceed or on how to get any guidance on the subject. To clear his mind, Judas decided to walk around his village and to explore the nooks, crannies and crevices of his new community.

After his meeting with Chrystal, Judas wandered around his village with the air of a visitor to the community searching the by-ways and alley ways. He strolled around the bustling harbour and the marina and was enchanted by their beauty. He strolled along the busy streets and lanes and was surprised at the thriving commercial activity taking place. During his walk, he passed an area of land shielded by timber barriers and a notice board which said "*Strictly No Entry, Archaeological Excavation In Progress*". Judas smiled as he reflected that this must be the location of the proposed building that Simon Lancaster had designed and was now consigned to history because of the discovery of Roman remains. Judas inwardly offered up a prayer to the Roman God of Fortune and chuckled.

It was at this time that Judas thought it a good idea to return to his workplace at Beaufort St. Vincent to see how his colleague Martin was coping with the work. He headed for the coastal path and was soon treading on familiar ground above the cliffs. It was the first time recently that he had been along the cliffs in daylight and he was enjoying the views. It was still cold, but the brisk walk soon warmed him. He enjoyed the views along the cliff path and he was sorry when his brisk coastal walk ended. He soon espied the lodge and, after a couple of minutes, he entered the building.

"Oh my God, look who it is. I thought you were in Biarritz. Can't you keep away?" asked a laughing Keith as Judas opened the door.

Judas replied, "As I was just passing, I thought I would drop in and see if everything was going smoothly." Judas then spoke to Martin, "Any problems?"

Martin shook his head.

"No problems, but it is good of you to come in and see how things are progressing. However, whilst you are here can I have a quick word?" Judas went over to the desk and sat down next to Martin, who continued, "As you know last night was our railway modelling club night and I showed your branch line terminus plan to three of our exhibition guys and they were suitably impressed. If the other two guys, presently absent on winter vacations, have no objection, or cannot provide plans that we like better, then we will proceed with the plan you provided. Thanks again."

Feeling embarrassed, Judas nodded and smiled, and as a vehicle approached the lodge, Martin returned to work.

Judas left the lodge and walked into the town of Beaufort St. Vincent. He reached a small park area and sat overlooking the ornamental gardens, where a groundsman was busy weeding. He took out his list of the work he needed to do today and saw that he had completed it, out of order, with the exception of the visit to the museum. He ate an apple, as he pondered how he would communicate his findings to the museum representative. He then had the thought that he might be regarded as an eccentric by the representative and the thought did not please him. He was still in deep thought when he heard a welcoming voice and he looked up to see the face of Gavin Melbourne smiling at him.

"Whatever it is you're worrying about, it can't be as bad as the problems that I have been worrying about. All my notes and slides about the Romans passing through this local area and not leaving any settlement remains are now completely wrong. I have to amend the course significantly and the first class is on Friday."

Judas smiled and said he had great sympathy with his friend and tutor. It was then that Judas had a thought.

"Can I pick your brains for a moment?" asked Judas and, without waiting for a response, he continued, "You do some lectures at the museum, therefore you might know who I should contact about an archaeological problem and possibly a theoretical solution that might be of interest to the museum?"

"That sounds very interesting and very secretive," responded Gavin Melbourne, "The person that deals with archaeological excavations in this area and also gets involved with other excavations in the county is Professor Robin Cooper. He is an authority on the Romano British period of history, but he, like me, was taken aback with the recent discovery of the ruins during building work. His time at the moment is taken up with his attendance at the newly discovered site and the various excavations taking place. Why do you ask?"

Judas was reluctant to reply, but he had known Gavin for over twenty years and he trusted him completely and so he began his outline of the story. Initially, Judas could see that Gavin was sceptical about the information, but after about ten minutes, Judas knew that Gavin was hooked.

After a further twenty minutes Gavin interrupted and asked, "God's honour, is this genuine?"

"God's honour, yes it's genuine," replied Judas and continued, "but I have worked it out that one of the locations is in the nature reserve and I need to have it confirmed by finding the stone and digging down."

"Thank you very much," said a smiling Gavin. "I am half way through a mound of paperwork at the moment, regarding the lost religious artefacts from the abbey, which needs to be ready for a course later in the year and now I have to re-write that as well. Again many thanks. We both need to see Robin and I know where he will be. Come with me."

With that Gavin stood up and walked away and Judas dutifully followed. After a short walk down a couple of streets, Gavin turned a corner and ahead, across the square, was a very imposing Victorian building, housing the museum. During the walk, not a word was spoken by either person, as they were in deep thought about the dialogue that had just taken place. Gavin entered the building and was greeted by the girl on the reception desk.

"Back again so soon? You must like it here," she said as Gavin entered.

Gavin nodded and asked, "Is Robin still here?"

This time the girl nodded, and Gavin signed in and invited Judas to do the same. After this exercise, Judas simply followed Gavin up the main staircase and along a main corridor and entered a small office at the end. Professor Robin Cooper looked up from his desk.

"Hello again, what did you forget this time?"

"Absolutely nothing," said Gavin, "but I have here someone who has been attending my courses and classes for a number of years. I saw him in town a few minutes ago and he asked me who would be the person to approach at the museum concerning an archaeological problem. When he outlined the problem and it concerned the abbey artefacts, I had to come here with him to get you two introduced. Therefore, may I introduce Judas Wells and this Judas is my brother-in-law Robin Cooper."

Both men shook hands.

"This sounds interesting and ominous," said a sceptical Robin Cooper, "I am all ears."

Judas began, "Thank you Professor Cooper, for the opportunity of laying before you my findings and my interpretations, concerning the lost abbey artefacts."

Judas thought he could see Robin Cooper frown as he said "abbey artefacts", but he carried on. He informed both men of his early days at the orphanage and of Adam, the gardener handyman at the home. He told them about the discoveries he'd made in the garden shed when the old man died and about how he had been fascinated by the stories told to the children of the orphanage by Adam. He told them of how he recently went to the orphanage during its transformation into a luxurious residential complex and discovered additional papers behind the skirting boards in Adam's old room. He also mentioned the name Albert Stonehaven, at which point Robin Cooper looked up and his bored expression changed.

"Albert Stonehaven, the researcher?" questioned Robin, "My old tutor said he once saw him with some sort of map that was completely wrong. Hang on a moment, my tutor drew a map from memory and he gave me a copy to try and solve what it meant. I was completely stumped. It's in my cabinet."

With that Robin Cooper got up and extracted the sheet from his bulbous file.

"Here it is," said the Professor and handed it over to Judas as he returned to his seat.

Judas looked at the paper and could instantly see that it bore no relationship to the correct map. He reached into his shoulder bag and extracted four sheets from his file and handed two to Robin Cooper.

"The first is a photocopy of the original drawing of the cross and the second is a photocopy of the original markings on the reverse of the cross. Both of the original drawings were done by the mediaeval monk."

"What?" said an incredulous Professor, who was suddenly very interested in the subject, "Oh Ye Gods."

Judas then said, "And the third is a photocopy of the original markings by the mediaeval monk with the addition of the deciphered work, which was possibly written by Albert Stonehaven."

He handed it over as Robin Cooper sat speechless.

Judas continued his story and could see that both men were now spellbound by his narration. He omitted some of the mundane minor details, but explained enough to keep his captive audience very attentive. He explained about the various maps he had seen, about the initials *C ROFT* and how he thought it stood for Centurion and for Roman Fort, and how he had enlarged the maps and drawings and seen a similarity of the positioning of the settlements in the area. He described how he had figured out the ancient coastline and had turned the Albert Stonehaven map, where everything seemed to be in the wrong place, through one hundred and eighty degrees and had figured out what he thought to be the location of the abbey property. Judas then handed Robin Cooper the fourth sheet of paper, which showed how he had deduced the positioning of the clues and his attempt to indicate them on the plan.

Judas concluded by saying to both men, "You now know as much about the possible location of the buried property as I do. I am therefore entrusting the information to you both, especially to you Professor, as you are the only one of us who can do justice to any excavating and not damage any items if they are found."

Robin Cooper, now gaining his composure, said, "Thank you for your comments. And yes, I will definitely keep this information under lock and key." Then as an afterthought he simply said, "Oh dear God, I do hope that you are right with your theory."

Judas then went into details about what the buried packages consisted of, but as he saw both men nodding he assumed they already knew these details, possibly better than he, so he cut short his talking. He then asked both Gavin and Robin if they wanted copies of his abridged notes and, assuming the answer would be in the affirmative, he picked up Albert's information from Robin Cooper, returned it to its correct position and went to the photocopier. The photocopier was a much more advanced machine to the one in the lodge, but was practically the same as the one he had used at his previous employment. Judas could see that Gavin and Robin were in deep and serious discussion, so he stayed by the photocopier. The machine seemed to take an eternity to complete the task, but eventually it fell silent. Judas went over to the men and handed them the required paperwork. Both men thanked him for the papers, but seemed to be in shock and Judas was at a loss as to what to do or what to say.

After a few moments of thought Judas said, "Gentlemen, the photocopies you have in your possession are the simplified and abridged version of my findings, but they do contain all of the essential information. One word of caution. Not all of the markings on the reverse of the cross have been understood or deciphered and other clues may have been interpreted incorrectly, so I may be completely wrong in my deductions. However, whatever you do gentlemen, do not lose these papers."

Robin then regained his composure.

"I need a drink, I'll put your papers with mine in the safe Gavin and then I have to think deeply about this. This really is genuine?"

This last question was put to Judas, who simply said, "What I have told you Professor, and you Gavin, is the truth. I have looked at this problem for years and the recent discoveries I have made and the conclusions I have reached are the ones you both know about. I sincerely feel the evidence I have put before you both is worth investigating, although if I am wrong in my conclusions I will be devastated. However, I think I have unlocked the key."

Gavin then spoke.

"Robin, I have known Judas for twenty years. He has been at my evening classes for the history subjects and other classes for the geography related subjects and has passed all of the numerous examinations he has taken. He is also a very knowledgeable person in historical, archaeological, geographical and geological matters. He is also honest and trustworthy and in spite of his name he is a true Christian, although he does not celebrate Christmas."

Judas looked at Gavin and nodded and thanked him for what he had just said.

"Okay," said Robin, "but I still need a drink. The name, by the way, is not Professor, it's Robin. Follow me to the bar guys and the drinks are on me, and believe me when I say that I need a strong one."

With that, he led the men to a nearby inn.

At the inn, Robin bought double whiskies for himself and Gavin and a lemonade for Judas, and the trio sat at a table in the large orangery. They were the only ones in there and Judas could see that Robin was still pondering how to proceed.

Judas eventually said, "I do not think that any progress can be made in the nature reserve, without bringing a lot of unwanted attention to the site, especially after the discovery of the Roman remains that you are presently investigating. Therefore, if my calculations are correct, there should be something under the soil at the other inland location. This inland spot is in the middle of nowhere and if the farmer or landowner is agreeable, then a sizeable trench can be dug to test the theory. If screens are put up to hide the dig, that should give privacy to the site. Is that feasible?"

"You've been watching too much Time Team on the television," remarked Robin after a few moments and then said, "but I must admit that I was thinking on the same lines. The trouble is most of the guys used by the museum are already out on the present excavation and there are no surplus staff to call upon. However, leave it with me and I will sort out something. After all, this might be an even bigger event for the county to boast about."

The group sat in quiet contemplation and enjoyed their drink, although Judas could see that both of his companions were troubled and deep in thought. Judas also sat in silence and gave deep consideration to the problem.

After a few minutes of quiet contemplation, Judas had a bright idea.

"I've just had one of those eureka moments. The Beaufort settlements, St. Clement, St. Vincent and St. Catherine, all have one common denominator: they possess ruined mediaeval castles. I used these locations as the base point for my calculations when the circles on the upturned map were used to indicate the base point locations of the other two circles, which showed one in the nature reserve and the other inland in a field. If the exact locations of the mediaeval castles could be established using a Global Positioning System, then it should be possible to project the exact coordinates and position of the other two locations. This should then eliminate unnecessary excavations. Does that sound realistic?"

Robin looked up and smiled, "You really have been watching too much Time Team. I had come to the same conclusion and I was planning to go back to my office soon and try to find out who owns the field. I will then telephone them and arrange to see them, hopefully tonight, to obtain written consent to go on site. If I can obtain permission, I will then arrange to mark out the spot tomorrow and get the work done in the inland field. This excavation should then establish if there is anything buried underground in this location, and if there is, we should eventually discover its identity."

Gavin looked puzzled but said nothing. A few moments later Robin and Gavin left the inn to return to the museum and both promised faithfully to Judas to keep the photocopied notes safe and not to discuss the information with others. Judas slowly finished his drink and hoped he had embarked on the correct course of action by involving the authorities in his project. It was too late to do anything about it now anyway.

He left the inn and walked by the river, back to the town centre. When he reached the central square it was just after one o'clock and it was still cold, although there was no blustery wind. The temperature had only slightly risen from the early morning. Judas was enjoying his day off work and was feeling happy and contented that he had managed to fulfil all of the tasks written on his list. He sat on one of the benches and was content to reflect on his morning's activity.

It was then that Judas decided to return to the museum and to buy an annual membership card to allow him to visit the museum as often as he wished. Earlier, when signing in with Gavin, he had noticed that yearly access cards were available and, as he would be working four days on duty and four days off duty, he would now have the spare time to really enjoy visiting the museum and to enjoy the delights of the exhibits. The same receptionist greeted him on his return and, when he had completed the application form, it was processed efficiently. After a few minutes Judas was presented with his electronic membership card and separate instructions detailing how it must be presented to the access and departure machines on every visit.

Judas returned to the coastal path and enjoyed a casual stroll back to Beaufort St. Catherine. He admired the inland hills, the rocky outcrops and the wooded valleys. In short, he was at peace with the world and he was content. Judas arrived back at the apartment block and went to the post room to collect his mail. He recognised Anita's writing and he opened the envelope to find a card wishing him well in his new home. The other envelope was typed and it was from Stephen and

Amanda's lawyers. It contained a legal document outlining the terms and conditions of the agreement and a letter asking Judas, if he agreed to the terms in the paperwork, to make an appointment to see the lawyer and sign the agreement in his presence. As the law firm was in Beaufort St. Catherine and was the same legal company used by Anita, Judas retraced his steps to the main road and walked to the lawyer's office.

After a five minute stroll, Judas reached the High Street and, after a further five minutes, he arrived at the solicitor's offices and entered. After outlining the reason for his visit to the receptionist, Judas was advised that the sender of the letter was available on Mondays and Thursday mornings only. As Judas was away from the lodge tomorrow, he arranged an early appointment with the lawyer for nine thirty in the morning. On exiting the office, Judas could see some small vessels in the inland harbour and he went to the quayside to admire the craft. From his vantage point he could also see some yachts in the marina and he also admired their beauty and form.

At this point Judas realized it was getting colder and he decided to return to his apartment fortress. On the way back, he passed a model shop and in the display window was a very compact model railway layout. This layout showed a small country station with very limited facilities and it had a tank locomotive orbiting the circuit and pulling six wagons. Judas watched it for a few minutes and then, feeling the cold, he returned home.

On entering, Judas decided to contact his friend Anita. He then telephoned the Poacher's Retreat and Anita answered.

"Many thanks for your kind thoughts," he said, "and for the card wishing me well in my new home."

Anita chuckled and said, "It was a pleasure. By the way I was going to telephone you later to let you know that the surveyor's report has been completed and accepted and the valuation has also been completed and accepted and therefore the Poacher's Retreat will soon be owned and run by Stephanie and John Faulkner. The lawyers are, at present, drawing up the property sale and transfer papers and also the financial arrangements for immediate part payment and for future instalment payments, which have already been agreed."

Judas was pleased that the future was looking so good for his life-long friend and he could tell from her voice that she was very happy and contented.

Anita continued, "When the finances are finally sorted out, I will pay you back in full for the loan, as soon as the money goes into my bank. Also, just to keep me sane for a while longer, I will keep popping into the Poacher's Retreat until my official retirement date in early March, just to help Stephanie during the transition."

Judas then advised Anita, "I have been off all day and I have enjoyed a relaxing time, wandering around my apartment block, visiting the nature reserve, walking to Beaufort St. Vincent and seeing Gavin Melbourne, my evening class teacher, in the town."

"I'll bet you visited your work lodge," said Anita, and laughed when Judas confirmed that he had. Anita continued, "I have also had a very pleasant and very busy day, sorting out my new apartment. I have been looking at bedroom furniture, dining room furniture and lounge furniture, and I have also been looking at curtains, blinds, carpets, rugs and countless other items needed for my new home. Actually, I am very tired, but I have enjoyed every moment, as this is the first time I have been able to buy brand new things for my brand new home."

Anita and Judas both laughed. The conversation ended a few moments later.

Judas sat down and thought through the actions he had done during the day. He also re-read all of his notes and was half way through the neatly presented folder, when he realized that it was getting dark. He looked outside and could see that the black clouds were gathering and, a few moments later, it began to rain. Initially, the rainfall was only slight, but after a couple of minutes the heavens opened and a torrential downpour ensued. Judas looked out of the apartment windows towards the village centre and could see the street lights struggling to illuminate the main streets. Numerous shops were also fighting to eradicate the darkness and drivers of vehicles on the highways must have been having great difficulty seeing in the heavy rainfall. Judas was pleased he was inside. He returned to his seat and switched on his reading lamp.

After another fifty minutes, Judas completed his reading and closed his folder. He decided that the action he had taken was the only reasonable action that he could have taken and he now knew that the possible discoveries he had made were being investigated by an authority that could do justice to the investigation. He also believed that both Gavin Melbourne and Robin Cooper could be trusted and neither would betray his trust and confidence in them. Judas returned his folder to his trusty case and locked it. He again looked out of his lounge window and could see that it was still raining heavily. He sincerely hoped that if Robin Cooper had obtained the written consent from the landowner to excavate, then the land would not be flooded in the morning.

After his late meal, Judas retired to his study and sat in silence and in the dark, contemplating the day's events. In his own mind he was certain that he had acted correctly. It would be interesting to learn of any developments in the inland field when the promised excavating began, which would hopefully be tomorrow.

To keep his mind off the problems of the excavation and his possible cataclysmic errors in the decipherment of the clues, Judas went to his inner study and pondered. He checked the space available and believed he could fit a model railway on an L-shaped baseboard into the area. After all, his main study – the outer study next to the balcony area – housed his computer equipment, printer and shredder and some new bookcases and he had plenty of room to "expand." The bookcases he had brought with him from the Miller's Retreat sat neatly in the inner study and were easily accessible, even allowing for the space required by the proposed model railway. Judas was convinced he could achieve a pleasing small layout to keep him entertained and occupied in the most pleasurable of ways. He found the miniature track formation pieces in a drawer and the miniature board and set to work. Initially he set up the small board to the model area length and width for the L-shaped layout that he hoped to plan, develop and model.

For the next two hours Judas was unsuccessful in his endeavours. He initially thought that he might try to adapt one of the plans he had already designed, but the adaptations either did not fit in the space he had available, or did not please him enough for him to continue with the compression of the original layout. His mind seemed to be hitting the proverbial brick wall again, so he put the pieces down, closed his plans folder and just tried to sketch some layout formations onto a notepad. After another twenty minutes of fruitless achievement, Judas silently said to himself, *enough is enough, bed beckons* and retired for the night.

CHAPTER 23

Thursday 15th January

Judas awoke at three thirty from a deep sleep and was unable to return to quiet slumber. After a few moments, he got up and went to his study and just sat there looking out to sea. Eventually he saw, in the pitch darkness, a dim light on a ship, slowly travelling from left to right, across the outer glass of his balcony. As the vessel disappeared from his vision, he began to feel sorry for every mariner at present on the high seas. Judas loved watching vessels, ploughing through the thunderous waves, but he had no ambition to leave terra firma.

Just for something to occupy his mind, he returned to his desk, picked up his notepad and tried to design a model railway layout that would fit into the limited space he had available. When he had designed the track formations for the book, in the majority of cases, he had done the plans and then worked out the dimensions of the baseboard. For most of the other cases, the track designs were compact and did not present too great a problem, although two track formations did require some serious thought to overcome the acceptable gradient and the locomotive height clearance in tunnels.

However, now having a limit on his baseboard style, length and width, Judas was having great difficulty in sorting out a suitable model railway layout that he could operate himself and enjoy in the space he had available. For a whole hour he toiled with various designs and styles of layout, but eventually he was forced to put down his notepad and admit temporary defeat. He returned to his seat and gazed out to sea, still thinking about various layout plans and how to fit them onto his baseboard area. Eventually he gave up this mental exercise and sat back to watch the dawn and to contemplate the infinity of the horizon.

Judas retired to his bedroom, showered and dressed and then went to his kitchen. After a frugal breakfast, he collected the papers the solicitors had sent him concerning the prospective agreement about the guest house development and placed them in his case. At the same time, he extracted from his case the notes he kept there on the lost artefacts, and these precious notes he put into his safe. He also made certain that he had a notebook in the case ready for his evening class tonight on the subject of "The History of Maps".

As Judas was about to leave his apartment, he suddenly realized that tomorrow Juliette, his cleaner, would need to access his home and she hadn't been given the alarm code to deactivate the machine. He made a mental note to contact her during the day. He also wrote the alarm code on a small sheet of paper and sealed it in an envelope simply addressed to "Juliette". He walked down the stairway and marvelled at the scenery on his descent. As he left the complex he shuddered as it was still cold and there was a biting inshore wind.

The sales office was locked, so Judas walked to the centre of the large village and again looked over the harbour and over the marina. He then retraced his steps and eventually reached the shop with the small model railway in the window. This time the engine and trucks were stationary, as the shop was not yet open. Judas peered inside, but he could not see any movement.

Suddenly a light was switched on in the shop and a man unbolted and unlocked the entrance and turned the sign on the door to "Open". Judas entered and was amazed at the amount of stock there was in the shop. There were numerous shelves by the walls holding all types of model railway engines, carriages and freight wagons and all of the different manufacturers had their own separate spaces in the shop. Along the centre of the shop, back to back shelves held the associated modelling equipment of station buildings, goods sheds, signal cabins and engine sheds. Judas was impressed and moved towards the front of the shop and the section dealing with model railway books, brochures, magazines and layout books. Judas saw the Beaufort Models brochure and smiled.

He looked at a competitor's brochure and could see that it advertised a very good product. He also saw that the same company produced three model railway layout books and, as he thumbed through them, he saw that the layouts inside were very pleasant and, in some cases, very attractive and functional. He took the four items to the sales till and purchased them. The man at the counter looked at the books and congratulated Judas on his purchases.

"This company produces excellent models of locomotives, rolling stock and track and it also designs very good and functional layouts. Do you have a model railway?" asked the assistant.

"Not yet," answered Judas, "but I hope to get one very soon."

Judas then walked to the solicitor's office and entered into the reception area. He introduced himself to the young lady and after a short wait he was ushered into a room where a stern solicitor welcomed him with a very firm handshake. He introduced himself as Marcus Forth, a senior partner of the firm Abbott & Forth. He was a short man, with a large waistline, black hair and he wore thick rimless spectacles.

"Any problems with the draft agreement?" he asked and seemed surprised when Judas replied:

"No problems at all."

Marcus Forth regained his composure and said, "I followed the information you provided on the outline of the proposed loan, to the letter, with one addition. That addition being that in the event of your death, occurring before the loan is repaid, then the repayments to continue and be paid to your estate until full restitution is made."

"I had seen the inclusion and I am pleased that you inserted it into the agreement," said Judas. "It was something I hadn't thought of. However, we are all mortal and it now does cover all possible angles," concluded Judas.

Marcus Forth smiled and passed Judas three copies of the agreement for him to sign and Judas dutifully complied.

"When Mr & Mrs Bailey have signed the agreements, I will get one copy sent to you for your information and retention, one copy will be held by Mr and Mrs Bailey and the remaining copy will be held in our strong room. And that concludes the agreement," said Marcus Forth. "However," he continued, "may I ask a question?" and without waiting for a reply, continued, "What's in it for you?"

For the next ten minutes, Judas explained to Marcus Forth, as he had explained to Amanda and Stephen, his reasons for helping individuals to achieve their dreams, when the financial institutions had dented their ambitions. He outlined that the proposed plans for the expansion of the guest house could only be made with a large infusion of capital and he believed that Amanda and Stephen should be allowed to fulfil their ambitions. Judas thought himself again quite eloquent when he had finished and Marcus Forth simply held out his hand and shook the hand of Judas.

"I had to ask. It's not exactly good financial practice and it's something I would never recommend, even to my worst enemy. That's why the agreement is watertight for my clients.

I sincerely hope you understand why I had to ask? Thank you for making their dreams come to fruition."

Judas simply smiled and nodded.

When he left the building, he headed for the village square and sat on one of the wooden seats, by the war memorial. He breathed in deeply and was relieved that the meeting with the solicitor had gone so smoothly. He simply sat for a while and enjoyed the day. It was still cold, but the biting wind had abated and the sun was making a great effort to influence the day. Judas took the model railway brochure from his carrier bag and scanned through it. He was very impressed by the content and also of the quality of the photography illustrating the company's products.

Next he selected the layout book giving ideas for track formations in small spaces and he was mesmerised by the layouts. They were really first class and Judas was deeply moved by what he saw. Unfortunately, the only layout that had the same footprint, in area and dimensions, as his proposed baseboard was the only one in the book that he did not like. To Judas, it did not look right, the scenery seemed to be out of place, the station was too compact, the engine servicing facilities were limited and the goods yard was practically non-existent. When Judas looked at the bottom of the layout he was dismayed to see that the designer of the layout was Stephen Lindsey. Other layouts in the publication were also by Stephen Lindsey and these could not be faulted. In fact most of them were absolutely brilliant and Judas was now realizing what a catch this man was for the Beaufort Models Company, even allowing for the layout he did not like.

The next track layout book he looked at was for medium sized layouts and all of these plans were superb and Judas again could not fault any of them, except for the size of the baseboards, which he simply could not fit into his domain.

Again a number of the plans were by Stephen Lindsey and they were again superb. The third layout book he eventually picked up was for large sized layouts and again superlatives failed Judas as he looked with awe at the designs. The only stumbling block was again the size of the baseboards. However, Judas was very pleased with his purchases and he was now certain that, with the help of the books, he should be able to take sections from certain layouts and put them into a compact layout of his own. Judas was very happy with his purchases and began his walk back past his apartment block and towards the coastal path to Beaufort St. Vincent.

On his walk along the coastal path, Judas put all thoughts concerning his model railway layout to the back of his mind and he began to think about Gavin Melbourne and Robin Cooper. He especially wondered if Robin Cooper had contacted the owner of the property and if consent had been given for the exploratory excavation in the inland field. He then began to have negative thoughts and realized that if nothing was where he had calculated it should be, then he would look a complete idiot. A sudden gust of wind in his face made him return to positive thoughts and he realised that the sun had failed in its effort to influence the day and it was getting colder. He quickened his pace and after a few minutes the lodge came into view.

As he entered the lodge Martin said, "Just the man I need to speak to. Can I please see you for a few moments?"

"Certainly," said a very concerned Judas, "what's the problem?"

"No work problem," replied a smiling Martin, "but last night one of our exhibition guys at the model railway club telephoned me at home. He simply said that he had sent, on his computer, a plan of the layout we had already agreed on, with the addition of the terminus you had prepared, to both of the absent model railway exhibition members. Both were very impressed by the layout, its operating potential and its beauty and they both agreed that they could not design anything better and therefore we are going to build this layout as our next exhibition entry." Martin sat back and smiled. "All of the guys asked me to thank you most sincerely for your input to the problem and they hope that when we have completed the building of the layout, you will visit out club and look at the finished article," beamed a happy Martin.

"It will be my pleasure" said a relieved Judas.

As Martin was coping admirably, Judas left the lodge and wished Martin and his colleagues a very pleasant and enjoyable day at the model railway exhibition at Cranston Market. Even though he would see Martin again before the exhibition, Judas passed on his best wishes just in case he forgot to do so tomorrow. He also wished the guards well and told them he would see them in the morning.

"And not before," shouted a laughing Colin, as the lodge door closed.

Judas walked into the town and sat down on a hard wooden seat overlooking the harbour. He remembered that he had not contacted Juliette and he reached for his mobile telephone to rectify the omission.

After the pleasantries, Judas began to explain: "The access card will allow you into the apartment, but the alarm will bleep for twenty seconds after the door has opened and during those twenty seconds you must go to the cloakroom and enter a security code to de-activate the system. On leaving the apartment the reverse procedure must be followed and you will have twenty seconds to exit and secure the door, before the alarms reset. I will leave an envelope with the sales office on site with the required information in it to gain access."

"Thank you for the security information," said Juliette, "I was hoping you would call and give me the codes. Also many thanks for all of the furniture you have given to Andrew, to me, to Mary and to our daughters. We are all very grateful for your generosity, especially Mary, who was really very depressed after her marriage breakdown."

In return Judas simply replied, "It is I who should be thanking you and your family for the help you have all given me during my very hurried move." Judas then changed tack and asked, "How is Andrew's model railway?"

Juliette laughed and said, "I see even less of him now than I did before."

The call then ended. After about twenty seconds, just as he was about to put his mobile telephone into his pocket, it bleeped and Judas looked at the screen and saw that it was Anita.

"Hello," said Judas cheerily, but the voice at the end of the line was Gavin Melbourne.

"Sorry," said Gavin Melbourne, "but I have been trying to contact you at the Miller's Retreat, without success. Then I saw Anita in the town, window shopping for furniture, and she let me use her mobile."

"I see," said a bemused Judas, "What's the problem?"

"It's a bit delicate," began Gavin, "but Robin would like to see you and me at the museum as soon as possible. Where are you now?"

"Only in town. Overlooking the harbour. I can be at the museum in ten minutes," said Judas.

Gavin simply said, "Okay, see you there," and rang off

Judas walked to the museum and was full of doubt. He could only think of some disaster befalling his calculations and he was not looking forward to seeing either Gavin Melbourne or Robin Cooper. He reached the main door of the museum and Gavin was there to meet him, and standing behind him was Professor Robin Cooper and a stranger. Judas placed his membership card to the electronic machine and the machine bleeped.

"Don't look so worried," said Gavin, "as I think there's no great problem. Yesterday afternoon Robin gave his son the task of pinpointing the correct map references of the mediaeval castles, at the three locations and then calculating the same map reference information for the sites in the nature reserve and the inland field. And here are the references." He handed Judas a sheet of paper and then continued, "The positions you projected were absolutely correct, within a couple of feet, so well done. After our group split up yesterday, Robin telephoned the owner of the field to obtain permission to dig an exploratory trench in his land and the farmer had no objection. Robin immediately got the address and drove over there to get the agreement in writing. Whilst there, the farmer told Robin that when he was putting drainage pipes into a "dip in the field" to release the rainwater to a lower ditch, he came across some type of structure. He was forced to put the pipes about six feet away in empty ground. Robin asked if he could see the structure and to cut a long story short, the structure was definitely Roman.

"Because it was unknown, the County Chief Archaeologist had to be informed and that is the gentleman over there and he was once Robin's tutor at university. When Robin sought permission to excavate this new find it was refused, as the archaeological fraternity is fully stretched at the moment because of the recent discovery of the Roman buildings at Beaufort St. Vincent. Therefore, Robin believes that the only way we can legally check out the inland site is for the County Archaeologist to be appraised of the present state of knowledge. If he can be convinced, then we can proceed. However, neither Robin nor I can do that, as we have undertaken with you not to broadcast the knowledge." Gavin finished and sheepishly looked at Judas.

After a period of profound thought, Judas nodded and a relieved Gavin took him over to meet the County Chief Archaeologist. Judas saw that Robin Cooper was also deeply relieved, as he gratefully introduced him to his boss, Professor Mortimer Stanhope, the head of the County Archaeology Department.

The two men shook hands and Mortimer Stanhope said, "If I am to believe young Robin here, you have done some work that is completely mind blowing and you have discovered some information that is going to make me a very happy man. Therefore, we will go to the board room and I look forward to being educated and impressed."

"Before we begin Robin," said Judas, "may I please have the use of the notes I gave you yesterday, as mine are in my safe at home?"

Robin dutifully went to his room and collected the notes and gave them to Judas as he entered the board room.

Judas realized that the talk he was about to give, outlining the work that he had done concerning the lost artefacts of the Beaufort St. Vincent abbey and his decipherment of the information on the cross, would be crucial in getting the resources necessary to do justice to the recovery of the items. That was, of course, if the items were where he thought they should be. Judas began his talk by simply saying that two of the audience already knew the content of what he was about to say, so he would add in pieces of information that they might find very interesting. At this both Robin and Gavin smiled and Judas could see that all three men had a pad of paper in front of them and had pens and pencils at the ready to take notes.

He began by telling them of his involvement with Adam at the orphanage and of the wonderful stories he told the children, concerning his life and the other stories he told concerning local legends. Judas outlined that he always listened intently to the stories he told and would write them up later. He then outlined Adam's favourite story – the loss of the artefacts of the Beaufort St. Vincent abbey church. Judas saw all three men lean forward at this point and he knew he had them hooked.

After half an hour of intense scribbling, Mortimer Stanhope suggested a short break to allow Judas to rest his voice and for the men to rest their weary writing hands. Judas went to the nearby drinks dispenser and put in coins for four cold drinks. He opened his can and presented one each to the other men at the table. Judas looked at Mortimer Stanhope.

"What do you think of it so far?"

Mortimer Stanhope looked stunned and simply shook his head.

"Thanks for the drink." he eventually said and continued, "Is all you are saying true?"

"Yes," replied Judas, "and in the next half an hour or so, you will know as much about the lost religious artefacts as Robin, Gavin and me."

True to his word, Judas continued with his talk and his audience was held spellbound by his narration and by his method of decipherment of the ancient parchment. When he outlined how he had obtained the Albert Stonehaven paperwork and enlarged it on the photocopier and seen the circular clues, Mortimer Stanhope simply sat there with his mouth open.

As he slowly regained his composure, Mortimer Stanhope admitted "I once met Albert Stonehaven, many years ago, but I was unaware of his involvement in the decipherment."

It was at this point that Judas decided to inform his attentive audience of Adam's involvement in the story.

"My dear friend Adam was the great nephew of Albert Stonehaven and the recipient of all of Albert's research papers upon his demise. When Adam passed away, I discovered some of the papers that had belonged to Albert Stonehaven and followed various clues and eventually discovered more papers and I then deciphered the clues."

Mortimer Stanhope became absolutely speechless when Judas showed him the paperwork, showing the markings on the cross and attributed to the mediaeval monk. Judas then divulged how he turned the plan through one hundred and eighty degrees and lined up the mediaeval castles with the circles to project the other locations and to reveal the spot in the nature reserve and the spot in the inland field and Mortimer Stanhope had tears in his eyes. Judas concluded by saying that if Robin had no objection, then it might be best if the County Archaeology Department representative had photocopies of his notes. Robin smiled, nodded, collected his notes from Judas and went to the photocopier.

Mortimer Stanhope sat in silence for a long time and only spoke when Robin placed the photocopied notes in front of him. Robin then returned his own copies to Judas.

Finally, Mortimer Stanhope said, "That was the most interesting and informative lecture I have ever attended. I have learned more in the last hour about the lost church artefacts than I had gleaned from other sources in the last fifteen years. Oh God, I am so chuffed. And we know that at one of the sites, the inland field, there are Roman remains. This really is getting better and better."

"I told you yesterday Mortimer that you would be educated and impressed," said Robin to his boss and continued, "Now are you pleased that I told you to drop everything and come over to the museum?"

"For once," replied Professor Stanhope, "you did not exaggerate and yes I am so very pleased that I came over to the museum."

Judas then interrupted the light hearted banter and said, "Yesterday I asked both Robin and Gavin to take great care of their notes and I sincerely request that you do the same Professor Stanhope. The work I have done on this project to reach this stage took me over forty five years and you now have the results of my labours in your possession. As I outlined yesterday to both Gavin and Robin, some of the markings on the reverse of the cross have not been deciphered and some may have been interpreted incorrectly, so I may be completely wrong in my findings. I sincerely hope not. Please do not lose the photocopies, as you now know as much about my findings as I do. If my calculations are wrong then I will sincerely apologise and try again to do a better job in the future to discover the whereabouts of the holy relics, the gold and silver plate and the other objects which include rubies, pearls and sapphires."

At this point both Mortimer Stanhope and Robin Cooper screamed in unison:

"What?"

Judas was stunned at the outcry and was relieved when Robin was the first to regain normality.

"How do you know about the precious stones?" he tentatively asked. "We only knew about the church plate and the holy relics."

Judas was taken aback and simply replied, "The notes I gave you Robin contained that information, although I did not mention anything about the items when I spoke to you yesterday. I saw you nodding and I just assumed you knew more about the subject than I did. Sorry."

He returned the notes to Robin and pointed to the part of the list showing the information.

Mortimer Stanhope had, by this time, regained his composure, but still seemed to be shocked by the information he had been given. He looked at the photocopies he had received from Robin and wallowed in the information he was reading. He then remembered that Judas had requested him not to lose the paperwork and he eventually spoke.

"I religiously undertake to protect the information I have received today and not to inform anyone of the contents."

Judas nodded.

Mortimer Stanhope then said, "I am so very grateful to you Judas for sharing with me the information that you have accumulated during your study of the mediaeval clues. I promise I will take great care of the information." He then addressed Robin Cooper. "You can have permission to excavate in the inland field. There is only one condition."

Robin Cooper's brow furrowed.

"Which is?" he asked anxiously.

"I am allowed to join the excavation. The team will just consist of both of us and if anyone asks we simply say it is a Roman structure and, if there is anything else there, then you and I will be on hand to make sure we do justice to the excavation. We are not treasure seekers, but by all that I hold holy, I want it to be the church artefacts. I will clear my desk of urgent work tonight and be here early in the morning."

It was then that Mortimer Stanhope realised that he had shunned both Judas and Gavin and he unreservedly apologised for his lack of tact and diplomacy.

"Ye gods, what must you both think of me," he said and continued, "here am I saying that we two archaeologists will be on site, perhaps discovering the find of the millennium and ignoring the lifelong work of the person who cracked the code and also ignoring the person who brought together Judas and Robin. What an idiot I am. My sincere apologies to you both."

It was a little bit awkward, but both Judas and Gavin smiled and both wished the professors a very interesting and fruitful excavation. Robin Cooper thanked both men and suggested that they all needed to relax and have a proper drink.

"You're always at the pub," said Gavin and everyone chuckled.

Mortimer Stanhope had his notes placed with Robin's in the museum safe and they all left the building following Robin.

"This must be your local," said Gavin to his brother-in-law, as they entered the same inn as yesterday. Robin bought himself and Gavin large double whiskies and bought his boss and Judas lemonades.

"Ye gods, if I wasn't driving I could definitely sink one of those whiskies," lamented Mortimer Stanhope as he sipped his drink.

They went to a table at the rear of the courtyard, with no customers nearby, and began to talk about the work done by Judas. Judas was embarrassed, but answered their questions fully and with good humour and, at the end of a very interesting hour, the group split up. Judas wished them well with their findings and all of the group shook Judas by the hand and thanked him for his attendance. Robin promised to notify Gavin of the outcome of the following day's excavations and Gavin took Judas' mobile telephone number and promised to pass on the information.

Judas walked back to the harbour area and sat watching the small boats as they were gently lifted and then dropped by the waves. It was definitely getting colder and he began to shiver. It was only four o'clock and his evening course on "The History of Maps" did not begin until six thirty. He therefore went into the shopping mall and found a seat in the central area and again looked at his model railway purchases. He was still fascinated by the quality of the publications, by the brilliance of the modelling, the complexity of the designs and by the photography of the finished layouts. They were magnificent, with the exception of one and this was by Stephen Lindsey. He kept looking at the book relating to the designs for small model railway layouts and after about half an hour, he had selected sections of about half a dozen layouts that he liked and juggled these bits around to fit into his available space and into the type of layout he required. He decided that, as he did not have the space on one level baseboard, he would have to make his layout multi layered.

After a little more juggling, he had the basis of a layout that he liked and he would use the miniature track pieces later today to confirm that his requirements could be accommodated on his stacked baseboards. He was happy that he had done some good work on the design, but he still had over an hour and a half before the start of his class. Judas went into a small café and had a drink.

He then thought very deeply about the events of the day. Somehow he felt very vulnerable. He had freely given all of the knowledge he had accumulated over the years, concerning the lost church plate and other items, to three knowledgeable people. All of them had initially known less than he on the subject and the two archaeologists of the trio were soon going to excavate where he had directed. Judas sat in profound thought and eventually decided that there was nothing now that he could do, other than accept and acknowledge that the professors were honourable people and the right people for the excavating work required. If his calculations were correct they would find something in the inland field, possibly under Roman remains. He began to relax and also began to look forward to tomorrow and hopefully to some wonderful news from Mortimer Stanhope and from Robin Cooper.

After a few more minutes Judas left the café and walked to the nearby college for his evening class. He was still early for his class, so he went to the canteen area and waited for other members of the class to arrive. He sat and pondered the day's events and was deep in thought, when he was interrupted by a familiar voice.

"What are you doing here?" asked Gavin, "The class on 'The History of Maps' has been cancelled, as not enough people enrolled on it to make it a viable proposition for the school to continue. You should have been advised by post of the cancellation."

Judas was disappointed.

"I bet they wrote to my old address and Simon Lancaster has not yet retrieved the correspondence from the post box."

After a few moments, Gavin said, "I am at the school to collect some notes for my class tomorrow evening. As you know I have been forced to amend my original scripts because of the recent discovery of Roman remains in the area." He then said very quietly, "Hopefully I will have to amend my notes again in the very near future, when more Roman remains are formally discovered in the local area..." and he smiled at Judas.

On this happy note, they parted and both men said they looked forward to the evening class tomorrow night.

Judas left the school and walked towards the coastal path. As he passed by the Lodge, Judas resisted the temptation to enter. He just kept on walking and eventually arrived at Beaufort St. Catherine. Judas continued to the sales office and was disappointed that Jennifer was not on duty. However, the young lady in the office greeted Judas cheerily.

He explained, "My cleaning lady will be arriving on Friday morning to do the domestic chores in my apartment and will call into the sales office to collect this envelope. May I leave it here please?"

The sales assistant immediately understood the problem and promised to make sure the person on duty would comply with his request. Judas left, after a few minutes of idle chatter, and walked over to the main entrance to the block. He entered the post room, unlocked his post box and extracted an envelope with the school name emblazoned on the reverse. Judas surmised that it contained the cancellation information on his Thursday evening class and a refund cheque and he was correct. He went to his apartment.

Judas took out the miniature track pieces from his study drawer and tried to sort out a track formation that fitted the scale baseboard on his office desk that reflected the dimensions of his actual proposed baseboards. He again looked at the layout book that contained all of the part-layouts that he had selected that morning. He then used the miniature track pieces to put together the small sections of the layouts he liked, with the intention of eventually putting them all together to form a good and functional multi level layout. That was the theory, but unfortunately, in practice, the exercise faltered very badly. After an hour Judas stopped and put the miniature track pieces, still in their track formations, back into his study drawer. He was feeling peckish and retired to his kitchen for a simple dinner.

At about nine o'clock Judas returned to his study. He thought deeply about his model railway requirements and concluded that he did not want a really complex layout. Apart from the fact that it would be beyond his capabilities to build, the layout would only be operated by himself, and therefore, as long as it satisfied his needs, a simple layout would suffice and that was all that mattered. However, he was still struggling to design even a simple layout, so Judas put down his note pad, full of simple and rejected layouts he had sketched, and again looked through his folder of designs he had prepared for Henry Brown.

Eventually, he came upon one design that could be the basis of a layout, albeit a truncated version of the original, with only a single main line instead of the up and down lines of the original. The only station on the new design was a fairly complex terminus with four platform faces.

Judas doodled various track formations and, eventually, he came upon one design that fulfilled his requirements. The new layout was still on two levels and involved a simple staging area under the terminal station. For single operative model railways, Judas preferred the simple single terminus option and not continuous running. The layout also involved numerous country activities, including forestry and a timber yard, a brewery, a quarry and a very small harbour at the lower level.

After sorting out the plan on his notepad, Judas repeated the exercise with the miniature track pieces and was delighted when he eventually got the design to fit the baseboard parameters. He was even more delighted when he incorporated some staging loops under the upper level, instead of the original plan to have simple buffer end sidings. This new arrangement allowed complete freight and passenger trains to be held in the loops. He jotted down on the notepad the code numbers of the rails used so that, in the morning, he could draw his layout to scale on graph paper and also enter the item numbers of the required track. He was really happy and, seeing that it was now only one hour before midnight, he decided to retire for the night. He reflected on the happenings of the day and slept soundly.

CHAPTER 24

Friday 16th January

Judas woke early, retrieved the notes on the lost artefacts from his safe and locked them into his case. On his way to work, Judas hoped that Martin had coped comfortably with all of the work that had been required of him. Near to the lodge, Judas quickened his pace and, as he entered, the heavens opened and a torrential downpour ensued.

Gordon and Richard were both at their desk and both seemed pleased to see Judas.

Richard said, "How was Biarritz?" and, without waiting for an answer, asked, "Are the slopes exceptionally good this year?"

Both guards chuckled and Gordon enquired, "I assume that you enjoyed your days away. The lodge didn't seem the same without you."

"Thoroughly enjoyable days away, but very busy" replied Judas.

The guards did not press him for any information on his activities during his absence, but seemed eager to pass on to him their news concerning the site.

Richard advised, "During your trip to the slopes, there was a development concerning the Beaufort Models complex and this information concerns you Judas. Henry Brown came into the lodge and announced that all new building work should be completed and all of the new equipment should be installed by the beginning of April. However, as some of the building work has already been completed, equipment has been ordered and will be installed, as a matter of urgency, to allow increased output by the company. Also a new and larger gatehouse will be built near to a new car park entrance, which will be near to the main offices and engineering entrances. When all work is nearing completion the guarding complement will be increased by one per shift to three persons."

Gordon then continued, "There is a meeting today and numerous board members are to visit the factory. We have been given a list of names and have been requested to let the named members onto the site and to present them with a site pass."

Judas was about to speak, when Keith entered the lodge and was followed by Colin a few minutes later. The night guards quickly left the complex and the day guards completed their paperwork.

After a couple of minutes Colin turned to Judas and said, "I suppose you have heard from Gordon about the developments?" Judas nodded and Colin continued, "Enjoy your time off?"

Again Judas nodded and was about to speak when the guard's telephone rang and Colin lifted the receiver. At that moment Martin arrived looking like a drowned rat – he had been caught in the downpour. However, his raincoat was long and had taken the brunt of the heavens' assault and only his head was unprotected and open to the elements. Martin dried his face and hair and sat at his desk, still breathing deeply. He had hurried the last part of his walk to work to try and beat the storm and had lost miserably.

Judas asked Martin how he had fared on his own and was delighted at the reply.

"No problems occurred or were encountered that I could not handle." Martin then asked Judas, "No doubt that you have heard the news about the new gatehouse and other developments?"

Judas confirmed that he had. At that moment the first vehicle of the day arrived, followed by the departure of the first local van delivery and Martin began to log the information onto his sheets. Judas looked at the completed sheets Martin had worked on during his absence and was pleased at the information he saw. It was neat and accurate and Judas was now content and happy to be working with his new colleague.

Judas got out his graph book and began drawing his model railway layout to scale and putting the item codes by the sides of the track. The exercise took about thirty minutes and at the end Judas was very pleased with the plan he had developed and also pleased at the operating potential of the design. He then looked out of the window and was relieved to see that it had stopped raining and the high winds had abated. However, the black clouds were still dominating the sky and it was still very cold. Judas wondered if the recent downpour had dampened the enthusiasm of Robin Cooper and Mortimer Stanhope towards the work they had to perform in the inland field and he secretly wished them success in their work.

Whilst thinking of the archaeological work, Judas extracted his notes from his case and he began to read them again, especially the ones on the way he had deciphered the location points in the nature reserve and in the inland field. He then had a disturbing thought and it really troubled him. It was completely basic and he was disgusted with himself for not thinking of it before. Although he had overlooked it, he was surprised that Gavin Melbourne, Robin Carter and Mortimer Stanhope had not seized on the query and challenged him. The problem was simply this. When the two brothers took the artefacts to the coast for hiding, why did the brothers at the coast bring the artefacts inland to hide and not conceal the items near to the coast? It was a problem that Judas pondered about for a long time and he was about to put the problem aside for a while, when a solution hit him like a thunderbolt.

Judas surmised that if the brothers taking the plate and other items to the coast for protection and hiding did not know where the items were hidden, then, if they were captured by the rogues, they could never divulge the whereabouts of the artefacts. The rogues themselves would deduce that the items had been taken to the coast and would be buried near the coast. Therefore, the brothers at the coast, possibly on the written instructions of the Abbot, had returned inland and buried the items in a prepared hiding place made available for such an eventuality. Judas sat and pondered his logic and simply could not fault it. He felt very relieved, as he was now convinced that the other three people having knowledge of the believed hiding place, had already thought through the problem and had reached the same conclusion, only very much earlier. Judas admonished himself for his stupidity.

At eight o'clock, Judas prepared drinks for the guards and took the mugs over to the men. The guards began to talk about the weekend's football match, so Judas excused himself and went over and sat with Martin. Martin had been very busy with incoming and outgoing traffic and was pleased to receive the beverage.

Judas looked out of the window and was relieved to see that the ground was drying very quickly. He was relieved as he now believed that Robin Cooper and Mortimer Stanhope would be able to go to the inland field and do the necessary work to substantiate his research into the whereabouts of the church artefacts. Alternatively, they could go to the inland field and discover nothing concerning the church artefacts and completely destroy his research and his credibility. Judas shuddered at the thought.

"I am looking forward to tomorrow," said Martin to a startled Judas, "We got everything ready last night at the club for the weekend model railway exhibition at Cranston Market. We all decided to travel down tonight in my van and stay in a guest house and we will go to the exhibition hall early in the morning and set up our layout. Last weekend it was a bit hectic and a bit of a rush to set the layout up on time ready for the visitors. We decided to do this on the journey home last weekend, when we only stayed in a guest house on the Saturday night."

"That sounds a very good idea," agreed Judas and was about to say more when a vehicle arrived and two local delivery vehicles departed.

Ten minutes later Henry Brown entered the lodge and casually announced, "Tomorrow the new contractors will be arriving on site with the new production equipment. These contractors will begin unloading and positioning the equipment in the new buildings that have already been completed and, as the car park and access roads will be fully utilised by the incoming vehicles, all normal company stores arrivals and local retail deliveries have been rescheduled for the middle of next week." Henry Brown stopped speaking to let the information be absorbed by the assembled company and also to allow himself to take a small break. He then continued, "Also next week, the electrical installation engineers will be on site to complete the work on the new plant." Henry Brown waited again for the news to register and after a few seconds he turned to Judas and said, "Did you enjoy your winter vacation to Biarritz? The guys told me that's where you went. We are definitely paying you too much."

The guards and Martin laughed and Henry Brown chuckled as he left the lodge without waiting for any response or confirmation from Judas.

A few minutes later, during a lull in the traffic, Judas went over to see Martin and asked if there were any questions that he had concerning the work. Martin simply smiled and shook his head. Judas then showed him the track plan that he had worked out for his own model railway in his study and Martin was duly impressed. He even asked for a copy of the plan and Judas duly obliged and went to the photocopier to obtain a print. Martin was still looking at the plan when his telephone rang and, on answering it, he passed the handset to Judas and mouthed, "Anita Wells".

"Hello Anita and how is my favourite girl?"

Anita laughed and confirmed that she was well.

"It is just a social call to see if you enjoyed your days away from the lodge."

"I enjoyed it immensely," confirmed Judas and Anita was very happy for her friend. He continued," I have now been around the village, getting my bearings, and I have enjoyed my exploration of some of the back streets, the harbour and the marina. I also met the local vicar, the Reverend Oliver Winchester, and I saw him cringe when I introduced myself. My Christian name really offended him."

Anita chuckled at the news.

She then announced, "The initial payment for the Poacher's Retreat is in my bank and the cheque will clear by about Wednesday. Therefore, I will clear my debt to you by the presentation of a cheque on Friday next week."

Judas could tell from her voice that it would be a great relief for Anita not to have the weight of the debt hanging over her and to be financially free.

After the call Judas turned his attention to the excavation in the inland field and he hoped that the earlier rainfall had not stopped Robin Cooper and Mortimer Stanhope from beginning their archaeological search. He secretly and earnestly wished them both well in their quest and he hoped to receive positive news during the day. Judas looked around for something to do, but was frustrated by the lack of work. He sat at the corner desk, away from everyone, and his thoughts again returned to the excavation in the field. He realised that he had not understood some of the information shown on the cross and he honestly hoped that the unknown information would not cause his deductions to be false.

It was still early and Judas felt completely surplus to requirements. He took from his case the evening class information on "Roman Britain" from the college and he began to read. He inwardly smiled, as the information outlining the content of the course, suggested that the Roman presence in the county was inland and not in the local area. The publication also stated that it was in the counties to the north and south that the Romans had the coastal forts and lookout stations, to protect their naval vessels and none were ever deemed necessary in the local vicinity. Judas could already hear Gavin Melbourne apologising to the evening class for not having more substantial and accurate notes on the subject.

Judas was interrupted in his thoughts by Martin.

"Your presence is required by Mr Brown in his office."

Judas put his papers back into his case, changed into his jacket and marched off to Henry Brown's office. He knocked on the door and was called to enter.

"Hello Judas," said Paul Gibson, who was standing at a desk with Henry Brown.

Judas returned the greeting.

Henry Brown looked up and said, "Here are the papers we are going to send to our printing section to be made into a fairly hefty volume. Our proof readers have read and re-read the pages and our technical services have tried and tested all of the layouts and also confirmed all of the item numbers required for each layout. Our legal people are as certain as they can be that we have not infringed, broken or slightly bent any laws and we are just about ready to go to press. We just thought that, as you are a major contributor to the content of the tome, you would like to see what the final draft would be."

"Oh God yes please," said Judas and he was ushered to a chair at the end of the large table and then presented with the weighty paperwork. Judas sat and began to read.

"I'll phone the gatehouse and tell them that you will be back after lunch," said Paul Gibson as he and Henry Brown left the room.

Judas began reading and was completely absorbed by the content of the pages, the brilliant photography, the historical background, the fantastic layouts of Stephen Lindsey and he was especially pleased at the way his own layouts had been made even better by the graphic design bureau's embellishments. He was absolutely mesmerised by the content, the clarity of the writing, the fine detailing of the layouts and the way the previously unknown information had been brought into the book without sensationalizing the events. In short Judas wholeheartedly approved of the proposed publication and spent the next three hours being educated, uplifted and inspired.

Judas was completely absorbed in his reading, when the door opened and in walked Paul Gibson.

"How did your reading of the pages go?" he enquired and before Judas could answer, he said, "Your presence is required in the canteen. Someone wants to meet you."

Paul Gibson held the door open and beckoned Judas to follow him. Sheepishly, Judas left the room and the door was duly locked. He followed Paul Gibson through various rooms and corridors, but instead of going to the works canteen, he was ushered into the board room. Inside were a number of senior managers, all in small groups and all talking quietly. He recognised Stephen Lindsey, Henry Brown and two other people with whom he had had dealings, but the remainder were unknown to him. Judas felt uneasy as he was being ushered towards the front of the room where Henry Brown was standing. As he reached the group Henry Brown smiled.

"This gentleman," said Henry Brown, to his nearest companion, "is Judas Wells and he is the person who has done so much work on the proposed publication and has also provided us with all of the new information, plans, maps and photographs, concerning the proposed Beaufort St. Clement station complex, about 1881. He also provided us with the previously unknown information, maps and plans concerning the extension line from Beaufort St. Vincent northwards to join the main line. This Judas is Dr. Oliver Rose, our Managing Director."

Judas was completely taken aback, but the MD held out his hand and firmly shook Judas' and greeted him like a long lost brother. Judas was then aware that the people in the room were applauding him, as they were all unaware of who he was by sight, but they had been privy to his name and the great service he had performed for the company.

Dr Rose said, "Judas I cannot thank you enough for the great service you have done for this company. The discovery of the Beaufort St. Clement station layout proposal and the previously unknown maps and photographs will make this publication a really special book. We all knew that there was a re-design of the station complex at Beaufort St. Clement and many of us have been searching for any snippet of information for years. I honestly did not think the information would ever be discovered. But you did it, so very well done and thank you once again for making our publication the vehicle to unleash this information to the world."

Judas was embarrassed, but just said, "It is a pleasure and a privilege to be of service. But gentlemen, the person who discovered the information was Adam Stonehaven and I just found it when he passed away."

The MD nodded and silently mouthed, "Well said."

Judas also received many thanks from other members of the board and senior managers for his magnificent contribution to the forthcoming publication. Judas began to relax and to answer questions that were being thrown at him and he answered them honestly, accurately and fully.

Dr Oliver Rose searched out Judas again and said, "I must also congratulate you on the magnificent layouts that you have designed. Some are truly inspiring. You really do have a great gift. Keep up the good work."

Everyone in the room at some point thanked him for something and Judas was really enjoying himself.

It was then that Dr. Oliver Rose said, "Gentlemen I think it is time for lunch. Judas you are my guest."

Judas was speechless and had to be guided out of the board room and into the small adjacent room where a banquet of cold buffet food had been prepared by the kitchen staff. Judas was ushered behind the MD, collected a tray and selected some mouth watering food from the vast array of various dishes on display. He was very sparing with his food selection, but others were ravenously hungry and satiated their gastronomic desires.

The MD then guided Judas to the main table and sat next to him. He began talking to Judas about model railways in general and told him about his own model railway located in his large attic.

"I designed my layout to fit the space available and having realized that my modelling skills were not of the highest quality, I employed a very competent modeller to construct the layout to my requirements. As a boy, I had been a very keen train spotter and had various books full of neatly ticked locomotive numbers. My school friend had a model railway and when I saw it, I'm afraid train spotting became history. My school friend also had a very pretty sister, who also liked model trains."

Both men laughed before the MD continued.

"I received my first train set a short time later and I was completely hooked. I bought model railway layout books and read then from cover to cover. I then began to design new layouts for my own model railway, but these were usually very complex layouts that were of no use whatsoever for the solo operator, as they were too large to operate enjoyably."

Judas was fascinated by the genuine, friendly nature of this powerful man and he contributed to the conversation by telling Dr. Rose of his own desire for a model railway for his study when he had properly settled into his apartment.

The MD said, "Judas, when you are designing your model railway, remember this simple fact. Do not make the layout too big for one person to operate. If you do, you will never be able to operate it to its full potential as a solo operator. When your layout is fully constructed I would like a copy of the track design and photographs of the completed layout and scenery."

Judas promised to complete the layout as soon as he could and promised he would send the required information and photographs to him via Mr Brown. Judas was feeling quite relaxed and he could see that Henry Brown and Paul Gibson kept looking in his direction and seemed relieved that Judas was not overawed by the occasion.

Dr. Rose then continued, "I began my working career in a simple model railway construction company and I worked myself up the promotion ladder. I developed new techniques in manufacturing and distribution and I eventually took over the present company. In my position, I can spend many vacations with my good lady wife, going to numerous international model railway exhibitions, in Europe and North America and in Australasia. I really enjoy these jaunts very much, although I have to admit that my wife only accompanies me if I allow her to have equal exhibition time and shopping time. My wife, by the way, is the sister of my school friend, although she grew out of enjoying model trains."

Both men again laughed.

All too soon the meal was over and the MD simply said that it was time to get back to the board room and to continue with the meeting. He stood up and all in the room followed his example. He then turned to Judas and shook his hand with a powerful grip.

"You have done this company a great service," said the MD, "and it is very much appreciated by all of us here. We have a very good product and soon we will have a very handsome publication, which I am sure will be a great success. Some of the information contained in the book will be a revelation, not only to the model railway world, but to the British Rail world as a whole. Thank you again for your massive contribution and for trusting us with the information. And don't forget – let me have a copy of your layout plan and photographs of the layout when you have completed it."

The MD again shook Judas by the hand and there was a ripple of applause as he walked to the exit door and was followed by the other men. Henry Brown and Paul Gibson both looked at Judas and both mouthed "Well done" as they followed in the crowd behind Dr. Oliver Rose. As the door closed various members of the canteen staff came forward and began to clear away the food.

It was time for Judas to return to the lodge.

However, as the ladies were clearing the nearby tables, Judas asked, "Ladies may I please purchase some of the food items for my colleagues in the gatehouse? They always seem to be hungry."

The ladies presented him with a box and invited him to take whatever items he wanted. Judas thanked the girls and took sandwiches, a selection of cakes and various packets of biscuits. Judas went to the cashier to pay for the items, but the offer of payment was declined. Judas therefore made a generous donation of coins into a charity box on the counter, supporting a local hospice.

"Thank you again ladies. Lunch was absolutely superb. I am certain my colleagues will also enjoy this unexpected feast."

Judas returned to the lodge, with his bounty.

"The wanderer returns," said Colin, as the door opened.

"The wanderer returns," echoed Judas, "and is bearing gifts."

He placed the box on the nearest desktop and the assembled guards and Martin swarmed around.

"Help yourselves to the food. The MD, directors, senior managers and I have just had lunch and I thought you might like to have some food also," said Judas.

The guards and Martin looked up at Judas. Colin was the first to react.

"You have just had lunch with the MD?" he queried.

"Oh yes," confirmed Judas and went on, "he is a very pleasant person. We sat together and he told me about himself and his life and his wife and even his model railway. In fact it was a very enjoyable experience. It was hard work, but somebody had to do it."

Judas looked at the trio and smiled.

"No drinks?" asked Keith, quite sheepishly.

"Sorry no drinks," replied Judas, "unfortunately, we drank all of the champagne."

Everyone laughed.

"Who is he trying to impress?" he heard someone say, but the men all helped themselves to the unexpected picnic.

Judas went to his desk and took over the work while Martin enjoyed his food sitting with the guards. After twenty minutes, Martin returned.

"Thanks Judas for thinking of your colleagues."

Judas nodded and replied, "I sincerely hope you and your colleagues have a very successful and rewarding time at the model railway exhibition at the weekend."

Martin was about to respond when the lodge door opened and in walked Henry Brown. He walked over to Judas.

"I'm really sorry about that Judas," muttered Henry Brown, "but the MD originally said it would only be a very quick meeting in the board room to agree a few minor points on the building alterations. Then he telephoned and said another bigger problem had occurred and this would need to be included in today's discussions. Therefore he and the board members would require lunch. When I had sorted out all of his requirements, he arrived and the meeting began.

"The first parts of the agenda were quickly resolved and agreed and everything seemed to be falling into place. The meeting stopped for lunch and the MD calmly said he wanted to meet you to express his gratitude personally for your input to the forthcoming book. Before I could warn you, the MD's secretary telephoned Paul Gibson and asked him to contact you and take you to the board room. Paul had no idea that you were to be presented to Dr. Rose. Paul sends his apologies. However, the MD seemed impressed with his meeting with you and looks forward to seeing the layout plan and the photographs when your layout is completed. Once again I really am sorry for what you went through, but you handled it very well. Well done. Did you enjoy your lunch, sitting next to the MD?"

"Oh yes," answered Judas, "I thoroughly enjoyed the lunch and the MD is a fine gentleman. We got on very well and I will definitely get my model railway up and running and get the layout design and photographs to him when it is finished."

Henry Brown left the building and silence reigned in the lodge.

Eventually Keith tentatively asked, "You actually sat with the MD, at his table and had lunch with him?"

Judas just smiled smugly, nodded and simply said, "These lunches can be hell sometimes," and everyone in the lodge burst into laughter.

For the remainder of the afternoon, Judas sat with Martin and quickly went through the work with him just to clear up any problems that he may have had. Vehicular activity had completely ceased, as all receipts and deliveries had been completed. Martin thanked Judas for the training and said that he expected more cakes and biscuits to be on his desk the next time Judas lunched with the MD. Both men chuckled.

In the car park, the vehicles began to leave and the drivers cheerfully waved as they left the site. At five o'clock the company receptionist entered the lodge and presented to Judas the lists from Henry Brown containing all of the details of the contractors vehicles expected on site on Saturday and Sunday. Both foolscap lists were completely full and Judas realised that the weekend would be very busy. He was consoled by the fact that being very busy would make the day more interesting and fulfilling. Therefore, he would not have time to reflect on the happenings at the excavation site.

The afternoon drifted on and at five thirty Martin made some telephone calls to his exhibition colleagues to confirm that everything was still okay with them for the weekend attendance at the model railway venue. He seemed relieved that there were no last minute hitches to cause problems for the remaining exhibitors. The clock ticked very slowly towards six o'clock and, just before the hour, Gordon and Richard arrived for their final night shift before their four day break. Martin left slightly early and was followed on the hour by Judas, after he'd extracted his uneaten meal from the fridge. As he left the lodge, Judas heard Keith inform the incoming guards about the MD visiting the site and also about the MD's luncheon guest.

Judas walked to the college for his evening class on "Roman Britain" and was pleased to see that many of the regular students that took classes in historical subjects had enrolled on the course. He surmised that many, like himself, were anticipating the course material to be somewhat in error, since the discovery of the Roman remains in the town. Judas also knew that the tutor, Gavin Melbourne, was aware of another Roman structure in the area, but at present could say nothing about it. The group of elderly students all seemed to sit together in the various classes they attended and all were very interested in the subjects. Many had found their school years to be a non-event and now wanted to rectify their ignorance.

As Gavin Melbourne entered the reception area, all of his class duly stood and filed into the classroom. After welcoming the attendees and running through the obligatory first aid information, the fire alarm procedures, issuing car parking discs for vehicle owners and a few other requirements, Gavin Melbourne began his lecture.

"Sorry, but as you all know by now, the Romans were a permanent presence in this area. I have taught many classes on the Romans in this part of the country and until recently it was assumed, as no settlements had been unearthed, that this area was considered a backwater by the Roman authorities. However, I will begin this week with the initial invasion of this island by Rome and the reasons for the invasion and the consequences of the invasion on the population."

With this opening Gavin neatly sidestepped the problem of the discovery of Roman foundations and would be able to educate his receptive audience.

The evening was a great success. Three pages of foolscap notes were presented to each of the assembled students and Gavin went through the notes, answering all of the questions put to him by individuals. At the end of the evening, Gavin outlined the course content for next week, allowing class members to do their own research if they wished to fully prepare themselves for the class.

As he was about to leave the classroom, Judas was stopped by Gavin, who simply said, "Please would you go to the college library? I will join you in a few moments, when the rest of the class have departed."

Judas complied. He entered the college library, where he was met by Mortimer Stanhope and Robin Cooper.

"Sorry for the deception," said Robin Cooper, "but we had to see you and try to resolve a problem."

"Sounds ominous," said Judas, "I was wondering why I had not had a telephone call today concerning the results of your labours at the farmer's field."

After a couple of minutes of idle talk, Gavin Melbourne entered the room and also apologised to Judas for the deception. Mortimer Stanhope then began to speak.

"You both know what Robin and I have been doing today and we have made very good progress. We have established beyond doubt that the structure is a Roman bridge with a small parapet on each side, including the part damaged by the farmer, and we have followed the line of the road for about five feet each side of the bridge. The road is a reasonable width and is in very good condition. As we said yesterday we are not treasure hunters, we are committed archaeologists and it was only this afternoon that we dug down at the side of the bridge. We were able to establish that the bridge crossed a now dried up river." Mortimer stopped to have a sip of water. "Underneath the bridge," he continued, "there is a lot of earth that we have to move and this is where we have a problem. We need more men on the excavation. I can divert some men from the existing excavation in Beaufort St. Vincent to the bridge and they will simply be told that we have found another Roman structure. These men will not be given any additional information and, when the earth has been removed, these men will return to their other excavation.

"Now, if we do find the items that are thought to be there under the bridge, both Robin and I think it would be unforgivable not to have a film crew on site to record the momentous event, which would be the archaeological discovery of the decade, the century and the millennium. We have a resident film crew at the museum, who regularly go to excavations with us and film the activities of we mere mortal archaeologists. We also have an artist who will sketch and do accurate technical drawings of whatever we find. Now this is the question. Will you allow us to have a film crew and artist on the site to record our activities as we go under the Roman bridge?"

All men were looking at Judas. Robin then spoke.

"If the items we seek are not there, then all the film crew will observe is another Roman structure in an area where no Roman structure was thought to be. If we do find what we all seek, then the film taken by the crew will be like gold dust and will be a real treasure in itself. If the items are there, fear not, you will be credited with the discovery of the paperwork relating to the gold and silver plate, with the decipherment of the clues and with the method of calculating the location of the items. This we guarantee."

Judas could see the pleading in the eyes of the eminent archaeologists and nodded.

"I am not the one who wants the plaudits for the discovery, I just want the items to be there. Adam and Albert Stonehaven are the ones to be credited with the discovery of the various pieces of information. All I did was bring together these discoveries and luckily I was able to decipher the clues. However, I do accept that if you find the items then numerous questions will be asked of me, so I suppose I will just have to get used to it. That is assuming that you find the plate and the other pieces."

Both Mortimer Stanhope and Robin Cooper were relieved at the outcome of the meeting and it was obvious that they both became more relaxed.

"Thank you for agreeing Judas," said Robin, "now let's go for a drink."

"You're always drinking," said Gavin to his brother-in-law, "but I think I will join you."

Both Judas and Mortimer Stanhope declined the invitation, as Mortimer was driving and Judas had things to do at home.

"I will telephone Gavin tomorrow and he will pass on the information about the dig," said Robin as the group split up.

Judas returned to the street and headed towards the lodge and then on to the coastal path. It was cold, but not excessively so, and on the walk home Judas had much on his mind.

On reaching his apartment block, Judas went to the post room, but his post box was empty. He hurried up the stairs and entered his domain. He could tell that Juliette had been cleaning as the fresh aroma assailed his nostrils and was very pleasant. Judas then took some notes from his wallet and put them on the breakfast bar under his tin mug. This was his standard procedure and it amused him. Judas then went to his study and neatly wrote out the notes he had taken at the evening class and filed the neat notes with the foolscap papers. He next consumed his uneaten lunch time snack. He was not hungry, but he just felt that he needed a little something to satisfy the inner man.

After this snack Judas went to his study and looked out of the window. He reflected on the day and he hoped tomorrow would be busy at work and would also be very rewarding for Robin and Mortimer Stanhope. An hour later he was in bed.

CHAPTER 25

Saturday 17th January

As he walked slowly along the coastal path, Judas listened to the gulls and their morning chorus. It was a very pleasant walk into work, where he arrived early. Gordon and Richard were busy scurrying around their desk, finishing their duty report and the entries into their logbook.

"Glad you made it in early," said Gordon, "vehicles have been coming in for the last hour. We have made notes of the vehicle and trailer numbers as usual and the first list is on your desk. I'll bring over another couple of pieces of paper in a few minutes when I have finished this report. The contractors unloading and positioning the equipment arrived at about four o'clock."

"Okay guys, many thanks," returned Judas, "I'll take over the incoming vehicle work and transfer the information on your sheets to the receipt lists. Thanks again. If I had known that the new equipment was coming in very early, then I would have been in earlier myself."

At that moment another vehicle arrived with equipment for the factory. Judas checked the driver's paperwork, checked his own list, entered details of the vehicle and trailer number and directed the driver to the correct area of the complex. A few more vehicles arrived in the next twenty minutes and were logged and directed to their unloading point.

Keith and Colin arrived for the day shift and, after a fairly lengthy hand over, Gordon and Richard left the site. Both men said they were looking forward to their four days away from the lodge, but did not disclose any details of what they were hoping to do. Judas wished them both an enjoyable break from work.

For the next three hours, the stream of traffic was not excessive, but it was constant. In between vehicles arriving and departing, Judas entered the information provided by the night guards onto his lists and by nine o'clock only one more vehicle was due to arrive. This vehicle arrived thirty minutes later and was duly processed. The car park was only half full with company staff transport and these cars were all parked by the perimeter fence, away from the areas occupied by the articulated vehicles that had delivered the new equipment. Judas prepared a coffee for the guards and was about to sit with them, when Henry Brown entered the lodge.

"Good morning gentlemen. It appears that the contractors are full of enthusiasm this morning. I just thought I would let you know that I am off to the model railway exhibition at Cranston Market and will return later this afternoon. Paul Gibson should already be there. If anyone telephones for me or Paul, we are not contactable, so the caller should leave a message on our respective voice mails and we will return the call later."

With that Henry Brown left and the guards went out on their various patrols with great enthusiasm. It was only when Colin returned to the lodge, with a large tray containing a selection of breakfast items, that Judas realized that the canteen staff were again on site. The kitchen staff had agreed to the company request and had opened the canteen facilities for the preparation of breakfasts, lunches and various snacks for the weekend contractors, who would be working until eight o'clock tonight. It was too good an opportunity to miss and both Colin and Keith made use of the canteen facilities regularly throughout the day.

At eleven o'clock Judas received a telephone call. He lifted the receiver with trepidation, as he was expecting a call from the excavation, but this call was from Anita.

"I will be moving into my new apartment very soon and I am very busy at the moment buying new items for my new home," she announced. "Initially I will only furnish my main bedroom, lounge and dining room and make the kitchen and bathroom serviceable. I am presently searching for furniture, but I don't know what type or style that I want, but when I see it, I will know that it is right for me and my apartment."

"That is great news. I wish you success in your searches."

Judas applauded her logic, but could not understand it.

Anita continued, "I will be assisting Stephanie at the Poacher's Retreat until my sixtieth birthday in March and then I will definitely retire gracefully to a life of leisure. Thank you so much for helping me to achieve this retirement. God bless you."

Judas was taken by surprise with this and stayed silent.

Anita then said, "When I finally move into my new home Judas, you will be invited to the grand opening."

Judas laughed and accepted the invitation and on that happy note the conversation ended.

Judas was expecting much more work for him to do, but very little was happening. He began to think much more about the excavation and it played on his mind that he had heard nothing from Gavin. It irritated Judas to know that Gavin Melbourne had the lodge telephone number, but Judas himself was completely ignorant of Gavin's mobile telephone number. At noon the guards again assaulted the canteen for provisions and each enjoyed an unexpected, bountiful harvest. The plates seemed to be groaning under the weight of the portions provided by the canteen, but the guards were easily equal to the task of doing justice to the cuisine. Judas also devoured his salad, but with much less enthusiasm and definitely with much less noise.

The afternoon progressed at a very slow and sedate pace for Judas. All vehicles due had arrived in the morning and had also left the site before lunch and he was, in all honesty, surplus to requirements. On completion of their afternoon patrols, both guards reported that the contractors were doing sterling work and might even be leaving the site early tonight to go to their hotel. In fact at three o'clock some of the contractors did exit the site as they had unloaded the equipment, delivered this morning, and placed it in the required location, ready for the electrical and power engineers to continue the work next week. If the deliveries tomorrow were dealt with in the same efficient manner, then the contractors would be finished by the early afternoon.

By four o'clock most of the remaining contractors had left the site to go to their hotel, leaving only a few senior contractors on site to tackle a rogue machine that was proving very difficult to fit into its allocated position. At thirty five minutes past four, the telephone rang on Judas's desk. Judas lifted the receiver and began to formally answer, when the caller interrupted.

"Judas, it's Gavin. Are you sitting comfortably?"

Judas was taken aback and answered in the affirmative.

"Good," continued Gavin, "because we are both summoned to meet Mortimer Stanhope and Robin Cooper at the museum at six thirty tonight. Before you ask, I have no idea what they want, although Robin sounded quite excited when he telephoned me and requested me to contact you. Can you be there please? I have to contact him and let him know if you can attend?"

"Yes I will be there," answered a confused Judas.

Before he could say anything else Gavin said, "Oh good, see you there," and rang off.

Judas inwardly thought that Gavin was using the expression, "Oh good, see you there," quite regularly lately.

For a few minutes Judas just sat at his desk. His mind was racing and it was still racing when the last contractors left the site to go to their hotel. Judas watched them as they drove away and his mind returned to the meeting tonight at the museum. Ten minutes later, when Keith returned from his final patrol, Judas asked the guards if they would hold the fort for a few minutes, as he had to go to the canteen for some supplies. Judas always made sure that the food containers in the kitchen area of the lodge were reasonably well stocked, usually with various packets of biscuits and cakes. However, with Martin in the lodge and Judas being away for two days, the supplies had reached a critical level. Drastic action was needed and this opportunity provided Judas with the perfect excuse to go and get some food items out of the vending machines. No objections were received and Judas left the lodge and walked to the canteen. On reaching the room he was disappointed to view a vending machine devoid of supplies.

Judas went to other locations in the factory and office areas and managed to get some packs of biscuits, a few packs of small cakes and various bars of confectionery that he thought would keep the lodge fraternity in good humour until he could properly replenish the depleted stores. Judas made a mental note to obtain a good selection of supplies on his next visit to his shopping mall.

Whilst in the main office area, Judas used the water dispenser and, whilst enjoying his drink, he looked out of the window towards the town. It was dark; the car park was empty, except for the guards' vehicles, and it was very cold. Judas looked over to the railway line as he heard the growl of a locomotive leaving the station. He thought of Adam and then immediately his thoughts returned to the excavation and then to his meeting at the museum tonight.

Judas returned to the lodge and replenished the practically barren food containers. Five minutes later, Adrian and Roy entered the lodge to begin their four days of guarding duties. The hand over was a very quick affair and Judas wished the departing guards, Keith and Colin, a relaxing and enjoyable break from their security work. Judas would normally converse with the incoming staff, but on this occasion he simply said:

"Sorry guys but I have an appointment in town and I cannot be late." He reached the exit, turned and informed the night guards, "I will be here about four o'clock in the morning, as vehicles delivering new equipment for the factory are scheduled for a very early arrival."

He left the lodge and walked briskly to the museum. It was still very cold and the quick walk helped him to keep warm. He entered the museum car park and was surprised at the number of vehicles standing in the car park. He was even more surprised to see one of the vans had "Museum Photographic Unit" emblazoned on the side. Judas went up the steps and was met at the door by Gavin, Mortimer Stanhope and Robin Cooper. After the initial greeting by Gavin, Judas was ushered into a small annexe off the reception hall and invited to sit. Sheepishly Judas sat.

"Sorry for the summons," said Robin Cooper, "but the museum film unit, with a cameraman, lighting technician and a sound technician, plus the artist draughtsman, came out with us this morning to the excavation we were conducting under the bridge. We have some footage that we are sure you will find interesting. Also at the bridge this morning, we had three senior archaeologists doing ordinary excavation work and I am certain that they began to think that something big was about to happen. These three gentlemen, together with Mortimer and myself, cleared away the earth at the right hand side of the bridge and then did the same exercise for the left hand side of the bridge. Mortimer and I then went under the bridge and we were watched by the eagle eyes of our colleagues. The results of our labours were captured on film and we would now like to show you and Gavin that film. We are sure that you will both find it very interesting."

Mortimer Stanhope then spoke.

"These archaeologists, who were with us today at the excavation, kept asking us questions, but we just kept pleading ignorance and eventually they stopped asking us anything. The film crew and the artist are not archaeologists, but enthusiastic amateurs and I am sure that they know that something historic is about to happen. We have therefore sworn them to secrecy and they have agreed. We will speak again of this after the film unit presentation."

With that, Judas was led to a nearby room where a small screen had been erected on the end wall. Six men were sitting in comfortable chairs in the room and were talking loudly. A seventh man, who Judas took to be the artist, stood behind the seated men. The chatter stopped immediately as the four men entered. Judas was introduced to the assembled crowd, the lights were dimmed and the film show began.

The initial footage showed the bridge parapet that had been damaged by the farmer and then panned to the bridge. It showed the work that Robin Cooper and Mortimer Stanhope had completed the previous day and the voiceover explained that the excavators today were going to remove the earth deposits from under the bridge. The footage showed the work beginning and the various archaeologists occupied on their allocated tasks. It also showed the artist busily sketching and recording every detail. Judas was fascinated by the film and was completely absorbed by its content. After a while the cameraman went under the bridge and showed the excavators carefully removing the accumulation of earth from the dried up river bed. After a few minutes the film showed that it was possible to see through the tunnel under the bridge and the lighting technician was seen placing lights to illuminate the underside of the bridge.

It was at this point that Mortimer Stanhope and Robin Cooper ventured to the centre of the underside of the bridge and the assisting excavators began to look at the activities of the senior archaeologists with a sceptical stance. Both Mortimer and Robin were engrossed in the search and cleared a pile of earth from the small alcove on the southern side of the bridge without result, and the film caught the sadness in the voices of the men. Next Mortimer and Robin applied their energies to the same procedure of removing another pile of earth from the small alcove, but this time on the northern side of the bridge. The sudden gasp from one of the men caused the cameraman to zoom in onto the ground between them and the lighting technician illuminated the scene. There in front of them was the top of a piece of pottery. Mortimer Stanhope, on his knees, gently picked the earth away from the object and then said with great delight that it continued downwards. Both Mortimer and Robin gently eased away the earth and eventually the top of a pot took shape. It could be seen on the film that both men were visibly trembling and there was a tremor in their voices as they spoke.

"Oh my God," said Mortimer Stanhope, "the pot lid is sealed."

Robin looked closely at the lid and with a quiver in his voice simply said, "Yes."

The next part of the film showed that the three additional excavators were at the side of the bridge, all eagerly looking at the antics of the two senior archaeologists. The artist was also sketching away and capturing the moment. They were all saying absolutely nothing, but were enthralled at the thought of being involved in the discovery of yet another Roman structure. It was only when Robin casually said that the pot was mediaeval, not Roman, that the mood of the three archaeologists changed, as they began to realise what the significance of the find could be.

The rest of the film outlined the work done by all of the archaeologists as they took it in turns, in the small space under the bridge, to try and free the mediaeval pot and its sealed lid from the enclosing earth. The film technicians, professional to the highest level, just kept filming and produced some spectacular footage of the pot being excavated, although it was still stubbornly refusing to yield after centuries of comfort and being embraced by mother earth. At last, as the whole group of archaeologists and the film crew were debating their next move, the pot moved. A startled cry came from Mortimer Stanhope, who was the excavator doing the work, and after a few more minutes of endeavour by numerous archaeologists the pot was free.

The film unit continued filming and showed many hands lifting the pot, now wrapped in protective cloth, and the assembled men just staring at it. Robin Cooper simply stated that the pot should be taken to the museum and the British Museum must be advised of the find and Mortimer Stanhope readily agreed.

The cameraman, who was taking final shots of the small alcove, said, "There's been a massive collapse of the earth from the wall at the back of the alcove and I think there's another pot."

Had the men been carrying the recovered pot they would surely have dropped it at that moment.

Robin was first to return to the alcove and confirmed, "Oh Christ yes, there is another pot," and he went down onto his knees to investigate further. After a few moments, he continued, "I definitely believe it to be another mediaeval pot."

This confirmation was agreed by Mortimer Stanhope. The artist began to sketch the new find in its natural glory, as the cameraman captured it on film.

The film ended at this point and the lights were turned up. Judas was impressed by what he had seen on the film, but he was still in doubt as to what was inside the pot. Were his calculations correct concerning the lost abbey artefacts, or was it just a fluke that mediaeval pots had been unearthed?

Judas looked up and saw Gavin, Mortimer Stanhope and Robin Cooper walking towards him.

Robin Cooper then said, "As I outlined on the film, we have to notify the British Museum and this I have done."

Robin Cooper then asked Judas for a favour. He explained that the archaeologists working at the bridge had known that something special was happening, as did the people working on the film and also the artist. They had asked questions of him and Mortimer Stanhope, but they could not enlighten them without breaking a promise. Robin said that the men should be told and Judas agreed. Robin then asked for another favour. He asked if Judas would allow the film unit to record on film his outlining of the research he had been doing, as this would be invaluable should the hidden artefacts be found. Robin guaranteed that the film would not be used if the present excavation proved fruitless concerning the holy relics. Judas again agreed.

Judas then walked to the front of the screen, introduced himself again to the men assembled and simply stated that he was about to put the audience out of its misery. Judas began slowly with an outline of the story of the abbey and its turbulent history. He outlined the attacks on the abbey and the drastic action taken by the monks to save the abbey gold and silver plate and the other valuable artefacts from the aggrieved robbers. Judas could see that the audience was hanging on his every word. He outlined the various clues that had been unearthed by Albert and Adam Stonehaven and how he had deciphered the mediaeval monk's clues. After forty minutes Judas took a break and asked if anyone had any questions. Robin Cooper left the room, but no-one else moved, so Judas continued.

Judas began again and was very pleased to see Mortimer Stanhope and Gavin beaming with delight in the audience and he was also pleased to see that Robin had returned and brought his notes, which were handed to Judas so that he could visually explain how he had arrived at his calculations. When he explained how he had turned the maps through one hundred and eighty degrees and had made various assumptions and followed these through to unravel the location, there was an audible gasp from the group. Judas continued for another twenty five minutes and neatly tied up his speech and opened up the floor to any questions. There was complete silence, even Mortimer, Robin and Gavin seemed dumbstruck by what had been said, as Judas had included information in this evening's talk that he had not mentioned before. Suddenly the room was ringing with the applause from the assembled men. Judas was embarrassed.

At this point Mortimer Stanhope thanked Judas for his lecture and he told the assembled audience that they had undertaken to keep the knowledge safe and not to divulge the information to anyone.

"It has taken Judas forty five years of hard work to reach this stage and loose talk could ruin everything," said Mortimer Stanhope.

The men all nodded towards Judas, who said, "Nothing is yet certain about the contents in the pots, or even if there is anything in the pots, but if it is proven that it is the missing ecclesiastical items, there will be time for celebration later." Judas continued, "There were also a number of symbols on the cross that have not yet been deciphered and I am still trying to understand these, but as yet I am completely baffled. Some of the information may be false trails to confuse any would be investigator. There is another pot to remove tomorrow from under the bridge and I look forward to receiving news of its content."

Judas then returned the notes to Robin Cooper. Mortimer Stanhope then stated that he had arranged for one of his men to be at the bridge site all night for security reasons and for another security person to be in the museum vault all night with the recovered pot. These men were museum staff and were completely trustworthy.

Mortimer also confirmed, "Representatives of the British Museum will be at the bridge site tomorrow. I have contacted an old friend and colleague at his home and have told him that the local museum staff were possibly hours away from the archaeological find of the millennium. This colleague asked for some additional details, but was simply advised, 'Beaufort St. Vincent abbey artefacts'. My old friend should be here later tonight, together with his assistant, and we have all been invited to stay with Robin at his home, ready for an early start tomorrow.

"God I have never been this excited about anything before. If the lost items are under the bridge, this will be the highlight of my archaeological career. And I still have a good few years of exploration left," he concluded.

"As do I," countered Robin Cooper and Judas could see that both men were eager for the morning to arrive.

The group began to disperse and Judas was once again thanked by Mortimer and Robin for his input to the evening's events.

"We are both very hopeful of the outcome tomorrow at the bridge site and look forward to the day's events," said Robin Cooper.

Judas left the museum; it was nine thirty and he realised that he was very hungry. He was also very happy and he was hoping that tomorrow would be the day that all of the hard work and research that had been expended on the project would prove fruitful and rewarding. He walked back past the lodge, along deserted streets and along the coastal path. Hardly a single soul had ventured out on this very cold and blustery night. He arrived at the apartment block, collected his mail from the post room, entered his castle and relaxed.

Judas reflected on the day's events, especially those at the field excavation and he was looking forward to tomorrow. He hoped that Mortimer and Robin and the rest of the archaeologists were successful in removing the second pot. He also hoped that the contents of the pots were abbey artefacts. It was at this point that Judas suddenly had a disturbing thought. Two pots were not enough to conceal the church plate and the other treasures. There must be more pots or there must be another hiding place!

With this thought still in his mind, Judas retreated to the kitchen, raided the fridge and prepared himself a large but simple meal. Afterwards Judas went to his bedroom and reset his alarm clock for three o'clock. He was about to retire for the night when he remembered his mail from the post room. He placed the three envelopes in his case and prepared for the night. In his darkened room he kept thinking about the pot problem, but ten minutes later he was past caring.

377

CHAPTER 26

Sunday 18th January

The next morning, Judas was thankful to reach the warmth of the lodge just before it began to rain. Adrian and Roy had both enjoyed a peaceful and uneventful shift. Both of the guards had been busy during their four day break.

Adrian said, "I went to a travel agent and arranged a summer cruise for my family in the Mediterranean. My wife has always been pestering me for a cruise and now I might get some peace."

Roy however had been busy at home sorting out his garage and loft.

"I can now get my car and the wife's car parked in the garage and the loft is practically empty," he said.

Both confirmed that they were glad to be back at work.

At four o'clock the contractors began to arrive and seemed pleased that over half of the work was completed yesterday. Judas checked them all into the complex against the paperwork supplied by Henry Brown. The first delivery vehicle arrived ten minutes later and this heralded the start of a very busy two hours. Judas did the necessary clerical work involved and directed the vehicles to the required locations. The operations all went very smoothly. Some company members began to arrive at five o'clock, together with the kitchen staff, and soon the various offices were emblazoned with light. However, the factory staff got their priorities right and the canteen area next to the vending machines was the first section to be illuminated. No doubt that the staff would all be disappointed to find the vending machine for confectionery, biscuits and cakes, devoid of all items. After another hour of solid work, the sheet containing all details of Sunday arrivals had been completed.

At this point John and Geoff the incoming guards for the day shift arrived and, after a fairly short hand over, Adrian and Roy vacated the lodge. As the incoming guards were completing their paperwork for the forthcoming shift, Judas retreated to the kitchen area of the lodge and prepared a mug of coffee for them. It was really cold outside and it was also raining heavily, and the new guards looked very cold and both had red faces. The coffees and the small packs of biscuits he associated with the drinks were warmly accepted.

As Judas returned to his desk he remembered the three letters he had collected from the post room. He extracted them from his case and neatly opened them. The first envelope contained a "Good luck in your new home" card from Juliette, Andrew and Mary. The second envelope was from the college, offering another course on maps, but later in the year, and the third envelope contained a copy of the signed agreement from Amanda and Stephen's lawyers for his information, retention and filing. Judas made a mental note to go and see the owners of the Ivy Lodge Guest House in the morning and to present them with the cheque they so richly deserved to fulfil their ambition and their dream.

Just after nine o'clock the last of the contractor's vehicles left the site, leaving only the contractors on the complex.

When Geoff returned from his mid morning patrol he said, "I have spoken to some of the contractors and they have confirmed that all of the equipment has been placed in its correct position with the exception of one, and this machine will soon be installed where it should be."

When John returned from his patrol an hour later he said, "Most of the contractors were in the canteen, sampling the delights of the kitchen staff."

From nine o'clock onwards, Judas did very little work and kept thinking about the excavation under the bridge. He kept hoping the telephone would ring and the caller would either confirm the accuracy of his decipherment of the clues and confirm the discovery of the lost church items, or tell him there was nothing there under the Roman bridge except a couple of empty mediaeval pots. Either way he just wished the telephone would ring. He sat there waiting for something to happen, but nothing did and it began to irritate him.

A few vehicles belonging to the factory workers began to leave the site at eleven o'clock and these returned to the car park just before noon. For something to do, Judas took from his case the model railway he had planned and studied it more closely. He was still pleased with it and even tried to better it with the addition of extra siding capacity, but this overloaded the original concept and he deleted the additional lines. At this point Judas recalled the advice given by Dr. Rose the MD, concerning large complex layouts and their unsuitability for the solo operative. This recollection troubled him and he thought deeply about his layout requirements in his apartment. He decided then and there that his design was too complicated for his solo use and consigned the layout sketch to his folder. He then began to think about another layout design, but every time he began to put pencil to paper, his imagination seemed to malfunction.

Judas heard movement in the kitchen area and saw Geoff preparing drinks for himself and John. Judas was about to get himself a drink when his telephone sounded and he snatched up the handset.

It was Gavin, calling from his mobile telephone, who simply requested in a very calm voice, "Mortimer and Robin would like you to be at the museum again tonight at six thirty for an update on the day's events." Unable to conceal his excitement, he blurted out, "The second pot has been released from its entombment and three others have also been discovered. All of the pots were located under the bridge, all were unbroken and all have now been removed intact from their initial burial place.

"We are taking them back to the museum in a few minutes, but we have no idea of the contents of the pots. The second pot was the same size as the first, but the third, fourth and fifth were bigger and were buried further back in the alcove under the bridge.

Hopefully, when you get to the museum tonight, we will have some more good news for you. Mortimer and Robin are as excited as schoolchildren in a confectionery outlet and are as happy as anyone can be," concluded Gavin.

"I'll be there as soon as I can tonight..." confirmed Judas and was about to continue, when Gavin simply said, "Oh good, see you there," and ended the call.

Judas sat for about twenty minutes pondering the news that he had just been given. Five pots had been unearthed, but Gavin had not said that pots three, four and five were mediaeval. That worried him. However, there was nothing that he could do, except continue with his work, and at six o'clock he would head off to the museum. The noise of the out barrier being raised made Judas look up and he saw a whole line of contractors' vans about to exit the site.

The foreman in charge told the guards, "All of our work has been completed and we are all going back to our homes."

Judas made a quick note of all the vehicle numbers as they passed and entered the time of departure next to the arrival time from this morning on the company sheet.

At two o'clock many of the factory staff began to leave the buildings and make for the vehicles in the car park. Twenty minutes later the car park was virtually empty, with only the two vehicles of the guards and two others remaining.

"Oh God, now what?" said a concerned Geoff as he saw Henry Brown's car enter the car park.

Henry meticulously parked his car in the white lines of the parking area and then walked into the lodge.

He explained to the guards and Judas, "As you know, Paul and I have been to the model railway exhibition at Cranston Market and have represented the company and we have answered numerous questions from the public. The company stand has been a great success. I have also seen Martin Holland and his club members demonstrating their layout and they all seemed to be enjoying themselves."

Henry Brown then continued on a completely different tangent.

"The new publication will be completed soon and going to the proof readers for a final check and, if everything is okay, it will then go to the publishers."

Henry Brown then walked over to Judas and spoke directly to him.

"I know that you are off tomorrow, but something has come up and Paul, Stephen Lindsey and I must speak to you urgently. Can you please come in tomorrow? There is nothing to worry about, but it is honestly very important, so could you please come in during the morning?"

Judas smiled and nodded.

"Okay Mr Brown, I will come into the lodge early and do the hand over to Martin and I will also find out from him how his exhibition layout was received at the venue. I will then come over to your office."

This time Henry Brown nodded.

When he had left the lodge, Geoff said, "You really are popular at the moment. If there is another MD meeting tomorrow, can you please bring some champagne back this time, together with the sandwiches," and he burst out laughing.

Henry Brown had gone into the main complex to collect some publicity material that he was going to deliver to some new client companies in the morning. Fifteen minutes later, after two trips to his vehicle with hands full of literature, he drove from the car park and with a cheerful wave he left the site. At that moment, John entered the lodge and announced that all staff had left the site, including the pedestrian staff, and the whole alarm system could be activated. Geoff complied and the shrill system sounded and set.

When Henry Brown left the site Judas thought about what he had said: *Something has come up... Must speak to you urgently tomorrow... It is honestly very important.* Judas could not think about anything that he had done that could cause the men any great problems, but it did give him food for thought. However, he tried to put this problem to the back of his mind and he concentrated on other things.

At three o'clock, Judas telephoned Juliette, but only activated the answering machine, so he left a message thanking her and Andrew, and also Mary, for their kind wishes concerning his new home. He then wrote out a cheque for the agreed amount to the Ivy Lodge Guest House and this he would deliver sometime tomorrow. Judas next wrote out a note to Martin Holland, simply saying that if Martin had a problem with any aspect of the work, then he could be contacted at any time on his mobile telephone. Judas then telephoned Anita at the Poacher's Retreat, but again the answering machine stirred into life and he simply put down the handset. He next tried her mobile telephone, but this was switched off. *Just my luck*, he thought as he had time to talk to anyone, but no-one was available to listen.

The afternoon was definitely beginning to drag and Judas went to the kitchen area to prepare coffees for the guards. He placed the steaming cups on their desk and all three sat and talked about everything in general and nothing in particular. The conversation, as usual, turned onto the subject of football and the desperate plight of the local team after its heavy defeat yesterday, and Judas quickly retreated to his desk. He began to think again about the archaeologists working at the bridge and he sincerely hoped that when he entered the museum tonight, he was given some good news. He kept thinking about the mediaeval pots and he really hoped and prayed that the other three pots unearthed were also of the same period.

As all staff had left the site, the guards concentrated on the external patrols and the guard left in the lodge concentrated on the internal office, canteen, kitchen and factory cameras. Judas was still searching for employment when the telephone on his desk sounded. It was Gavin again, on his mobile, giving an update on the excavation.

"James Priestley and Giles Anderson are here and are looking forward to meeting you this evening. The camera crew have had a field day, no pun intended, and have some wonderful footage of the day's events. All the pots have been liberated and taken back to the museum for examination. All of the archaeologists are in a very positive mood and are looking forward to seeing you this evening."

Gavin stopped to take a deep breath, but before he could begin again, Judas asked "Who are James Priestley and Giles Anderson? I have never heard of them."

"Oh sorry," said Gavin, "James and Giles are the British Museum representatives and both have been involved in the excavations today. They kept asking Mortimer and Robin questions about the site, but both men said that all would be revealed tonight. I think you may have to do your speech again for their benefit and again I think the cameras will be running."

Gavin again stopped for breath, but before Judas could say anything, he simply said, "See you later, at the museum," and ended the call.

That ending makes a change, thought Judas.

The rest of the afternoon seemed endless. Both guards completed an external patrol and, on completion of the second, they prepared themselves for an early exit from the site. In case he forgot later, Judas wished both guards a very pleasant and enjoyable evening and the guards in return hoped that Judas had a very relaxing four days away from the lodge. The final twenty minutes definitely dragged for Judas. He got himself ready for a quick getaway and when Adrian and Roy arrived just before six o'clock, he was at the exit ready for departure. He wished the incoming guards a very peaceful shift and walked swiftly out of the site.

Judas was not expecting it to be cold. Normally when it was cold, the guards complained about the low temperatures after each patrol, but today they had not enlightened him. He walked to the Beaufort St. Vincent museum at a quickened pace and, when he arrived, he was surprised to see the building lit up and the car park perimeter lights all blazing. Judas entered the reception area and was met by Gavin, Mortimer and Robin.

After a quick "Hello" from all of them, Judas was introduced to Professor James Priestley of the British Museum and his assistant Giles Anderson. Both of the new men shook hands with Judas and it was the professor who spoke.

"Giles and I arrived here last night and stayed with Robin and his lovely wife at their beautiful home. Our questions were not answered, but we were told that we would not regret being here. Today, after a fabulous breakfast, we have all been working under a bridge in the middle of no-where, built by the Romans who were not supposed to be in this area. We all excavated under the bridge and surrounding area today and found three mediaeval pots to add to the two that were found yesterday. Giles and I have persistently asked questions, even of the people on the film unit, and have received no information. I am told you have the answers. For the sake of my sanity will you please enlighten us?"

Mortimer Stanhope then spoke, "Judas, I hate to ask this of you, but would you please allow the talk that you did last night and filmed by our museum staff, to be shown again to enlighten James and Giles and to thoroughly entertain Robin, Gavin, me and the rest of the guys who were here last night. Our film guys have done sterling work in the field again today and have film of us finding the three additional pots and extracting them from under the bridge. When this information goes public it would be unforgivable not to have complete film evidence to substantiate the discovery."

Judas could feel the pleading in Mortimer's voice and agreed. The group, including James Priestley and Giles Anderson went into the same room that had been used yesterday. The audience consisted of the same archaeologists and film crew that were there last night and a slight ripple of applause began as Judas entered the room. The main difference tonight for Judas was that he was now part of the audience.

The film began with the talk by Judas as he introduced himself to the men assembled. Judas was surprised at the content of the talk and he was also surprised at the superb quality of the film. Judas thought his outlining of the events of the mediaeval period was a bit lengthy, but everyone else in the room seemed to be enjoying the talk and also seemed to be hanging onto his every word. He cast a casual glance over to the professor and his assistant, and he could see that they were captivated by the information they were receiving. Mortimer, Robin and Gavin were also smiling at the look of sheer pleasure on the faces of the British Museum men. When Judas outlined how he had deciphered the mediaeval information a cry of "Brilliant" was heard, and when the photocopy of the markings on the original cross were shown, there was an audible gasp.

The talk went on for about one hour and then the lights came on and the film stopped.

"The film will continue in about ten minutes," said Mortimer and then asked, "If there are any questions, these will be answered later." James Priestley was about to speak when Mortimer said, "Now do you see why we were so reluctant to say anything."

James Priestley simply nodded as did his assistant. The film show continued after a short interlude and initially outlined how the calculations to produce the positioning information for the lost artefacts were determined. The film showed the damaged Roman bridge before excavation and the digging down at the side of the bridge and under the bridge to expose the first pot and the discovery of the second pot. The film continued with the releasing of the two pots from under the bridge and the taking of the pots to the museum.

The next part of the film was of the day's events, which Judas had not seen. It showed the men returning to the excavation and continuing with the delicate work under the bridge. When the next three mediaeval pots were unearthed, the film unit captured the event and also the wonderment of the occasion.

Mortimer Stanhope was heard to say, "This will be the highlight of my archaeological career, assuming the pots contain the abbey church artefacts."

Robin Cooper could also be heard reiterating the same sentiment and, in one shot on film, both men could be seen with tears in their eyes. All of the extra pots were removed and bandaged up and very carefully taken to the museum where the second part of the film ended.

"Now, any questions?" asked Mortimer Stanhope.

James Priestley simply looked at Judas and said, "That was absolutely brilliant. A marvellous presentation. How you deciphered the markings on the cross and how you reasoned that the maps should be turned through one hundred and eighty degrees was sheer brilliance and I sincerely applaud your knowledge and expertise. Well done."

Judas was completely taken aback and smiled and looked away.

"If the pots are found to be empty, you may change your opinion," said Judas and a slight murmur of laughter was heard in the room.

A few questions were asked and Judas answered them all completely and honestly and after about thirty minutes Robin suggested that they all went to the foyer drinks machine for refreshment. Mortimer told the assembly that no more work was to be done until the morning and then most of the people declined drinks and left the museum. This left James, Giles, Mortimer, Gavin and Robin with Judas in the foyer.

The group sat for about forty minutes and Judas was bombarded with questions, especially by Giles and James and he again answered them all with great clarity and insight. As the questions petered out, Mortimer again reiterated that it had taken Judas over half a lifetime to arrive at the conclusions that he had and therefore secrecy was required for a few more days.

However, he concluded, "I am convinced that when we start work tomorrow morning, at nine o'clock sharp, we can do archaeological work on the pots, as well as discovery work, and we will reap the rewards that Judas so rightly deserves. Hopefully, when we open the containers we will discover the lost abbey church artefacts and the archaeological world will go ballistic. I will consider it an honour to be there, as I am sure Robin, James, Gavin and Giles also will be honoured to be there."

Judas was again embarrassed and simply said, "I sincerely hope the mediaeval pots contain the items we are all seeking."

After drinks the group left the museum and the guards made the building secure. James and Giles, together with Mortimer, returned with Robin to his home for another night and Gavin walked part of the way through town with Judas.

As they parted, Gavin said "A great day today and I am sure tomorrow will be even better. I will keep you posted by telephone."

"No need," said Judas, "I have four days off work and I will be at the museum early." Judas then recalled that he had to see Henry Brown and added, "I have to see my boss at work at about seven o'clock, but I will be at the museum as early as I can."

The walk home was a very solitary affair, but Judas enjoyed it. He reflected on the happenings of the day and he was content. He was certain that tomorrow would be a momentous day in the local archaeological community and he was pleased to know that he would be part of it. It was getting colder and Judas was pleased to be near to his home. He walked up the stairs, entered his aerial fortress and relaxed.

After a ten minute rest Judas prepared himself a simple meal. He wasn't hungry, but just needed something to munch. He sat in his study overlooking the coast and was pleased to be indoors. He could hear the wind howling outside and this brought a shiver down his spine. He thought about tomorrow and hoped that the archaeologists would be able to confirm his findings about the lost abbey artefacts. He then turned his attention to the meeting with Henry Brown, Paul Gibson and Stephen Lindsey. He still hadn't a clue as to what it would be about, but it began to worry him. Even Henry Brown's assertion that there was nothing to worry about did not pacify his trepidation. However, there was nothing that he could do about it now, so he reset his bedside alarm to five o'clock and surrendered to the world of dreams.

CHAPTER 27

Monday 19th January

Judas was awoken by the alarm and was immediately fully awake. He made leisurely use of his en-suite bathroom and whilst using his mirror to check his hair, he was disgusted to see that he needed a haircut urgently and his beard needed trimming. Judas got himself ready for the day and had a simple breakfast. He ventured to his study and pondered his activities for the day.

As he sat looking out towards the horizon, at nothing in particular, he made a mental note of what he had to do during the day. He had to see Henry Brown at work. It was imperative that he saw Amanda and Stephen at the Ivy Lodge Guest House to present them with the cheque. He also wanted to contact Martin Holland at the lodge to make sure everything at work was okay and he had to be at the museum to be present at the opening of the pots and hopefully he would be present at the discovery of the lost artefacts.

At six thirty Judas walked to the coastal path and began the journey to his work. *No peace for the wicked*, he thought. Judas enjoyed walking on the coastal path and this morning there were a number of joggers and dog walkers active along the path. One dog in particular took an instant dislike to Judas and growled and barked persistently at him. Judas stood still, not wishing to antagonise the beast, and the dog owner profusely apologised to him and led the animal away, admonishing it severely. Judas continued his journey without any further problems and reached the lodge.

Martin was at his desk and was surprised to see Judas. John was at his desk but on the telephone.

"I just popped in to see how the exhibition went," said Judas.

"Absolutely brilliantly," replied Martin, "it was a great show and was a pleasure to be involved in."

Judas was pleased and then asked, "Has Henry Brown arrived yet?" and was relieved to receive a positive reply.

John's telephone call had ended and he casually asked, "Biarritz still crowded?"

Judas nodded and smiled.

"By the way, many thanks for the note giving your mobile number in case of any problems – it was very thoughtful," said Martin, as Judas exited the lodge and walked to the office block.

Judas asked the receptionist to advise Henry Brown that he was on site and, on completion of the call, he was requested to go into Mr Brown's office. Judas complied and after a short walk he was standing outside the required door.

Here goes, thought Judas as he gently knocked on the panelled door, which was opened immediately by Paul Gibson.

"You really must enjoy your days off," said Paul Gibson and invited Judas into the room.

Seated at his desk was Henry Brown, telephone in hand, and standing at the side of the table was Stephen Lindsey. As the call ended, Henry Brown looked up and thanked Judas for attending.

The following conversation related to Beaufort Models.

"As you know," began Henry Brown, "the new company publication is undergoing its final proofread and will soon go to the printers. We have an earlier proof copy here and we are all thrilled at the outstanding information content, the quality of the photographic work showing our products and also the wonderful layouts and diagrams. In short, we are as certain as we can be that this book will be a great success and this is, in no small part, down to you Judas for your contribution concerning the previously unknown photographs of Beaufort St. Clement, the missing layout design of the revised station at Beaufort St. Clement, the Beaufort St. Vincent harbour extension and of course your contribution with the model railway layouts. The dedication of the book will also be of great interest to you.

It reads, "This book is dedicated to the memory of Albert Stonehaven, a historical researcher, and also to Adam Stonehaven, a signalman of the Great Western Railway and great nephew of Albert, who discovered the long lost maps and plans of the Beaufort St. Clement station complex. May they now rest in peace."

Judas began to feel the tears in his eyes and he just mouthed "Thank you" to Henry Brown.

Henry Brown then continued: "The book has a very good selection of layouts of all shapes and sizes, but it was only after the initial printing that we realized that we had omitted to cater sufficiently for the novice railway modeller. We hope to rectify this omission by publishing a separate layout book aimed at the junior modeller and also aimed at those older people entering the hobby for the first time. This first book will contain simple layouts and we will show how these simple layouts can be expanded, as and when space and finances allow. We will then publish a second book of more complex layouts and show how these can also be expanded to allow more complex shunting manoeuvres and to help the operator to develop his modelling and design skills. If these books are a success, and we are all confident that they will be, then a third book will be introduced showing very advanced layout designs and demonstrating how these complex plans can be improved upon by a little thought and energy."

Judas listened with great interest, but he was also wondering where the conversation was heading, when Henry Brown came to his main point.

"This is where you come in Judas. As you have done such good work with the simple layout plans in the new book and also some of your moderate plans are impeccable, we were hoping that you would please join our Design Bureau and help Stephen here and his new assistant Matthew Forrester to produce the required publications and do the publicity work. That is, you will be the person responsible for the company's publicity stands at exhibitions, for transportation to the exhibitions and for the accommodation at these events for our staff. In addition, we hope for future exhibitions to have a layout at these venues promoting our track, locomotives, rolling stock and buildings. Your duties would also be to design layouts that one of our company teams will construct in the factory, so that they can be developed into better layouts in stages. We then hope to sell these initial layouts and, later on, the owners will want to add to the layout and they will buy the additional track packages from us and develop the layout in stages." Henry Brown paused to take a few deep breaths and then finished by asking, "Would you please give this proposal your consideration and let us know your decision as soon as possible please? By the way, we will formally introduce you to Matthew Forrester at a later date."

Judas was completely taken aback by this offer and his shocked expression was seen by all present.

"You are the perfect man for the job," interjected Stephen Lindsey and continued, "Your layout designs are first class in the present book and I am sure you will not have any undue problems performing all aspects of the new post. It will be challenging, but it will also be very rewarding."

Paul Gibson nodded and then whispered to Henry Brown, who then spoke to Judas and outlined that on this new post he would have additional leave and when he mentioned the initial salary figure, Judas was astounded.

When he had regained some composure, Judas asked the assembled company, "You do realize that I am nearly sixty years old?"

"We did know this statistical fact," said Henry Brown, "and it will not be a problem for the company."

In view of this, Judas accepted the offer and was greeted by all of the men with a very firm handshake. Henry Brown then became serious.

"Judas, do not broadcast the information to the security lodge personnel or Martin Holland, until the paperwork is made official. However, my name, by the way, is Henry, he is Paul, and over there is Stephen. Welcome to the club."

Judas could not help but smile and simply said, "Thank you."

Henry Brown then became defensive.

"Now, if I may ask a very personal question, how in God's name did you get christened Judas?"

All three men were looking at Judas and he smiled. It was a question he had often been asked, but ironically until now, no-one at Beaufort Models had.

Judas resigned himself to the question and answered, "My parents were both at the local orphanage when I was born, but three days later they both absconded, leaving me there. They never contacted the orphanage again. A lady helper at the orphanage saw a book by the side of my mother's bed, written by Thomas Hardy, called 'Jude the Obscure'. This lady notified the authorities and it was decided to name me Jude.

At the christening the vicar, very old, partially deaf and suitably inebriated, asked formally for the name of the child and was advised 'Jude, as in the Obscure'. The vicar just heard the 'Jude, as' part and here I am."

Henry, Paul and Stephen all collapsed with laughter, but Judas was again not amused. As the meeting was now at an end Judas left the three men in the office, sorting out the problem that he had interrupted when he entered the room and went to the company canteen for a cool drink. He sat at a table by the window and began to ponder his very bright future.

He was still deep in thought thirty minutes later when a middle aged man approached.

"Are you Judas Wells?"

Judas nodded and the man introduced himself.

"I'm Matthew Forrester." He shook Judas by the hand and sat down next to him before continuing. "You really are to be congratulated on your discoveries of the lost station plans. Henry Brown is as chuffed as hell that they have been discovered. I have also seen the drawings and plans prepared by you for the new publication and they are absolutely superb. I have just seen Stephen Lindsey and he gave me the wonderful news that you will be joining the team. Welcome.

"Stephen and I had worked together many years ago at a production company, which unfortunately suffered in the recession and was forced to close. On the company's demise, our paths parted. I came south to another job and Steve went north. It was only by mere chance that we re-met recently, when Steve and his wife moved here from the north of England. As I was seeking employment and Steve needed an assistant at this company, the die was cast.

"The job you are being employed on is a great opportunity for you to gain experience and knowledge and there is also the added bonus of additional leave and higher salary."

Judas thanked him for his kind words and said he looked forward to working with him.

As his new colleague was about to leave the canteen, he turned to Judas and stated, "On Friday, Saturday and Sunday, auditors will be on site, together with company staff on stock taking duties, so it should be quiet for a few days in the lodge." Matthew Forrester then left the canteen, calling over his shoulder, "I will tell the guys in the office that that I have seen you."

Judas just sat at his table and continued to ponder his future. He was certain that he had made the correct decision and he was looking forward to doing more work planning model railway layouts. He accepted that his layouts would not be as large or as complex as those designed by Stephen Lindsey, but he was confident that he could accomplish the requirements of the company. Also the thought of designing layouts that could be enlarged, doing publicity work and being associated with the exhibition work excited him, and he looked forward to his involvement in the projects.

He resisted the temptation to return to the lodge to see if there were any problems and instead he headed towards the town centre. On his way there, he passed an old corner shop that had recently been refurbished and changed from its former use to that of a model, hobby and craft shop. The shop next door was, at present, being refurbished and the windows were covered in white dust and grime, as the contractors inside were busy with building alterations. Out of interest, Judas entered the model shop.

The shop frontage was not excessive and in all honesty the shop itself seemed to be very cramped, but it did have a large quantity of stock. Judas walked along an aisle that displayed First World War models and was fascinated by the numerous types of models that were displayed. On another shelf, Second World War kits were available, showing the same types of weaponry and personnel, only this section had more kits available and Judas surmised that modelling equipment for this war was more popular in the modelling fraternity. The whole of the right hand side wall was dedicated to craft work and when Judas reached the rear wall of the establishment, he was engulfed in model railway equipment. The shop in Beaufort St. Catherine was small, but well stocked. This shop in Beaufort St. Vincent was slightly smaller, but it was bursting at the seams with modelling equipment associated with model railways.

Before he began in earnest to rummage through the shelves, Judas looked at his pocket watch and saw that it was ten minutes to nine o'clock. He retreated to the shop entrance and was about to leave when he saw an advertising flyer on a notice board. Judas quickly read the paper, outlining a construction service available to build a model railway to your own design and giving a local contact telephone number. Judas was very interested in the proposition and it would provide him with a complete model railway much quicker than he could construct it himself. He decided to investigate later with a telephone call and wrote down the name and number displayed on the flyer notice.

Judas hurriedly left the shop, promising the proprietor that he would return in a few days, and walked smartly to the museum. The museum car park was fairly full and a number of people that he recognised were milling around the museum entrance, waiting for the main door to be unlocked. Judas walked towards Gavin, who was standing at the rear of the crowd, and as he reached him the museum doors were unlocked and the assembled group were allowed in. Mortimer

Stanhope and Robin Cooper were standing near the entrance and when they saw Judas they walked towards him.

"We didn't expect to see you until this evening," said Robin, "but you are more than welcome and we have some good news."

At this point, Mortimer and Robin were joined by James Priestley and Giles Anderson and an expectant hush followed the earlier idle banter of the incoming museum staff. As Robin was the resident archaeologist at the museum he was the one elected to speak. Robin began and the audience was all ears.

"As you are all aware, recent events have allowed the museum staff to excavate a site in the middle of an inland field and we have retrieved five mediaeval pots. The location of the pots was the brilliant work of Judas Wells, who deciphered the clues left on the ancient cross by the monk who possibly buried the pots. Also this monk was possibly the one who placed the various contents of the pots into the containers."

Another gasp was heard from the assembled group as the information that various contents were in the containers could only be known if the pots had been opened.

Robin continued, "Very early this morning, Mortimer, Giles, James and I had only been asleep for about three hours, when our curiosity got the better of us and as we were all wide awake and raring to get back to the museum, we decided that is what we would do. We telephoned the guards, told them to expect us and we duly arrived. We all went to the basement where the pots were kept and began our quest to detach the lid from the earliest pot we excavated. This delicate operation was filmed by one of the guards, who did a superb job as it is one of his many hobbies and, I must say, he is a very gifted person. If you would all please go to the room we used yesterday for the film, you will be enlightened with the results of this morning's exercise."

With that, Robin marched away to the film room, followed closely by Mortimer, James and Giles. The rest of the group followed, all excited at the prospect of discovery.

Inside the film room Judas and Gavin were stopped by Robin, who simply apologised for the melodramatic events of the day.

"Mortimer, Giles, James and I simply could not sleep, so we returned and we are all so happy that we did. You will both love this film, so prepare to be entertained as you have never been entertained before."

Robin then saw that everyone was in the room, so he waved to the rear of the room. The lights darkened and the film began. Initially, it simply showed the archaeologists entering the room and working on the smallest pot and after a few minutes they delicately detached the ill fitting lid. All of the assembled eminent men were wearing white coats and were also all wearing face masks.

With the removal of the lid, Mortimer Stanhope gingerly peeked inside and was heard to confirm that the pot did contain something. A powerful light was used to illuminate the contents, but only centuries of dust could be seen with any certainty. Mortimer's gloved hand entered the neck of the pot and, after what seemed an eternity, it was withdrawn, clasping what looked like small dark pebbles. The exercise was repeated and more dark pebbles were released from the pot. After four more attempts, a sizeable collection of pebbles were assembled on the table.

The next object to be released from incarceration in the pot was unmistakably a metal plate of some kind and was followed by four more plates. The only sounds were the archaeologists mumbling on the film; the audience was simply mesmerised. However, when the pot had been emptied and Mortimer, Robin, James and Giles had examined the finds, the senior member of the group was heard to say, "Gentlemen we have found the long lost Beaufort St. Vincent abbey Treasure."

The film then ended and the lights were switched on. For a moment, the audience were stunned by the gravity of the news and then the enormity of the find registered and the small room exploded with the cheers and rapturous applause of the viewers. After a couple of minutes, Mortimer Stanhope appealed for calm in the room and congratulated Judas on his decipherment of the clues and congratulated the members of the teams of archaeologists that had unearthed the pots.

He then asked the assembled group, "Do you wish to see the next film and the identifying of the contents of the first pot?"

Silence reigned until eventually Gavin asked, "You have identified the contents?"

"Oh yes," replied Mortimer, "and the results are staggering."

With that, darkness fell upon the room and the next film started. It began with the gentle washing of the small dark pebbles and one of the people in the room suggested that the items were pearls. Whilst these objects were being cleaned, the metal plate objects were being examined and were found to be in very good condition, considering their age and also where they had been kept. The cameraman panned over the pearls and the plate objects and the archaeologists in the audience were spellbound by the content and the undamaged state of the finds. Various plate objects were shown and all were highly decorated and engraved with religious scenes and some had precious stones embedded in the actual plate. The cameraman was enjoying his work and was being very precise, giving each object his full attention. After forty minutes, the cameraman panned onto the face of Mortimer Stanhope and he was in a very serious mood. Mortimer then began to speak, directly facing the camera.

"Sorry viewers, but we must stop. We have established that this is the treasure that has been lost for over five hundred years and we must now inform the authorities of our find and we must announce to the archaeological world that one of the greatest mediaeval mysteries, the whereabouts of the Beaufort St. Vincent abbey Treasure, has now been discovered. On a personal level, I can only say that the past few days have been the highlight of my archaeological life and I will never forget how I feel at this moment."

The film then stopped and the lights were once again turned on. A great cheer went up in the room when everyone present realised that they had been involved in what was possibly the high point of their archaeological careers. It was at this point that Mortimer Stanhope called for order and, as silence descended upon the room, he spoke directly to Judas in front of the assembly.

"Judas, the work that you have done to decipher the clues has been absolutely fantastic. I know it has taken over forty years, but it is a magnificent achievement. When I first met you I must admit that I thought 'here comes another treasure seeker', but after five minutes of your talk, I was certainly hooked and when you produced the plans and maps, I was convinced that you knew something about the hidden plate that I didn't.

"However, I must now apologise. Robin and I had to advise the responsible authorities of the discovery. I telephoned my old professor in the middle of the night and told him what we had unearthed, and he and four colleagues, plus their emergency investigation team and cameramen, arrived about two hours later. These people are, at present, in the building examining the pots and sorting out the contents.

"There is one more thing I have to tell you all. Not all the treasure is in the pots that we recovered. Some of our guys have been back under the bridge to make certain that we have not missed anything and I am relieved to say that nothing was missed. Therefore, the rest of the treasure is somewhere else. 'Where' is the question?"

There was a deep silence in the room and Judas simply said, "I expect it must be at the other location I mentioned in my talk."

Mortimer's jaw dropped and he was silent for about ten seconds.

He then spluttered, "You know where it is? How? What other location? Where?"

Judas carried on speaking, but he was embarrassed that such an eminent archaeologist had forgotten something that was so important. He outlined how the other location had been determined, how he had observed the triangle of the three mediaeval castles in the settlements, plus the outstretched arm and the two clues and turned them to formulate his hypothesis. After five minutes of intense explanation Judas stopped talking.

A dumbstruck Mortimer simply said, "I am so sorry Judas, but Giles and I simply missed the meaning of what you outlined and we simply misunderstood the symbols. It's a damn good thing that you are here to correct such a buffoon as myself. I'm afraid that my mind must have been in treasure trove mode and my brain must have been absent without leave."

"And mine also," echoed Giles Anderson.

Judas continued, "Robin has the co-ordinates of the position where I believe the remainder of the abbey artefacts will be unearthed. They will be in the nature reserve in Beaufort St. Catherine, possibly near to a standing stone that may now be buried."

Mortimer regained his composure and asked Judas, "May I have permission to take Robin and this information to the people presently examining the pots and advise them where we believe the outstanding artefacts are located. They will no doubt allow us all to join them in the search, when permission is obtained from the necessary organization. They are the national authority on this period of history and they also have the knowledge and ability to circumnavigate red tape and to quickly obtain the necessary authorization to enter the nature reserve and to commence searching for the remainder of the artefacts. Personally, I am looking forward to doing more intensive excavating."

Judas nodded and Mortimer, Robin and Giles all looked relieved as they departed and sought out the experts who were engaged in the emptying of the pots. As a parting gesture Mortimer suggested the men all went to the café area and had coffee.

In the museum coffee shop Judas refreshed his parched throat with a lemonade. After five minutes, Mortimer returned with his old professor and Judas was introduced to Julian Fitzroy, who clenched his hand so tightly that he thought it would stop his blood circulation. Julian Fitzroy must have been in his eighties; he was white-haired, bearded and he was only about five feet tall.

"Young man," he said to Judas, "when Mortimer here telephoned me early this morning, I could have killed him for interrupting my sleep. But when he said, 'We have found the Beaufort St. Vincent abbey church treasure', I was very forgiving. I immediately contacted other colleagues and the leader of our emergency investigation team, all of whom, I am sure, could also have killed me for interrupting their slumbers. Like Mortimer, I was also forgiven when I outlined the events and the reason for my call and we all arrived here within two hours. When we arrived the first pot had been opened and the contents extracted. When you have time, my colleagues and I would love to be informed on how you deciphered the information and how you arrived at your conclusions. In the meantime, we have been very busy opening the pots and filming the operations as we emptied the containers."

"All the containers have been emptied?" questioned Judas and Julian Fitzroy smiled as he nodded.

"As you know the first pot contained pearls and various small plate objects of silver and gold," said Julian. "The second pot contained sapphires and more small plate objects of silver and gold. The third pot contained rubies and even more plate objects. The larger fourth container held larger plate objects of silver and the larger fifth container held larger plate objects of gold.

"Many of the silver and gold plate objects were highly decorated with religious engravings and some were ornately decorated with pearls, rubies and sapphires. Also in the last pot to be opened, there were early Viking objects, including a dagger, necklaces, wrist bands, brooches, pins, buckles and armlets and some of these are exceptionally rare objects. All of the objects recovered are in a remarkable state of preservation and are mostly undamaged. May I just congratulate you Mr Wells on your achievement, on deciphering the information, which allowed we mere mortal archaeologists, the opportunity for finding so much of the lost treasure and also for making an old man very happy."

"You will be even happier Julian, when we bring in the rest of the buried items" said Mortimer Stanhope, looking at his old professor and smiling.

Julian Fitzroy gazed at Mortimer and asked, "What did you say?"

"That's what I came to the basement to see you about," said Mortimer, "but you directed me to bring you here to see Judas. He knows where the rest of the treasure is buried. We need you to get through the red tape of officialdom so that we can do the excavating and get the objects out of the ground. Judas has calculated that the rest of the buried items are in the nature reserve at Beaufort St. Catherine and we therefore need permission to excavate. You never know, but it might be another Roman settlement in an area previously thought not to have any Roman activity."

"Consider it applied for and consider it granted. I do so hope it is another Roman structure," said an official sounding Julian Fitzroy, with a wicked gleam in his bright blue eyes. He then continued, "And now Mortimer, please lead me to a telephone and I will sort out everything. However, when you go to the nature reserve to open up the ground, I demand to be with you. I need to be there at the actual opening. Like our politicians often say, 'these terms are non-negotiable'."

Mortimer smiled again and just nodded. Julian Fitzroy and Mortimer left the café area, both old friends and happy to be involved in the discovery that would be the highlight of both of their illustrious careers. The assembled group left in the café area split into smaller groups and Judas found himself with Gavin Melbourne.

"You seem to be discovering Roman remains with unfortunate regularity," said Gavin, as he drained his mug of coffee. "If the information about the discovery of the lost treasure is released in the next few days, I will have to consider emigrating. My reputation as a competent tutor will be shot to smithereens and I am going to look a complete imbecile at the class on Friday. As you know, I have outlined on many occasions that the Romans did not consider this part of the country worthy of their military presence."

Judas did not know what to say to his friend, but then saw that Gavin was chuckling away quite merrily.

"However," continued Gavin," if the information about the abbey treasure is released and the nature reserve is covering a Roman structure, I will be one of the first to congratulate you on the discovery. I will also be sitting in the classroom on Friday as you take the lecture and explain how you did all the deciphering work."

"You jest of course," said Judas, but Gavin shook his head.

It was when Gavin began to smile that Judas, with great relief, realized that his friend and tutor was in fact joking.

Judas and Gavin found a vacant table and sat together. After ten minutes of talk associated with the possible reason for the Roman activity in the area, they were interrupted by the museum cameraman, who had done such a superb job with filming the excavation of the Roman bridge.

"Gentlemen," he said, "may I ask you, if you have the time, to accompany me to my office? It is located at the rear of the building."

Both Judas and Gavin duly followed. Whilst walking with the cameraman, Judas noticed that the museum was still open to the general public. He realized that the museum had to keep the face of normality alive, whilst protecting the treasures just discovered. He saw that various individuals and school groups were wandering around the numerous museum exhibits, completely unaware of the impending revelation being investigated in the basement.

In the small office, the men sat and Judas and Gavin were formally introduced to Charles Sibley of the museum records, camera and photographic section.

"Sorry to drag you away, but I have something to ask. I am going through the film that we have taken of all of the recent events and Robin, Mortimer, James and Giles think it would be a great idea if you, Mr Wells, would please do the voiceover on the film that we have taken. After all, it was your discovery and, in all honesty, you do deserve the credit."

Judas was stunned and was brought out of his reflective mood by a slap on the back by Gavin.

"A brilliant idea," said Gavin and continued, "you really do deserve to be the one on the film and you could do it very well."

Judas was not convinced that his abilities were good enough for the task, but decided to give it a go, with the proviso that if he was not satisfied with his performance then someone more proficient would take on the challenge.

"When do we start," asked Judas, "as I am not required back at work until Friday? The name by the way is Judas."

"We start right now," said Charles Sibley, "and we will begin with the film I took of your lecture to Mortimer Stanhope."

And so it began. Judas and Charles Sibley, watched by Gavin, went through all of the film that had been taken so far by the museum staff, and Judas, where necessary, spoke over the original film. The initial film was the outlining by Judas of how he had obtained the written information, how he had deciphered it and how he had rotated the information to reach a possible location of the Beaufort St. Vincent abbey treasure. This first film was only slightly amended to give the subject more clarity, and it was definitely better than the original.

Gavin listened to the work being done by Judas on the next films and at times made suggestions on how to improve the script. His input was very much appreciated by Judas and by Charles Sibley and the changes he suggested were all used. Judas also made certain that his dear friend Adam and his great uncle, Albert Stonehaven, were given full and lasting credit for the initial collection of papers relating to the lost relics and for the discovery of the information in the abbey archives, including the information from the ancient cross.

Other films followed and Judas felt a complete fraud as he did the voiceover on the excavation of the inland bridge and the discovery of the various pots. He felt even more uncomfortable when he spoke about the opening of the pots to reveal the various types of gold and silver plate and the pearls, rubies and sapphires.

As he said to Charles Sibley, "I was nowhere near the inland Roman bridge when the articles were found and I was not even present in the museum when the pots were opened and the relics retrieved. Others should be doing the talking."

However, his protestations fell onto deaf ears. Judas therefore carried on.

The one piece of film that was left without additional speech, was the part when Mortimer Stanhope looked at the camera and simply announced that the lost Beaufort St. Vincent Treasure had been found. At this point the film just showed the various gold and silver articles, the pearls, sapphires and rubies, with no voice to aid the viewer and this continued for a whole two minutes. Judas thought that this was a superb piece of theatre and he wholehearted supported the actions of Charles Sibley for this silent masterpiece.

Other films were used and Judas dutifully spoke the narrative given to him, and the end product was appreciated by both Gavin and Charles. To Judas, some of the films seemed out of sequential order, but Judas assumed that Charles knew his art better than he, so he just continued as instructed. Gavin was very attentive to the proceedings and his input was invaluable.

At one o'clock, the work was nearly finished, so they all carried on for ten more minutes to complete the task. It was then that Judas realized that he was parched and he went with both Charles and Gavin to the museum café for a refreshing drink. They all sat together and Charles said that during the afternoon they would run the film again and do any adjustments necessary to correct any faults they found in the production.

It was whilst they were sitting in the café that one of the museum receptionists entered the room and quietly informed Charles Sibley, "All of the other archaeologists, assembled earlier in the café, have gone to the nature reserve. I do not have any other information, but I was told by Robin Cooper to pass the information to you and he said you would understand."

Charles Sibley thanked the young lady and she left.

"It simply means that Julian Fitzroy has wangled verbal permission to do an exploratory excavation in the nature reserve," said Charles Sibley when the receptionist was out of earshot. "God that man must have some very powerful friends in exceptionally high places to be able to get permission to do the work at such short notice."

"I just hope the calculations and assumptions I have made bear the fruits of discovery," said Judas, "otherwise I may ruin the reputation of some very eminent archaeologists."

"Oh no!" cried out Charles Sibley, "everyone on the excavation is bursting with pride to have been involved with the discoveries under the Roman bridge and I am sure everyone is very confident that the remainder of the missing items will be there in the nature reserve. Even if we take the worst scenario and there is nothing in the nature reserve, it is still a fantastic discovery. You will be the person who has the honour of decipherment of the various clues and the archaeologists will have the honour of being involved in the unearthing of the items. Believe me, whatever happens, this is a stupendous success for everyone involved, especially for you Judas."

"Well said," interjected Gavin, "I completely agree. Well said."

After a leisurely break and two drinks, Judas, Gavin and Charles returned to the small office to continue. Judas and Gavin sat looking at the screen and Charles ran the film that had been prepared with the voiceover that morning.

The film had been running for about fifteen minutes when Gavin nudged Judas and said, "This is really good."

Judas was about to reply when Charles stopped the film and said, "That last part needs doing again, it isn't quite right."

The afternoon continued in the same vein and Judas dutifully corrected the work that was thought to be substandard by Charles Sibley. Just after four thirty, Judas did his last correction and when played back by Charles Sibley he received a nod to signify that it was acceptable. Judas relaxed and was about to invite Charles and Gavin to the café area for a cold can from the drinks dispenser, when the door opened and a flood of jubilant archaeologists entered.

"We have found it, all of the missing items, and they are still intact," cried out Mortimer Stanhope.

He had his arm round the waist of his old tutor Julian Fitzroy, who had tears running down his cheeks. A large cheer reverberated around the very cramped room and the assembled company began to applaud. Judas was embarrassed, but he was also very happy for his friend Adam and for Adam's Great Uncle Albert.

"Gentlemen," yelled out Mortimer Stanhope, "decorum please," and the noise began to abate. After a few more seconds, Mortimer continued. "Today we have been privileged to be the discoverers of one of the greatest mysteries of the mediaeval period of English history. So far, everything Judas has told us has come to fruition and we have the lost treasure of Beaufort St. Vincent abbey finally unearthed, literally as well as metaphorically, and it is intact. The film we took today will be added to the film that was taken yesterday and we will soon be able to release to the world the knowledge that I never in my wildest dreams ever thought I would hear, let alone be part of. Tomorrow we must properly examine the items that we released from the three pots and do a thorough check of them. After all, we are archaeologists, not treasure seekers, although at times today I'm afraid I succumbed to be a member of the latter, for which I apologise. The items will be under guard again and tomorrow will be another glorious day."

At this point Charles Sibley said to Mortimer Stanhope and all others in earshot, "Today Judas, Gavin and I went through the film from yesterday's excavation and discovery and we have done a voiceover of the main points and done the editing of the work. It will be ready for your observations and comment in the morning. We also did the section about how the information was deciphered from the markings on the cross and incorporated all of the necessary information to allow the viewer to realize the enormity of the challenges that had to be overcome. It is ready now but I just want to view it for perfection just one more time."

"I look forward to seeing it in the morning," said Mortimer. "Remember gentlemen that we are still keeping quiet about this discovery, but when news is released, it will cause shockwaves around the archaeological world. Just keep it to yourselves for only a couple of days please."

With that, the assembled group left the small office. Judas was about to follow the men, when he and Gavin were called over to the group of Mortimer Stanhope, Julian Fitzroy, James Priestley and Giles Anderson, by Robin Cooper.

"This looks ominous," said Judas as he reached the group of eminent men.

Robin then said, "I just wanted to say a very big thank you to you both for helping us all to make the greatest find of our archaeological careers. Had you not returned to the museum with Judas a few days ago, these pots would still be dormant and incarcerated under the Roman bridges."

"Bridges?" questioned Gavin and then went on to say, "not more Roman bridges?"

"Oh I forgot, we didn't tell you, so therefore you don't know," said a forgetful Robin Cooper and then he spoke again. "Yes there is another Roman bridge. You will see it in the film tomorrow. Your calculations were exceptionally accurate Judas and two feet down we came upon another bridge, again Roman in origin. We again carefully dug down by the side of the structure and then went under the centre of the bridge. Underneath the one span of the bridge, over another dried up river bed, we eventually removed the earth blocking access to the underside of the bridge and here we successfully excavated down and liberated the three mediaeval pots. Mortimer and Julian were the actual liberators, but we all had a hand in the discovery."

Gavin groaned, "For years I have stood in front of various classes and informed my students that the Romans did not consider this part of the country worthy of their occupation. Now you tell me that there is not one, but two Roman bridges carrying Roman roads across the county. Oh the shame of it all. I will just have to grovel to my class on Friday night, but hopefully if the news of the Beaufort St. Vincent Treasure find is released, Judas can take the class and outline to his fellow students how he cracked the decipherment." After a few seconds to catch his breath, Gavin began again. "I blame Robin and Mortimer for the wrong information, because both men have written excellent books about the Roman occupation of Britain and both have openly stated in all their writings that no Roman presence was considered necessary in this part of the empire. Oh the shame of it all."

At the end of his outrage everyone began to see the humour in the situation and then began to smile and eventually to laugh. Finally, when sanity had prevailed, all of the eminent archaeologists assembled decided to blame Judas, Adam and Albert Stonehaven for the decipherment of the clues and for the discovery of the Roman structures, which had made them all re-evaluate their knowledge of the Roman activities in the local area. However, they were all very happy and content to accept credit for the discovery of the lost Beaufort St. Vincent treasure, which would nullify any dent in their reputations.

Judas left the museum, having agreed with Mortimer and Robin to return in the morning, to continue with any work required of him. It was just after six o'clock and Judas was feeling peckish. He walked towards the harbour and sat looking out at the small boats bobbing about on the water. It was getting colder and the twinkling lights seemed helpless in the gathering gloom. Storm clouds were gathering and it looked as if there would be a torrential downpour very soon. Judas retreated to a nearby shopping mall, made various food purchases and decided to speedily return home to his apartment.

On his walk, Judas concentrated on the day's events and was very relieved that his positional calculations were correct for the discovery of the outstanding abbey items. He shuddered to think of the outcome if the nature reserve had not yielded its entombed artefacts and rejoiced that Adam and Albert would now receive recognition for the discovery. Again Judas was very pleased to see the welcoming lights of his village and even more pleased to enter his apartment block. He checked his post box and extracted his mail. It was a solitary envelope.

Judas entered his home and prepared dinner. Afterwards he opened the envelope and was pleased to see that it was a typed note from Anita, requesting his company the following evening at eight o'clock for an exploration of the pool area and a possible dip in the water. Judas laughed and telephoned Anita's mobile number, but was disappointed that Anita did not answer. Judas left a message accepting her invitation and saying that he looked forward to the experience, even though he could not swim.

After a substantial meal, Judas spent the rest of the evening pondering the events of the day at the museum. He was elated that the Beaufort St. Vincent abbey treasure had been located and was now in the museum under guard. He realized that he would now have to get himself another project, although the treasure would still occupy his thoughts and his time for a few weeks more. At the moment he was completely unsure what project would replace the practically completed one and the thought disturbed him.

He then remembered that he still had to see Amanda and Stephen to present to them his cheque. This fact also disturbed him and he resolved to rectify this omission in the morning. It was still early, but Judas was very tired from the day's exertions and he gracefully surrendered to sleep.

CHAPTER 28

Tuesday 20th January

Judas woke very early. It was still dark and he went to his outer study and looked out of the window, towards the nature reserve. Nothing was visible inland, so he looked out to sea and in the distance he saw the lights of a passing ship. He also saw the comforting flashing beacon of the lighthouse and this gave him a certain satisfaction. Outside it was still blustery and the wind was howling. He thought of his invitation from Anita for an exploration of the pool area that evening. He was looking forward to it, although the thought of being immersed in water did not appeal and secretly he knew he would fight against it.

Judas sat in his study, in deep contemplation of the recent events at the museum, until the fingers of heavenly light began to dispel the outside gloom. He had a small but leisurely breakfast and then returned to his study and looked out of his window. He immediately saw the sheets covering the area the archaeologists had excavated yesterday and was sorry that it looked so small. He was also sorry that he could see absolutely nothing to suggest the reason for the presence of sheeting. At twenty minutes past seven, Judas exited his apartment and left the building.

He walked towards the Ivy Lodge Guest House and was relieved to see two cars parked in the roadside parking spaces and even more relieved to see lights on in the hallway. As he approached the garden gate, two men exited the guest house door, got into the cars and drove off in opposite directions. Judas pressed the bell button and waited. The door was opened by Amanda, and Judas was greeted as if he were her long lost brother. Stephen was summoned from the kitchen and he also warmly welcomed Judas back to the guest house.

After a few moments of idle chatter Judas said, "I have here a cheque for the agreed amount and I have great pleasure in presenting it to you." He passed it to Amanda before continuing, "And I have here a simple receipt document for the loan."

This he presented to Stephen. Both looked at the paperwork and Amanda broke down and openly wept. Stephen also had tears in his eyes, although he did manage to control his emotions.

After a few moments Stephen signed the receipt document and handed it back to Judas, again shaking his hand and thanking him profusely for allowing them to fulfil their dreams, extend their guest house and secure their future.

Eventually, Amanda recovered sufficiently and said, "We can never thank you enough for what you have done and as soon as our bank is open, the cheque will be presented and the money will be put to good use. God bless you."

After a few more minutes Judas wished them well and left the premises.

He walked quickly towards the harbour of Beaufort St. Catherine. He knew of a hairdresser near the harbour and sought out the establishment. On finding it he was surprised to find the shop open and the hairdresser busily cutting a client's hair. After a few minutes, Judas was invited into the chair, where he outlined his requirements and sat awaiting the buzz of the hair and beard trimmers.

The hairdresser was a man of about fifty and his hair and beard were snow white. He was a very pleasant individual who did not ask questions and only spoke when replying. However, as Judas paid for the man's excellent services, he wished Judas "a very pleasant and enjoyable day" and said that he hoped to see him again soon. He even shook Judas by the hand. Judas was embarrassed, but thanked him.

Judas had a leisurely walk out of the village and, on reaching Beaufort St. Vincent, he once again resisted the temptation to go into the lodge. Instead he walked to the harbour to view the waterside activities. He saw small boats anchored close to the shoreline and a small fishing boat chugging out of the little harbour onto the open sea. After a few minutes he walked to the museum and, along with others, entered the building.

He was joined by Gavin and was about to speak, when Charles Sibley came over.

After a few words of greeting, Charles said, "I carried on working yesterday, checking through the film that we had produced and I am as sure as I can be that everything we did was acceptable. From now on though the film footage will be from more professional sources and this will no doubt provide a more dramatic conclusion to the discovery. The various films taken of the discovery are being viewed as we speak and the best footage will be incorporated into a spectacular production. It will definitely put this museum on the archaeological map, for providing the excavation teams for the discovery of the century," concluded a very proud and happy, Charles Sibley.

Mortimer Stanhope and Robin Cooper then joined the group and both looked at Judas a little defensively. Robin then began to speak.

"All of the films are at present being looked at and, with your agreement, we would like to put together a complete production to show the full history of the missing Beaufort St. Vincent abbey Treasure – the reason for its burial, the monks involved, the clues on the cross, the decipherment, your meeting with Gavin, your meeting with me, the discovery of the Roman structures, the discovery of the treasure and anything else we can think of," said Robin.

Judas replied, "If everyone else is agreeable, then I have no objection, but I would like Adam and Albert Stonehaven to receive the credit for amassing the documentation that was eventually deciphered."

"They will receive full credit for that," said a relieved Mortimer Stanhope. "The films are being processed at the moment and I will not spoil your later enjoyment, but at three o'clock this afternoon we will be showing some footage in the cinema room. It will be the first attempt by our production people, but it should contain everything that we wish to convey to the general public about the discovery. Your comments will be invited and appreciated."

With that Mortimer Stanhope and Robin Cooper left the group and Charles Sibley invited Gavin and Judas to the café area for a drink.

Drinks were gratefully accepted and when the group were seated in the café, Charles casually asked both, "What are you both doing until the showing of the film this afternoon?"

Gavin answered first.

"I am going back to my school to concentrate on some coursework."

Judas then said, "I am going to a model shop to organise some construction work for a model railway. I work for Beaufort Models so I think it would be appropriate for me to have a layout."

Charles then told them that he was going back to his office to catch up on some paperwork that had not received the attention that it should have had during the past few days. After a few more minutes the group split up. Charles retreated to his office, Gavin returned to his school and Judas walked to the model shop.

As Judas walked, he realized that today was going to be a very proud day for him. He also understood that if everything went smoothly at the museum, then it would not be long before the whole world would be advised of the discovery of the long lost abbey treasure. Judas just hoped that the film production team were able to piece together the historical events in chronological order, followed by the diagrams on the mediaeval cross, the decipherment and finally the events that had happened in the last few days to discover the location of the lost abbey artefacts. He then realized that when the film was released, his activities involved with the search would be over. More important for Judas, however, was the knowledge that his friend Adam and Adam's Great Uncle Albert would receive the acclaim that they so richly deserved.

Judas walked towards the model shop at a fairly sedate pace and took in the surroundings. He had always thought of Beaufort St. Vincent as a very pretty town, with some beautiful buildings and a very bustling market square in the town centre. However, at present, it looked drab and unappealing and the gathering storm clouds only added to the prevailing gloom. Judas reached the model shop and exchanged greetings with the proprietor. He slowly walked to the rear of the shop and was again stunned by the amount of model railway equipment on show and available for purchase. Initially he just stood there and admired the quantity and the quality of the goods on offer. There was everything on view that a modeller of the railway scene could possibly require and Judas stood there absorbing the contents around him. Eventually he remembered the layout construction service he had spotted the flyer for on his last visit to the shop and he returned to the front of the store to see the proprietor.

The proprietor was a very friendly person. He was completely bald but had a well trimmed grey beard and wore a black storekeeper's overall. His badge indicated that his name was Rupert and, for some unaccountable reason, Judas inwardly smiled.

"You said you would be back and here you are," commented Rupert.

"Indeed I did," confirmed Judas, "and here I am. I work on the goods reception duties for Beaufort Models, but I have no model railway of my own and I was thinking very seriously about rectifying this very glaring omission. I have already designed a multi level model railway layout, using my company's miniature templates, but I had to discard this layout as it was too complex for solo operation. However, I still want a layout and I hope to design a simpler one in the very near future. Do you have any more information about the actual person who is involved in the model railway construction services as advertised on your notice board?"

"Oh you mean Rudolf," said Rupert, "he's the man you need to speak to. He is a very gifted model builder and he has a small workshop close by. I think I should mention that he is my elder brother. When the building work next door is completed I will move my stock there and Rudy will take over this place. I will have more space for my stock next door and Rudy will continue to construct model railways to the purchaser's requirements in this shop. Also when Rudy has the time, between constructing for other people, he will then design his own model railways on his own baseboards for sale to the general public. Our shops will have access to each other by three archways that are at present hidden by the racks in this shop and by protective sheeting next door."

"I have his telephone number and I will contact him when I have designed my layout," said Judas.

A concerned Rupert looked up.

"That could be difficult. Rudy has a voice mail system and sometimes doesn't get messages until days later. When you decide you want his services it would be better to contact me and I will pass on the message. I have some photographs of his work if you want to look at them?" Rupert offered.

Judas nodded and the shop proprietor reached under the counter and produced a photograph album and presented it to Judas. The album had a short outline of the requirements of each of the clients and about half a dozen photographs of each of the finished models. All of the baseboards shown in the album were constructed by Rudolf and all were completed to a very high standard. The photographs also showed the finished layouts and although a couple of them were basic and intended for young children, all of the layouts were beautifully finished and absolutely superb. Judas was impressed. However, the MD's words regarding layouts that were too complex for solo operation came flooding back to Judas and he dismissed many layouts. Some layouts were also too large to fit into the space he had available. However, there was one layout that Judas saw that he thought was absolutely out of this world and he had the space that it could fit into. This layout utilized two baseboards in an L-shaped design along two walls and consisted of a complex branch line with an out and return loop configuration. He thought again of the MD's words and reluctantly decided that the layout he favoured fell into the category of being too complex for his solo operation.

However, he still looked at the photographs and liked what he saw. The high level terminus occupied part of wall one and the approach line from the valley circled upwards in three loops, using wall two of the layout. Travelling from the terminus, using the descending loops and out of sight staging, the line travelled downwards past industrial complexes, comprising of a forestry compound, a saw mill, a slate quarry and at the lower level there was a dairy and a creamery. The base of the layout was the part of the railway that the modelling fraternity considered to be the "rest of the railway network" and on this occasion it contained the reversing loops and hidden staging. This main line then continued its journey and rejoined a spiral at a higher level, via more hidden staging and holding lines and returned to the terminus.

As an added bonus for the modeller, Rudolf had fitted in, at the base of this layout, a small harbour, and railway lines radiated to the local canning factory, to a holding bay for the storage of timber, to a separate wharf warehouse and also to a jetty. The operating potential for this whole layout was enormous and Judas was enthralled by the endless possibilities available. In fact there were so many industrial complexes on the layout that most could be used solely in an operating session and give enormous pleasure to the operator. However, a solo operator could not do justice to the operating potential of the very complex layout.

Judas looked again through the album, but could not see any layout that impressed him like the one he had dismissed as being too complex for his requirements and he presented the album back to Rupert.

"Sorry," said Judas, "but the layout that I like the most would be too complex for a single person to operate. Again I am very sorry."

"There is another album," said Rupert after a few moments, "but there are only about a dozen smaller layouts shown in it." Rupert again reached under the counter, only this time to the back of the shelf and retrieved the album. "Here it is," he said and presented it to Judas.

Judas opened the book with little enthusiasm and the first two layouts were very good but not outstanding. Again they were beautifully constructed and well planned, but lacked that special something. Judas continued scanning through the book and although all of the layouts were very good and the outline information very informative, none of the layouts he saw were exciting him. He turned the last page to the final layout and was again mesmerised by what he saw.

This smaller layout showed a fairly important terminus station, stipulated by the client as serving a medium sized inland village, supposedly sited in a fairly mountainous location. The layout itself was again L-shaped. The station had all of the facilities required to operate the layout with great interest, including Engine Sheds and Turntable, Carriage Siding, a Private Siding, Bay Platforms, a Parcels bay, Loco Spur and sidings for Coal, Cattle Dock, Goods Shed and End and Side Loading. Also included in the layout were various industrial complexes sited around the lower slopes of the layout, which was built on three levels and the layout also had three separate and hidden, staging yards. The lowest staging yard finally spiralled upwards to another industrial complex and then into the reversing loops under the terminus, to allow the locomotives, carriages and wagons to reverse their journey and return eventually to the terminus and the upland parts of the layout. It was a beautiful arrangement and a superb concept brought to reality on the layout. It was also a very novel design that Judas had never seen before. In short he thought the design was absolutely brilliant. The layout was very compact, it was pleasing to the eye and it was also manageable for a solo operator to enjoy. Judas studied the associated photographs and again admired the workmanship of the designer and constructor.

Judas liked the design so much that he asked for copies of the photographs and Rupert duly photocopied the prints and presented them to Judas, who placed then in his small case. Judas looked at the layout, checked the dimensions again to make sure the layout would fit into the space he had available and decided that this was the layout for him. As an added incentive for Judas, he recognised that the track and line side equipment was that of his own company and this somehow was a relief to him. Judas advised Rupert of his decision to purchase a layout like the one in the photograph and he again showed the selected layout to Rupert. Rupert was surprised and also relieved that he had helped his brother and said he would get his sibling to telephone him and arrange a meeting to finalise the plan and any changed requirements. As Judas left the shop he gave Rupert his telephone number and said he would be home about nine thirty tonight.

"And the name please?" asked Rupert and it was his turn to inwardly smile as Judas provided the answer.

It was still only ten o'clock, but Judas did not feel like going all the way back to his apartment and having to return along the coastal path to the museum. Hopefully he would be able to view the screening of the film being put together today. If there were problems with the editing of the film, then the final version of the production could be delayed. Judas tried not to think negatively and offered a prayer towards heaven, requesting that no insurmountable obstacles were encountered by the museum staff regarding the delicate work.

Judas walked back towards the harbour and enjoyed the view. The anchored boats were gently moving in the water and although there was sunshine at present, in the distance, dark clouds were massing. Judas sat at one of the numerous seats protected by a retaining wall and looked out to sea. He took from his small case the photocopies of the layout he so admired and just looked at it. He still thought it was a marvel of design. In fact he liked it so much that he even thought of incorporating the main part of it into his own layout that had yet to be constructed, but then decided against it, as it would make the final layout too complicated. However, he continued to look at it and marvelled at its simplicity and its fascinating operating potential. In fact, the more he looked at it the more perfect it became.

At eleven o'clock Judas was still sitting by the harbour. However, the dark clouds were gathering and a few specks of rain began to fall. Judas walked quickly to the nearest shopping arcade and sought out the obligatory newsagents in such a complex. He was scanning through the various racks of magazines, when he was startled to read that the local weekly paper, *the Beaufort Gazette*, would soon be releasing information on the lost Beaufort St. Vincent abbey treasure. Judas re-read the advertising board and his blood ran cold, but he then remembered that the paper often published articles about the lost items, just to keep the information in the public domain and also to update any new knowledge available.

Judas was beginning to relax when he received a tap on the shoulder and on turning he saw Anita Wells. Anita was smiling and looked happier than he had ever seen her before.

"What are you doing here?" she asked and not waiting for a reply, said "I'm glad to see you, as I have something for you."

Anita then rummaged through her large and very old handbag and retrieved an envelope and passed it to Judas. On opening it, Judas saw it was a cheque and it cleared the loan that he had given Anita long ago.

"Thanks for everything," she said, "I feel so much better now that I have cleared that debt. It really was beginning to worry me, but recent events, thanks to you, have made my life a complete pleasure. And soon I shall retire and I have a good pension all arranged. Lucky me."

Anita looked at Judas and he could see that tears were in her eyes, so he just smiled and looked away and placed the cheque into his wallet.

After a few seconds he turned again and asked, "Do you fancy lunch?"

Anita declined gracefully.

"Unfortunately for us I am meeting Stephanie Faulkner a little later and we are going to look at some furniture for my new apartment. However," she said, "I would love to have a coffee and a slice of cake and I know just the place."

After a leisurely stroll to the rear of the arcade, Anita entered a small, unassuming restaurant and the aroma that filled the nostrils was sensational.

The restaurant was the one that Anita and Stephanie had lunched at recently and it was nearly full. They sat at a table at the rear of the dining area, overlooking a beautiful walled garden and a perfectly manicured lawn.

Anita said, "Stephanie and I have been doing a lot of window shopping recently, but now I think it's decision time and I am going to buy the things I require." Anita looked at Judas. "Thanks for everything. It really is appreciated and I cannot thank you enough. At one stage recently, I honestly thought I would never be able to retire until my early seventies. Now, thanks to you, I retire at the beginning of March, aged sixty and I do have a reasonable income with my pension. Thanks again." As an afterthought Anita added, "Are you sure about the rest of the money for the apartment?"

"Quite sure, it was a gift to a very special person."

Tears were again in her eyes. Judas began to speak again, but the waitress came to the table and Anita ordered her coffee and cake and an orange juice for Judas.

She then said, "Have you seen the Miller's Retreat recently?" Judas was again about to speak, but Anita continued, "They are building on the site and extending everything. It will look completely different when it's completed. You really did well out of that deal and I am so pleased for you."

Judas made another attempt to reply, but the waitress returned with the drinks and the cake. Anita then became preoccupied with eating the large slice of carrot cake and Judas just enjoyed seeing someone at peace with the world and enjoying themselves. After twenty minutes of idle chatter, Anita left the restaurant to meet Stephanie, with the parting remark, "See you later in the pool."

Judas also left the restaurant and decided to visit his bank to deposit Anita's cheque. The pavements were wet, but it had stopped raining, although it looked as if it would begin again at any moment. Judas walked to his bank and deposited the sum into his current account. Whilst at the counter he cancelled the standing order to his gardener, as promised, for the shortage of notice to terminate their work contract at the Miller's Retreat.

At noon Judas's mobile began to ring and he saw from the screen that it was Gavin.

After the initial greeting Gavin said, "I have been contacted by Robin and requested to go to the museum. He also asked me to contact you and ask you to join us there. Are you available?"

"Yes," said a bemused Judas, "I am in town and will be with you very shortly."

"See you there," said Gavin and he then rang off.

Judas retraced his steps and arrived at the museum a few minutes later. In fact as he reached the main entrance door of the building he saw Gavin walking across the car park towards him.

"I wonder what the problem is," said Gavin, as they approached the reception desk to register in.

The receptionist, stern faced, simply asked them to go to the office of Robin Cooper. Gavin and Judas meekly complied and a few moments later entered the inner sanctum of the professor. Robin Cooper, Mortimer Stanhope, Charles Sibley, Julian Fitzroy, James Priestley and Giles Anderson were already there and all stopped talking as Gavin and Judas entered.

"This looks very ominous," said Gavin and then asked, "Any problems?"

"Yes, there is a problem," said Robin Cooper, "and it's a big one. As you may have seen on the advertising board for *The Beaufort Gazette*, the grandly titled local weekly paper, the publication will soon be releasing information on the lost Beaufort St. Vincent abbey treasure. It's an annual thing with the paper; it churns out all of the known facts and any new theories regarding the whereabouts of the lost items. This year the reporter went to the receptionist, only this morning, and asked to see me concerning the update on the lost abbey treasure. The receptionist then said, 'It's good news, but I didn't know he had told you about the discovery.' After this unfortunate slip, the secrecy element had been lost and the knowledge could not be contained.

"The local reporter is still at the museum in the projection room. The film has been completed and is now ready for showing. At this point I feel I must own up to a little deception. The film crew of the museum have been actively involved in the excavation work, and in all of the other aspects of the work, since the first day of my seeing the Roman bridge in the field. It was necessary to have film documentation of the events, to record for posterity, if in fact we discovered lost items.

"Everyone involved in the excavation is waiting in the cinema room, so if we join them we can see the film in its entirety. Some of the initial part of the film, we have all seen, but the rest of it is new and we may need to re-do part of it if it is not quite right. Charles will see to that."

At this point Charles Sibley said, "Sorry Judas, but because of the rush to get the film completed ready for the release to an unsuspecting world, we have had to get the guy from the museum to do the voiceover for the complete film. However, your contribution in outlining the events leading up to the actual decipherment is still there and is absolutely first class. If anyone present finds any fault with the film please advise me, so that corrections can be made before the public are allowed to see the finished article."

With that, the whole group went into the cinema room and, as they entered, the idle chatter subsided and silence reigned. Charles Sibley then repeated to the assembled what he had said in Robin's room.

"If anyone present finds any fault with the film please advise me."

Robin Cooper then collected the reporter for the local paper and introduced him to the assembled company. The member of the press looked completely bewildered, but simply said that he looked forward to the film. The lights were then turned off and the film burst into life on the screen. The production was grandly called "The Beaufort St. Vincent Abbey Treasure".

The actual production was magnificent. The film began by outlining the events that occurred in mediaeval times and the reasons why the abbey artefacts were taken to the coast for safe keeping. This outline was shown in script on the screen with a voice over reading it. The film then showed an area of coast, wild and windswept, representing how the Beaufort St. Vincent coast was thought to have looked at the time of the loss. The film outlined the actions of the Prior and the brother who had taken the items to the coast and their actions on discovering the bodies of the slain brothers who had hidden the items. At this juncture the narrator made a special point about the Prior, who had carried the items to the coast and who had swapped his simple wooden cross with that of the senior slain brother. This was the cross that had random markings on it and these were shown on the film. The Prior believed the random markings on the cross were the directions to the buried parcels and although he studied the cross for the remainder of his life, he was unsuccessful in deciphering it.

The film then showed Gavin, talking directly into the camera, about a meeting with Judas Wells, concerning a theoretical archaeological problem and Judas asking Gavin if he knew of anyone who could advise him. On outlining the problem Robin Cooper was contacted. Robin Cooper then took over the narration and simply said he was introduced to Judas Wells, who outlined his theory on the lost abbey artefacts and from that moment archaeology took on a very different meaning for him and the museum staff. Robin then said that Judas began to outline his theory and it was absolutely spellbinding.

"Judge for yourself," he said as the camera faded out and Judas appeared on screen. The screen was then taken up with Judas going over how he obtained the information, from Adam and his great uncle, Albert Stonehaven, and how he had deciphered the markings and calculated their positions. This part of the film was embarrassing for Judas, as he had not seen it before and he did not seem to be at ease on the film. When Judas arrived at the point relating to the turning of the plan through one hundred and eighty degrees, the graphics on the film applied the movement and the end result was a simplification of the event. It was very effective. When Judas had finished, his picture was slowly faded out and the film stopped. The film so far had lasted for two hours.

Robin Cooper then suggested that all of the audience had a break in the museum café and all in the room dutifully filed out. Judas sat with Gavin and Charles for drinks and both of the men were very happy with the film so far.

Judas said, "My own performance left much to be desired," but Gavin and Charles both disagreed with his opinion.

After twenty minutes of idle chatter, the café emptied and the men returned to the cinema room. The second part of the film began with Robin Cooper simply saying that he went to the inland field and found the bridge and under the bridge two pots were found. He explained: "Mortimer Stanhope was then contacted and advised that we had another Roman structure in an area that was thought to be devoid of such things. When Mortimer came to the museum, Judas was requested to outline to him the same speech as earlier and Mortimer and I and a few other archaeological excavators eventually found five pots under the inland bridge."

Robin then admitted on film that he and Mortimer were absolutely staggered to unearth another Roman structure and even more staggered to find some unbroken pots under the bridge. The film then continued in silence, except for the sound of the excavators clearing away the earth covering the pots. The next part of the film showed the first of the pots being opened in the museum and the contents it had released. The rest of the film carried on in the same vein, with the other pots being emptied and the contents being catalogued.

Again Robin Cooper called for a break in the proceedings and Judas checked his pocket watch and confirmed that another two hours had elapsed since the start of the second film. The café was invaded by the audience and again Gavin and Charles joined Judas for a drink. All the men were fairly quiet in the café, although all agreed that the second part of the film was very absorbing and also very interesting.

Back in the cinema room, the nature reserve was the next area excavated and the film showed the initial trench unearthing the Roman bridge and the Roman road. Judas was supremely happy when he saw on the side of the bridge, at the top of the arch, the Roman *C*. He thought over in his mind *C ROFT*. He still did not know what the *C* stood for, but he assumed that it might be for a Roman emperor. He then surmised that others could now figure out that problem. The road was followed for about ten feet each side of the bridge and on the coastal side there was a structure at the side of the road – presumably another Roman building and this would drive Gavin even more towards emigration.

Under the bridge, the film showed three further pots, numbers six, seven and eight, being discovered. Judas and a few others present had not seen this part of the film and were enthralled by the content. The sixth pot contained large silver plate, the seventh pot contained large gold plate and the eighth pot contained more large gold plate with sapphires, rubies and pearls inlaid. They looked magnificent. It was at this point that James Priestley and Gavin Anderson had their moment of fame on the film and also added their input on their involvement in the excavation. Finally, Julian Fitzroy had his moment on film and he simply outlined that this was the highlight of his career and he was involved, albeit only very lightly, in the excavation of the greatest archaeological discovery of the past five hundred years. He simply concluded that he could now retire very happy and contented.

Finally, the film scanned around the basement of the museum, showing the items recovered from the two sites and the pots that had contained the items for the past few centuries. The film credits then ran and Judas was very pleased to read that Adam and his Great Uncle Albert were recognised as the discoverers of the information on the cross. Judas was credited with the decipherment of the information and the archaeological excavators were all mentioned by name. As the film finally ended, there was rapturous applause from the audience. Judas noticed that the final film had also lasted for two hours and the credits lasted for an additional three minutes. He then thought that it had taken him over forty five years to decipher the clues and he chuckled at the mathematics.

"Did anyone see anything wrong with the film?" asked Charles Sibley very casually and was relieved to have no response. The man from the press was absolutely mesmerised by what he had just seen. Robin then spoke to him.

"This information will be released tonight, so you can publish it in the weekly paper tomorrow, that is, if you want to?"

The press man smiled, nodded, looked at his shorthand notes and asked Robin, "May I have your mobile telephone number in case of questions on clarification?"

Robin gave him his card and the press man exited the building very speedily.

"Gentlemen," said Mortimer Stanhope, "all of the pots and contents are at present being loaded onto vehicles and are being transported to the British Museum, where a special exhibition will no doubt be staged in the very near future. The departure of the items is being filmed as we speak and will be added to the last part of our epic production. May I thank you all for your attendance and help during the past few days. We can all now have a break from treasure hunting and get back to the serious work of archaeology."

This attempt at humour was greeted with applause and groans. The group slowly departed the room and Judas was about to leave with Gavin, when Charles, Mortimer, Robin, Julian, James and Giles confronted them.

"We just had to see you before the news gets out," said Mortimer Stanhope, "to thank you, Judas, and you, Gavin, for the work you have done to allow us all here to reach the pinnacle of our careers. We will live off this discovery for the remainder of our days and we will all enjoy every second of the adulation poured upon us.

"James and Giles of the British Museum will release the news of the discovery in a few minutes and this will give the newspapers the time to produce their headlines and information and to put together a special pull out supplement for the morning. It will also allow the television companies to produce a programme outlining the known facts about the lost items and to supplement these facts with the exciting news of the discovery. The film we have just seen will be shown to the television companies and may be accepted for their release to an unsuspecting world.

"Whatever happens, we cannot thank you enough for what you have done for archaeology and we will be forever in your debt."

With his speech over, Mortimer Stanhope reached out for the hands of Judas and Gavin and shook them both. Julian, Charles, Robin, James and Giles followed Mortimer's example and both Judas and Gavin were practically mobbed.

The eminent archaeologists and the museum staff retreated to the inner sanctums of the museum. Judas and Gavin joined the exodus and exited the building. As they left the museum, two pairs of eyes looked at them from an upper corridor window. Robin Cooper turned to Mortimer Stanhope and suggested that Judas should now turn his investigative attention to the discovery of King John's Lost Treasure in the flatlands of Norfolk as his next project. Mortimer Stanhope was silent for a few seconds and then turned to his friend and said, "You never know, but he might just find it."

Judas and Gavin walked together for a few minutes in silence, each with his own thoughts.

At the centre of town, Gavin simply said, "Back to work to amend my course notes," and laughed as he went to his school.

Judas smiled and continued walking along the pavement towards the coastal path. It was nearly seven twenty and it was cold. There was a biting headwind as he reached the coastal path and he could hear the waves crashing against the rocks at the foot of the cliffs. After a brisk walk he saw his village and he was relieved to be nearly home. As he entered his apartment block he went to the post room, but as nothing was in his post box, he climbed the stairs, entered his domain and silenced the alarms.

Judas was very tired. He was meeting Anita at the pool in about twenty minutes, but he needed to rest, so he prepared himself a drink and just sat at a stool in his kitchen. He reflected on the events of the day and he was suddenly hit with the enormity of the void in his life. He had spent so much of his time thinking about the lost treasure, reading about it, searching for any clues, sometimes even dreaming about it, and now the search was over; the treasure had been found and he realized that there would be a large hole in his future existence. He pondered for a while on what project he would venture into, but as the clock kept clicking meticulously forward, he came to no conclusion.

He retreated to the bedroom, collected some shorts, a bath robe and a large towel and descended to the pool area. He expected to see Anita there waiting for him, but the pool area was empty. He entered a cubicle and changed. After a short while a security guard looked in on the pool area and seeing and recognising Judas, he waved and retreated.

Ten minutes later Anita arrived and asked, "Have you heard the news?" and without waiting for a response, continued, "the Beaufort St. Vincent abbey treasure has been found." Judas was about to speak when Anita turned and advised him, "Stephanie will be collecting me at nine o'clock."

Anita then rushed to the cubicle area to change. She emerged and promptly dived into the pool. Judas walked down the steps at the shallow end of the pool and just walked on the tiled floor. Anita was enjoying herself and completed a few lengths of the pool and then joined Judas at the shallow end.

"A few months ago I could never imagine me doing anything like this," she said, "but thanks to you, I now have a wonderful future. The sale of the Poacher's Retreat has gone through and I am working with Stephanie for a short while to sort out any transition problems that might occur. After that I will just enjoy myself. By the way, I have bought some beautiful furniture and it has been delivered to my apartment. I will move in very soon. Oh I nearly forgot. I also bought myself a very posh handbag."

Anita then realized that she had not received any response from Judas concerning her question about the recent discovery and asked, "Do you have any knowledge about the museums recent excavation activities? It's all over the news channels and also on the radio."

Judas nodded and confirmed that he knew about the discovery and was about to elaborate when a security guard escorted Stephanie to the pool area to meet Anita.

"Thank you," yelled Anita to the guard, who just smiled and waved.

"Now this is what I call living," said Stephanie and burst into laughter as Anita tried to splash her with water.

At a few minutes past nine, Anita changed and she and Stephanie left the pool area and Judas wished them both a very pleasant evening. He then dried off, collected his clothes and walked up the stairs to his apartment. He saw no-one and was inwardly relieved. He entered and prepared himself a simple meal. He was still munching away when the telephone rang and a number he did not recognise showed on the screen. It was Rudolf, the model railway builder and arrangements were made for him to call at the apartment at eight o'clock in the morning. Judas gave him the address and received the usual response.

Rudolf then went on, "Rupert showed me the layout in the book that you liked and it is actually for sale. The person who commissioned it unfortunately died and I just couldn't morally contact his widow about it, so I kept it. It is 'OO' gauge, so it isn't too big, but it does have a very good operating potential. The baseboards are bolted together and are held up by numerous upright supports that contain storage drawers for any excess rolling stock. The photographs that we took and placed in the album honestly do not do justice to the layout. Although it is not anywhere close to the largest layout that I have built, it definitely is one of the more interesting layouts that I have designed and constructed. Should I bring it all over in the morning for you to have a look at it?"

Judas was surprised and simply said "Yes, I would love to see it, as it were, in the flesh and if we can agree on a price, then I would like it installed. I look forward to seeing you. Would eight o'clock be okay?"

Rudolf agreed.

Judas returned to his meal in a very happy mood and completed his munching. After he had cleared away the pots, he turned on his kitchen television and was shocked to hear his name being casually mentioned. The programme was a special edition and was being presented to mark the discovery of the long lost treasure from the Beaufort St. Vincent abbey.

Mortimer Stanhope, Robin Cooper, James Priestley, Giles Anderson and Julian Fitzroy were all in turn interviewed and cross questioned by other eminent archaeologists and they all answered the questions honestly and fully.

The programme went on for an hour and at the end of the questioning the senior man present, Julian Fitzroy, simply said: "Gentlemen, we have found the treasure, but we are not the ones who deciphered the clues on the cross, or calculated the exact positioning of the lost artefacts. That honour goes to a Mr Judas Wells. He did all the hard work and it took him over forty five years of painstaking dedication and research to accomplish this monumental task. Mention must also be given to another researcher, Albert Stonehaven, who unearthed the information on the original cross, but could not decipher it so it was passed on to his great nephew Adam upon his demise. These two men and Judas Wells deserve the credit for pointing we mere mortal archaeologists in the right direction, so that we may, in our small way, also bask in their shining glory and achievement."

Judas was surprised, shocked and stunned. As the credits began to roll, Judas saw the names of all the eminent archaeologists involved in the work and also the names of the excavators who did the initial work to unearth the lost artefacts. Also mentioned was Charles Sibley and his photographic and recording team and Judas was amused and alarmed to read that Gavin Melbourne was a Technical Advisor. At the end of the credits, Albert and Adam were given the credit for their dedication in locating the clues to the location of the treasure and Judas Wells was given the special credit for deciphering the jumbled up clues, relating to the treasures buried location.

When the credits of the television special had ended, the camera returned to the presenter of the programme, who simply said that a film of the events leading up to and including the discovery of the lost items, was being shown at the Beaufort St. Vincent Museum from eight o'clock in the morning and from three o'clock in the afternoon, for a period of six weeks, starting on Monday next. The presenter indicated that bookings were at present being taken by the museum receptionists as space was limited.

Judas was still in a daze when the telephone rang. He recognised the number of the Poacher's Retreat and answered.

The caller was Anita who said, "You kept that quiet. Why didn't you tell me?"

"I did try to say something when you told me that the treasure had been found, but you didn't give me a chance. Did you like the programme? I only saw the last twenty minutes," said Judas.

"I only saw about half an hour," admitted Anita, "but what I did see was absolutely fantastic. You really are a very dark horse concerning archaeology. Very well done. Will I see you tomorrow? How about lunch?" she queried.

"You're on," answered Judas.

Before he could say anything else, Anita continued "I will see you by the church at noon and we will walk to a superb restaurant I know by the harbour. After lunch I have some more shopping to do. See you tomorrow," and with that she hung up.

After a few more minutes of thinking about the events of the day, Judas decided that it was time to relax and he retired to his study.

CHAPTER 29

Wednesday 21st January

The alarm went off very early and Judas still felt tired, but got up and went to his study. He sat there and pondered the happenings of the past few days. He also began to wonder what project he would do now to occupy his time and to exercise his mental ability. He sat for fifteen minutes pondering the question, but was not getting any nearer to a solution, so in desperation he turned on his television. He was immediately assaulted by the national news concerning the discovery of the local abbey treasure. The presenters showed the newspaper headlines. Some of the quality newspapers' headlines were very serious and dealt with the subject with due care and attention, remembering that it was a serious subject and a national sensation. Other tabloids were more sensational, with headlines that debased their profession and brought archaeology into disrepute as treasure seekers. Some foreign newspapers even carried the news that the lost artefacts had been found, although these countries were mainly in the commonwealth and were aware of the history of the items.

However, when the news programme showed the film of the pots being liberated from their burial places and the treasure being liberated from the pots, Judas felt that the whole exercise, lasting for over forty five years, had been worth all the toil and trouble. Also when the presenters mentioned the names of Adam and Albert Stonehaven, Judas felt an inner pride that his old friend and his friend's great uncle had at last been recognised for their contribution to the discovery. In short he was happy for them both. His only regret was that neither man lived to see the results of their research.

Judas watched the programme for about thirty minutes, but when it began to be repeated, he turned off the machine and just sat in the dark. Outside the wind was howling and the clouds were low and black. Rain was forecast, but not until about midday. Judas looked out to the sea and saw a few lights twinkling on various ships. The lighthouse beacon was flashing its warning light and the village was beginning to arouse itself for another day of expectation. For some inexplicable reason, Judas went to his case and took out the various notes he had on the lost treasure. He began to read and for a complete hour he was engrossed in the content of the pages. As he came to the photocopy of the cross, he suddenly realized that the markings on the cross had still not been deciphered and were still unknown. This thought worried him, as the markings must relate to the location of the treasure. The thought baffled him and also upset him, as he was not a person who took shortcuts to anything, yet the lost treasure had been located and still vital clues could not be understood.

At seven o'clock, after breakfast, Judas took out the model railway plan again and was still enthralled by its design and operating potential. Judas retreated to his inner study and looked at the area where the layout was to be sited. He imagined the layout when erected and in place and was looking forward to seeing this perfection in miniature installed into his home.

At eight o'clock sharp, the door bell sounded and Judas greeted Rudolf and Rupert, each carrying a fully constructed and scenic section of a model railway baseboard.

Rudolf introduced himself and then shyly asked, "Are you the chap on the news who found the treasure?"

"Not exactly," replied Judas, "I am the chap who unravelled the mediaeval clues, which gave directions leading to the location of the hiding places, which allowed the eminent archaeologists the pure pleasure of unearthing the buried artefacts."

"Told you," said a smug Rupert, as he and Rudolf were escorted up the stairs to the inner study. Ever the businessman, Rudolf said the price he had agreed with the deceased and said he would be prepared to sell the layout for slightly less to get it from his cramped workshop. Judas agreed to pay the price, as the sections of the baseboards he had seen were absolutely first class. He was certain that when the exercise was completed he would have a fabulous layout in his new home.

After six more trips to the van parked by the main door, all of the baseboards, cabinets and battens were grouped together in the study area.

As Rupert was about to leave the apartment, to drive his car back to his shop ready for the opening, Judas said, "I will see you this afternoon, hopefully, or tomorrow to purchase more equipment, including locomotives, carriages and wagons for this layout. I really like it and I am certain that I will eventually be able to operate the layout to its full potential."

Rupert smiled, nodded and said, "It may take a short while to gain the necessary knowledge concerning the operating of the electrics, but it is definitely a wonderful hobby."

As Rupert exited the apartment he turned to Judas and said, "By the way, you have a very beautiful home and you have a layout to match. I look forward to seeing you at my shop."

Judas looked on in awe as Rudolf bolted together the sections, placed them onto the storage cabinets, which acted as supports, and screwed battens onto the walls to secure the baseboards. The removable sections of track were quickly re-united with the baseboard and the whole layout suddenly came to life with the electrification of the whole system; the signals, the turntable, the crossing gates, the points, the windmill and the watermill all obtained operating power. Also barriers to factory entrances and lights in workshops became operational, together with cranes in the goods yard. Rudolf then took from a small case a tank locomotive and let it run around the layout to test the track and to iron out any poor rail joints. To Judas, the layout looked even better than the photographs in the album held by Rupert.

After an hour of intense work Judas said, "You deserve a coffee and some biscuits," and this offer was eagerly accepted by Rudolf.

After another stint of forty minutes the layout was installed, the curtains were attached to the facia to hide the cabinets and the operating literature was outlined and presented to Judas, together with some copies of the layout photographs he so admired. Judas then presented the cheque to Rudolf, who profusely thanked Judas for his custom.

"If there are any problems, just give me a call, via Rupert and I will come back and rectify the faults?"

After letting Rudolf out of his home, Judas returned to his study and just looked at his new acquisition. It was superb and it was a masterpiece of design and construction. Judas read and re-read the operating literature involving the master control booklets, the instructions on the signalling and point switches, the staging loops and all of the other items that had to be mastered, before the system could be operated to its full potential for pleasure.

At eleven o'clock Judas exited his apartment. He walked towards the village and, on reaching the church, he went inside. He sat at the rear of the church and just marvelled at the peace and serenity the place exuded. He offered up a silent prayer for the guidance he had received, to aid him in his research and for the money he had received for the sale of his old home and for the gift he had received in the form of his apartment. Judas was feeling relieved and, he did not know why, but he felt close to God and this seemed to comfort him. He sat for ten minutes, simply looking at the statues and the stained glass windows and was about to leave when he saw the Reverend Oliver Winchester.

"Hello there, Mr Wells isn't it?" said the reverend gentleman and held out his hand to Judas who eagerly shook it.

"I was just admiring your beautiful church and having a few quiet moments of meditation and reflection. How are you Reverend?" enquired Judas.

Ignoring the question Oliver Winchester simply said, "That was an absolutely brilliant piece of archaeological decipherment you did with the chaps at the museum. My wife and I were glued to the television programme last night and we are both eager to visit the museum to see the film outlining the events leading up to the discovery of the lost artefacts. Very well done." He again held out his hand to Judas, who shook it.

Judas was embarrassed but replied, "Thank you for your comments reverend, but in all honesty it wasn't brilliance on my part. It was fifty per cent luck and fifty per cent fluke. The museum staff did all of the hard work, it is they who deserve much of the credit." Judas then deflected the conversation towards the church and said, "This building is absolutely beautiful. I look forward to being at your church service when I am next off work on a Sunday."

This statement pleased the vicar.

Judas left the church and stood by the wall protecting the building. He looked along the road inland and saw Anita striding quickly towards him.

She took his arm and said, "Onward to the harbour."

The clouds were dark and the expected rainfall looked imminent. As they passed a newsagent's, Judas read the advertising board of *The Beaufort Gazette*, which proudly boasted: "Our Reporter has seen the Treasure." Judas then heard his name being called and, as he turned to face the caller, he recognised the reporter he had seen at the museum and who by his name tag was called Edward Eastwood.

"Hello again," said Judas and held out his hand to the reporter.

"I just happened to be in the area, having interviewed the local winner of the Art competition we held last month. I'm very pleased to see you again," said the reporter. "As you know I was at the museum yesterday and by a fluke I saw the film concerning the discovery of the treasure. The weekly paper had already been prepared for printing and it was too late to add anything concerning the news of the discovery. However, we are in the process of doing a special edition of the paper and would love to have an interview with you and also an interview with Robin Cooper. Mr Cooper has been contacted and will be at our main office in Beaufort St. Vincent at two o'clock this afternoon. Would you please join us, to give us your most valuable input to the archaeological discovery of the century? Please?"

The last "Please" was really a pleading one and Judas could not find it in his heart to decline.

Judas and Anita continued their walk to the harbour and Anita said, "You really are getting the star treatment at the moment aren't you?" and smiled. She then said, "It couldn't happen to a nicer person. You deserve it," and she squeezed his arm.

After a few more steps Anita stopped, turned and guided Judas into The Harbour View Restaurant.

"This meal is on me," she said, "just to thank you for the loan, for helping me to purchase my dream apartment and for just being a very special person."

Judas was lost for words and this amused Anita, who just smiled.

The forthcoming meal was a very welcome interlude for Judas after a very hectic few days. After ordering lunch, Anita stayed away from the subject of the treasure and just talked about her working at the Poacher's Retreat for Stephanie.

"I will just help out where needed, but Stephanie knows as much about the place as I do," concluded Anita. The talk then changed again and Anita continued: "I am still in shock concerning ownership of my new apartment, but that hasn't stopped me from buying some new furniture and curtains for it. I have also bought some new clothes, where previously I had been forced to make do and mend. Thanks to you Judas, I can now see a very bright future and a very pleasant retirement in front of me."

Judas was about to speak, when Anita again continued.

"I will be moving into my new apartment on Friday and I will be spending Thursday morning packing. This packing shouldn't take very long to accomplish as I have very few items that I want to transport to my new home. I have even booked a holiday for myself," said Anita, as the waitress delivered their meals and continued, "on a coach to Cornwall. I am going in May for a whole fortnight. I have never been away for more than three days before. I am really looking forward to it."

Judas could see that Anita was very happy and this comforted him.

He simply said, "I am sure you deserve a very healthy, happy, peaceful and prosperous retirement and I wish you every success in all you seek to accomplish. Just don't forget to send me a postcard from Cornwall."

Anita smiled and said she would do as ordered.

After the meal, Anita left the restaurant for her shopping spree and Judas sat for a while enjoying his drink. When he left the restaurant he was dismayed to see that it had been raining, although it was now fine. The ground was still very wet, the clouds looked ominous and black, and further rainfall was expected. The walk to the newspaper building at Beaufort St. Vincent was very invigorating and Judas enjoyed the exercise. On reaching the offices of the local weekly paper, Judas entered the reception area and was met by Edward Eastwood, who had Robin Cooper standing behind him.

There being no need for introductions Edward Eastwood guided both men to a small office, barely big enough to hold the three seats and a desk that it held.

"Thank you gentlemen, for agreeing to this meeting, which I am sure will be a great boost to the gazette's circulation," said the host.

"Better still," interrupted Robin Cooper and reached into his small case, "for I have here a copy of the film from the museum and it is now on loan to the gazette for a period of four days, to be returned on Monday."

The small package was handed over to the press representative, without ceremony. Judas had said absolutely nothing and was impressed by the offer of Robin, to allow a copy of the film to be used by the gazette for its literary scoop.

Edward Eastwood was also suitably impressed and simply blurted out, "Oh my God in Heaven. What a prize," and carried his new prize possession to his nearby editor, who was even more impressed by the temporary possession of the film. Everything that Judas knew was on the film and he had no doubts that if any queries needed resolving by the press, then Robin Cooper would be the first port of call.

After a few minutes, both Robin and Judas were requested to stand against a white walled background for photographs and, on completion of the snaps, Judas was asked various questions by Edward Eastwood, concerning his discovering the papers of Albert Stonehaven in the room of his dear friend, Adam. Judas answered fully and honestly and after about twenty minutes the conversation turned to the decipherment of the markings on the cross.

After another twenty minutes, Judas deflected the praise being given to him by saying that the heroes of the exercise were Adam and Albert: "Albert for discovering the original papers and Adam for keeping the papers safe," suggested Judas. "Also the archaeologists were the actual people who had done the spadework, literally, and had found the hidden artefacts. And when the printed copies of the cross were enlarged and the positioning of the circles at the end of the lines had been recognised as being representations of the local settlements, then the hiding places were a simple and logical deduction."

At this point Edward Eastwood switched his questioning to Robin Cooper.

Judas then asked, "Will I be required further today?" and as he received a shake of the head he opened the door to leave.

"By the way," said Edward Eastwood, "we are producing a Special Edition of the paper on Friday, with a world exclusive for *The Beaufort Gazette* regarding its local lost treasure and its discovery."

Judas concluded that Edward Eastwood did not consider that the national newspapers reporting of the finds were in any way challengers to the local papers exclusivity.

"Remember," said Judas, "some of the items were found in Beaufort St. Catherine, although the main items were discovered in Beaufort St. Vincent."

"A minor detail and a miniscule glitch," commented the reporter.

"Journalistic licence," muttered Judas.

Judas bade both men a pleasant afternoon and evening.

Edward Eastwood stated, "I will be working late at the paper, to help with the Special Edition on Friday."

Robin replied, "I will be returning to the museum, to continue making inroads into the backlog of work that I have neglected during the excavation process. Both James Priestley and Giles Anderson are still at the inland Roman bridge, excavating the road towards the coast, and Mortimer Stanhope is still at the nature reserve, excavating the bridge and also the newly discovered guard house. All of them are really enjoying their work and are basking in their popularity."

Judas and Edward both smiled and then Judas, having wished Robin luck in clearing his backlog of work, headed for the model shop run by Rupert.

It was raining as he reached the pavement and Judas walked quickly to reach his destination.

"You made it then," said Rupert cheerily, "Rudolf has already told me that the layout is up and running perfectly. I am sure you will enjoy operating it. The layout itself is the best one, in my humble opinion, that my dear brother has ever designed and built. The four staging areas, hidden under the scenery, are really something that Rudolf is pleased about."

Judas agreed.

"It is a fine layout and I am sure that I will enjoy operating it," he advised.

Judas then went to the section of the shop dealing with his company's products. After a long search, Judas selected a small tank locomotive, a larger tank locomotive and two mixed freight and passenger locomotives with tenders. He also selected eight carriages and twelve various sized goods wagons, all of the Great Western Railway and joined the queue of three at the pay point. He eventually placed his overloaded basket onto the counter. He was certain that to operate the model railway effectively he would need more stock, but he had to get used to the complicated operating of the layout and his present purchases would have to suffice for the time being.

"This should keep me entertained and educated tonight," said Judas as Rupert began to put the items through the till. "Tomorrow I may be in for some more equipment, but I will see how events pan out this evening. It looks like being a long night."

Rupert finished putting the items through the accounting process and Judas promptly paid. He picked up the three carrier bags and exited the shop.

As he departed, Rupert said, "I hope to see you tomorrow."

Judas retraced his steps to the coastal path and resisted the temptation to visit his workplace. He reached the coastal path and, because it looked as if it would soon rain, he hurried forward. The welcoming lights of the village came into view and Judas soon reached the sanctuary of his apartment block.

As he entered the building he heard the distant sound of thunder and a few moments later the heavens opened.

Judas checked his mail box and retrieved an envelope. On entering his apartment he opened his post and saw it was a note from Gavin, his history tutor. It simply said that he had definitely not been serious about Judas giving a lecture to the class on Friday night, concerning the decipherment of the clues to the lost items. It also said that he had told some members of the class what he had proposed to Judas and they were all very pleased with the false suggestion. Judas just smiled.

Very soon he was in his study unpacking the carrier bags of their contents and then emptying the boxes of their railway equipment. He carefully placed all of the boxes into the cupboards under the layout and placed the locomotives, coaches and trucks onto the tracks of the layout. Judas read and re-read the instruction manuals left by Rudolf and slowly the fog of ignorance lifted from his mind and understanding replaced it. After a few more minutes Judas began to operate the layout, albeit only tentatively, but it was working and there were no red lights flashing to indicate imminent catastrophes. Judas then remembered the MD's request, to be given a track plan and photographs of his layout, when completed. He retired to his printer and copied the required information from the operating manual ready for presentation to the MD. He then used his own camera to give an indication of the layout in situ in his study and printed off the photographs. He then wrote a covering note to his MD.

Judas then looked through all of the paperwork he was passing to the MD and, on the photographs from the instruction manual, he saw various locomotives and rolling stock displayed. Some of the items he had already purchased and he made a note in his pocketbook of the identity of those items that he still needed. He concluded that a model railway was not a cheap hobby, but then reflected that most people entering the hobby took years to reach the standard of his present layout and the cost per week would therefore be manageable.

After a quick snack, Judas retired to the study and continued the familiarization exercises with his new hobby. He tested his locomotives on all of the tracks and he tested all of the points, slip points and crossings. He tested the isolating sections of the staging tracks and he tested the signals and their relationship with the points, slip points and crossings. He was enjoying himself and he was lost in a new world of absolute pleasure. He also lost all track of time and was surprised when he looked out of the windows and saw only blackness and a few distant twinkling lights. He checked his pocket watch and was confounded to see that it was nearly nine o'clock.

Judas suddenly felt tired and he switched off the power to the layout. He decided to have an early night and went to his bedroom. He began to read an autobiographical tome, but his mind kept wandering and he decided that he needed his rest. As he settled down in bed his mind wandered back to his *C ROFT* problem and he tried to figure out the reason for the *C*. He entered sleep without reaching any conclusion.

CHAPTER 30

Thursday 22nd January

Judas was wide awake just a few seconds before the alarm sounded. He had slept soundly and awoke completely refreshed. After a giant yawn he looked out of his windows seaward and saw absolutely nothing but blackness. Not a single light on a single ship was in view. The sky was also black, with thick cloud obscuring the myriad of heavenly stars, circulating in their orbital majesty. He went to his new model railway and just looked at it with great pride and pleasure. He marvelled at the perfection of the layout and the endless possibilities of the operations available. He returned to his bedroom and then descended to his kitchen.

Judas prepared for the day and then went to his outer study and just looked out to sea. There were still no lights to be seen on any ship. The heavens opened and the inshore wind threw the downpour onto the windows, with a violent force. Again he looked at his new model railway and this time he activated the controls and a steam Tilbury Tank locomotive pulled out of the terminal station with a rake of coaches.

After ten minutes of watching and operating various locomotive journeys around the compact layout, Judas heard himself say, "This is the life, a wonderful home and a good job. Great!"

He was happy. He was pleased. And he had made Anita happy. What more could anyone want?

He looked out of the windows overlooking the village and decided that he would soon set out on a mission to investigate his surroundings. He knew some of the highlights of the area, but there were many more of them to discover and learn. Before leaving his apartment he ventured outside to his rear-facing study balcony, overlooking the nature reserve and surveyed the views. Strangely he could see the expansive cover over the section of the archaeological excavation, that he had a hand in opening up, although his involvement was only indirectly. This fact amused him.

Judas looked again out over the sea and this time he could see cargo ships plying their trade and travelling north along the coast. He watched them for over half an hour and he was fascinated by the slowness of the boats and pondered that it must sometimes take weeks to complete a journey. The day began to brighten up and he retreated to his inner study. Judas looked on his computer screen for any messages, but there were none. He checked his pocket watch and it digitally showed 7.22 a.m. It was still early and it had stopped raining, so Judas decided it was time to leave and go into the village. He collected his shoulder bag, containing the information for the MD, and left the apartment. Through the glass panes of the stairwell he could see the village slowly embracing the challenges of a new day.

As he passed the church, Judas again felt the need to enter and he duly opened the heavy wooden door. Inside, the church was dimly lit and he sat in the rear row of pews. He was the only person in the church and he felt uncomfortable. It was eerily quiet. After a few minutes the day brightened and the stained glass windows reflected the day's majesty. He spent a few moments thanking his maker for the bounty he had received recently and he somehow felt more calm and relieved than when he entered. A short while later, Judas left the church and walked to the harbour and sat looking out at the small boats, casually tossed about by the relentless waves.

After a few more minutes, idly watching the waves lapping onto the boats and onto the numerous jetties, Judas stood and walked back into the village square. He remembered that he had to purchase a, "Good Luck in your New Home" card for Anita, who would be busily packing today and would move into her new apartment tomorrow. He went into the nearest newsagents and made the necessary purchase. On exiting the shop he was hailed by Amanda Bailey.

"Hello Judas," she said warmly, "lovely to see you. I still have goose pimples when I look at my bank book and see the amount in there. We are both looking forward to the better weather when building work can begin. We are still in shock, but it is honestly a good feeling. We can't thank you enough."

Judas was embarrassed and simply asked, "Where's Stephen, is he not with you?"

"No, the poor man is working, as usual. However, he now has a spring in his step, just like me," and Amanda attempted a small hop.

Judas smiled. "You both deserve to fulfil your dreams and I am pleased to be of help," he said.

"Bless you," said Amanda, as she turned away with more tears in her eyes.

Amanda then turned and asked, "How is your apartment? Have you settled in okay?"

Judas was surprised, but answered, "The apartment is absolutely first class. It really is beautiful and the views from the windows, seaward and landward, are stunning. I really am fortunate to have such a wonderful home. Anita also likes her–"

"Anita?" questioned Amanda, "your wife? I honestly thought you were a career bachelor."

Judas laughed.

"No, not my wife. She is going to be –"

"Oh that is good news. Congratulations," said Amanda.

"No. No," said Judas quickly, "what I was going to say was Anita also likes her apartment and she is going to be one of my new neighbours. I have known her practically all of my life. We are great friends and we look after each other, in the purest of senses."

"Ah I see," said a disappointed Amanda, as she turned and left.

Judas was embarrassed, although he was pleased to see Amanda. However, her presence seemed to unnerve him and he abandoned his wanderings around the village. Instead he would go to Beaufort St. Vincent. He decided that a long exercising walk would help him and he set off towards the coastal path. The walk to the nearby town was bracing and he enjoyed the beautiful views from the cliff tops. Beaufort St. Vincent came into view and Judas again saw the security lodge and resisted the urge to enter. However, he knew that he would enter the lodge later in the day to see if Martin had any problems that needed resolving. However, that was for later and he headed for the main square.

On reaching the town centre, Judas was about to enter a café, when he was hailed by Henry Brown from his car.

"Judas, just the man, can you please come to my office sometime this morning as I have something important to ask you? Don't go to the receptionist, just come to my office."

Judas was about to answer, when a noisy vehicle passed, so he just nodded.

"Nothing to worry about," yelled Henry Brown as he waved and drove off.

Judas could think of no reason for his presence, but the request intrigued him and he headed for the company. Judas mused that "nothing to worry about" seemed to be Henry Brown's favourite saying.

As he passed the gatehouse Colin shouted out, "Biarritz crowded again?"

Judas just waved and yelled back, "Yes. Bloody tourists!"

Colin laughed.

Judas knocked on the bureau door and was invited in. Seated in the room were Paul Gibson, Stephen Lindsey and Henry Brown.

"Thanks for being here so promptly," said Henry Brown and continued, "I was going to call you later, but thankfully I saw you in town. I have only just returned from a breakfast meeting with the MD and some senior members of the board and we had a very good meeting and an even better breakfast. However, we now have another proposition to put to you."

Now what? thought Judas as Henry Brown prepared himself for a speech.

"Don't look so worried," began Henry, "I think you will like what I am about to say. As you know we have been to two model railway exhibitions recently, exhibiting our company items on a makeshift stand and I think we made a good impression to the attendees. When those other stand members discovered that we were a last minute replacement for the deceased gentleman, we were actually congratulated on our performance. Yesterday we had confirmation that we would be allowed to go to another model railway exhibition, again in place of the deceased, and this time at a larger venue in the town of Chalfont Springs. It's about forty miles away. This is where you come in Judas."

Judas was still trying to make sense of what Henry was going on about, but decided to carry on listening and not to interrupt.

"We propose to go to the Cleveland Centre, in Chalfont Springs, tomorrow morning and set up our display and, as we have been allocated more space, we will be taking a small model railway with us to operate at the venue. The company people going are the ones that did such sterling work at the other two exhibitions, but as you know these exhibitions were both very rushed jobs.

"This latest exhibition will not be rushed. The model railway selected for exhibition is an L-shaped layout and it was designed by you Judas. If you have no objections, the company would like you to go with the other four people and set up the stand with all of the associated literature. Also the stand with the various products of the company and, of course, the layout. The layout is on a single solid baseboard so it can be transported easily and it does not require bolting together at the other end.

"By going, you will sample what it is like at these venues and we, as a company, expect to be involved with about twenty five exhibitions every year. These exhibitions will be all over the country and will involve weekend working and days off during the week. The people that will be involved at these various exhibitions will consist of a group leader and four others, presently two girls and two guys. This existing group are very hopeful that you will join them on this trip to get an insight into your future involvement with exhibition work and your other duties. Your duties will also cover arranging hotel accommodation for your crew, but this has already been sorted out for this exhibition." Henry stopped speaking and took a drink before continuing, "The MD would like you to do this and so would we three. You are very talented."

Judas was stunned. He knew he was going to be involved with this work, but he had never expected it so soon.

After about ten seconds, Judas enquired, "Is Martin okay with this, as he should be off tomorrow for four days?"

"I have already spoken to Martin and enlightened him about your new duties and he is very pleased for you," said Henry, "and he is happy for you to go away tomorrow and represent the company.

"However it would be appreciated by us all in this room, if you could keep an eye on Martin, as he is being thrown in at the deep end. He will also be training your replacement on Wednesday next, after the newcomer's induction course. His new colleague will be Aaron Miller and on Monday Aaron will go through the induction course and be with Martin later in the week. As Martin is fairly new on the job I have told him that if he has any problems you will be on hand to assist. Is that okay?"

Judas nodded.

"In that case gentlemen, it seems that I now have to be introduced to my new team," said Judas.

Henry, Stephen and Paul all shouted, "Yes."

When the men had settled down, Henry said, "If you can be in my office at seven o'clock in the morning I will introduce you formally to the team. It is just as well that you agreed to go, as I had already arranged hotel accommodation for you."

This remark amused Judas.

"In the meantime, I see you are also something of a live wire in the archaeological sphere," chided a smiling Henry Brown. He then said, "My wife was so engrossed in the television news programme on the lost Beaufort St. Vincent treasure that she forgot to go to her evening class on cookery. I, of course, got the blame for not reminding her of the class. However, on a serious note, we all here congratulate you on your work to decipher the clues allowing for the discovery of the lost items. At my wife's insistence I have booked two seats for the film show on Monday afternoon."

"Thank you for your comments," said Judas, "but I just got lucky and was able to see a way forward. Thankfully the small part that I played was crucial in the unravelling of an important piece of the jigsaw and the museum staff were able to extract the items from their entombment. There are still a lot of things that we do not know about the markings on the cross and it will require the services of a number of very gifted people to understand and decipher the remaining hidden information."

At this point Paul Gibson stated, "My wife demanded that I get seats booked at the museum as early as possible and we go on Wednesday afternoon. She never liked archaeology before seeing this item on the TV news."

Stephen Lindsey then added, "I go with my wife to the museum on Thursday afternoon. She is also now very interested in archaeology."

Judas smiled and said, "I sincerely hope that you all like the film. My involvement was not expected, but it was thrust upon me and I had to do my speech concerning the decipherment. I only hope it doesn't ruin the remainder of the film for the archaeologists."

Judas then deflected the conversation away from the museum, by stating, "I have here some photographs and a layout plan, which the MD requested me to supply when my own layout was up and running."

Judas presented the file to Henry Brown, requesting him to pass the papers on during his next weekly meeting with Dr. Rose.

Judas continued, "If you wish you can all look at the layout plan and photographs."

Henry, Paul and Stephen did all wish to see the paperwork and all looked in awe at the contents in the file.

Judas explained, "The layout I now possess was originally built to order for a client who unfortunately died just before its completion. The constructor of the layout had been left with it. I saw photographs of the layout and a plan of the layout and thought it was superb. I checked the area I had available for a layout and as it would fit into my study, I had it installed yesterday. Later today, I am collecting the remainder of the locomotives and rolling stock that are needed to operate the system to its full potential."

All of the men were impressed by the layout, but they all said that Judas had a very beautiful study and they were all envious. They were even more envious when Judas admitted that the layout was situated in the smaller of his two studies.

Judas looked at his pocket watch and, as it was approaching eleven o'clock, he decided to visit the lodge and to see if Martin Holland had any unresolved problems that needed his help.

As he entered the room he was greeted by Colin, who simply repeated "Biarritz crowded again?" and he again laughed. Judas forced a smile and went over to see his goods reception colleague.

"Any problems?" asked Judas, and Martin shook his head.

"Everything is under control, although tomorrow, Saturday and Sunday, should be quiet days because of auditors and stock takers on site."

"Thanks for doing the extra shifts, Martin. I honestly didn't know anything about it until I arrived earlier," confided Judas.

Martin just nodded and then asked Judas the question that all in the lodge wanted to ask. "How on earth did you arrive at the solution to decipher the clues to the local treasure?"

"In all honesty, said Judas, "it happened when I enlarged a copy of the cross details, to the same scale as other maps I was using and I saw the small dots at the end of the wavy lines. I originally believed these wavy lines represented the coast or the sea. When I looked at them upside down the relationship of the dots was the same as the three local small settlements. I then reversed the cross details and things fell into place. It was a fluke and the rest is history."

Martin and the guards looked at each other and were not convinced that they had been told the truth. However, at that moment a vehicle arrived and whilst Martin was occupied Judas left the lodge.

He also remembered that he had to obtain more equipment from Rupert and he again smiled at the name. The afternoon was not cold but the temperature was dropping and at noon he decided to return to the model shop and complete his purchases. As he entered the establishment he was greeted by the owner.

"Hello again," said Rupert, "As you have returned, I assume that you have worked your way through the complexities of the layout and have decided to add more stock to complete the designs operating potential."

Judas simply replied, "In a word, yes."

Rupert continued, "I can honestly say that I did expect to see you again today, so I took out the stock that I could see on the photographs of the layout and it is here on the rear counter. With this additional equipment, the layout can be operated to its planned potential and you should have plenty of pleasure operating it. That is, of course, if you wish to purchase it all."

Judas thanked him for his thoughtfulness and walked to the section of the shop exhibiting various boxes of model railway equipment, directed to the younger generation just beginning in the hobby. He was amazed at the number of items directed towards this section of the modelling fraternity. However, he noticed that in the boxes containing a locomotive and trucks, or a locomotive and carriages, that there was only a simple oval of track supplied with each set. This set him thinking and he was convinced that he could provide simple plans in his new design bureau work, to rectify the barrenness of the basic purchased oval, with the addition of a few points and lengths of track. This discovery pleased him and he set his mind into design mode to begin planning.

After a few minutes in deep thought, he retreated to the main counter and Rupert. Judas checked his notebook list against the items selected by his host and requested an additional two items of equipment that Rupert was only too happy to provide. After payment Judas collected his three carrier bags of equipment and retraced his steps to the coastal path. The walk was a solitary affair. Half way along the coastal path Judas sat huddled on a wooden bench for a rest and watched the distant ships ply their cargo trade and also saw the clouds swirl and get darker. He continued his journey and very soon he reached the main street. He entered his building, checked his empty post box and walked up the stairs.

Judas entered his apartment and went straight to his model railway in his study. He emptied all of the contents from their packaging and placed the empty boxes in the cupboards under the layout. He placed the locomotives and rolling stock onto various sidings and onto various loops and just enjoyed the scene. However, for some reason he did not operate the system, but sat at his desk and sketched various layout diagrams onto graph paper. He was enjoying this exercise as he tried to enlarge the basic purchased oval and incorporate a passing loop and siding facilities, to provide basic operational potential to a basic concept. He thought he was succeeding.

After an hour of mindful endeavour, he had eight different sketches and all would improve the basic oval of the original train set package. Judas then used the miniature track sections of his company's layout product to ensure that his designs would work. As each one of the layouts he designed was proved to be geometrically correct, he drew the layout to scale and placed the item code of the track next to the rails. Judas was now getting into the meat of the hobby and was enjoying his new found expertise at designing layouts. However, he was getting slightly peckish and he retreated to the kitchen. Whilst there he placed the money for Juliette onto the kitchen breakfast bar and then wrote her a note saying that if she wished to bring Andrew to view his new layout, then he had no objections. At the end of the note he wrote, "We model railway engineers have to stick together."

On a sudden whim, Judas telephoned Anita at the Poacher's Retreat. Anita answered with her receptionist voice and changed to her normal voice when Judas spoke.

After the initial banter, Anita said, "I have everything packed in two small cases ready for my move to the new apartment tomorrow. Packing did not take long, as I have very few personal possessions that I want to keep. Stephanie says that she will get rid of the items I leave behind. It's a very sad day for me to be leaving a place that has been home and a workplace for a number of years. It is also an exciting day as I am about to fulfil an ambition and live in a beautiful home and also look forward to retirement. I am very happy, thanks to you."

Judas was very happy for her and it pleased him to know that Anita would soon be retired and able to have a comfortable future. Judas then informed Anita of his latest news. Although he was not supposed to broadcast about his new position in the company, this was Anita and she was special and very trustworthy.

"I have been offered and accepted, a new role at the company organizing our attendance at model railway events, publicity stands, accommodation and a few other titles and I start tomorrow."

"I am very happy for you," confided Anita, "and I am sure that you will do justice to the work and uphold the confidence the management have shown in you. Well done."

Anita then turned the conversation back to her new home. "I love my new home and I have purchased lounge, dining room and bedroom furniture, together with the curtains and other items that are essential to complete my dream abode."

Anita was completely in "Information" mode and Judas just listened. Finally Anita said, "Thank you Judas for your help and support and for being such a good and generous friend. I will treasure your friendship always."

Anita then rang off and prepared for her last night's sleep at the Poacher's Retreat.

Judas ate a very simple meal. Half way through the snack he had a thought about track formations and retreated to his study. He looked at all of the eight layouts he had designed earlier and then set about expanding them to a higher degree of operating potential and then expanded them all to their final layout formation. Each of the layouts had three stages. This was a long and arduous task, but Judas stuck at it rigidly and completed the exercise. He then checked that the miniature track sections fitted correctly and was relieved when they did. Judas then simply coded them *1A, 1B* and *1C* up to *8A, 8B* and *8C* and this gave him twenty four layouts.

He then had another thought and in his mind he combined one track plan to another, to create a model railway with two stations. On a small baseboard, Judas concluded that this would not work scenically, but on a larger support it would work very well. However, as his initial layouts were developments of the basic circle, Judas decided that two stations were not necessary, but he believed that small industrial complexes would add considerably to the operating potential of the layouts. He therefore designed two factory, forestry or waterside activities to complement the initial layouts. Judas was really getting into the meat of the subject and spent the rest of the evening drawing the layouts and industrial additions to scale with the rail item code adjoining. He also joined various layouts together, to see if these would work and these did work perfectly, but he did not develop them further, as this could be done on the second book of larger layouts. Judas then packed his papers and plans he had prepared into his small case and retired for the night.

CHAPTER 31

Friday 23rd January

The alarm woke Judas, who had not stirred all night. After a sparse breakfast he wrote out the "Welcome to your new home" card for Anita, saying "I look forward to having you as a near neighbour" and sealed the envelope. He placed the envelope in Anita's post box. On his walk to work his thoughts were on new layout plans and he had a few thought out in his mind. He was happy and very content with life. He only hoped that Anita's move today into her new apartment would go smoothly and that she would enjoy her new social surroundings.

He arrived at the lodge and was greeted by Gordon and Richard, who both congratulated him on his fine work for the museum.

Gordon said, "Today there is a special edition of *The Beaufort Gazette,* according to my newsagent's, with a world exclusive on the treasure find. It should be very interesting."

"And informative also," added Richard.

"Yes, I did know about it," admitted Judas, "as Edward Eastwood dragged Robin Cooper and myself into his office and drained us both of information about the decipherment of the clues and also the information relating to the actual discovery of the Beaufort St. Vincent treasure. We were lucky to get out of his office with our sanity. The fact that some of the treasure was found in the nature reserve at Beaufort St. Catherine was, to Edward, a minor inconvenience."

"Well done anyway," said Gordon, "and also my very best wishes with your new job. It is well deserved. Good luck."

"And from me also" said Richard. Keith arrived for his day shift, followed by Colin a couple of minutes later. After the handover, they also congratulated Judas on his archaeological achievement and also on his promotion.

Keith eventually said, "Archaeology has never been interesting to me, but that was something different. Well done."

Judas simply said thanks and returned to his desk. Judas had a few words with Martin when he arrived and wished him luck in his new job. Martin reciprocated.

Until Henry Brown arrived, Judas could only sit and wait. However, he did keep looking at the designs that he had done and thought about having some stations at different levels on the layouts, but then decided that as the prospective operators were not proficient modellers, single level baseboards would be the preferred option. Judas then photocopied all forty eight layout plans, plus the rail requirements for each sheet and awaited the arrival of his new colleague.

At six fifteen the telephone rang on Judas's old desk. It was Anita and, after the greeting, she said she had some important and wonderful news.

"I have arranged for my few meagre possessions to be transported to my new apartment and the removal van will be here in the next half an hour. Stephanie has kindly volunteered to drive me over to Beaufort St. Catherine, following the van. I will have today and the weekend off work to try and settle into my new environment. I already have new furniture in the apartment, but there are a few things I have here that I just cannot get rid of, as they are like very dear friends to me. I will return to work on Monday next and work through until the evening of Saturday 31st January and then I will be as free as a bird and will stop work and retire."

Judas was about to say how happy he was for Anita when she continued, "As the Poacher's Retreat has only a few bookings until the beginning of February and then none until the 16th February, Stephanie and John have decided to take the opportunity to re-decorate the whole building and the contractors are arriving on Monday next and will initially be decorating the unused rooms. I feel that I will be surplus to requirements, as Stephanie honestly does not need my presence at the guest house anymore, and therefore I have decided to end my association with the building. Stephanie has great plans for this property and I have great plans for my retirement."

Anita then waited for a response from Judas and he simply said, "That's marvellous news. I am so pleased for you. I sincerely hope the move goes smoothly and you get the apartment sorted out the way you want it to be."

Judas was about to say more, when Anita said, "Thanks and good luck in your new job. Bye."

Colin eventually asked Judas if he had enjoyed his first bout of freedom away from the lodge and was pleased to receive an appreciative response.

It was then that Colin said, "On one of my recent days away, whilst visiting my sister, I went on a guided tour around the stately home of Ashfield Manor and its associated garden and I enjoyed the experience. In fact I enjoyed it so much that I am planning to return during the summer with my grand children, who will absolutely love to travel on the extensive narrow gauge railway which wanders around the grounds and garden."

Colin then presented Judas with the Ashfield Manor brochure, outlining the history of the stately residence from the early sixteenth century, the various owners and their numerous mishaps, the landscape architects and the assorted attractions, including a motor museum, an important art collection and some priceless furniture items.

As Colin retreated to the kitchen area for a coffee, Judas scanned through the brochure and when he reached the centre of the publication he was transfixed by the map, showing a plan of the house, its extensive gardens and the route of the miniature railway. Judas photocopied the centre pages. The railway began at a simple terminus, which had a loop release line, a carriage shed for the passenger stock, a workshop and repair building, and a coal and oil siding, which also had a very small turntable for the use of the two steam locomotives on the enterprise. The line also had two diesel powered locomotives.

The first route from the terminus was a simple out and return line, going through a small wood and passing a small lake. The second route utilized the majority of the first line, but had an additional wood to pass through and an additional lake to cross on a wooden bridge, before rejoining the main line and returning to the terminus. The third route utilized the majority of the second line and then passed through another two woods, travelled by two more lakes and crossed over another lake, before rejoining the main line to the terminus. Routes two and three had their own return entry points to the main line outside the terminus. All routes had their own pricing codes for the journeys and varied considerably.

Judas was captivated by the map. He was so captivated that he decided, there and then, to try and produce a model railway layout depicting a replica of a narrow gauge railway in the grounds of a stately home, although it was not based on Ashfield Manor as this location was so vast. He began sketching and soon he had the semblance of a small finite plan, although much more work needed to be done to satisfy his perfectionist tastes. It was whilst pondering the work required that he suddenly realized that it was not feasible to continue. There was no operating potential with the layout. Locomotives would go out and return to the terminus, or simply travel round the track, stopping only at vantage points, or at supposed organized events on the layout. This disappointed him, but he filed these sketches for review later.

Judas was still in design mode and he decided to continue with the narrow gauge theme and to try and plan a layout for a forestry complex, transporting felled trees to a despatch point, situated by a trio of main line sidings. This scenario interested him greatly. He doodled some designs without hitting on one that he liked enough to develop. However, he kept persevering. After ten further minutes of hectic sketching, again without success, Judas decided to stop for a drink when he saw Henry Brown enter the car park. Henry waved towards the gatehouse as he exited his vehicle and rushed off to the office. Judas followed, after returning the brochure.

Judas was in Henry Brown's office dead on seven o'clock and in his hand he had the folder containing the plans he had designed for the proposed project.

Henry Brown welcomed Judas and said, "Before I introduce you to your team, I just thought you might like to see the office you will be in when you start your new job in the design bureau."

Judas smiled and followed his host along two corridors and into a very plush new office.

"This is it. Your desk is there, your team are over there, Stephen will be over there and Matthew's desk is that one," said Henry as he pointed to the other side of the room.

Judas was impressed. He looked at the desk where he would be sitting and the filing cabinets located by the rear wall and he could never believe that they would be necessary for his paperwork.

Henry smiled and then said, "The MD was impressed by your layout and asked me to thank you for the layout plan and for the photographs. He, like us, was also impressed by your study."

Judas regained his composure, nodded and said to Henry, "Thank you for the tour of my new office. However, I do not think I will need all of the filing cabinets."

"Don't be too sure," chided Henry, "I thought the same when I started and I now have double cabinet space to what I had then."

"When we get back to your office, may I see you on another matter?" asked Judas and Henry nodded.

In Henry's office Judas presented him with the folder containing the forty eight plans that he had drawn up and photocopied. Henry opened the folder and, after a few seconds, he looked up at Judas and smiled. His host then slowly looked at all of the plans and, still smiling, telephoned Paul Gibson, requesting him to come to his office. Paul Gibson duly arrived and was surprised to see Judas.

"Are these plans any good for the proposed first book of simple layouts?" asked Henry as he passed the photocopies over to Paul.

Paul accepted the photocopies and sat in front of Henry, looking at each photocopy and eventually nodding.

Paul looked up and simply said to Henry, "Absolutely first class. Just what is needed."

Paul then turned to Judas and said, "Very well done. They are all superb and when we have put proper stations and line side features onto the plans, they will look even better. Again well done."

"Can I keep these to show Stephen Lindsey at our meeting later?" asked Paul.

Judas nodded and said, "The papers are yours."

Henry then said, "I will take you to meet your team in a few minutes. They are, at present, in the publicity department and various store rooms, collecting brochures and various company books. They will leave about ten o'clock and set up the exhibition of our company products, the publicity stand and of course the operating model railway. Two of you will travel in the truck and the other three will travel in the company car. The guys are very gifted modellers, but not layout designers and the girls did sterling work on the two displays we have done. I am sure you will all get on very well together. They are all looking forward to meeting you.

"However, on this trip we don't expect miracles from you. Just go to the exhibition, help where you can and absorb the environment and pleasure of the exhibition. Go around the various stands, competitors and exhibitors and just enjoy yourself, get as many brochures as you want and get a good grounding for the future and for future events. On Sunday the exhibition closes and packing away our exhibits takes less time than setting it up. You will get back here late on Sunday. The crew will unload the truck on Monday and you can help them to store away the equipment. At least you will know then where everything is stored. Also on Monday I will show you the requirements of your duties. You already know about some aspects, but everything will be revealed on Monday. Now go and enjoy yourself."

Judas politely thanked him for this information and walked to the office door with Henry.

"By the way," he said, as he turned to Paul, "I have spent a fair amount of time this morning trying to design a batch of narrow gauge railway plans, but without any success. The designs are for forestry complexes, quarry lines and slate mines. I also tried to incorporate a small harbour into all of the plans, but I simply couldn't fit them into the design. Hopefully, I will have some success later."

Judas was introduced to his team by Henry and recognised them by sight as he had seen them all crossing the car park. He now knew them by name, as he shook the hands of Gillian Ross, Kirsten Hartmann, William Anderson and Richard Marshall. They knew him as the goods reception person and also now as the decipherer of the Beaufort St. Vincent abbey treasure clues. They were not aware of his involvement in the company book, as it had not yet been released to the unsuspecting modelling world. According to Henry they all got on very well together, both work wise and socially. William had written some guidance notes, collected from their attendance at the previous two weekend exhibitions, and presented a copy to Judas.

"I hope it helps to launch you into the ocean in a leisurely fashion," said his new colleague.

Judas started his new job by helping his new group to load the company products from the store rooms onto the truck, as well as the various brochures and pages of company literature required for the publicity stand. Lastly, the model railway was delicately loaded onto the vehicle. Judas was then asked by Richard if it was okay for the group to visit the canteen before departure. As his team retreated for refreshment Judas sat at the nearest desk and looked at his guidance notes. It was a thick tome and Judas was impressed. It contained some photographs of other exhibits at the venues and details of competitors' forthcoming developments. After a quick scan, Judas placed the notes into his case and then saw in his case the notes from last week, given to him by Gavin Melbourne, about the Roman occupation of Britain.

Judas realized that he would not be able to go to his class tonight. He telephoned the school and requested the receptionist to leave a message for Gavin Melbourne concerning his absence. Judas still found the subject of the Roman occupation of the country absolutely fascinating and absorbing. He then began to wonder how Gavin was going to rectify his notes, especially now that it was definitely known that the Romans were not only present in the local area, but had even built roads in the local vicinity. Judas smiled as he remembered Gavin's attempt at humour and trying to get Judas in front of the class to do the lecture.

At nine forty his mobile telephone rang and on answering it he was pleased to hear Anita.

"Hi," she said, "I am now in my apartment. The small amount of furniture that I required taking from the Poacher's Retreat was collected earlier and is now in my beautiful apartment and most of the new bought furniture has already been delivered and is in situ. I am absolutely chuffed and very happy and I am surveying my new domain with a critical eye to create perfection." Anita paused to take breath and began again, "This afternoon I am going out to walk about the new village and to discover my new surroundings more intimately. Honestly, Judas, I cannot thank you enough. You are a real diamond in a sea of sludge."

This remark amused him.

"I will assume that means I am not too bad a person to know?" queried Judas and Anita laughed as she hung up.

Judas was pleased that Anita was very happy and was more positive, now that she knew that she would be retiring very soon. Judas was very pleased for her. He knew that when she did retire she would have a very interesting future without any undue worries.

The horn sounding on a slow moving freight train made him look at the signal box once manned by his friend Adam. He recalled his time at the orphanage with great pride. The regime was harsh, but Adam made it bearable. At the orphanage it seemed that Judas was either at school, on his paper rounds or doing other work for the orphanage authorities. However, he always knew that he was under the protective eyes of Adam, who was always available to listen, to impart good advice and to entertain the children with his wonderful stories. Whilst he was treading in the footsteps of his friend and searching for the treasure, he always felt close to him and sometimes even felt his presence. Now the lifelong quest of Adam's Great Uncle Albert and, to a lesser extent, the quest of Adam was over. Judas had a new job, but still seemed lost. He just sat there and mused that if Adam was "up there," he would be shouting at him to get a grip on reality. This thought spurred him on.

At the prescribed hour, Judas and his new crew departed the company complex and headed for the Cleveland Centre, Chalfont Springs. Judas sat with William, the van driver, and the other three had the luxury of travelling in style in a company vehicle. Judas chose the van as William was the person who had presented him with the guidance notes. He was a very interesting person who had been employed at the company since leaving school.

"I worked in the graphics department until recently, but I was 'volunteered' for exhibition work and actually I am thoroughly enjoying it. I never thought I would, but I really do like the work."

He told Judas of his ambitions and aims in the company and Judas had a very pleasant, interesting and informative journey.

On arrival the crew took over the operation and entered the Cleveland Centre Exhibition Hall and were directed to the area allocated to the Beaufort company. In his ignorance, Judas just helped with the unloading of the vehicle and the setting up of the publicity stand. When the whole exercise had been completed, Judas spoke.

"Many thanks guys for all of your hard work today and for helping me to realise that I have made very little contribution to your efforts. Thanks again for the installation of the publicity stand, for the setting up of the stand exhibiting the company products and lastly erecting the stand containing the model railway. It is very much appreciated."

The actual layout itself, being on a solid baseboard, presented no difficulty to the team when being erected. It was covered by a cloth and all anyone could see initially were legs poking out from under the cloth. When the covering was removed Judas was amazed. It was definitely his layout, but it now had the station building, signal cabin, goods shed and engine shed built up and the layout was also fully landscaped, with roads, fields, rivers and a back scene. It looked magnificent and the whole group, even Gillian and Kirsten, congratulated him on its design and operation.

"That is a beautiful layout," said Richard, "I have operated it and it is definitely a pleasure to control. It is something that modellers will definitely want to copy and have as their own home layout."

Judas was embarrassed, but thanked them all again for their work and apologised for his lack of contribution. His new group just smiled.

Gillian then said, "Next time we will make sure you definitely know what to do."

On completion of the setting up exercise, they all retreated to their hotel. In his small room, Judas returned to his problem with the narrow gauge layout design and after a few attempts to rectify his lack of progress, he found that he still had a problem. He just could not get it to work how he wanted it to and it began to worry him. He put the problem layout back into his case, awaiting inspiration, and began designing other layouts to enlarge the basic ovals of the initial purchased model railway packages. He had some success and during the next two hours he produced a dozen new layouts, all confirmed to work by using the track templates, and also provided the layout items required to enlarge the basic oval. Judas then returned to the hotel receptionist and obtained photocopies of all the papers.

Back in his room time slowly dragged on and Judas was in a deep and contemplative mood. He liked the goods reception work, but he thought he would like the challenges of his new work better. It was more demanding and he relished the challenges ahead. As he thought of this, he also reflected that he had still not completed the design of the narrow gauge model railway plan and he reached into his case to withdraw the papers. Judas struggled with the plan and simply made no headway and was unable to put anything remotely satisfactory onto the page.

Judas was interrupted in his work by another telephone call on his mobile, by Anita.

She excitedly said, "I have explored Beaufort St. Catherine and really love the village and its amenities. I was collected by Stephanie Faulkner and taken to Beaufort St. Vincent for a wonderful lunch. Afterwards we both visited the museum and had a look at various exhibits, but these exhibits had nothing to do with the recent discovery of the treasure. We both found the trip to the museum absolutely absorbing and thrilling. After this we went shopping and the day was absolutely wonderful. How was your day?"

Judas was again very pleased for his friend and in a few words simply replied, "Not as good as your day, but I thoroughly enjoyed it."

Judas retreated to the hotel bar looking for his colleagues, but they were not there. He looked into the restaurant and saw all four having dinner. They were all in deep conversation and he decided not to encroach on their evening. He returned to his room. As he prepared for sleep, Judas had deep thoughts, but he was happy. He knew that, even though he was approaching the senior age of sixty, the next few years of his working life would be very enjoyable. He knew he would relish the challenge of exhibition organization and of designing model railway layouts for various books planned by his company. He was respected by his colleagues, by the company management and even the MD knew him by name. He had been involved with a new discovery concerning the disastrous floods at Beaufort St. Clement and had unearthed some lost station plans and photographs relating to the lost village. Lastly, he was proving to be good at planning model railway layouts and he was also fairly knowledgeable about some aspects of archaeology.

He also knew that Anita, his friend of many years, was about to retire and she had a home that she absolutely adored. He had a new home also and he was very pleased that he lived in complete comfort and luxury. He had no financial worries, or health worries, or employment worries and his future with his company was secure. The fact that he had, in some small way, achieved a great archaeological breakthrough for his friend Adam and for Albert now seemed to pale into a background of insignificance. In short he was happy and content.

CHAPTER 32

EPILOGUE

Judas continued working at the company, designing layouts and doing publicity and exhibition work; he took to the tasks involved like a duck to water. The guards and Martin were sorry to see him leave the lodge, but wished him well in his new enterprise. Henry, Paul, Stephen and Matthew were all happy to have Judas on board as a colleague, as he was exceptionally good at layout designs, exhibition requirements and did sterling work for the various publications he was involved with during the rest of his working life at the company. The company publication, which included the Beaufort St. Clement tragedy, was a great success and was popular with railway historians.

All of the subsequent annual layout plan books, for small spaces and for extending the basic oval, all designed by Judas, were a great success and were eagerly awaited by the modelling fraternity every year. Judas never disappointed the modelling public and his designs for model railway layouts in small spaces were always well received. Some of the layouts he designed worked very well and were always included in the publication. Some layouts unfortunately did not work very well; the complex track formations refused to fit the space available, but the sketches were never scrapped, just kept and filed. Judas was always reluctant to destroy any of his sketches, as they might be useful for incorporation into larger layouts, at a later date.

Judas also had a great aptitude for sorting out the requirements of the exhibition attendances and he was always congratulated by the display staff for his contribution to the smooth running of the exhibition stands. He organized the staff, the transport, the route, the erection and dismantling of the stands, staff accommodation whilst away and any other problems encountered during the exhibitions. Judas absolutely loved the work and was exceptionally good at his job.

Everyone at the company continued to call him Judas, but in the literature generated by the company, his title was Exhibition Organizer and Layout Designer. This was followed by the name Jude Wells. The reason given was apparently the fact that Judas was not considered an appropriate Christian name for an employee, working in a country with high Christian values.

Mortimer Stanhope, Robin Cooper, James Priestley, Giles Anderson and Julian Fitzroy became major celebrities because of their involvement in the discovery of the treasure. All of the men wrote newspaper articles, pamphlets and even books on the subject. The film of the excavation, orchestrated by the museum, was also a great success and was well received by the general public. Because of it, both Beaufort St. Vincent and Beaufort St. Catherine had a great influx of tourists, but if they were hoping to see the treasure they were very disappointed. All of the items recovered were housed at the British Museum and were on permanent display there. Also on display at the British Museum were the original papers held by Judas, which allowed him to decipher the clues, which led to the discovery of the long lost treasure. Judas however did keep photocopies.

Judas never did have the status of celebrity for his involvement in the treasure story, as he did not seek publicity, but he was nevertheless elevated to the status of minor celebrity for a short while.

Martin Holland did train Aaron Miller on the goods reception duties and did not have to involve Judas in the process. The new gatehouse was constructed and the new security guards installed on completion of the building work. The company expanded and became a major constructor of model railway equipment and its products were considered to be amongst the finest available on the market.

Martin and Susan at the timber yard were very successful in their working environment and reduced the debt every month until the required payment to Judas had been repaid. Their business was successful and they had a wonderful future together. Amanda and Stephen Bailey also benefited from the loan made by Judas and they expanded their business along the agreed lines and repaid the debt at the agreed sum and at the agreed time. The guest house was eventually considered amongst the best in the area and the couple were famed for the homely cooking and for the excellent service given to their guests. The timber yard and the guest house were the last business ventures to receive financial assistance from Judas Wells.

The Miller's Retreat was extended by the purchasing company and developed into a fine hotel and conference centre. Judas often walked past the old place that he once owned and it filled him with joy to see how it had developed. The old orphanage site was also developed and Judas and Anita frequently walked past the new and expanded complex with fond memories of people that they knew in their youth, especially an old man who told wonderful stories and made people believe in themselves and in a very positive future.

The Poacher's Retreat was another success story. Stephanie and John Faulkner eventually extended the building and created a superb guest house that even Anita looked at with admiration. Anita was never jealous of them for developing the property to a standard that she was never able to achieve and she and Stephanie were great friends and often had lunches out when the guest house work permitted.

Sometimes, at weekends, Judas was allowed to join them and he enjoyed seeing two friends sharing the simple pleasure of good food and good company.

On Sundays, Judas was a constant member of the congregation at the Beaufort St. Catherine church, exhibitions permitting, and became a personal friend of the Reverend Oliver Winchester, as did Anita Wells. They both enjoyed the services and on occasion Judas did the bible reading. However, Judas never did celebrate Christmas as he considered that Christ was not born on that day and no amount of arguing by the illustrious reverend could convince him otherwise. The vicar also refused to call him Judas, but reverted to Jude.

Anita Wells had a wonderful and pleasant retirement. Also she had numerous coach vacations to various locations in the United Kingdom and enjoyed them all. Her attempts to persuade Judas to join her on these outings were unsuccessful, but she kept trying. On his vacations throughout the years he was employed, Judas enjoyed walking holidays in the local area and sometimes he attended specialist weeks bird watching, or doing conservation works in forestry, or just visiting the local churches and stately homes, gaining as much knowledge as he could on the subjects.

Judas also continued his evening classes in history and geography related subjects, when work permitted, and became very knowledgeable in these arts. His tutors were exceptionally gifted men and both were a credit to the teaching profession. They were able to put meat onto the bones of their subjects and it was a real pleasure to be in their classes. Sometimes Saturday classes were arranged, especially when it was the centenary of some momentous event in history and Judas was always happy to attend and to be entertained and educated.

As for the model railway in his inner study, Judas was completely satisfied with the layout and it was in constant use. Judas made a special point of going into the "Railway Room" for thirty minutes of pure pleasure before retiring for the night, only to find that an hour later he was still trying to sort out shunting movements on one of the industrial complexes. However, it was a wonderful layout and it gave him immense pleasure. On one Saturday afternoon, on a rota day off work, Martin Holland was invited over to see the model railway. Although he had viewed the plan of the layout, he was completely taken aback by the sight of the actual model railway. He complemented the designer on the beauty of the layout, on its operational potential and on its sheer perfection. He was also enthralled to be allowed to operate the layout and Judas just watched as his friend and colleague was immersed in pure pleasure.

Judas Wells heard about Robin and Mortimer suggesting he turn his attention to searching for the lost artefacts in East Anglia. However, he never did find King John's Treasure, although he did read up about the subject, but in all honesty he never did any more than read about it. He also never did discover what the *C* stood for in *C ROFT*, although he did keep reading through the notes he had amassed on the subject, hoping for another Eureka moment. Various books were written by eminent authors, on the subject of the markings on the mediaeval cross, but no-one was able to decipher the remaining unknown symbols. Eventually the "experts" stopped writing about the treasure and to date no additional information has been forthcoming.

One amusing incident occurred when Judas and Anita were walking towards the harbour at Beaufort St. Catherine. It was a very hot day in summer and Anita was in need of an ice cream on a stick, duly purchased by Judas. On finishing the refreshing item Anita was about to consign the redundant stick to a bin when she was stopped by Judas who pocketed the stick.

When asked by Anita the reason for this action, Judas simply said, "It's for my model railway. These sticks make fine ballast for my lumber trucks and I have quite a collection."

Anita collapsed into a fit of giggles and with tears running down her cheeks, she had to sit down. Judas could not see the joke!

As for the treasure, the subject of the treasure trove was often mentioned, but to date the legal standing of the recovered items has not been resolved. On a personal note, Jennifer never did marry a millionaire and Judas never did learn to swim. Also Judas was never able to design a suitable narrow gauge model railway layout that he considered to be acceptable for publication. This fact irritated him.

LIST OF CHARACTERS

Archaeologists
> Giles Anderson
> Professor Julian Fitzroy
> Professor James Priestley
> Professor Mortimer Stanhope

Architect
> Simon Lancaster
> Helen Lancaster
> Alan
> Susan (Secretary)

Bank Financial Adviser
> Chrystal

Beaufort Gazette
> Edward Eastwood

Beaufort Model's
> Dr Oliver Rose (Md)
> Henry Brown (Head Of Department)
> Richard Foote (Design Bureau)
> Matthew Forrester (Design Bureau)
> Paul Gibson (Head Of Department)
> Robert Grey (Design Bureau)
> Stephen Lindsey (Design Bureau)
> Judas Wells (Design Bureau And Goods Reception)
> Martin Holland (Goods Reception)
> Aaron Miller (Goods Reception)

Beaufort Model's Exhibition Team
> Jude Wells (Group Leader)
> William Anderson
> Kirsten Hartmann
> Richard Marshall
> Gillian Ross

Beaufort St. Vincent Model Shop
> Rudolf
> Rupert

Church
> The Reverend Oliver Winchester

Monastery Personnel

Abbots
> Etienne
> Laurent

Brothers
> Bernard
> Stephen
> Tancred

Prior
> Tatwin

Museum Staff
> Professor Robin Cooper
> Charles Sibley (Photographic Unit)

Orphanage
> Adam Stonehaven

Researcher
> Albert Stonehaven

Sales Office
> Jennifer

School
> Gavin Melbourne

Security Guards
 Adrian
 Roy

 Colin
 Keith

 Gordon
 Richard

 Geoff
 John

Solicitor
 Marcus Forth

The Ivy Lodge Guest House
 Amanda Bailey
 Stephen Bailey

The Miller's Retreat
 Judas Wells

The Miller's Retreat (Cleaner)
 Juliette Gilchrist
 Andrew Gilchrist (Husband)
 Mary (Sister-In-Law)

The Poacher's Retreat
 Anita Wells
 Stephanie Faulkner
 John Faulkner (Husband)

Timber Yard
 Martin
 Susan

Vending Machine Operative
 Allison